As Leaves are Prey to Wind

JOHN F MCGOWAN

Front cover image: Helicopters' © Binh Danh
Chlorophyll print and resin 2005, USA Immortality: The Remnants of the
Vietnam and American War Series
Back cover: Mother and Child © Binh Danh 2005

ISBN: 978-0-646-81468-1

First published 2020

For enquiries, contact:
Email: johnfmcgowan1@gmail.com
Facebook: JohnFMcgowan
www.johnfmcgowan.com

This book is fiction. Every attempt has been made to avoid mentioning particular dates, Infantry Battalions or lesser known battles in which Australians fought. The village described in this book is deliberately not named and its description altered to avoid comparison with any existing village.

Some military procedures, signals procedures, tactics and equipment descriptions are intentionally altered.

Any similarity to particular events, soldiers names, nick names
or to particular personalities is coincidental.

Contents

PART TWO

PART ONE

The God's mark out the destiny for each people

as they do for each man

and we must walk down that pathway

without ever turning back

What is it to be a man!

Poor mortals, prey to sickness

to misfortune

As leaves are prey to wind

Departure

THERE IS AN old man just standing quietly by the exit door. He is all alone.

His wrinkled hands, one atop the other, fondle the worn cane walking stick upon which they are resting. There is a nervous twitching of his fingers. He wears a battered Australian slouch hat not unlike that which sits atop my youthful head, but the old man's hat is worn and frayed. On the top right side of the hat there is a hole that appears to have been chewed by a rat or a mouse. This is a hat that spends most of its days in an attic or shed. Why is he wearing it now?

Like the hat, the old man's weather-worn face shows no emotion, just neglect. All wear and tear. There are deep ruts and canyons carved into his tough leather skin by a lifetime of hardship, but his hands are trembling, he is stressed.

Why is he here, all alone? Who does he belong to? Who once belonged to him?

I must concentrate all my attention on this lonely old man as it enables me to avoid staring at my mother. It is too painful.

She stands there rigid as a statue, holding in her emotions as she always does when difficult moments enter her life. I feel her eyes burning into my soul. She would have stared at her own two brothers when they were about to go off to war against the Japanese. Only one returned. The other left to rot in the jungles of Kakoda. No grave. No chance to say farewell.

I can sense, almost taste my mother's anguish. I am her baby boy, named Brian after her brother lost in a distant war. I cannot find the emotional strength to stare back at her. The old man is my only focus. I concentrate on every minute detail, every movement.

The old man reaches into his pocket and retrieves a handkerchief. He wipes his gnarled, pockmarked nose with a trembling hand. He has a huge liver spot, or maybe even a skin cancer, making an ugly presence on the lower right cheek. Both cheeks sag, empty potato sacks, beside elongated elephant like ears. The old man's trembling hand does not replace the wrinkled cloth from where it had come but screws it tightly in his fist which he rests atop the other hand placed upon his cane. Ancient, almost colourless eyes stare from below rice paper thin eyelids camouflaged behind untidy bushy grey eyebrows, their ancient hairs poking and protruding at all angles. Why is he here? All alone.

Robert walks past my parents. 'Hi Mr Fronton', he calls to my father. 'Dad said you were making the trip to say goodbye to Brian.' He points to Emily, the girl at his side. 'Have you met Milly before? Emily, my fiancée.'

My father clears his throat. He ignores Milly standing beside Robert. 'Well young Robert, are you looking forward to the flight?' he enquires.

'I guess so Sir', he shuffles on his feet for a moment. 'It's a bit strange seeing parents and family here at the air base and my mum and dad are back in Sydney, but I said my goodbyes on leave last week. I just want to get going sort of, err if you know what I mean.' He looks nervously at Emily. She stares back at him through watery eyes.

'Your father is proud of you Robert, I know that for a fact. You didn't volunteer for this war but when your number came up on the ballot you did the manly thing and now you are about to serve your country just as your father did.'

I am listening to their conversation as I stare at the old man. So Robby's father is proud of his son is he? Are you proud of your son dad? Have you ever told me that you are proud, that you love me? Have you ever let me inside your head or your heart? I change my gaze from the old man to Peter Van Housten who is talking to his uncle, a Catholic priest. Peter's widowed mother is cuddling Peter so hard he stares around embarrassed that the other lads will tease him when they get on the plane. I wish my mother would cuddle me like that, but I can't ask her. I can't even look her in the eye. I am afraid we will both cry if I do. You are a lucky man Dutch Van Housten. Beyond Dutch I can see Ray holding his two year old daughter. His wife is crying uncontrollably, she is almost ready to give birth to their third child. I wonder if she ever imagined that her husband would go back to Vietnam a second time. Would she have married him?

Just 76 soldiers are all that is left of the Australian Battalion here in Australia. The rear guard. Our job was to pack up the barracks after the battalion had left for Vietnam by the old aircraft carrier HMAS Sydney for a ten day voyage. The job completed, we now fly to the war and arrive just days after the main body had disembarked in the war zone.

A whistle blast causes all to stop and stare at the sergeant major who calls, 'Load up!' The room fills with a sudden burst of activity, hugs and kisses, a child screams and another starts crying for daddy. Milly is crying now, 'Please stay safe, please come home to me.'

Finally I gain the emotional strength to face my mother. She is frozen, an alabaster statue, fighting back tears. She gives a quick hug then pushes me back, 'Be a man son, like your uncles, be strong and take care.'

My father pushes in front of her, sticks out his hand and gives me a crushing firm hand shake, 'Come on son, man up for Christ's sake, give me a firm handshake, you're not holding a limp dick in your hand are you?' I feel my face glowing red with humiliation and then grip his hand hard. 'That's more like it. Now for God's sake keep your bloody head down and stay safe, your mother would be devastated if something happened to you.' What about you dad, would you be devastated? Have you ever shown me or my brother or even our mother any emotions?

We form a line and walk to the Boeing 707 with the QANTAS flying kangaroo emblazoned on its tail. How strange to be going to war on a commercial jet. But no soldier will ever complain about that. To travel to Vietnam on a C130 transport would be a terribly long haul. I shudder with humiliation as my father calls out above the crowd, 'Stay close with Robby son, he will look after you, just do what he says.'

Robby is beside me, 'Your old man is a weird one ain't he? How the hell could I look after you any better than you could look after me?'

We are among the last group through the door. I look back to catch a final glimpse of my mother but she and my father have already walked back toward the car park. Emily is waving a hanky toward Robert, her quivering lips mouthing silently, 'I love you darling, please stay safe'.

Suddenly I see the old man with the walking cane. He is staring at me. There are tears running down the canyon wrinkles on both his cheeks.

ARRIVAL

THE BOEING IS cruising at high altitude. We are tired but unable to rest due to the excitement of anticipating our destination. Robby is sitting beside me staring out the window to the ocean below. I have known him since we were young teenagers. Our fathers are close friends and drinking buddies at the RSL Club and members of the club's golf team. Robby and I played rugby together in our teen years. I am still a teenager, 19 years old, I will turn 20 while in Vietnam. Robby is a year older. He is a national service man, not a volunteer. I chose the army as a career and volunteered two years earlier. I assumed the war in Vietnam would be over by the time I was old enough to serve. But wars never turn out the way people assume they will.

I decide it is time to open my small but thick notebook. Not a diary but a pocket-sized scribble pad, its cover is artificial leather. I purchased this size because I can carry it with me at all times, the cover provides some protection from the elements and there is a simple pen or pencil holder behind the ring binding. I unclip the pen and consider my first entry. The first two lines must be about how the war happened. How could I do that in just two short lines?

It was Joseph Heller I think, who wrote that Aristotle knew what Plato did not, that politics and good intention do not mix. He also wrote 'Catch 22'. So what is the catch for us? I guess I will find out soon enough.

I study this first entry with pride, then scribble a few more lines.

Day 1 departure - There was an old man standing…

I love to read, any book is a gem for passing quiet times. I would never admit it publicly but I hope one day to be a great novelist myself. My mind is filled with quotes and anecdotes gleaned from the pages of a thousand writers, some famous, many just struggling wordsmiths. Famous or not, their words have been committed to memory as best I am able. Words I try to equal whenever I put pen to paper.

'What are you writing Brian?' Dutch calls out from across the aisle.

'Just some short notes, memory joggers, I want to be able to recall this trip to war in detail.'

'I doubt you will ever forget it mate.'

'Yeah, but I want to remember the detail.' I turn the page of scribble in my pocket notebook toward my friend. 'See I have written about that old man by the door. If I read this many years from now I will remember everything else. All I do is pick out an interesting thing that happened and it helps me remember the rest in detail. That's how I used to study for exams in school.'

Dutch shrugs his shoulders. 'What old man at the door? I didn't see no old man.' Dutch scratches the bottom of his nose and I notice that he still has some pimples on his chin and one on his right cheek. Until this moment I felt old and grown up but Dutch is my age, do I still have pimples? My hand rubs the side of my face. Yes!

'You planning to write a book about the war young fella?' Ray calls out from beside Dutch. 'It will be a bloody boring book, I know, I've done one tour and it's just hard fucking work.' I like Ray, he is older than most of us young men on the plane, a corporal. He was on the first ever tour of duty with first battalion 1RAR. After that he went to Kapooka as an instructor but within a few years they sent him over to this battalion. He does not seem to mind though, he just figures he is a soldier and that soldiers serve where and when the government decides.

'No I wasn't planning to write a book, I just wanted the details for myself, maybe my kids and grandkids if I ever have them.' I feel myself blush at my own little lie. 'It's not a hero war story thing. It's… well, it's sort of strange that my own father went to war four years and never told me anything about it. When I asked him he used to just say it's in the past boy, I don't remember much and don't want to talk about it. Anyway I don't want my kids growing up with a dad like mine that's all. That's why I am writing some memory joggers.'

Ray's face turns a shade paler. 'Well I think your old man may have the right idea, I only saw one bad contact on my first tour of duty, there were others but only one was real bad. I wish I could find a way to forget that day that's for sure.' There was something cold and strange in Ray's voice that caused us all to stare away in discomfort, we did not talk again for another hour.

Suddenly there is a stirring amongst the soldiers on the right side of the plane, I grab my notebook and quickly scribble.

> *The pilot announces that we are about to fly over the Vietnamese coast.*
>
> *All of us young men try to find a window to stare out of. It's not like we thought it would be, we first timers thought that Vietnam was full of jungle but what we see is mostly clear, there are dark green areas in the distance and we can see some rice paddies and a river. But we spent our entire training on jungle warfare. Maybe there are just bits of jungle where the enemy hide and the rest of the country is safe. I guess we will find out soon enough.*

'Fuck, get a gander at that will you', somebody calls out and we stare agog as three Phantom jets seem to just fly up beside the QANTAS jet then shoot off into the distance at amazing speed. The pilot flicks on the 'FASTEN SEAT BELT' sign and advises us to get ready for landing at Tan Son Nhut Air Base. The aircraft joins a holding pattern and from the window we can see all sorts of aircraft circling around with us waiting their turn to come in. Another two Phantom jets scoot past us in the opposite direction and suddenly the big Boeing 707 tilts and drops quickly toward the tarmac as if the pilot wants the shortest and quickest way to the ground as he can possibly take. My ears ache and I try to pop them by holding my nose and blowing air through. It doesn't work and the pain is terrible. Everyone is complaining until Ray calls out, 'The less time we spend getting on the ground the less chance of a missile hitting us.' We all stop complaining instantly and sit quietly pretending that we are not scared. The plane hits the runway with a hard bump, bounces twice before the landing gear seems to grip the tarmac and bring the beast as rapidly as possible to a halt. A cheer starts up and all start laughing. A first taste of short sharp stress followed by a need to express the tension.

A wall of thick humid hot air attacks us as we leave the plane. We left South Australia to land in tropical Saigon, the shock to the system has us all sucking in extra oxygen. A cacophony of engine noises assault our ears as hundreds of aircraft jostle for space amongst the aircraft hangers, bunkers and fuel sidings. With under-exercised stiff legs we climb down the stairway and are herded like cattle to a shed with no walls and told to stay loose until moved to our next transport. We stand around confused, with summer dress uniform and no weapons. Ray calls out to us members of signals platoon under his stewardship, 'Another cluster fuck, hurry up and wait, that's the army for you. We are supposed to be in a war zone for fuck's sake and all we get is, 'Hurry up and wait'. Ray ought to know about things, he is a lifer in this man's army.

'When do we get our weapons?' Some digger calls out to the sergeant wearing a blue beret. 'Soon enough son', he replies. 'You will be sick o' the sight of them soon enough, just sit tight, don't let any Yank try to sell you some crap souvenirs and don't wander away, I will be back with a bus shortly.' A pallet stacked with our soldiers' kit bags is dropped at our feet and we rummage through to find our individual bag.

There is a steel stores container on the tarmac some 50 meters from us. An American soldier is standing on top of it waving his M16 rifle around and calling out to the Australians. He is the first Black American most of us diggers have ever seen in the flesh. I am curious so I break rank and walk over to see what he is saying. The man is babbling incoherently about the lord Jesus and the devil. He sits down then jumps up again and starts babbling about three horsemen coming to get us all. 'Don't mind that dumb Nigger boy jest get back with your Aussie friends now why don't you.' I turn around and find a six foot five Afro-American wearing a Military Police helmet and resting his hand on a large colt handgun strapped to his side.

'Is that man stoned on drugs or is he just a looney?'

'He sure as hell's on some bad shit son and we don't want to excite him while he got a damn M16 rifle in his hand else I might have to shoot the son of a bitch. You go on back to your Aussie friends boy, this here is Nigger business not yours white boy. Go on, git!'

Bewildered I wander back to the lads under the shed roof. 'Hey Ray, you ever seen anything like that last trip?'

Ray is staring and shaking his head, 'I heard about it and that it has got a lot worse over the years since I was here last but that's the first time I've ever seen it.' He shrugs his shoulders, 'So now you know why we ain't won the war yet Brian, have a good look at our allies.'

'They ain't all like that surely', Robby remarks.

'Not all, most are okay', Ray replies. 'But it don't take more than a few bad apples does it?'

The QANTAS 707 is already taxiing along a runway for a rapid departure. A mighty roar as the engines hit full throttle and the delivery bird disappears in the wavering heat haze. The group stares after it.

> *One hour in this country. Hot! Watching jet fly out - a last link with home. Black guy, drugs I think. Black MP big gun told me to piss off. I hope all Yanks aren't like them two. I should write more, a better description of this place but I am a bit too excited at the moment.*

A green bus pulls up and the sergeant with the pale blue beret steps out, 'Grab your kit bags and climb aboard.' There are no glass windows in the bus just open air spaces covered in thick mesh to stop an enemy lobbing a grenade in amongst the passengers. For a moment I wonder if it would also stop the occupants escaping from a burning vehicle should the bus be hit by a Molotov cocktail fire bomb. I soon discover there is no need to worry as the bus does not leave the massive air base. It simply drives around the edges past a countless number of C130, Fairchild and even two huge Starlifter air transports. The boys' notice and make various comments about even more Phantom jets parked beneath concrete bunker hangars. The number of helicopters, both Huey and Chinook, leave us dazzled. Never could us soldiers from a scarcely populated Australia imagine that so much high performance war technology could be gathered together in one location.

Why haven't the United States won this war by now, surely the Viet Cong cannot beat this mighty war machine?

The bus grinds to a halt. We are told to jump out. I stare at a hut with a kangaroo emblazoned on its side 'Wallaby Airlines'. There is a USAF C130 on the tarmac with all four engines revving, its rear load door is dropped and a sergeant loadmaster is waving us to come up the ramp. One by one we scuttle past him and step up the rear loading ramp into an empty aircraft, no seating, just a metal floor with load rollers down its centre. As we each pass him, the loadmaster yells, 'Hold your kit bags close and squat on the floor. Find something to hang onto because when we land at Nui Dat the pilot will reverse the props pitch and slam on the skids so hard that you will be smashed against the forward bulkhead if you are not grabbing some part of the airframe. He's got no choice, it's a goddamn short runway.'

I sit and grab one of the roller stays bolted to the floor and look out the back ramp as the aircraft taxis to a take-off station. 'I wonder if this is how the cattle feel as they are loaded into semi-trailer trucks to be taken to the slaughter yard?' I call out to my companions thinking it would be a funny statement. No one laughs.

The ramp remains only half closed as the C130 turns and accelerates before rising into the air at a steep angle. The tropical climate causes the transport to bump and drop several times before it can reach a few thousand feet altitude. The load sergeant lowers the rear ramp until it is flat and walks out to the end where he sits with his feet dangling over the edge. He has no safety harness. Within minutes we are descending at a steep angle, the load master climbs off the back ramp, raises it slightly and grabs hold of a piece of the airframe. The C130 hits the runway at Nui Dat with a massive bump and the four engines roar as the plane desperately tries to pull up in a short space. Several soldiers slide past me and career head first into the bulkhead. There is much cursing and swearing. The load master is already lowering the ramp to a foot or two from the tarmac as we confused occupants feel the aircraft begin to do a quick U turn. The plane is still moving slowly and the load master is waving at us diggers to get off.

Each man scrambles down the rear ramp and steps onto the tarmac with the plane still moving and already revving its four giant engines ready for takeoff. As the last digger leaves the rear of the plane, the ramp begins to rise again and the C130 accelerates down the runway before making a steep climb back into the sky. We stand in a gaggle, confused and disorientated. A Land Rover pulls up on the tarmac and Lieutenant Hinkled the battalion transport officer, climbs out and approaches us with a beaming smile

'Grab your kit bags and head through that gap in the rubber trees. Signallers to the left, the few anti-tank diggers to the right and the assault pioneers will be met by Sergeant Hallebin and told where to go.' Each man picks up his meagre kit and wanders into the shade of the rubber trees. I see Captain Jacobson the regimental signals officer and move over toward him. The officer stares at me, Robby, Dutch and Ray. 'Welcome to Nui Dat.'

POGO

THE BATTALION SIGNALS platoon is like no other in an infantry unit. A group of 40 or more trained radio operators who are then divided amongst various company commands and specialised units. Of the signallers on the rear guard flight, Dutch is allocated to Delta Company and Robby to Alpha Company. Ray and I are allocated to the Administration Company as command post signallers for the Zero Bravo Command Post (CP).

CP's role is to organise all resupplies, or resups, for soldiers in the field. I have a second task as an air traffic operator on the battalion chopper pad. My days are filled doing shift on the helipad, clearing Hueys to land and take off and ensuring there are no mid-air collisions above the battalion area of Nui Dat. At night I do a command post shift. It's a cushy job as I can sit and read a book when there is no action in the field. I also enjoy command post work as it allows me to decode and encode messages from the various company commanders and the battalion commanding officer, intelligence officer and operations officer. I am one of the few diggers who remain in the know when it comes to what is happening and that gives me a certain status amongst other Nui Dat soldiers. I enjoy the privileges of inside information but am also professional enough to self-censor any information that diggers should not have access to.

I am also known as a pogo, or person on garrison orders. For the diggers in rifle companies out in the field of operations I am one of the lucky ones with a bed to sleep in, surrounded by barbed wire and set machine gun posts.

Nui Dat is great, it has electricity, bucket showers, access to a company boozer for my ration of alcohol each night. I even have some movies to watch one night each week. If this is war, it sure ain't what I expected it to be.

I share a tent with Ray and Graham, or Buckets as the lads tend to call him. Why not? His pear shaped body lends itself to a tag like 'Bucket Arse'. When not on signal duty the boys collect empty artillery and mortar ammunition boxes and make furniture for their Korean war vintage tent, one of many that are spread along a narrow road under rubber trees. I am a little embarrassed when the Rifle Company boys tease and call me pogo but I did not choose the job, the regimental signals officer (RSO) put me in this position because he believed that I was skilled in both CP work and had a calm disposition when handling the many chopper landings and take offs from the battalion pad.

Why should I risk getting killed after spending endless days patrolling in leech-infested jungles with 50 kilograms of radio, rations and ammunition on my back? When this war is over I will have the same medals, the same entitlements as all the poor diggers in the rifle company. My life is an adventure not a lot of hard work and undue risk. I am happy.

I have my first bit of excitement just three weeks into my tour of duty. A gun post spots two Vietnamese wandering into the exclusion zone around the Nui Dat perimeter so an armoured personnel carrier (APC) is sent out to investigate with a squad of infantry soldiers on board to do a quick ground search. I am just coming off a chopper pad shift when told by the RSO to grab a signal set and get on the APC as the radio operator.

The rapidly formed patrol belts out of the perimeter and speeds toward the two Vietnamese who begin to run. The APC commander fires a burst of

50 calibre machine gun fire at them so they stop and raise their hands. The armoured vehicle pulls up and the infantry squad consisting of two anti-tank diggers, the administration postal clerk, two drivers from transport platoon and me as signaller, jump out of the APC and point our rifles and M16s at the two trembling souls. The patrol commander screams for them to lie down or be shot. The two Vietnamese are confused so a digger from anti-tank platoon pokes his rifle into one of the poor soul's abdomen with such force the Vietnamese bloke buckles over and falls to the ground. The other soon follows.

After a quick search of their now bruised and winded bodies and the surrounding area, no weapons or any suspicious items are found so two patrol members man-handle them onto the APC. The patrol roars back to the safety of the perimeter where the two Vietnamese men are dragged over to the dog compound and chucked in with a growling black labrador. The Vietnamese squat down cowering. 'We sorry not to go on your place, big mistake', one calls. 'We no be bad people, we look for rats to eat.' The intelligence officer tries to speak to them with little result so they are handed over to two American men who I am told are spooks, better known as CIA.

I never see or hear about what happens to those two terrified souls after they are driven away. I hear stories of how prisoners are treated by South Vietnamese and US interrogators. But it's not my concern, I just have a job to do. At night I write a short letter home to my father.

> *Dear Dad,*
>
> *Today I saw action for the first time, I was part of a small patrol and we attacked and captured two enemy soldiers.*

I fail to mention to my father that the enemy were unarmed and terrified and were last seen being dragged into a van by some rather mean looking CIA men for a terrible interrogation. But I did end the letter.

> *Well dad I was scared but I did not let down my mates, I hope you are proud of me.*

Give my love to mum,

Brian

'Do they always kill prisoners in this place?' I ask. Ray looks up from the Playboy magazine he is studying. 'Nah! Of course not. Some go to a prison camp for the duration of the war and some agree to come over to our side as guides. Bushman scouts is what we call them.'

'I heard these stories about the CIA and their helpers', Ray just shrugs his shoulders and without raising his eyes from the naked centerfold he responds with bland indifference. 'Some get a hard time, it's called water torture or boarding or something. And there is some actual footage going around of Gooks getting chucked out of helicopters at a few thousand feet. I suppose if it gets good information to help win the war then it might be okay to chuck one out the chopper door and ask the next one if he is willing to co-operate. Shit I would! I would tell any sort of bullshit to some burly Yanks sitting on the chopper door if I thought they were stupid enough to believe me.'

'But would you tell the truth, I mean dob on your own army and mates just to stop getting chucked out a chopper door?'

'What the hell would I know that the enemy can use to win a war? I am just a bloody digger, that's all', Ray responds. 'I'd just tell them any bullshit. I bet 99 out of every 100 Gooks they put through the grinder are no different from me. Just poor dumb pricks in the hands of fanatic wankers.'

He raises the magazine to show me a picture of a naked woman laying on her back, legs apart and fingers caressing her vagina. 'I get my rocks off from real pussy Bri! Them interrogators get a hard-on by being dumb fuck cruel bastards. They believe the end justifies the means. Get used to it mate. War is not like your daddy told you it was.'

I lie back on my pillow. 'My father told me nothing Ray.'

> *I don't like thinking that one of them little fellows we caught is going to take a dive out of a chopper. It would mean I helped put him there. Fuck I am confused!!!*

UNCLE HO'S HAT

'So, WHERE DID you get that Brian?' Graham asks. 'Is it a real NVA helmet?'

'Real? Did you ask? Real? Let me tell you my good friend, it actually belonged to Uncle Ho himself', I reply with a cheeky grin.

'Nah, bullshit. How do you know it was Uncle Ho's?' Graham asks. He knows I am having a go at him, but he's drunk enough to give me the benefit of the doubt.

'Bought the thing off a Green Beret colonel when I was doing the messenger drop and picking up some replacements at Tan Son Nhut Air Base. And trust me mate, Green Berets never lie, it's part of their code of honour, ya know?'

Graham stands, thinking a moment, swaying back and forward in his drunken state. 'Nah, bullshit, ya pullin' me leg, ya bastard.'

I turn to the mortarman beside me at the bar. 'Well that's nice ain't it, me best friend Bucket Arse here calls me a liar. After all we've been through together, Ingleburn, Canungra and now Vietnam and ya callin' me a liar. I'm hurting Buckets, I tell ya I'm hurtin'. Don't know what else to say.'

Graham is having second thoughts. He puts the beer can up to his mouth to take another drink but misses his mouth completely, the beer runs down his shirtfront.

'Fuck it! Who moved me mouth anyway?' He mumbles as the lads laugh at him. 'Not funny', the drunken Graham retorts, 'and not my fault, it's these cans, they make the thing so ya spill it everywhere.'

'Communist plot', mortarman replies. 'Uncle Ho probably designed the can himself.'

'Nah, that's bullshit', Graham responds, 'I know you're bullshittin' 'cos you just screw mortar tubes, but I am willing to believe Brian 'cos he's me mate, aren't ya Brian?'

'That's the truth Buckets.'

Graham now manages to get the lip of the can up to his mouth with the aperture correctly positioned to allow more brown fluid a chance to disappear down his gullet. He looks at me and asks, 'tell me about this Green Beret fella. Who is he anyway?'

With tongue in cheek, I look back at him with a stunned expression. 'Ya mean ya don't know?'

'Nah.'

'He really doesn't know', I say looking around the company boozer, at the mixture of diggers gathered there, and then glancing back to Graham. 'John Wayne himself, in person. He's over here to win this war for all of us and he started by sneaking into Ho's secret base camp and pinching this very pith helmet right off the old bastard's head.' I stop for breath then continue, 'John Wayne said he coulda killed the old Uncle Ho but thought it would not be the right thing to do. Ho bein' an old man and John Wayne bein' a young un' and all. Gotta respect yer elders don't ya?'

The bar group is now in an uproar of laughter. Graham looks around, drunken mouth wide open.

'Bastard, you sucked me in big time.'

The sound of the Nui Dat artillery suddenly interrupts the group. 'Wow it's on out there', someone remarks. 'Got the howitzers firing in support of some of the boys.'

'Hey shuddup a sec will ya', mortarman calls.

The bar goes silent. The group can hear small arms fire in the distance.

'Only two klicks away, I reckon.'

I was off radio shift but knew who was out there. 'Alpha Company must have found some Gooks. Must have sprung an ambush.'

'Give the bastards hell boys', remarks one of the Support Company drivers. 'Cheers to Alpha Company', he calls as he raises his can of beer.

'Alpha Company, Oi, Oi, Oi!', the group calls out together in their drunken state.

'Time for Uncle Ho's pissaphone competition', I yell above the continuous eruption of the artillery firing in support of the company in battle.

The boys in the bar cheer and unbutton the flies on their army issue green baggy pants. I place the North Vietnamese soldier's pith helmet upside down on the ground and call for chalk. The barman throws me the piece used to keep score of the nightly darts competition. I take three measured steps back from the helmet and draw a line. Standing and swaying in a slightly drunken state, I produce my penis, aim and squirt in the direction of the helmet, arching my back to gain extra trajectory. The stream of steaming urine snakes across the floor and into the upturned helmet.

'Beat that ya piss heads', I call out loudly over the cheer. 'Let's see who is really weak as piss shall we? If you miss you have to put the fucker on ya head.'

Singo the postal clerk steps boldly forward, takes the chalk and makes one valiant stride further back from my line, draws a new line and produces his member. He stands swaying on the spot. Singo is a slightly overweight, sad little man with a lustful desire for cheap whisky, which once satisfied, turns him into the military equivalent of the village idiot. Penis in hand, concentration on face, he takes careful aim. Nothing.

'Weak as piss, weak as piss', the crowd chants.

Singo's concentration turns to facial contortion as he strains to make something happen. Fftttttt comes the sound from the back end of his trousers.

The crowd erupts in cheers. Singo presses on with his task. Red faced with effort and little result. Finally, a trickle spills down his trouser leg.

'Ohhh!' screams the crowd, who then pounce on him and hold him down while Ben the cook picks up the helmet and turns it right way up over Singo's head. My earlier deposit trickles over Singo's eyebrows.

'Bad luck mate', is the sensitive response from Ray. 'Better luck next time ya tiny pricked little farter.' Ray then returns the helmet to its rightful place on the floor.

The crowd cheers again as Ray undoes his fly. 'It's an art form', he screams out. 'Years of training and endless drills have honed me to the peak of ruthless accuracy and distance. Turned me into a pissaphone king and I'm going to piss all over Uncle Ho's head.'

A jet of fluid shoots skyward, not a drop touching the floor as it hits the targeted pith helmet. 'Direct hit, first mortar tube', calls mortarman, as he steps forward with penis in hand. 'Two guns - fire!', he screams as his own urine splashes over the helmet.

The real artillery has slowed its rate of fire and is now pounding out the occasional illumination round. Back in the bar we are tiring of the game with Uncle Ho's helmet. Talk returns to the battle out in the boonies with the boys from Alpha Company.

'Wonder how many Nogs they got, aye?' I ask the veteran Ray.

Ray is not so casual about this matter, drunk yes, but not casual. 'All I know is I'm glad it's not me out there.'

'Ya done it before ain't ya Ray, One Battalion, first tour?' Singo asks, his hair wet with urine.

Ray looks at the young pogo for a moment, his sunken eyes suddenly turning dark, lips drawing tight and thin across his rugged face. 'Yeah, I done it before, Hobbo Woods, out there as scout with an old F1 sub machine gun that couldn't kill a fuckin' flea and a heavy backpack, wondering if I'll get home alive with both legs still working. I ain't doin' it again! It's safe behind a wire for me on this tour of duty mate. I got kids now. None of the hero shit!' he pauses and swallows down the last drops in his beer can. 'No heroes out there just dumb grunts and scared kids. I'm a proud pogo', he pauses and sniffs the air in Singo's direction. 'and a dry one, you smelly little piss head.'

Singo is now looking at me and Ray, too drunk to care about his state.

'Come on you two, you can get into the command post. Why don't yas go up and get the news about the contact? See what the Alpha Company boys have shot up.'

'I don't need to know', Ray replies. 'I just hope it's Gooks not diggers who caught the lead, that's all.'

I am drunk and amused by this comment. 'C'mon mate, it has to be a sprung ambush. We must have caught the bastard out, our boys are fine', I say trying to sound like a real veteran, when in fact I have not seen any combat at all.

Ray is now serious, downright miserable in his facial features. 'It's not a game Brian. This shit in the bar is a fucking game, out there people die.'

He walks off, grabs his SLR and heads back to his tent. The group stands silent for a while. Finally, Graham the linesman speaks out. 'Never could handle his booze could he? Might be able to piss further and higher than most men but get the bastard drunk and he gets all miserable.'

'Hey Brian!' Singo calls out. 'Go on, slip up to the CP and get the word on Alpha will ya?'

'I'll do it. I'll risk me career and do it for you blokes and do ya know why?' I call out in true Mickey Mouse Show fashion.

'Why Brian?' Call back the group of drunks.

'Why? Because I **like** you!' I reply as all the boys cheer.

I stagger away from the bar and up the hill to the Zero Bravo Command Post while rearranging myself to look at least half-sober. Behind me, I can hear the drunks singing 'M-I-C (pause) K-E-Y (pause) M-O-U-S-E.'

I am standing quietly at the door of the command post. The Admin Company second in command and the battalion operation's officer are standing looking at decoded reports. Gary and Pom are the two signals operators on shift. Gary is working madly decoding the encrypted message sent by Alpha Company. As he decodes he calls out each new item, 'M60 two thousand.' I am stunned but impressed. The boys must have expended almost all their machine gun ammunition and are now requesting a re-sup.

'ANPRC 25 set by one', Gary calls out as he decodes.

Shit, they need a new sig set, I wonder what happened to the one in the field? The radio speaker crackles into life and I can identify the voice, it is Macca one of the A Company Battalion Signallers. His voice seems tight and edgy.

'Zero, bravo this is one, the information you require is as follows: two, seven, four, niner, (pause) niner, six, initials Romeo, Delta, Kilo, India, Alpha (pause) three, six, eight, zero, four, one, (pause) initials Juliet, Tango, Kilo, India, Alpha, Over.'

'Roger that, one zero', Pom replies.

My heart skips a beat. I realise I have just overheard the military serial number and first initials of two soldiers who have been killed in action. Suddenly I am in a war. Not the Mickey Mouse Clubroom.

Pom runs his pencil down the roll call list of Alpha Company soldiers, matching the serial number to the name. He draws one circle around a name, continues then finds the second amongst a separate group of names, the company add-ons, field sappers, medics and battalion signals operators. Pom draws a circle then shakes his head.

He passes the list to the operations officer, looks back at me, shakes his head again. 'It's Robby mate, they need the sig set 'cos Robby was on the thing when the RPG came in. Poor bastard took an almost direct hit.' Pom stops to let out a long sigh of sadness, his face pale and eyes drawn. 'They're putting bits of his body together and stuffing what they can in a body bag. God I'd hate to die like that, in bits and pieces.'

I turn. I am drunk and the alcohol is not helping me come to grips with what I have just heard. I walk away, not toward the boozer where a gang of clowns are waiting for news. I walk instead to my tent. My close friend, a fellow signals operator, died within hearing distance while I was getting drunk and pissing in Uncle Ho's hat.

Suddenly this war does not make sense to me. I'm shrouded in guilt that I had been laughing while Robby was dying. I get my notebook and with trembling pen scribble…

In an Australian ocker man's world, there is an unwritten code of behaviour. Loyalty, honour and mateship but never the word love. To love another man is to break the code. Yet how can I feel such painful loss if I had not also loved Robert. The English language is so barren of words to describe the grey areas of a man's emotions and I feel numb and shocked, knowing only that I should not be fighting an urge to burst into tears.

Real men don't cry, so I won't cry! Somehow, I will hold back the tears.

Ray is wiser than I realised. His previous war experience has given him good reason to be a miserable drunk.

Welcome to the Real War Son

The RAAF Pilot

Whop   Whop   Whop   Whop   Whop

The UH-1C speeds across the treetops, destination somewhere near Long Khanh Province. At its controls, Flight Lieutenant Trevor (Surf) Marshall is doing the thing he loves almost more than life itself, flying the Huey by the seat of his pants. He has grown up loving stories of the Red Baron. His favourite movie as a kid was John Wayne in the 'Flying Tigers' and at night he would lie in bed fantasising about chasing North Korean bandits in Mig Alley. Surf put aside his Jackson surfboard and joined the Royal Australian Air Force as soon as he was able, fulfilling his childhood dream of being a jet jockey, flying Sabre jets for the Royal Australian Air Force.

Just when he was about to move into French Mirage jets the call for extra chopper pilots sent him out of curiosity to examine the early model Huey choppers. One short stint at the controls and his need for speed was rapidly replaced by his love of sheer versatility and manoeuvrability. The jet's joystick replaced by the chopper's cyclic. The early smaller birds were great to fly, simple but effective, all control left to the pilot but these newer larger and more powerful models allow new technology to take away some of the pilot's skill.

Not Surf's skill, he would never simply roll on 100% of the power through the collective to engage the computer which balanced the power need with the cyclic demands. Surf just loves to juggle both controls manually while playing the foot pedals that control the rear rotor.

Flying by the seat of his pants is the real joy of flying choppers. It is just like riding his six stringer Jackson Special down a steep wave over a shallow rock reef, or driving his ancient MGTF sports car through the Blue Mountains back in Australia. It is never about power or speed, it is about balance and manoeuvrability. Picking the revs before rapid gear change then hurtling into a hairpin bend, feeling the road inches below his bum. Surf drives by the seat of his pants and he flies by the seat of his pants. There is not a pilot or crew member that would disagree that Surf is the best pilot in 'Nam.

Sitting behind the pilot, I am taking in the experience. I have a chart in my leg pocket but no idea exactly where I am going and don't care. Right at this moment I am very close to the open door of a chopper scudding through the air at break-neck speed, swinging occasionally left or right in a lazy casual evasive manoeuvre. I feel my stomach lurch upward into my chest as the force of gravity responds to the aircraft dropping down to just a few feet off the ground to cross the larger jungle clearings and then shooting back up to treetop level as the next piece of jungle springs up before us. I am sitting on the alloy floor of the Huey chopper. The light framed canvas seat has been folded back to create the extra floor space for any re-supply task the Huey might have to perform.

Whop   Whop   Whop   Whop   Whop

The air is buffeting my face. Engine vibrations run up through my body and treetops career beneath my feet just meters away. Suddenly the chopper lurches at a 40-degree angle to change direction and I instinctively grab the cargo ring set in the floor to steady me as I stare almost straight out the open door to the tree canopy below. Another bump of air turbulence has me grabbing the cargo ring even tighter as the aircraft levels out again and speeds onward toward its destination.

What a rush, this is better than any roller coaster ride at Luna Park in Sydney. With my back against the pilot's armoured seat, I glance across at the door gunner propped precariously behind the machine gun mounted at the right side of the rear cockpit. Another door gunner is on the left. They, like the pilot and co-pilot are on a basic MEDEVAC run, just another pick-up and delivery job, and quite casual about it all. This is not a combat mission unless things changed unpredictably. I am the cargo and Delta Company is to be the recipient.

The pick-up will be an injured company signaller. Not exactly injured, not by gunfire. The company signaller has an infected elbow. A small cut with little attention can become a serious infection within days in the tropical jungle environment and the company signaller is now at risk of permanent damage from his infection, possible gangrene. I am his replacement.

The blast of humid air continues to thump rhythmically in my face from the open rear section of the chopper. The rhythmic sound of the rotor blades and internal whine lull me into a trance-like state, soaking up the exhilaration of high speed tree surfing.

Whop   Whop   Whop   Whop   Whop

From where I am perched I can see the heavy dark clouds forming, ready to unleash a tropical downpour with monotonous regularity. These particular clouds seem larger and darker than usual. Come on boys, get me there before the bucket drops on us. These clouds are signalling zero visibility in the air, possible thunderclaps, strange down drafts and water droplets the size of cannon balls. I know the pilot will be just as keen to deliver me and be homeward bound before the downpour. Choppers have crashed when hit suddenly by tropical thunderstorms. The chopper will not turn back unless necessary but time is running out quickly. A decision is only minutes away.

The death of my friend, the surreal way I had been partying while others were facing peril so close by, has left me with a deep sense of selfishness. I feel so guilty and I believe I have failed in my duty. Not my duty to the army - my duty to Robby, to Robby's parents and to poor Milly.

From the moment I found out about Robby's death I have requested, argued and pleaded for a transfer to a rifle company. Until now, my problem has been my training and skill level. I've been too useful in command post areas and the battalion's regimental signals officer has not been willing to release me to any rifle company just because of my newly found gung-ho attitude.

A month has passed since my first request for transfer to a rifle company - how things change in war. Soldiers become injured, sick or dead. As with infantry machine gunners, signallers are high-risk soldiers when it comes to ankle, knee and back injuries simply because of the extra weights we are required to lug through twisted vines and jungle undergrowth. In addition to the extreme weights we carry in food water and ammunition, signallers also carry the ANPRC-25 VHF radio set and a couple of heavy spare batteries.

The sick and slightly injured can serve in safe areas such as Nui Dat, healthy men are needed in the field. As the battalion signallers limped and hobbled their way back to base from each field operation, the regimental signals officer ran out of options and in me he actually has a man stupid enough to want to be sent into the field. Into the sharp end.

Whop   Whop   Whop   Whop   Whop

As I sit here in the chopper I begin to reconsider the weight I am about to carry. Strapped to my web waist belt are four water bottles. A munitions pouch hangs by my left hip containing twin sets of 20 round 5.56 mm magazines. They are taped together upside down allowing me to quickly reload after a burst of fire by unclipping the empty one and flipping it over to engage the full one. This gives me quick access to 80 rounds of ammunition. A plastic cigarette case consisting of two halves shaped to fit a pack of 20 smokes protects the exposed rounds on top of each magazine. Each half of the case slips snugly over the mag forming a watertight and dust free barrier. There is also a hand grenade with electrical tape around the safety lever. An extra precaution against accidentally getting the pin pulled out and having the thing blow up in my face. There are no magazines in the second pouch positioned over my right hip on the web belt. Instead, I carry snack food, a bit of hard dark vitamin enriched no melt chocolate, coffee, sugar and hexamine (hexi) fuel tablets used to cook a meal or heat some water. These are nearby in case I have to drop my main backpack in a combat pursuit, I would need some energy food to snack on. The final tool of war attached to the belt is a pair of simple garden secateurs. These will clip and quietly snip my way through jungle vines and undergrowth, machetes are too loud and cumbersome.

Over my shoulder and around my waist are two bandoliers of seven M16 magazines, ready loaded with 20 rounds each, heavy but not as heavy as the SLR 7.62 ammunition carried by the rifle sections. As a signaller with the extra weight from the radio, the army issued me a lighter M16 assault rifle, capable of semi or fully automatic rapid fire. Its black plastic butt and handgrip are splashed with green and brown paint to help break up its silhouette lines and camouflage it. A shell dressing is taped on the butt which each soldier carries in case they are wounded. Under the front handgrip I have taped the bayonet sheath and bayonet rather than having it hanging on the overcrowded web belt. Not that I will need the bayonet for actual combat but the bayonet is a useful, multi-purpose implement. It cuts strings and cords, digs holes, cleans mud from boots and opens cans. If needed the bayonet can be used to prod the earth in search of land mines.

Also attached to my M16 is a sheep counter, positioned at the point where my left thumb can click over a new number each time my left foot touches the ground. I am a keen bushman and love to navigate when on operations even though it is not a strict requirement of my role. Counting steps give me the ability to estimate distance travelled, a compass tells me approximate direction. This simple information marked on my map gives me a reasonable dead reckoned position. It helps me as a signals operator to identify possible blind spots for VHS radio communications. It is that extra effort and professionalism that helped me finish top of the class at advanced signaller training back in Australia.

Propped on the chopper floor in front of me is a backpack consisting of an aluminium A-frame. At the top of the frame is the space for the VHF 25 sig set which I will strap on once on the ground with the company. Attached to the sig straps are two more water bottles and a lightweight entrenching tool. I can dig in the radio at night harbours or dig a shell-scrape or shallow trench. At the bottom of the frame is a large canvas pack with side and rear pockets. The pack attaches to the A-frame by quick release straps so that it can be dropped off quickly, leaving only the radio set on the frame to carry into combat.

Within that pack is my home, a lightweight hooch or one-man tent that can clip together with another soldier's hooch and create a two-person tent. I have a string hammock that can be slung low between trees to keep my arse off the ground in tropical downpours and a silk which is a thin sleeping bag liner. A heavier ground sheet and second hooch are packed tightly into the bag. No sleeping bag needed in the tropical heat. All extra space filled with rations, insect and mite repellents and a variety of knick-knacks designed to make life in the jungle bearable. Finally, the two spare radio batteries and a spare collapsible bottle of water sits packed at the top, ready to access when needed. On the actual shoulder straps are clipped an army issue torch, a second shell dressing and two yellow smoke grenades, again taped to guard against accidental loss of the safety pin. Pack pockets are filled with quick grab items including waterproof matches, spare smokes, waterproof pens, plastic liners to keep any codes and other papers dry, C ration and an extra box or two of hexi. A dipole aerial is neatly coiled and packed at the top of one pocket ready for use along with the obligatory plumb bob with its length of cord ready to be launched into the treetops to raise the dipole aerial for better communications with HQ.

Like most Australian soldiers I choose to wear American issue shirt and trousers because both are festooned with extra pockets unlike our poor quality equivalent uniforms. I fill the shirt pockets with waterproof pens of various colours, a codebook in pages of plastic sheaths, the always-ready pack of smokes and Zippo lighter slipped into a waterproof plastic case, Band-Aids, pain killer tablets 'acquired' from the Nui Dat regimental aid post, strong rubber bands, some string and a penlight torch.

In the larger pockets on each side of my legs are more codes that are changed each day; a topographical map of the general area the company is patrolling; a flat plastic orienteering compass; and finally, more string or green com-cord pushed into any spare spaces. My notebook has pride of place, a quick grab and scribble can happen in short rest moments when patrolling.

Apart from the most vital ammunition and sig set batteries, it is the rations and the water that provides the greatest weight for all soldiers. We could be five to seven days without a re-supply and must carry it all on our backs.

I should re-think just how much water I need. In the wet season, instead of the heavier cans, the advice is to carry plenty of dehydrated rations. 'They taste like crumbed dog shit', the quartermaster had told me, 'but they are lighter to carry and you won't need all those water bottles in the wet season, just fill up with the rain as you go, catch it off your hooch each night.' I glance at my waterproof plastic army issue Mickey Mouse watch noting that the aircraft must be in the general location by now. I make a final mental check that I am ready to drop-in to the jungle below.

After reconsidering the enormous weight, I decide to detach two water bottles from the backpack and push them over to the back floor area of the chopper as it continues its erratic dash across the treetops. I have between 35 to 40 kilos to carry in addition to my weapon.

Whop   Whop   Whop   Whop   Whop

The RAAF Crewman

Beaver Hamilton looks at Brian and smiles. Beaver has been 'in country' six months and has worked mainly slicks and Dustoff runs as a crewman, come door gunner. His nick name 'Beaver' comes from having two overly large front teeth that dominate his smile. Poke a crew helmet on his head and Bucky Beaver, the cartoon character, is instantly in the minds of all airmen who know him. The Bucky has long since been dropped, he is now just Beaver.

Beaver has a deep respect for the grunts. Sure, there is always the friendly rivalry, jocular little jibes between army and air but Beaver had seen these grunts leap off choppers into a hailstorm of enemy fire. He's helped drag the tired filthy bodies of exhausted men on board at the end of a gruelling operation in the bush. He has also had the horror job of holding and trying to comfort a grunt with both legs blown off by enemy mines as his Dustoff flew hell-for-leather to Viper hospital.

Beaver checks that his monkey belt is attached and free enough to allow him to move over to the solitary grunt before climbing around the side post and pushing his face close to Brian's to be heard over the whop, whop and air buffeting.

'I don't know how you grunts do it', Beaver calls out, 'but I do know why they call you grunts. It's the sound you bastards make when you lift that weight onto your fucking back.'

I look at the aircrew member and nod and smile in agreement. Every infantryman has heard this tired old joke a million times, but RAAF chopper crews are allowed to lack new and creative humour. After all is said and done these flyboys are sometimes all that stand between a wounded digger being in a hospital and a body bag. Like all diggers, I love these chopper crews, they sometimes take enormous risks to help their army comrades. But on low risk flights like this it is not uncommon for only one trained crewman to be behind a gun, the other spot taken by aircraft maintenance men, RAAF base guards and even cooks with a hankering for a bit of the action. Me? Well I figure that any combat service member who can get a break deserves it so I do not really care if I am talking to a trained crew-member or a sit in.

'How long have I got?'

The crewman with big buck teeth shrugs his shoulders then pulls his pilot helmet microphone down to his mouth and talks to the pilot before again leaning close to me. 'Not long, I'll get the winch ready', he yells. He then gives me an inquisitive look, 'Have you ever sat on one of these jungle penetrators?'

'No, I have abseiled out of a Huey and I have been winched down in a sling but not a bloody contraption like that.'

'Well, just hang on tight mate. You fall, you're dead and we don't get any bonus drinks back at base for delivering dead grunts.'

The Pilot

Up front Surf double checks the map board strapped to his thigh, places the point of his pencil on his location and looks to his co-pilot for confirmation. Thumbs up from the 'co', so he eases back the cyclic and rolls on the collective's throttle to 100% and kicking in the flight computer. The chopper begins climbing up from the jungle treetops as Surf grudgingly makes his bird ready for a standard procedure drop off. He pushes aside his talk piece and grabs the small water bottle from between his legs. A habit now implanted into his flight procedure is to wet the throat before each drop into bad land territory. After a quick gulp he pushes the bottle back between his thighs. 'Keeps my throat moist and my balls cool on hot flights,' he quips to the pilot beside him as he banks the aircraft toward its destination.

Behind the pilot, I get my first good look at the landscape I will soon be walking over. A sea of dark green stretches below me with any number of unusual small water holes dotted through it. At first, the sight confuses me until I realise they are bomb craters that have filled with water now the wet season has arrived. The area must have been blanket bombed by B52 bombers at some stage a couple of years ago. The 500 pounds of explosives in each bomb has decimated the general area, leaving behind this myriad of craters some 10 to 15 meters wide and probably as deep. The jungle has since reclaimed the decimation. In only a couple of years it has regrown, not as a pristine tropical rain forest, but as a tangled mess of vines and under-growth growing over and around the shattered and knocked down trees. No doubt the bamboo and lantana vine would have a head start on the other native undergrowth. I can see from the air that I am about to be lowered into a hellish place through which Delta Company is undertaking search and destroy patrols.

Like all trained soldiers, I understand why the Huey has climbed high. The pilot's navigation to the area would be accurate and the D Company navigation on the ground reasonably accurate. But in this terrain there are too many variables working against a dead-set six or eight figure grid refer-ence where chopper and troops can meet. The pilot is up high scanning the area for some tell-tale coloured smoke to be rising up from the jungle below.

In the distance, I make out a purple smoke signal drifting upward from a B52 crater. I assume the pilot has also spotted it and confirmed the colour with the D Company signaller on the ground. The Huey now swoops down and away from the smoke, flying in a large 1000 meter arc to get back onto the treetops before skimming back toward the D Company position.

I take a few deep breaths and grab the winch line then throw my legs over and around two of the four penetrator arms, my bum sits uncomfortably on a third. Beaver helps put my pack opposite to me, resting it on the remaining penetrator arm. Somehow, I am supposed to hold all of this and my rifle in a precarious balancing act. I am swung out to the side of the chopper to be lowered before the chopper is over the landing zone (LZ). I look up and am gripped with a sudden panic attack.

'Hey, is that a damn wire cutter attached to this winch line?' I scream.

'Yeah', Beaver screams back over the whop, whopping. 'If you get stuck in them trees it's either you get cut free or we all come down. Sorry buddy, just an occupational hazard.' He winks at me as I swing helplessly suspended in space. 'Don't worry we got the one and only Surf Marshall at the controls, the best chopper pilot in the force is in charge of this bird, he can drop you on a zac.'

'Surf Marshall!' I yell back. I cannot believe what he has just told me. 'Same Surf Marshall that hung out with Bobby Brown at Voodoo Reef down the end of Cronulla?'

'Yep. Same Surf Marshall. Him and Bobby were legends.' Beaver screams back, 'His brother ain't bad either, you know him do you?'

'Well how about that, the people you cross in a war. Tell Surf I remember him, I was much younger than him but some weekends I used to camp on the clifftop, above Voodoo, at the old farm. I loved watching those guys surf the Voodoo reef man.' I laugh aloud as I visualise my young adolescent hero riding a left break. 'Good old Surf Marshall and his Jacko six stringer. Man he was almost as good as Browney and that is really saying something.' My panic disappears as I smile back at Beaver and give him a 'thumbs up'. He begins lowering the winch line.

With new found trust in the pilot and too preoccupied to be scared, I am now looking at the drop site, some 90 feet down into a bomb crater half-filled with water.

Whoosh   Whop   Whoosh   Whop   Whoosh   Whop

The chopper's down-draft is causing the treetops around me to sway to and fro, flicking small leaves off their branches which swirl around, often hitting me in the face. Down and down I descend, slowly turning clockwise on the end of the winch wire. I can make people out now. A soldier is lying to one side of the crater in a defensive position. Squatting at the edge of the crater is another soldier with black and green camouflage make-up on his face and hands. I suddenly realise I have forgotten to 'cam up'.

Just within the edges of the dark jungle, I can make out a few ghost-like figures squatting at the ready. Probably the injured signaller with a few helpers. As I near the bottom of the treetops, I look up at the Huey in admiration as its pilot, my hero Surf Marshall is skilfully and most considerately moving the chopper in a gentle rocking motion. Has Beaver told him that a fellow Cronulla surfer was on the end of the winch line? Is he doing me a favour? I like to think he is. Surf has just a few feet in which to manoeuvre his aircraft without crashing the bird into the upper tree canopy. Yet his concern is for me and he uses all his skill to get me to swing over to the edge of the crater rather than be lowered into the water below. As I swing toward the crater's edge the soldier squatting nearby reaches out and grabs at me.

'Let go and fall', the digger calls out. I do as instructed, falling heavily onto the crater's edge while protecting my M16 from sinking into the mud and somehow stopping the backpack from sliding down into the giant puddle at the bottom of the crater. I struggle to my feet, already covered in mud down my back and one side. The winch line and penetrator is now swinging back toward the assisting soldier who grabs it and makes frantic motions toward the jungle where I can make out a signaller talking to the pilot above, calling for more line to be let out.

Suddenly from the darkened jungle comes three more soldiers. Jock, the injured signaller in the middle with his right arm heavily bandaged. Even with the bandages, I can see Jock's arm is swollen like an elongated party balloon. Jock wraps his legs around the jungle penetrator and clings on tight with his good arm while the other two string his rifle, pack and webbing under the metal contraption and tie it loosely by a toggle rope. Suddenly Jock is airborne. The chopper already lifting away before Jock is half winched into the cockpit.

In an instant the chopper disappears from above us, its sound fading through the jungle canopy as it flies toward its home base in Nui Dat.

Whop   Whop   Whop   Whop   Whop

The diggers quickly melt back into the dark jungle undergrowth with me following. I suddenly find myself staring in the face of the D Company sergeant major. A black, green and brown face. The CSM has a handful of black cam cream and smears it over my nose and cheeks.

'You know who I am son and you know I can be a mean mother feckin bastard if I don't like some piss-arse little pogo who wants to play soldier', The CSM starts his lecture. 'So you better make sure I like you because you and I are partners from this moment on, you are never more than 15 feet from my arse and never closer than 10. Got that?'

'Yes Sir.'

'Not feckin Sir, not in the feckin jungle son. In the jungle my name is Sandy. You call me Sandy out here and Sir back at base.' He turns his face to one side and spits out a piece of stick he had been chewing. 'Get that right straight away and I won't have to rip the face off the front of your head and use it as an arse wipe.'

'Yes Si…Sandy'.

'Good, you are now officially my best feckin friend, now strap Jock's radio on that A-frame 'cos we are moving out as we talk.' The CSM takes one step back, pauses briefly to admire his handy work as a make-up artist on my newly blackened face. 'Get the backs of your hands cammed soldier', he spits then turns away and walks off into the undergrowth.

I bend down and lift the 25 set to the top section of the A-frame propped against a tree. Wrapping the two retaining straps around it, I pull them as tight as possible, unscrew, fold, slip and secure the ten foot aerial between the set and the frame, and attach the short whip aerial to the set.

Finally, I check the entrenching tool will not be loose enough to knock against the metal back of the 25 set. All human noise is strictly forbidden when patrolling.

Already the perspiration from the stifling heat in the thick tropical jungle air is running down my forehead and into my eyes, causing discomfort. I reach into my shirt where I had tucked my 'giggle hat' to stop it from blowing away in the chopper's down draft. I use the hat to wipe my forehead before wrapping a green sweat rag around my neck to try and absorb the moisture gathering under my chin and down each side of my neck.

In my shirt pocket, I find my small tin of cam cream and put black and green strokes across the back of both hands. As a last thought I flip open my notebook and quickly scribble…

23rd 1100 hrs: Surf Marshall flew the chopper – wow! I don't think CSM likes me - shit I am in for it - what have I got myself into?

I don't really have time to collect my thoughts nor my bearings. I quickly tuck away the notebook and look around to get some sense of what is happening. Shadowy figures are already moving slowly past me and I am able to identify Nunga the support section commander moving past Dutch the second company signaller. From this I can guess where I will need to be on the patrol line. I obviously have the task of back up or zero bravo signaller, close to the CSM but far enough away from the command group in case they are taken out by enemy fire. I can now identify the company commander standing with a company-trained signaller called Jacko nearby. There is also someone else with a sig set. I assume he is the artillery forward observer or FO. From this quick visual reconnaissance, I know I will probably fall in behind the CSM in that general area of the patrol line. They are beginning to move now so I heave the heavy backpack up and slip my arms one at a time through the shoulder straps.

The sky suddenly opens in a torrent of rain. Gigantic droplets of water smash against broad jungle leaves in a thunderous roar, others smash into any solid objects and disintegrate into a myriad of tiny water darts that sting bare skin, causing me to turn my face sideways while looking through squinting eyes. Steam begins rising off the dank jungle floor creating a sauna, heavy with the stench of decayed jungle matter. I am instantly soaking wet and sucking thick humid air back into my lungs, leaving a horrible feeling that each breath isn't getting me the oxygen levels my body craves.

Only moments ago I had been lowered into a jungle, imagining myself to be some kind of hero, coming to the aid of an injured comrade. Since then I have been dressed down by a CSM, wet through, covered in mud and the heavy backpack shoulder straps are cutting painfully into my neck muscles. I know it will be about two hours of patrolling in this jungle before we set up a night harbour. I am beginning to question why I agreed to this insanity and whether I will survive the next two hours without collapsing from the heat and weight.

Sandy re-appears through the downpour and steamy heat haze. The camouflage cream causes his features to take the form of an evil nemesis, an anti-Christ or a wild beast bearing down on me as if I was a helpless fawn. He stands looking at the sodden and confused young man in front of him. The sergeant major leans over closely and stares directly into my face, his steel grey eyes boring into my soul. Suddenly his lips curl upward in a strange half smile, half sneer, exposing dark yellow teeth.

'And you thought this war was about Charlie didn't ya? Well it feckin ain't, it's about being tired, sore, wet and feckin miserable', he spat out the words in the low whisper used by soldiers in the field. 'Welcome to the real war son, now fall in line and earn your feckin pay.'

THAT'S WHAT GRUNTS ARE! THAT'S WHAT GRUNTS DO!

Two days have passed since my less than heroic entry into Delta Company ranks. In those two days the company has only managed to travel some 2000 meters through the tangled mess of jungle. At the end of the first day patrolling, I note...

Day 1: This jungle is foreboding yet beautiful in a strange sort of way. A conglomeration of greens and browns. Endless vines, bushes and amazing trees with twisted gnarled trunks and wide buttressed bases. All around me life mixes surreally with death, new shoots sprout up all over the jungle floor and struggle toward the sun somewhere high beyond the menacing green canopy, old trees are slowly strangled by this new growth, devoured by mites and moss. The jungle floor is thick with the mulch of a million dead plants and animals. Ants, insect beetles, scorpions, spiders and snakes compete ferociously for their tiny piece of jungle. They survive by killing and devouring until they are killed, devoured or rotted into the jungle mulch. I hear all sorts of bird calls, but bird life is heard more than seen, they are just some of the many creatures of the jungle's upper canopy moving about calling their territorial chants. I saw monkeys this afternoon. Little ones, they live up there in the canopy. On the lower parts of the trees, bloody snakes and giant spiders. I saw my first bird eating spider this morning. Looked like it could eat me it was so bloody huge. As for snakes! I have sighted two green tree snakes and one huge python, it just hung in the branches two lousy feet above my head.

Dutch reckons there is the occasional Asian elephant out here and wild boar scuttling through the undergrowth. Wild cats, Asian tigers. What do I do if I come face to face with a bloody tiger???

Bamboo is impenetrable and we get stuck in vines that cling to our clothes. Wait-a-while vine - the boys call it hell vine. It's out to get me and trap me long enough for a bloody big spider or snake to come along and have its way with my exhausted body.

This is hard bloody yakka!

I have become fascinated, if not seduced by my new environment. The jungle is a living entity. It is gradually drawing me into its web like a black widow spider. I know there is a risk of certain death if I fail to move away quickly and yet I instinctively move deeper into the trap.

Wet season rains are thunderous downpours, at times so heavy I have to push my head downward to avoid large blobs smashing into my eyes. This and the reduced visibility make patrol work more dangerous. Any contact with the enemy will be in very close combat as the enemy is in exactly the same situation. Death at five meters! I am afraid but I am mesmerised. I am living on adrenalin. I am already nearing addiction.

Day two: Somehow I have survived the heat, the downpours, the weight and constant exhaustion. My right shoulder is almost red raw where the backpack strap keeps digging in and rubbing, as are both sides of my hips. This is the result of my web belt rubbing each time I bend, twist or step over, under, or around the tangled mass of the once bombed jungle. Jesus, I am hot, dehydrated and hoping for another downpour one moment, then sodden, muddy and cursing the rain the next. The heavy rain can wash a soldier clean of mud and sweat in an instant. It passes as abruptly as it arrives, leaving a waterlogged bushland in its wake, dripping constantly. Occasionally a small puddle full of water pours down my back as a cupped broad leaf is disturbed.

For a brief moment, the rain leaves the jungle cleansed. For that same brief moment a clean smell lifts the spirits of all who experience it. The stench and decay of rotting leaves and fallen foliage disappears for a brief post-downpour moment. A moment only!

Humidity rises within minutes of the rain passing, perspiration begins re-staining the underarms, back and crotch-lines. Mud soon finds its way back up my legs. Knees, hips and bum soon become stained black and brown when I squat or take up temporary rest positions.

I gradually adjust straps, location of equipment and weight distribution across my body until the least damaging mix is found. I'm resigned to the fact that pain and discomfort will be my constant companion each day. Aches are my bedtime partner and stiff muscles are a breakfast companion.

Sandy proves to be all his reputation claimed him to be; mean as mustard but fatherly to his troops. He has taken me under his wing, gradually easing me into the harsh reality of counter insurgency jungle warfare where little is said and monotonous days of patrolling tests each soldier's will to remain alert and vigilant.

Sandy is the consummate soldier's soldier. In his late thirties, the company sergeant major has 20 years' experience in this business including active service in Malaya and a prior tour of Vietnam. He is medium height and carries a slight pot belly under his barrel chest, these features disguise his strength and tenacity. Unlike me, Sandy sweeps his overloaded backpack up onto his shoulders and wanders off with little more than a muffled grunt and a jovial 'nother day, 'nother dollar comment.

Sandy's darker-than-Caucasian skin hints of an Aboriginal heritage. Army life can be harsh but it is equal, at least in the ranks. Everybody is shit in the army and everyone is judged on their performance, not their colour or religion, particularly in times of war. This does not mean racism does not exist. Heck I tell plenty of Irish and for that matter blackfella jokes myself.

But that is the one-on-one racism that can be sorted out with a beer, or at worse a fight at the back of the barracks. In fact, Sandy is not unusual in this army, many Aboriginal people wear the baggy green uniform. Most are of mixed blood, others like the dreaded Nunger are blackfellars as they like to call themselves in this unit.

I'm told that Sandy returned from the Malayan conflict a lance corporal and started his first tour of Vietnam as a corporal, returning as a sergeant. He was awarded a Mention in Dispatches for bravery. Promoted to warrant officer class 2 and transferred to the next battalion preparing for a tour of duty in 'Nam.

My greatest problem with Sandy is his love of cooking. In the patrol buddy system, Sandy and I are teamed up together. We share all sorts of tasks. Only one of us can be cleaning a weapon at any time, so the other one would be on sig watch and making a brew of tea or coffee. Sandy however insists on preparing all the hot meals. His culinary skills are simple. Take a can or packet of whatever and heat it rapidly over a piece of hexi or C4 explosive and mix in liberal splashes of hot Tabasco sauce or curry powder, which he carries in great quantities.

'The meat in these ration tins ain't feckin dead you know, you gotta kill it with the hot red stuff before you munch on it', he often whispers as he prepares our poison.

'It's so hot it makes my mouth and throat go numb', I once replied.

'Exactly as it's meant to do! Kills the feckin taste so you don't know you're actually eating feckin dog shit.'

The man scares me. How does a buck private tell a bloody CSM that he is a shithouse cook? If only he would let me cook my own food. War is hell in ways I never imagined.

'Hey Sandy, you're part Abo aren't you?'

'The best part of me is son... got a problem with that? If you want to spend the rest of this war eating my cooking without any teeth you can tell me that being what you call an Abo is not a good thing.'

'Hey cool down, I was just wondering where you come from. That's all.'

'Koonibba I think, or coon-what-ibba for pricks like you.'

'What do you mean "I think"? And where is this Koonibba place anyway?'

'I got took from my mum when I was an ankle biter, I don't remember. But the foster folk that tried to give me a Christian upbringing said I come from Koonibba. It's a mission or some sort of place near Ceduna, you know, that place down near the Nullarbor Plains. They said I got a mum there somewhere.'

'A Dad?'

'Nah, just some prick of a white man that put his dick in me mum and pissed off and left her I reckon. That ain't exactly a dad is it?'

'Ever going back? I mean ever going to look for your mum?'

'Never you mind about me ya little twerp, my business is my business, okay?'

'Sorry Sandy, well I just was thinking that, well I would hate not to have a mum that's all. You should go find her, that's what I reckon.'

'Yeah, maybe one day. Look son I know you mean well and I sort of appreciate that you are the first digger in 20 years ever asked me… but I don't want to talk about it again… understood?'

I nod, it's all I can do when Sandy gives me his scary look. As I eat I can see Dutch, the other battalion signaller. He is buddied with the company commander whom we all refer to as OC. Then there is the artillery forward observer or FO as we call him. He doesn't have a separate sig operator and carries his own 25 set. He's buddied with the company signaller, nicknamed Jacko who is an overly good looking, dark skinned, gentle sort of a person. I learn from a brief whispered conversation that his mother is Timorese and his father is an Australian teacher. They met while he was travelling in the Portuguese outpost. I can't help but notice how Jacko's dark skin accentuates his balloon-sized white eyes with their sparkling deep dark brown centres. They match or at least accentuate the young boy's shiny white teeth which live in two perfect rows between pinkish brown lips. He is good looking alright, too good looking for most women. I figure he is gay. Jacko is no soldier, just a gentle young boy who dreamed of playing concert cello at the Sydney opera house. But for now he is simply a part of Prime Minister Menzies' conscription fodder for the war in Vietnam. Yet despite his gentle nature and slim effeminate build Jacko is never heard to complain about the enormous weight a signaller has to carry. He always does his turn of night watch or additional gun shift without so much as a murmur of discontent.

'Do you think that Jacko is gay, Sandy?'

'Never mind that ya pogo, 'less ya want a bit of him for yourself. It don't matter what he is, what matters is, will he do his job? Let me assure you that Jacko won't let you down if and when the shit hits the fan. Behind his pretty face is a young man with the balls to do his job so I don't give a tinker's feck what else he does with his balls when he ain't on patrol.'

The HQ group also consists of the company medic who automatically carries the tag of Doc. He's buddied with the ever smiling and slightly insane army engineer affectionately known as Wingnut. I have yet to get into any conversation with these two strange characters.

Moving along with the HQ group is an Infantry Support Section, supposedly of six men, but rarely more than four or five. Their section commander is the infamous Nunger, a full Initiated Aboriginal complete with the missing tooth and chest scars from his tribal initiation. His infamy stems from history of soldiering punctuated by a history of binge drinking and bar brawling between patrols. He has been promoted and demoted more times than most diggers have enjoyed a hot breakfast and if it wasn't for Sandy being his constant guardian angel, he would no doubt be a private again.

Sandy and Nunger are a team. They served together in 'Nam on Sandy's last trip. On that tour, Nunger was Sandy's forward scout and no better scout had served in warfare as far as Sandy was concerned. Sandy used his influence with the company commander to put Nunger in charge of the support section as a tracker with the reconnaissance team. Trained in the ways of his elders in northern Queensland, Nunger can track an ant across a rock face and easily adapted his tracking skills from the Queensland tropics to the terrain in 'Nam. He should have been attached to the anti-tank or tracking platoon but they didn't want him due to his drinking binges and because he had broken the nose of the tracker's platoon sergeant back in Australia.

But not just Nunger, all infantrymen, Sandy, the forward scouts, machine gunners, the specialist soldiers and me, we're all here in this jungle for one purpose, and that is to seek out and destroy the enemy. We literally hunt them down, ambush, track, or stumble upon them, as a result of constant jungle patrolling.

If the enemy force is small, we engage and kill them using infantry weapons alone. If large or in a fortified bunker system we find them and keep them busy for long enough to enable artillery, air power, or in the right circumstances, tanks to close in and destroy them with the infantry mopping up the pieces.

I am an infantry soldier trained and re-trained in contact drills and immediate actions that would make me react instantly to a situation before thinking about it. Trained to think and respond in the most aggressive and violent manner possible.

Surrounding me in this jungle are young men of 19 to 24 years and young officers of similar age guided or led by the older sergeants. Taken from their civilian lives as accountants, students, farm hands, apprentice tradesman and labourers and turned by army instructors into trained killers. I am afraid sometimes, but I feel confident that I will survive.

'Green clad jungle killers, trained to the peak of ruthless efficiency', Sandy often says, 'and God help any bastard who gets in our way because that's what grunts are and that's what grunts do!' It is the impossibility of the area that makes it such a useful place to build base camps and training areas. The Viet Cong and North Vietnamese soldiers are used to war against American or South Vietnamese soldiers, most of whom would avoid such areas. Australians are that little bit different, more professional and hungry for enemy contact on our terms. We are trained to traverse

these conditions quietly, our patrolling methods almost silent. Americans push and shove their way through the jungle or walk along tracks where they are easily ambushed. We use hand signals rather than talk to each other. When we do talk it is always in a whisper. We quietly snip and move vines aside, rather than crash and hack our way through them. The Aussie grunt is a hunter, not just a warrior.

This silence and extra care give the enemy no warning of their impending peril. It gives the Australian grunt an edge. It is this edge Delta Company is attempting to exploit. I am confident we will win any encounter with Charlie.

The enemy too is cunning. Masters in the art of camouflage, they can cover tracks from being sighted by aircraft and are, to the untrained eye, difficult to recognise from ground level. Their defensive bunker systems, magnificently camouflaged, made from the very jungle material they hide within. More often than not, such systems protected by land mines or booby traps set out about 50 meters from the bunkers as deadly early warning devices.

This is the Australian infantry forward scout's main fear. To tread on a mine or trip a booby trap doesn't always mean death is the instant result. Often a leg and genitals are blown off, or you suffer a painful death as you lie waiting for other soldiers to slowly clear the area before coming to your aid, knowing that if they rushed forward to help you they too could trip a mine or booby trap.

The other fear all scouts live with each day is the fear of leading your section and platoon into an ambush or directly into a bunker system.

Scouts fall into two categories. Those who have to take their turn in a rotation system amongst the section, or as is often the case, those who are just good at it and choose to stay up at the front. Probably because they don't trust any other digger to do the job properly.

Either way, I can always tell at a glance which digger has been the forward scout when dusk calls an end to patrolling. They are the ones with dark eye sockets and eyes that dart across the bottoms of eyelids in jerking non-stop motions. They live on the very edge of their nervous system and you can see just how close to insanity they are travelling, even if they themselves do not know it. War is a drug, most full time scouts are well and truly addicted to the high levels of adrenalin.

Today we are lucky, our forward scout is finely tuned to his task. He has noticed the slight change in the jungle canopy, more cover from prying aircraft. This is bunker country and he is taking extra care in his search for tell-tale signs.

On this day, his professional skills are rewarded. He sees the signs and reacts quickly and quietly. Dropping to one knee and sending back the watched for hand signal. Fist clenched, thumb facing down, possible enemy to the front.

He has not sighted an enemy. What his keen sense of survival has noticed is the ever so slight and clever thinning of the undergrowth. It is not obvious to an amateur but to a skilled eye it is unnatural. Nature is random, particularly in this type of re-growth, nothing is neat, tidy or structured. The scout knows he is on the edge of a bunker fire lane. The area has been carefully cleared just enough to allow the enemy in a bunker to get a clear view of any enemy soldier walking within the fire lanes of the bunker. The scout is certainly not walking, he's squatting and hidden. Looking around him the scout can make out the inter-locking fire lanes from another bunker. This supports crossfire so that each enemy position can defend the other from a frontal assault by a large force. He cannot yet see the actual bunkers but he knows they are there.

He sends back the three-fingered landmine and booby-trap signal to get every soldier to freeze in his current position, in case he has missed seeing a booby trap or mine on his way into the current fire lane.

I am well back from the forward section but the signal passes rapidly to me and I now feel the first tang of fear in my stomach. But I am trained to react, so react I will. Just as I have been drilled too.

I slip my bayonet from its sheath under the M16 handgrip. Slowly I clear my immediate area for mines by carefully sliding the bayonet into the ground, gently prodding at about a 30-degree angle, feeling through the wet season's mud for the metal or plastic casing of a mine, clearing a circle area around me. At the same time, my eyes are scanning my immediate area for any trip wire or unnaturally strung vine. Nothing!

Now my training as a sig must take over. I scan the trees for a possible branch from which I can suspend a dipole aerial in case I am unable to get a good comms with zero alpha or bravo. My pulse is racing. I must try comms with my whip aerial. Stay calm, depress the talk button on the handset and whisper to zero bravo for a radio check. Don't let them hear your voice tremble, quiet, calm, slow words.

'zero bravo this is call sign four… radio check. Over.'

A short silence is rewarded with a 'loud and clear' reply from 'the Dat'. I let out a slow sigh of relief, then whisper into the handset, 'Roger zero bravo, we have possible enemy situation here, alert zero alpha. Over.'

'This is zero bravo wilco. Out'.

A strange metallic taste starts in my mouth as the adrenalin surges through my body. Nature ensures that I am primed and wound tight, ready for whatever I might be about to encounter. It's happening to me just like my jungle warfare instructor told me it would. I have passed my first test, I feel strong.

So what are We Doing in this Place?

Anticipation is gradually turning into confusion, the other soldiers and I are just squatting or lying where we've been stopped by the forward scout's signals. Time is eating into nerves and curiosity. Minutes seem like hours.

Eventually a signal comes down the line: two fingers on the upper arm then a tap on the head. This is followed by a second signal: pull on the left ear, poke out the tongue and again a tap on the head. The first signal is a common and simple one for any trained grunt to understand, it's a signal to the section commander, Nunger, to move forward and check out the situation ahead. The second signal has quite confused me, but I mimic and pass it back to the rear troops.

Quietly Nunger slips past me, moving up the line toward the forward scout and the two sections of soldiers up ahead. Next follows the army sapper, nicknamed Wingnut. I now realise what the second signal represented. D Company's sapper from the army engineer detachment has little ears poking almost at 90 degrees from the side of his scone.

More moments pass slowly. I practise slow deep breathing. Finally, thumbs up. I receive a signal to move forward to the company commander. I struggle to lift the weight of my backpack off the broken bough where I've

condition ready for use when needed, which means there is another base camp or something nearby.'

With the stick, he scratches out the details.

'Each point of the star is a machine-gun bunker with two bunkers behind on each side like a triangle. If we hit the enemy head on, we will be faced with gunfire from three fortified positions, if we sweep around to the right or left to make a flank attack we will be caught between one-star point and the next point beside it. The cross fire will cut us to pieces.' I can see OC is admiring the piece of handiwork scratched in the ground.

'Damn clever, never seen this before, but I tell you here and now it was not designed by a bunch of local villagers for two reasons. Firstly, there is no local village. Secondly, the dimensions and layout is close to perfect. My guess is North Vietnamese sappers designed and built this bastard.'

Sandy now cuts into the conversation. 'You will notice that there ain't no crawl trenches between bunkers, this means each bunker will be connected by tunnels to the other and back to the central area where I am dead sure Wingnut will find a command centre. We already know he found a field surgery and post-operative recovery room down there.' He makes a sweeping motion over the slightly cleared area in the system's centre.

'This area immediately in front is set up as the airing space for wounded soldiers to lie in the fresh air after their surgery. You can see the short stumps around where we are sitting, these hold up the stretcher bunks. If you look up to that tree there', Sandy points, 'Nunger advises me that the scuff mark is a spot where they tie a low slung canvas which is stretched over this area to provide cover from rain or whatever sun gets through them feckin trees.'

The OC turns to his CSM, 'Sandy, there must be some tracks out of here?'

'I've got Nunger onto that little task as we speak. He has found something off the gun bunker to your right, heading north-west from here.'

The OC now studies the map in front of him, 'They probably have a base camp over here in the east. My guess is it will be near this creek-line here. It might be wet season now but they will need to be close to water in the dry.'

'Why leave it empty?' A platoon commander officer inquires.

OC has the answer, 'They don't want it found. Noise, smells from cooking fires or a sniffer flying by to pick up bodyheat would give the place away but if they send in a small maintenance crew each week they keep it ready for when they need it, after a big op or battle. I reckon it's been built ready for a big surge of activity against us.'

The second lieutenant from Twelve Platoon now enters the conversation, 'I thought the tracks Nunger found were over on the northern side.'

Sandy snorts and responds. 'What would you do if you were Charlie and didn't want anyone to find your precious feckin hospital? Charlie is just as cunning as we are you know sonny boy. He will have all sorts of tracks leading in different directions and just one of them sneaking into here, most likely from the opposite direction than dumb, wet-arse young lieutenants would consider.'

I watch amused as the officer blushes. It's obvious that Lieutenant Robert Dowelment feels uneasy in the presence of the sergeant major. Most young officers would. Many of their tough and often abusive instructors at the military academy were sergeants and warrant officers. They were taught to jump when told, to obey and above all, to swallow as much wisdom as their instructors could force down their throats, for theirs was the wisdom of experience, not theory and history books. Now this officer is a commissioned and theoretically his commission is higher in rank than the tough non-com but he dare not challenge this CSM, particularly as the Major would always back Sandy in any disputation of authority.

I can see Robert is trying to hide his embarrassment, the young bloke tries to ignore the CSM and impress his company commander and asks, 'So we get our own sappers in and blow this place to kingdom come do we?'

OC is more patient than Sandy with his junior officers. 'No Robby, we do that and Charlie will know we are here. What we are going to do is let Nunger finish snooping around that track today and bunk down until morning. Tomorrow we go after the support base these Nogs have got hidden out here somewhere', he points to his map. 'We can blow this bunker to pieces after we find Charlie.'

OC pauses and then continues, 'Sandy, I want you to make sure the boys have got the area secure for the night. You personally take charge of every perimeter gun sighting and make sure there is an extra claymore mine or two on the edge of that track.'

'On the way now', Sandy moves off to his task.

My immediate thought is one of relief. Enemy soldiers are not my priority anymore. I am physically exhausted and no more travelling today means I can rest my aching back and treat the raw skin on these shoulders and hips.

The company can camp on top of the bunker system but not inside the underground system. Our well-rehearsed night routines would be useless if carried out inside those tunnels. As the afternoon passes, the other signallers and I set up HQ for the impending nightfall. Each radio is dug into their individual hole to prevent them being damaged by gunfire or shrapnel. The radios are more important than the soldiers. Without them there would be no artillery or chopper support. A wide shell-scrape is dug about 20 inches into the ground to allow two people to lie in relative safety if the shit hits the fan. As long as two men and the radios survive in combat, the HQ can keep functioning.

Two low slung hooches are joined together and suspended over the HQ shell-scrape to keep soldiers and their equipment dry. From this location each soldier operating the radios at night has strung up green com cord from the HQ area, back to where they will set up their own individual hooches once dusk turns to night. In the pitch black of jungle nights we can only find our way by grabbing the com cord and following it on hands and knees.

Wingnut has finished his task of clearing the bunker and is his usual smiling self. He sits next to me and introduces himself, 'G'day, you're Brian ain't ya?'

'Yeah that's my name. I got to ask you, what's it like inside that underground bunker?'

'Bloody brilliant, one of the best I've ever crawled through and the surgery down there is amazing, better than our own M.A.S.H. unit in Vungers.'

'What Viper? I doubt a hole in the ground could better than our hospital.'

Wingnut stares back at me for a moment and then passes me the second Browning handgun and three spare magazines of 9 mm ammo, 'Leave the M16 with Dutch, you're all set up and not on picket, come with me my man and I will blow your fucking mind away.'

I hesitate, this is not what I should be doing, but I am being offered a chance to see inside one of these infamous bunker systems and know I may never get a second opportunity. The OC and the CSM are not to be seen so I decide to take a chance and have a squiz. Wingnut leads me over to the trap-door entrance to a secondary bunker in the northern star point.

'They sometimes booby trap these doors but nothing in this system at all. On your knees and follow my torch light.' He drops down a small hole before squatting to his knees and disappearing. I follow.

The underground tunnel is about one meter high and no more than about 80 centimetres wide, definitely not designed for larger European bodies carrying equipment. The walls of the tunnel are like hard packed clay with the occasional damp patch emanating the smell of rotting compost giving me early symptoms of claustrophobia. I can feel the excitement of the unknown and anticipation of new experiences, it helps drive the primitive fear of a confined space from my mental focus. I peer through the gloom at my guide and nod, 'Wow! Lead the way'.

Wingnut leads me to the actual bunker position. Half standing I peer through the gun slot and am amazed at the clear vision of fire. 'How do they do that? Out there it looks just like jungle but down here it's all clear.'

'Clever bastards aren't they? It's their jungle and they know what to cut and how to cut it.' Wingnut is again on his haunches and moving down another tunnel. At the intersection of two more tunnels is a larger area with a cooking hearth.

'The Nogs call this a Dien Bien Phu kitchen. It's got exhaust vents up through there.' Wingnut points to the vent at the back of the hearth. 'Smoke is drawn up and back then dissipates and comes out a couple of meters away. As a bonus to the design, if we try and get at them from the top the vents protect the Nogs below. You could drop a grenade down the kitchen vent and it would not cause any casualties back here, even gas grenades are useless because the natural air flow just pushes it back to the vent opening.'

'Gas! Is that legal? I mean… well you know Geneva Convention, legal?'

'Don't know, don't fuckin' care.' Wingnut crouches again, turns left and scurries along. I follow in awe. We pass through a door obviously used to seal one section from another in case of gas attack. Suddenly we are standing in a larger area where a table has been constructed and many shelves are built into the walls. Natural jungle materials and some pre-sawn timbers provide carefully constructed structural supports.

'Command post', Wingnut announces as he moves the torch around for my benefit. 'By the way you probably didn't notice but we passed over a hatch leading to a second layer of tunnels even deeper down. It's just sort of sleeping quarters and very fucking stuffy so no point me taking you down there.' I nod in agreement. I am feeling closed in as it is and have no desire to go deeper. Through the next entrance I can see a blaze of bright light just past another ceiling door, which is pulled open.

'What's in there?' I ask.

'The piece de resistance!' Wingnut replies. We slip into the next room and are confronted by the OC.

The company commander is simply called Sir, Skipper or OC by the troops and John by his junior officers and CSM. Six feet tall and a former rugby centre half, he is the image of a dashing soldier. Ruggedly handsome, blue eyes and a strong dimpled chin supported by a powerful neck protruding from broad shoulders. The kind of person who would naturally emerge as a leader in any group, the alpha male. The OC has a quiet arrogance and a potent aura of self-confidence that assures all around him that he is in charge and that's the way it should always be.

'What's this, you running a tourist service are you sapper?'

'After the war I might do just that.'

The OC shakes his head, 'Not you Sapper, some retired Viet Cong hero maybe but not you or me, we won't be welcome here after the war, not for many years.'

Wingnut looks surprised by the Major's comment. 'You figure we won't win this war Sir?'

'No way son, just look around you. Look at this workmanship. You have to be hungry for victory to build this, fanatical. America isn't hungry, just bloated. The South Vietnamese army have lost their capacity to survive without massive American support and there simply aren't enough Australian soldiers to fight these bastards the way they have to be fought if they're ever going to be beaten.'

I am probably as shocked as Wingnut. Having a senior officer say we could not win the war is quite disconcerting. I have never even considered defeat. But here I am looking around me at the underground surgery. The OC seems not to mind my being here so I take out my notebook and pace the room.

No more than three meters wide and maybe four meters long and obviously carefully constructed with reinforcing pillars and walls. The whole room is lined with American C ration container tins that have been opened out and flattened, then skilfully joined together to make a complete ceiling, wall and floor lining. The shiny and polished metallic side of the tin walls reflect light all around the surgical room. In the centre is an operating table constructed of jungle material and the workmanship is thoroughly professional. Dovetail joints carefully hold the table together, the top lined with perfectly joined tin. The joints are remarkable, each sheet folded along a crease and slipped together with machine like precision. The surgery table comes complete with skilfully grooved blood drains, not dissimilar to a mortuary table. The drains are angled to the table edge and along to a hole where buckets could be placed. Above the table is the source of light. An ingenious piece of engineering. It is again made of tin but constructed in such a way that a torch, in this case the OC's, placed in its centre and facing upward reflects bright sharp light beams from mirrors set at different angles, which then reflect off the polished tin walls. Brightly lighting up not just the operating table but the whole theatre.

The smell of disinfectant is strong. I realise what the above-ground conversation was all about now. The enemy must be coming to this place at regular intervals and keeping it spotlessly clean, ready for immediate use after a major battle somewhere in the Phuoc Tuy, or Long Khanh Provinces. Several coconuts are stacked on a shelf. 'What's with the coconuts?' I ask anyone who might know.

'These boys can't just ring up the Red Cross and ask for a couple of pints of plasma or blood. Coconut milk is sterile inside its shell and is used as a temporary transfusion, it holds up a wounded man's blood pressure, hopefully long enough for their medics to drain blood from other soldiers who aren't wounded. Damn clever bastards, you have to respect them son, never see them as anything less than damn clever. They are very brave and determined to win at any cost.'

The Major lets out a sigh, 'I sure wish they were on our side instead of fighting against us.'

'So what are we doing here? if we aren't going to win, what the fuck are we dying for?'

'Your country son. We aren't here to win, we are here to protect our trade links with America, and through American arrangements, our trade links with Japan. That's why we are here', he pauses a moment then imparts more wisdom. 'The European Common Market will all but destroy our arrangement with mother England, its America or national bankruptcy. These days we live off the Yanks' back, not the sheep's back, so if America asks us to send some boys over to get killed, we send boys over to get killed, otherwise America may punish us through international trade.'

'That's nice isn't it?' Wingnut responds.

The Major smiles. 'It's okay sapper, it's our job as soldiers. We are protecting the wealth of Australia by being here. Ours is a very lucky country, we keep Australia lucky by putting our arse on the line for our trade partners, winning and losing has nothing to do with it. This is our ANZAC legacy and tradition.'

'I thought ANZAC tradition was linked to Gallipoli?' I ask.

'Exactly! Sent to fight a war in a strange country without any control over where or how we fight, forced to follow orders and deploy stupidly by some foreign generals who don't know shit from sugar and eventually we will have to withdraw with our tail between our legs. That sounds like the ANZAC tradition to me.'

The Major runs his hand over the magnificently constructed operating table, 'I only hope the bastards who got us into this war come up with a load of propaganda that makes us look like heroes in much the same way they did with Gallipoli. If we must die, it is best we be remembered as heroes. Not as more of Kipling's fools.'

'Kipling?'

'Yeah, a little poem, a short ditty, look it up when you get back home.'

I feel instantly disillusioned if not downright depressed. This Major is an educated man, Duntroon Military Academy and no doubt a university degree in international something or other. Suddenly I did not want to be here anymore.

'Kipling huh! I'll remember to do that. By the way, how do I get out of this place?'

'Up through there', Wingnut points.

'I wasn't talking about the bunker Wingnut. I was talking about the fucking war.'

Once above ground again, I make my way to Doc, the company medic who has been busy all afternoon treating a thousand nicks, cuts, festered boils and awkward rashes as diggers from the platoons take advantage of the company-sized harbour.

I pull back my shirt to show Doc the raw skin on my shoulder. Doc glances casually at it, 'Come back when it's really sore.' He has a slight cockney English accent. He smiles at me and grabs some white powder from his medical kit, sprinkling it onto my sore skin.

'Good to see someone with enough sense to get things treated before they get badly infected. I now recommend a long hot bath followed by a day or two in bed with a healthy young woman.'

'I'll do that as soon as the OC can organise it for me. Hey, you've done a lot of schooling haven't ya?'

'I suppose, well, yes I managed to get half way through university, that counts for something. Why?'

Doc's 'why' answer seems more guarded than curious in its tone. 'Do you know much about Kipling?'

'The writer,' Doc responds. 'A bit, why?'

'I assume it's that Kipling, I haven't read his work. OC said he wants me to look up some little ditty he wrote about dead fools and war.'

'Limerick, it's a limerick I think. I remember some short lines about a fool's grave. Guess you'll have to wait 'til you get home if you want to read Kipling. Stick books are about all that diggers like to read over here.'

'So do you remember the limerick?'

Doc reaches over and takes the notebook from my hands and produces his own pencil and begins to scribble. Once done he hands back the notebook.

'I think this is how it goes but I may not have got it exact. I haven't read any Kipling since I was about thirteen.' He rubs an itch on his camouflaged nose. 'You like to read and write Brian?'

'Sort of, I want to keep a record of things so I write stuff down in this book. It helps me remember details when I read back the notes.'

'Good! Keep writing Brian, keep writing. We need people to keep a bit of the actual living history of this war.'

I liked Doc the instant we met. A certain calm maturity is present in the man. Doc says little but does a lot and never complains about doing his turn on radio shift at night, or carrying an extra 25 set battery in addition to his bulging medical kit. Doc returns my smile, but it disappears instantly when Wingnut sits down beside him. Wingnut and Doc are buddied up but clearly Doc has little time for the sapper who is now cutting in on the conversation.

'That OC don't know what he's talking about', Wingnut says to me, ignoring Doc completely. 'This war is going on forever mate. I know it for a fact. Mick back at the Dat told me and he isn't ever wrong.'

'Who in God's name is Mick?' Doc responds.

'The company storeman. He knows everything. He is a 'nasho' with university studies in economics, and he said America has to fight this war.'

I am curious enough to listen to what Wingnut has to say, even if Doc is showing his contempt, 'Go on, tell me why America has to fight this war?' Wingnut immediately points at my M16 assault rifle.

'What's that stamped on your 'Gat' man? G fucking M, get it, GM. Think about all them APCs, tanks and jeeps man, not to mention the choppers and jets and stuff. America needs a war so it can make more war shit. Mick says that Detroit City would go bankrupt if America stops fighting this war.'

'What a lot of wank, they just make more cars and washing machines if they don't make war material.'

'Not so according to Mick, he says any country that has an economy with more than five percent of its manufacturing base being used to make war shit, has to have a war somewhere to keep up supply and demand. He says America has about 20 percent of its economy based on making war shit.'

'So I am beginning to dislike America', is all I can say in response.

Doc cuts back into the conversation, 'Don't listen to Wingnut mate, he's a war monger, he likes this war and wants it to keep going.'

'So will you eventually. Trust me mate, you will go back to Aussie and be chaffing at the bit to get back to 'Nam, just like me and the Major and the CSM. We belong here, we don't belong back in Aussie.'

Doc's anger is now obvious, 'Don't put yourself in the same league as Sandy and the Major, they are professional soldiers serving their country because that's what they believe in. You just plain like this war. That's what makes you a dirty arse wipe, not a professional soldier.'

Wingnut smiles back at him through what I am now seeing as crazy man's eyes. 'We'll see if I am right. Trust me on this one. You belong here in 'Nam now. There is no place for us back home. I know, I've been back and I fucking know they don't like us diggers back home.'

'Hey cool it you two. Get a grip for God's sake. It's a long time before we need to talk about home anyway.'

I stand and walk back to my night area to check all is ready for 'stand-to'. I am rapidly becoming disillusioned and depressed. This is not what I assumed war was all about - mud, rain, and sore body parts. Politics and economics are a different proposition to domino theories and communist aggression taught at Kapooka Military Training Centre. I open my notebook and read Doc's pencilled in memory of Kipling's verse.

> *At the end of the fight*
> *a tombstone white*
> *with the name of the late deceased*
> *The epitaph drear - a fool lies here*
> *who tried to hustle the East*

Until now, I had never thought about my possible death in war but suddenly I am afraid. I do not want to die because Australia needs to keep trade relations with America. I take my pencil and print below Doc's version of Kipling's limerick.

> *G fucking M. I think I am scared but I don't know for sure – I mean it*
> *isn't like I am in a battle or stuff, but I just feel on edge– I will never forget*

that tunnel system. OC is right, how do you beat that sort of commitment? Not with B52s and napalm that's for sure.

I look at the environment around me. My black widow spider nest called jungle. I hate it, yet I feel it sucking my soul. I jot down some more short notes to describe this environment. I decide I will fill many lines with descriptions of this environment almost every day. It is both beautiful and overwhelming at the same time.

The late afternoon jungle sounds begin their regular chorus as cicadas, lizards and birds go about a pre-dusk frenzy; a last minute shop for post dinner snacks. This sudden increase in jungle noises is no concern to diggers as it happens with monotonous regularity. It does however warn us that last light is soon approaching. Around the defensive perimeter soldiers' quickly carry out last minute checks of equipment or puff a final cigarette before stand-to routine commences.

Just on dusk the outer listening-post sentries come back into the defensive perimeter and each soldier takes up a firing position as if ready to repel an enemy attack. The tactic was born in the Korean War where the Chinese soldiers would launch their assaults at first light or last light. The Viet Cong do not generally do this, but the North Vietnamese Army trained with assistance from China and Australian soldiers are not in the habit of being caught unprepared. Stand-to also sets up a ritualised routine for night practice. When dark descends, each soldier sets up his pre-prepared hooch and bunks down until called upon to do gun picket or radio shift.

I have scored the first light morning shift. I can look forward to a decent rest if no enemy comes near the perimeter tonight.

Word comes by whisper to stand-down after darkness has engulfed the jungle. I pull up my hooch first, then string the hammock tight between the two thin trees, just enough to get my back off the ground. The afternoon downpour is over but at this time of year, more rain will fall at night. Water will inevitably run under my hooch when the tropical rains dump buckets on me. I am glad that tonight I can slip into the hammock's netting.

In only a matter of minutes, another tropical downpour thunders on the hooch in a deafening crescendo. In the darkness, and feeling with my fingers, I check that my water bottles are catching the water running from the hooch. Already one is full. I screw the lid tight and slip it back into its pouch on the web belt.

Wrapped in my silk, and drier than I could possibly have hoped for, I lie here waiting to slip into my new light and fitful sleep pattern. More than ever before, I wish I had not joined the army as a young 17-year-old. I had assumed the Vietnam War would be over by the time I turned 19. I wonder if any person back in Australia appreciates the irony that their Americanised lifestyle is protected by having young men die in other people's war. A war that even a professional soldier like the Major believes cannot be won.

No Longer a Boy
but Never to be a Man

THE NIGHT PASSES without incident. I am sitting enjoying a hot mug of coffee, sipping it slowly from the kidney shaped mug.

Nunger approaches me, 'You're coming with me white trash', he whispers with his ever-present cheeky grin. Pointing over to the group in the HQ briefing area Nunger silently wanders off to join the OC and platoon commanders. I stand, weapon in right hand, mug in the other and walk over to the briefing to be acknowledged with a brisk nod by the OC.

'Good, now that we are all here, this is today's plan of action.'

The Major starts his briefing by pointing a short length of stick at the map on the ground before us. 'Twelve Platoon is going to sweep this area along the creek line. Ten Platoon will hold back at this point as a ready response group between Twelve Platoon and Eleven Platoon.' His stick is pointing to a space on the map where a six figure grid reference is scrawled. 'HQ will be with Eleven Platoon and we will split.' The OC then looks at Eleven Platoon Commander, 'You leave two rifle section, platoon sergeant and batman with me to secure the hospital and use the other section to set up an ambush on the track we believe the enemy are using to get in and out of this hospital.'

The OC now looks at Nunger, 'After what you told me about the usage of that track I have decided to use your section to recce a good ambush site. If Charlie is coming today, I think you will hear him before any other scout. Follow that enemy track no more than a couple of hundred meters until you find a perfect ambush site for Eleven Platoon's ambush party. When you find it, come back and lead them in. Once they are in position, return here and help secure this place.'

The Major then looks at me. 'You young fella are going with Nunger, just in case the shit spills and he needs back-up artillery support. So go talk to the forward observer and get the details of the silent DF we logged out there last night.'

I try to look as calm as I possibly can, stand and move over to the artillery officer who smiles and spreads out his map. The FO does not look at all like a veteran soldier. Thin build and wearing steel-rimmed glasses, his mannerisms are more that of a science nerd wandering in the jungle looking for butterflies. But I've heard scuttlebutt that this man is a pro, calm in contact and deadly accurate with his directions. I produce my own map of the area and fold it in such a way that it resembles the one before me.

'We are right here', the FO remarks. 'Last night I had the Yank 155s sight two guns onto this grid square as a silent defensive fire or DF location'.

I examine the map and note the eight-figure grid reference marked DF on it within one of the grid squares, then transfer the information to my own chart. The FO continues his briefing.

'They are still set and ready to fire. If the shit spills, all you need to do is call me up and ask for the fire mission. I will get first sighting rounds on the ground within 30 seconds.'

I nod, trying to look calm and professional but my thigh is starting to tremble uncontrollably. The term 'sighting rounds' means little in the jungle, as you can't see where the shells are exploding. You have to be guided by the sound, I understand what the FO means. It is a big responsibility to make a judgement that may kill your own men if you get it wrong.

The FO continues, 'As long as you are heading left or right of this approximate bearing, down that track, it will be a simple matter of calling the shells right from the original zone first, then dropping the shells toward you.' He pauses, I think he has noticed my leg shaking.

'Bear in mind the 155s are a long way off and there will be a pretty long beat zone, so only 'walk in' the guns until dead shrapnel starts falling on your position, no 'danger close' calls, got that?'

I shuffle nervously. Already my throat is dry, my pulse increasing.

'I had FO training back in Aus Sir. Live firing practise at Shoalwater Bay, last thing I want is a situation where I am bringing artillery down "danger close."' I begin to silently question whether I will handle the responsibility if tested.

'Hopefully you won't even need a fire mission', the FO replies, then he smiles at me. A calming smile that eases my nervousness. 'You will be okay mate, remember, if the shit spills, the artillery is only there to scare the bastards while you lot bugger off out of harm's way, leave any close call heroics to me.'

I hurry back to my kit and unclip the quick release straps on the backpack leaving just the radio attached to the A-frame. I quickly pull it onto my shoulders. I'm amazed at how light it seems with just the radio and no pack.

My mouth is filling with the strange taste of fear and anticipation. Suddenly I need to swallow a mouth full of the nervous liquid excreting from glands somewhere inside my throat, one minute bone dry, the next dripping with adrenalin. I am about to become a hunter and the adrenalin is surging through my body like an opiate rush.

I join the support section at the edge of the defensive perimeter and take instruction from the section commander. Nunger's tracking patrol technique is simple enough. He will lead, looking for signs as he goes. He will have his M16 set on auto. More importantly, the MX148 attached under the hand-grip will have a M79 shotgun shell in its chamber and Nunger can fire that in the general direction of any possible enemy he comes upon, then drop to his stomach. Tim the support section machine gunner will be right behind him with a 50 or 60 round belt attached ready to spray the jungle if Nunger suddenly drops.

Behind the gunner is a second digger with an M16, which puts maximum automatic firepower to the front. Two more riflemen and I take up positions at the rear of the patrol as tail-end-Charlie. My automatic M16 will protect us from any enemy contact from behind us as we patrol.

We are standing at the start of the track. I have no idea what track the boys are looking at, all I can see is mud, leaves and twigs. Nunger on the other hand, can see enemy marks as clearly as I can see my own two feet.

'Okay boys I'm not pissing with you lot about this', Nunger starts in a low whisper. 'Like I told the OC, I make three and sometimes four people walking back and forth along this trail about every couple of days or so.' He then picks up a small broken twig, looks around for a similar sized and aged twig and breaks that, comparing the two ends for a while.

'That spider web on that short tree was broken just past the curled dead leaf and a new joint re-spun, my guess is about two days ago but I might be wrong. That means Charlie is due back here in the next 24 hours for another maintenance check on the hospital, so don't be thinking this is just a stroll, we could walk right into him while we are planning our own little surprise.' With that, he stands and starts his patrolling, looking back one last time and puts his finger to his mouth, 'Shush!' We move off slowly.

Some 20 minutes have passed and my tension is easing, not increasing. I feel a little exposed out here with only five other men, but trust Nunger implicitly and am allowing myself to believe in my own immortality again.

The jungle has thinned slightly as we move clear of the B52 devastation. Light is filtering through the top layer of jungle canopy high above; it seems to bend and dance its way toward us soldiers below. Birds occasionally dart across a light beam causing a flicker of light and a flutter of fright as tense diggers snap their weapons toward the movement, satisfy themselves it is not enemy, then return to the task of covering their individual arc of responsibility in the patrol line. The day's rain is yet to arrive but already the humidity is sucking perspiration from our bodies, turning the jungle green clothing into sticky sweat soaked cloth.

This is a world of shadows and dampness. Despite the thinning of undergrowth Nunger is still moving slowly, he is taking no chances this morning.

I am automatically counting how many paces I take to give me an approximate distance from the company harbour, which will also give me an indication of where to bring in artillery if called for. By my best estimate, we have moved some 130 to 150 meters. I am now experiencing actual patrol conditions as taught in jungle training back in Australia.

Each person is moving from possible fire position to fire position, pausing, scanning their arc of responsibility, sighting their next point and slowly moving toward it. Only two are moving at any one time while the others remain at the immediate ready to cover. Being a company sig, I am usually too far back in the patrol line to experience this tension. Back in my usual place it is more of a jerking, stop, start affair, still covering arcs but no fear of the immediate action to the front.

This tension of patrolling is a wake-up call for me. I now have a greater respect for those grunts who normally go before me on the patrol line. Particularly when I consider that platoon grunts must patrol with full kit or about 30 kilograms strapped to their backs. Not as much as me, but bloody heavy.

Regardless of the tension, I now see a similarity to the tropical forests in northern Queensland. If it were not for the war this would be a beautiful land to walk through. Suddenly a hand signal comes back down the line. Up ahead Nunger has squat down on one knee his M16 held tight into his shoulder by his right hand, finger now inside the trigger guard and safety catch pushed toward auto. He has cupped his left hand behind his ear: the signal to freeze and listen.

My ears strain, nothing… suddenly I realise that this is exactly what Nunger is hearing. Nothing!

Jungles don't sound like nothing. There are always sounds but right now only silence. Suddenly several birds are heard in the distance darting in the treetops, calling to each other. Are they ducking for cover or returning to protect their young? Just like Australian kookaburras when a goanna is climbing in the trees.

A signal quickly comes back through the group to me: a hand over the mouth and a point to the left side of the track. This means Nunger is thinking, sensing or hearing the enemy ahead and wants the section to set up an instant ambush.

Amazingly, I am feeling no fear. Like my fellow patrol members, I simply turn left and slowly move silently off the track line and into the undergrowth's thicker cover. I find a good place to set up, turn around, squat, then silently lie down facing back the way I had come, weapon ready to fire.

By the patrol moving in single file, and then suddenly turning off the track like this, we had formed a straight-line killing field on the very track we had been following.

How many times had I and every grunt practised this simple manoeuvre? I respond like a trained robot, still thinking as a soldier not a scared young man. I adjust my position to get maximum view of my personal killing zone. I slide the half plastic smokes cover from the bottom of the taped upturned magazine so I can empty 20 rounds into the ambush, and then flip the mags over, ready for 20 more on short bursts.

I know this is not the time to call back on the radio. Maximum silence is of utmost importance. Any noise could give our position away and I know that instant ambush drills are only safe if you have the upper hand. If the enemy realises we are here, they can sweep around our flank and we are completely exposed in a straight line rather than a defensive circle or triangle.

Now all we can do is wait. I lift the radio handset from its hook on the shoulder strap and place my thumb over the earpiece to muffle any sound should someone decide to call. Finally, I remind myself that I am here to communicate not kill, this is a time to ensure self-discipline and control the desire to shoot instead of talk.

I look across to the support section machine gunner. If ever a man had a square jaw Tim's is a perfect example. It pushes out almost as far as his hooked nose, which had obviously been broken in a fistfight or a rugby match. Right now, that square jaw rests on the butt of his M60. Deep brown, almost black eyes staring through the gun sights at the killing field to his front. Below that square chin with its canyon like dimple is a thick-set body with huge nuggetty hands attached to muscle-bound arms. Hands and arms that had lifted and set in mortar a hundred thousand bricks on building sites all over Melbourne before the dreaded conscription put a uniform on his back. But if ever a man was designed to carry a GPMG M60 Tim was it. A task he accepted willingly. Tim carries the additional weight without complaint and assumes the extra responsibility of providing the support section's main firepower. He seems without fear, a man focused on his duty with a cold determination that he will never let down his mates. It gives me a comforting new confidence to have Tim to my left side at this very moment.

I take my finger from the M16 trigger and rest it against the outer part of the trigger guard, my weapon is there only if needed. As I peer through the undergrowth, the immediate environment becomes suddenly confusing. Threatening.

There is no other place like a tropical jungle to stimulate the human survival instincts and sharpen the senses of that predatory beast lurking inside us. In the dappled light of the undergrowth, the shadows begin creating images of possible enemy. My eyes scan for those recognised images of face, arm or weapon carried at the ready. A slight breeze causes the shadows of the undergrowth to dance and shiver, my eyes dart toward each movement, a new possible threat? No, back to the scanning technique so powerfully drummed into each soldier at the Infantry Training Centre. *Look through the foliage, not at it, look through it.* I repeat this mantra over and over in my mind as I scan slowly from right to left. *Always scan in the opposite direction you normally scan a book page with.*

I am now straining to identify new sounds. Was that a falling leaf and twig from a tree or was it a soldier stepping on a twig as he came along the track? Suddenly, movement to my left, a flash of the sun's reflection from an un-camouflaged wrist.

'There, got them!'

I have stopped breathing, frozen in concentration for what seems an eternity, aware of my heart beating loudly within its chest cavity.

Thump   thump   thump   thump   thump

Along the track-line comes three enemy soldiers. One with a green, grey uniform the others in simple black shirt and pants. They appear to have only one weapon, an AK assault rifle carried by the uniformed first man in line. The others carry a small satchel each and what appear to be rags bundled together. They are not talking but walking at a fair clip. Rather than carefully checking the area for hostile soldiers, each is looking down at their feet, treading very carefully as they go, trying not to leave any obvious sign of their movement.

I lie waiting.

Thump   thump   thump   thump   thump

It forms just above my right eyebrow, small beads of perspiration gather and then as one, cascade into the corner of my right eye. I blink, firstly to ease the stinging sensation caused by the mixture of salt and cam cream, then repeatedly to try and clear the blurry vision caused by the murky mixture of sweat, tears and fear.

I do not just feel my heart pounding within my chest cavity, I can hear it thumping between my ears. I am excited. I am a beast of this jungle. A hunter about to claim his prey.

Thump   thump   thump   thump   thump

As the three men move along the track toward the patrol I am now measuring their distance to the killing field, not in meters but in pounding heartbeats.

Thump   thump   thump   thump   thump

The jungle's silence is shattered by a rapid burst of fire from Nunger's M16 and the machine gun beside me. Finally one loud boom from a rifleman's SLR. Three enemy soldiers fall to the ground.

I grab the radio handset and depress the talk button, 'Four this is four minor in contact, wait out.' I lie silently with the others, straining to hear any sound of more enemy soldiers reacting to the gunfire. Nothing! Except the strange gurgling sound from one of the enemy lying shot in the killing field.

'Four minor this is sunray four, what's happening? Over.' The radio crackles in my ear. 'This is four minor, I request wait-out.' The patrol continues the silence, we are listening for signs of more enemy in the area.

'Four minor this is four, call sign eight wants to know do you need a fire mission? Over.'

'This is four minor, I said … fucking … wait-out.'

Suddenly Nunger starts barking commands to the patrol, 'Gun, up the track. Johnno cover behind you. Mick over the other side. Tiny you got the Gooks in front.'

In an instant, the machine gunner is on his feet and moving quickly up the track the enemy had walked. Dropping to a defensive fire position and extending the bipod legs on the machine gun, he clips a 100-round belt to what was left of the ammunition dangling from the left side of the machine gun. Next, Nunger is up the track behind the gunner a high explosive gold top pushed rapidly into his grenade launcher, ready to support the gunner if more enemy arrives. One of the section riflemen leaps across the fallen enemy soldiers and takes cover on the other side while another turns away, moves a couple of meters out from the track behind me and takes up a defensive fire position. The small section can now defend itself from a small to medium enemy attack.

'What do you see Tiny?' Nunger calls to the remaining rifleman.

'Three down, two not moving, one on his back and bleeding bad, hes trying to sit up, he is unarmed, do I drop him.'

'No, those ones not moving, are they on their backs or stomachs?

'Stomachs... I can see one of them is shot full of holes but not a mark on the other Nog'.

'Okay, so why don't you just put a little fucking mark on him', Nunger sarcastically comments.

Tiny is a six foot two inch tall ape-like figure of a man. Under his sweat saturated giggle hat his hair is rusty, reddish brown, matted and filthy with accumulated sweat and grime that's sticking to his body after two or three days in the humid jungle environment. His once childlike face now shows hard lines cut too deeply, too quickly, by recent stress and experiences. It is obvious to me that Tiny no longer carries the appearance of a little boy lost amongst men, coldness emanates from his deathly distant stare, the grim stare of a man who had witnessed or participated in acts alien to his childhood teachings. The stare of a man no longer able to align his social conscience with the grim reality of his current existence. A stare he will probably carry the rest of his life

I watch half horrified, half excited as one of those cold, distant eyes peer through the rear aperture sight of his SLR. Callously he sights his weapon carefully at the prone soldier and squeezes the trigger. The enemy soldier's head explodes like a smashed watermelon, bits of brain splashing over the leaves nearby.

'He has just a little mark now Nunger', Tiny calls back in a dead pan, emotionless tone.

'Okay sig, call up support.'

'Four zero alpha this is four minor, we have three enemy down, two Kilo India Alpha; one Whisky India Alpha. No friendly casualties, no requirement for Fox Mike. Over.'

The OC is immediately on the blower, 'I'm moving two sections from call sign four three up to support you, how far? Over.'

'One five zero meters. Tell them to keep their fingers off the trigger, we have no other apparent enemy and I don't want them shooting at us accidentally. Over'.

I reply before calling out to the patrol, 'Friendlies sweeping up the track line to support us. Look before you shoot. They will do the same.'

The small patrol lie waiting and listening. Finally, from our rear come the sounds of movement through the undergrowth. The first Australian soldiers move up toward us in an extended line, behind them the platoon commander and his signaller. A second section follows, also in extended line, ready to pass through the front section in a leap-frog sweep if needed.

'Four three this is four minor, I have you visual, keep the finger outside the trigger guard.'

'They are just ahead, eyes open and careful with the trigger finger', I hear the platoon commander yell to the forward section.

Aware that they will now be looking for the patrol I raise my M16 high and move it from side to side.

'We got them visual', calls the lead section commander.

The sweeping sections pass over the ambush site and keep moving forward to clear the area for another 10 to 20 meters before stopping and setting up a defensive area.

'Okay we're set. Support section, make safe, then go check 'em out', the platoon commander calls back to Nunger.

'Sound off when safe', Nunger screams to his section.

'Safety on', each soldier calls back one at a time.

'Pronto! Fuck you pronto! Are you safe?'

Nunger's scream snaps me back to reality as I suddenly realise I have failed to sound off. 'Yeah, sorry, sig is safe… Pronto has safety on.'

Nunger can now move back and check the bodies more thoroughly. With Tiny standing by the two dead enemies and his rifle pointed at the surviving soldier, Nunger is able to move in and kick clear the one enemy weapon. He then goes down on his knees and slides his arm carefully under the two bodies lying face down in the mud, feeling for any grenade that might have stuck under there by the dying soldier in the hope that it would explode and kill his searchers.

'I thought you said this bastard had no marks on him. Stitched up the middle with my M16. Thought I got the bastard and that the gun brought down the other two.' He strips them of their satchel bags filled with cleaning equipment and some meagre rations. He searches their shirts and pants for any documents before turning his attention to the wounded soldier.

'Well you sure must be hurting my little friend', he says, looking down on the young man at his feet.

My curiosity gets the better of me now the area is swept and cleared by the other two sections. I get to my feet and come over to view the wounded soldier. I can immediately see what Nunger was referring to. The young man was hit three times by 7.62 machine gun rounds, one has literally smashed his upper leg bone to splinters, there is a gaping hole consisting of reddish white flesh with bits of broken bone protruding. Thick, dark red blood is pasted over the wound and slowly pumping from a torn vein. The bullets have obviously hit him on his right rear side. The second round had passed through his pelvis and come out around his testicles. I cannot see the damage through the bullet-torn, dark-red, blood-soaked pants he is wearing but it is obviously extreme. The young man is struggling to breath and has pulled himself instinctively up onto his good side to stop the one remaining lung from filling with the blood from the other. Regardless of his efforts, bright red blood is now starting to bubble and froth from his mouth. His shirt is unbuttoned and I can see the damage from the third round. I also know where the strange gargle-like sound is coming from. The bullet has entered his back and blown a hole the size of a ping-pong ball in the front of his chest; a piece of rib bone is protruding from the hole.

I stand mesmerised by the bright, frothy red bubbles blowing in and out, through what appears to be an old piece of sponge poking through the hole, forming a foam around the edges and over the piece of rib bone.

Doc arrives with Sandy and the company commander who is mumbling his disappointment that they don't have an interpreter. As Doc examines the wounds, the OC looks on.

'Can we get him back to a base hospital? He might have some valuable information on this hospital bunker and why it's here.'

'Looks bad, I doubt he is going anywhere skipper', Doc replies as he pushes his thumb into the leg wound from where the blood is pumping in an attempt to stem the flow.

The OC is agitated. 'Well we are going to give it a try son, this boy is valuable to us if he stays alive', he turns to Sandy.

'Get some boys to work clearing a helipad, or at least a space big enough for a litter drop.'

Nunger now cuts in, 'Hey boss this Nog isn't worth saving, he is no more than a kid. He won't know shit and he's in too much pain. I would rather put a bullet in his head if you don't mind.'

'I do mind corporal!' The OC snaps back angrily at his support section commander. 'I want any info he might have and I would remind you the Geneva Convention is there for all captured soldiers not just us if we get caught.'

The tension of the moment is broken by Doc. 'He's in a lot of pain Sir and it will get much worse. He will go into a bad case of shock soon. If I shoot some morphine into his arm to ease the pain, it will make it harder for the doctors at base to stem the blood flow. They do not like surgery on a morphed CASEVAC.'

'Do your best to ease his pain Doc, but I want him alive.'

Doc shrugs his shoulders and with his bloody finger scrawls 'M' on the enemy soldier's forehead then reaches for morphine. Sandy looks down at Doc and gives a subtle wink, before turning to the OC, 'Let's have a look at your map Sir, there might be a clearing nearby where we can get him lifted out.' Sandy then manoeuvres the OC in such a way his back is now turned to Doc and they both squat down to examine the map.

With the OC's back turned, Doc reaches for the string of morphine needles he has strung around his neck. He pulls one off and removes the protective sheath over the needle's point. With his left hand he feels for the young man's jugular vein before lunging the short needle into it, squeezing the little bubble of morphine at the top of the needle. Almost instantly the young enemy soldier's eyes roll back into the top of their sockets revealing blood-lined grey, white balls. Doc now takes the soldier's soft cloth hat and places it over the young man's mouth and nose and presses tightly. A large, bright red bubble forms on the outer edge of his chest wound, and then nothing. He is dead in an instant. Doc pulls out the needle from the jugular and pushes it into the dead boy's thigh.

'Skipper! Sorry Sir, he just didn't make it. I did the best I could.'

The OC comes over and looks at the dead soldier, 'Never mind Doc, you did your best, that's all I can ask of you.'

Doc and Sandy make brief eye contact, then Sandy looks around at me, Tiny and Nunger. The 100-mile look that says without any words: Shut up about this, we do what we have to.

I look down at the dead young soldier. He is no more than 16 or 17 years old. No longer a boy but never to be a man.

I wonder if he has a brother or sister, a girlfriend maybe. I try to imagine myself lying there shot to pieces, the combination of shock and pain must have been horrific. I look over to Doc who stares right back at me through cold hard eyes. I nod my approval, turn and walk away. I will not write any detail of this in my notebook because I already know this memory will haunt me for the rest of my life.

Professional Soldiers and Career Soldiers

BECAUSE OF THE enemy contact, the day's plans are no longer in place.

Any enemy within a couple of thousand meters of that short violent confrontation will now know the Australians are in the area. They would have taken a compass bearing on the sound of gunfire and realised that the hospital has been discovered.

For D Company this can mean only two things: either there was a large enemy force making its way to attack the Australians or more probably the small force in the area was clearing out of their base camp and disappearing into the jungle before they too are found.

The OC has decided to sit tight in a company-sized defence and to call in live artillery strikes on several locations about 1000 meters out from the hospital to let Charlie know that they would be stupid to mount a major assault if that was what they might be planning.

Noise is no longer an issue now that shots have been fired, so the OC calls for some Support Company assault pioneers to fly in with extra C4 plastic explosive. He also requests someone come in and examine the few meagre contents found on the dead enemy soldiers.

The first chopper delivers the assault pioneer soldier by winch. In addition to his rifle, he is armed with a chain saw which is quickly put to use cutting down trees. Within 20 minutes a large landing area is created in the jungle and the next Huey is landing with two more pioneers and Hun, the Vietnamese interpreter from Support Company. He will look at the enemy documents.

I am sitting in the HQ area on radio shift, watching with some amusement as Wingnut excitedly describes to the newcomers the underground network of tunnels he and they were about to blow to kingdom come. I remember Robert, my childhood friend who loved poking two-penny firecrackers into ant nest holes and lighting the wick. It is the first time Robert has entered my mind since joining the rifle company. The amusement disappears instantly as I look across at the three enemy bodies. The enemy bodies have been dragged back into the defended bunker area next to HQ and the interpreter Hun is examining them with OC and Sandy.

The Interpreter

Hun is short, wiry and thin. A shock of jet-black hair flops untidily on top of his narrow, brownish-yellow face. A tiny upturned nose separates the razor thin eyelids from the tightly drawn thin lips. Hun is 50 years old and has lived his entire life in a country at or between wars and yet he is loyal to the South Vietnamese government. Their current leaders supported the French and it was the French who had allowed Hun to develop a distinguished education at the City of Hue. Hun had the good fortune to win a 12-month study scholarship, which took him to London. Upon his return, he completed his PHD in arts, poetry and literature and commenced his career as a lecturer teaching the works of great Vietnamese scholars such as Che Lan Vien and his favourite scholar Te Hanh who had taught in his very same class room at the Thuan Hoa School. War changed his world of poetry and literature. The Americans needed interpreters and Hun was drafted into the Army of the Republic of Vietnam at the rank of captain to work as an interpreter. Five years later he clashed with his American commander over the treatment of prisoners and wrote a report to his ARVN commander outlining his anger and contempt and detailing the American breaches of the Geneva Convention. To his shock, he found himself before a military court charged with disobeying a lawful order. 'We are not signatories to that convention', his ARVN commander had angrily pointed out to him.

Hun was demoted to a junior officer and transferred to the Australian Task Force in Nui Dat then allocated to an Australian battalion as their interpreter.

Hun found the Australians much easier than the Americans when it came to him performing his duties. He found them arrogant as all westerners seem to be and the general soldier seemed completely ignorant of the history and culture of his beautiful land. Hun soon realised that most Australians seemed happy to stay ignorant. But they seem more willing to take his advice when planning to enter villages. They treat him in a friendly manner, they show no respect for his officer rank but they seem to respect him as a person with skills they need. The Australians share their food and water with him and like all soldiers are hardened and emotionally calloused by war experiences. Australians at least attempt to maintain rules as to the treatment of prisoners and the dead whom they have the decency to bury instead of stacking the bodies and leaving them for the pigs to feast upon as he witnessed the Americans do.

So here he is once again standing before three dead enemy soldiers and being asked to read and explain any documents found. He sighs, closes his eyes long enough to regain his composure. He then begins his gruesome task.

I watch as Hun points to the young boy. Blue-grey skin and contorted face, eyes rolled back to expose lifeless grey balls and one leg now twisted at an acute angle by rapid onset of rigamortis.

'This one is a NVA porter boy, H'Moung boy from Ho Binh maybe. Unusual for him to be this far south, probably kidnapped by NVA and brainwashed to hate American and Australian soldiers or just forced to carry arms and supplies down the Uncle Ho trail.'

He then looks at the uniformed body next to the boy and kicks the distinctive boots on the dead man's feet. 'This one NVA and this one over here maybe a local boy, VC from Baria maybe'.

'How do you know that one is H'Moung?' the OC asks, pointing to the boy.

Hun looks back at him in amazement, 'He looks H'Moung. Skin different colour. Shape of head different, make face look broader.'

'They all look the same to me', OC replies as he looks inquisitively at the corpses trying to differentiate their skin colour and facial features.

Hun bursts into laughter, 'You all look same to me. I can't tell a Kiwi from Uc Da Lai. even when you speak English. But you can tell different speak can you not?'

'What are the documents about?' OC enquires.

'This one just Uncle Ho bullshit, like China has its Red Book, Quyet chien, Quyet thang mean determined to fight determined to win,' Hun replies picking up the old well-worn booklet found on the North Vietnamese body. He reads the words on the second page. 'Doc Lap, Tu Do Hanh Phuc. It means independence, freedom, make us all happy.' Hun throws the booklet onto the body in front of him. 'He is not Hanh Phuc, he is dead now.'

Next, he reads the papers found on one young boy. 'Other bits, just letters to people, maybe intelligence can follow up names here on this letter', he points to one piece of paper. 'Could be name of a contact in Baria'. Next the final corpse 'These two papers are poems. He is H'Moung boy for sure. They are his poems.'

'Poems?' the OC enquires, 'You mean poetry?'

'Yeah poems.'

Sandy cuts in now. 'What the feck do they carry poems for?'

Hun lets out a slow sigh, 'In Vietnam there is no TV, not many movies. Vietnam only has songs, books and poems. We like books and poems.

Before I was forced into uniform I taught poetry. H'Moung people are very good at reading and writing poems. They sing family and tribal songs lot of the time, tell stories and write poems. They write poem like this one.' Hun is pointing to a sheet of paper taken from the young man Doc had relieved of his pain. 'H'Moung have a slightly different dialect so I can't translate it as accurately as it would deserve but it is a special poem to a special girl about flowers. He is not NVA or Viet Cong, I think the NVA took him from his village and made him come south as a porter to carry ammunition and stores. This poem is a mix of a famous poem from Doan Thi Diem maybe three hundred years ago. ..a mothers or woman's lament.. I know it well.. it say

Do you remember now the day you went away?

The apricot buds had barely opened to the western wind..

I asked when would you come back ..

and you assured me ..when the peach trees bloom..

Hun let a sad sigh pass his lips, 'The boy add to poem, say he loves and misses his mother and his promised girl who he will marry. He says when he comes home peach blossoms will be everywhere and he will give flowers to this special girl.'

My stomach knots, I feel faint, fighting an overwhelming desire to vomit. Jesus!

OC looks at me, noting the pale white face, then over to Sandy. 'Get Dutch to take over the radio and look after your new boy, he is about to discover that war tastes just like vomit.'

Sandy replies in his usual manner, 'I'm doing it as we speak.'

I sit by my gear where Sandy had dragged me. Sandy pulls a small piece of C4 explosive from his pocket. He places it in a carefully cut empty ration tin and sets fire to it with a Zippo. A bright blue-white flame bursts into life and Sandy places a kidney shaped army mug over the intense white heat. In no time the water is bubbling. Sandy pours half into a spare mug filled with some broken up biscuits, mashing them into a bland soft paste. In the original mug, he adds some coffee and a couple of sugars.

'Eat and drink boy.'

'I'm not hungry', I can taste the vomit in the back of my throat and in my nostrils where some has forced its way from within.

'Exactly, that's why you gotta feckin eat. You need something in your stomach and I am personally gonna make sure you get something in your stomach, even if I have to hold you down and shit in your feckin mouth then poke it down with a stick.'

With that threat hanging over me, I try to force the paste down my throat, I still have a strong desire to vomit. Slowly I am able to swallow without fighting the urge to throw up. Next I wash it down with a mouthful of hot bitter coffee, 'This tastes just as bad as your hot chilli stuff.'

Sandy smiles at me, 'Welcome back to the real war son. I'm going back to HQ but Nunger wants to talk with you.' With that said, Sandy walks off and leaves me with my coffee. I sit alone for some time before Nunger finally approaches.

Since joining the company, I have not had a chance to chat with Nunger and am now staring at the infamous corporal. Dark black skin indicates that Torres Strait or Papuan blood has mixed with his father's Northern Queensland Mob. Nunger's short bristle hair seemed to accentuate his broad nose, obviously broken on several occasions. Not one but two deep scars over his left eyebrow and another on his right cheekbone hint of his brief history as a travelling side-show boxer before he found his way into the army. Nunger is tough and sinewy, no wasted fat on his tight muscled bones. He makes a good friend but a bad enemy. Nunger is not one to stray from direct statements.

He squats down beside me, 'Sandy tells me your name is Brian, typical white name if ever I heard one. Can't do much with Brian as a name so I will have to call you Turkey.'

I look back at him, 'White meat the turkey, aye?'

Nunger now shows a bright friendly smile. His knocked-out tooth accentuating his distinct tribal features.

'Now you got it white trash, you and I are gonna be good friends.'

The smile disappears from his face. 'You okay about what happened back there today, with Doc and that Gook?'

'Yeah Nunger, I'm sort of okay about what happened, that's why I kept my mouth shut.' I look into my half-filled mug of bland, mushed biscuit. 'What Doc did and all that. I kept thinking to myself how bad he was, the damage was unfixable and he needed to be put out of his pain. I was imagining that it was me in his place and I was wondering what he would have been thinking and feeling. I would want someone to take me out of this life. It ain't really an honourable thing to do, killing a wounded enemy like some dog in pain. I feel kind of okay, but sort of dirty at the same time. You know what I mean?'

Nunger nods, his facial expression quite serious. 'This is my second tour Turkey. I learned the hard way that doing what you called 'the honourable thing' is easy when you sleep in a warm bed at night back home instead of a Gook-infested jungle. I'm going to do you and every digger around you a big favour, I'm going to give you some good advice.' His eyes burn into my soul, 'Never try to wonder what the Noggy feels, he isn't a human like us, he is a Nog, a Gook, or Slope or whatever filthy name you might like to give him but he isn't a human like you or me. Got that?'

I sit silently feeling the blood drain from my face, not about to challenge anything Nunger says.

'You ever shoot rabbits or foxes back home?'

'Sure', I respond nervously.

'Well think of Charlie like he is a vermin fox, not like he is a human being. You think of him as a human and you might just hesitate before you squeeze your trigger. Give Charlie a split second and he will make you pay for it. If not you, one of your mates. Maybe even me.' He picks up my M16 and shoves it into my hands.

'I want to know right now that I can trust you to use this little fucker to shoot them bastards instead of taking a moment to think about 'em.' Nunger pauses as he watches his message drive home and then adds, 'You're right about the pain though, even a mongrel sheep-killing dog deserves to be put out of pain.'

I nod to indicate I understand the message. Nunger smiles again and continues, 'Now I gotta tell you one thing, you did okay out there. I always use Jock as sig on short patrol because Dutch is too fidgety. You're as good as Jock so expect to get more work. And by the by, when you told the OC to fuckin' wait on the sig set, you did good. He will respect you for that call.'

I take that as a compliment but am not about to let Dutch go undefended. 'Dutch is a good battalion sig, mate. Wish I could code-up as quickly as him.'

'He might code-up alright but he patrols like shit, more noise than an elephant', replies Nunger before looking at my food mug. 'Are you surviving Sandy's cooking?' he asks sympathetically.

'This ain't so bad', I respond pointing to the bland mashed-up biscuit in his mug. 'I can handle a bit of hot curry but that Tabasco sauce is giving me heartburn day and night.'

'Only heartburn?' When I buddied up with him last tour the red stuff gave me constant shitting. Jesus wept, I could squirt soft shit everywhere. Practically bend over, take aim and squirt shit through the eye of a needle at fifty paces I could.'

Suddenly I hear a chopper in the general area. A smoke grenade pops and bright yellow smoke is rising above the cleared landing zone. Within moments a Bell Bubble chopper is descending through the trees with three people jammed into the tiny contraption.

'Fucking tourists', Nunger comments.

The battalion commanding officer and a stranger decamp and the little chopper climbs up out through the hole in the jungle and disappears. I am amused at what I see. The CO in pressed clean army greens with his silly looking side-kick. Both clean-shaven, without cam cream. They have clean boots and are wearing unused webbing with the ammunition pouches poking out the front where they would be impossibly uncomfortable to a soldier forced to lie on his stomach for lengthy periods. Of most amusement are the fancy cameras around their necks, they really did look like a couple of tourists. Diggers often carry small cameras in the field but these two have the best big cameras money can buy.

'They call him 'career man' out here', Nunger says. 'A half-wit of a Colonel who got his promotions back in a desk job somewhere in Canberra or as an attaché in some safe foreign country. Just our luck to score a career man instead of a professional soldier', he snorts angrily.

'Career man! Back in the Dat they call him the singing Colonel. Rumour has it he flies around in his chopper singing old songs from the fifties/sixties. Who is the other one, the clean skin?' I ask pointing my mug at the clean, baby-faced 40-year-old with his Yashica camera dangling from his slender neck.

'Probably one of his cock sucking mates from Canberra. They spend a couple of weeks over in 'Nam just to get the first gong to pin on their chest. Makes them look like real soldiers', Nunger's voice fills with contempt. 'The CO is real smart, he wants both gongs which he gets from being here six fucking months or more and he knows that every CO gets a Distinguished Service Cross just for being here. Add a long service medal and he looks like a hero to any dumb arse politician who don't know what all the ribbons mean or what he did to earn them.'

I don't care what Nunger thinks, I am suddenly feeling strong in the stomach and want to get close to the two strange looking clowns that have dropped in on the war. 'This will be fun, I'm going over for a squiz', I say to Nunger and I wander over to HQ.

The CO is squatting beside the OC, 'Well done John, we really caught them with their pants down didn't we? Got their hospital.'

The OC replies dryly, 'They'll just build another one and another if needed.'

'Yes, but we have dealt a terrible blow to their morale haven't we?' The CO replies before looking at the three bodies. 'Mind if we get a few shots of these fellows? He asks. Err... for the battalion history records.'

The OC just grunts, the CO and his companion take up positions around the dead enemy soldiers. The second clean skin asks if he can get a photo of himself squatting beside the enemy bodies holding the captured AK 47 Chinese assault rifle. The CO obliges, standing back and adjusting the lens on his Yashica before saying to his companion, 'That AK would make a good souvenir.'

The OC cuts in angrily, 'Already claimed, Sir.' It'll be recorded as captured so you can't souvenir it, I'm afraid.'

'Oh, sorry John, just thought, you know?' Meekly replies the CO, who then turns back to take a few more photos.

The OC looks over to Sandy and makes a hand gesture in front of his crutch imitating a masturbation action before silently mouthing the word 'wanker'. This is a side of the OC I did not know existed. It is unusual for a Major to display such contempt for a senior officer and the Major was of high breeding, a Duntroon man, yet he obviously dislikes his immediate commanding officer.

The CO finishes his photo shoot and returns to sit beside the OC. 'I have arranged for sniffers to fly over the area and see if their infra-red can pick up any body heat in the jungle out there, might give you a bead on the base camp.'

'Might also give me a bead on a bunch of wild pigs', the OC responds.

The CO looks at his company commander, obviously aware of the edge in his reply. 'You're looking exhausted John', he says. 'Probably need to take a bit of rest after this op.'

'The Company could do with a bit of R and C in Vungers', the OC replies.

'I'll be glad to approve that John. My boys work hard so they should be allowed to play hard.'

Dutch draws me away from listening to the conversation. 'Hey Brian, if you manage to get your guts to settle you can help code up this re-sup. We are having a nice little opportunity to get fresh greens and food delivered before we push on.' I move over to Dutch and examine the re-supply request that

Sandy is planning. Fresh fruit, clean greens, more rations and filtered water. 'This would be better than Christmas right now!' I grab my codebook and go about helping Dutch translate words into code phonetics.

The career man and his associate are now returning from Wingnuts' adventure tour of the underground hospital, obviously annoyed that neither had thought to bring a flash unit for their cameras. The clean skin asks the OC, 'Where did they get all those ration container tins from John?'

'Any American firebase or base camp from here to the DMZ', replies the OC. 'They scrounge them out of rubbish dumps and re-use them as waterproof containers to transport material up and down the Ho Chi Minh trail. Or, like this place, they use them to build clinics. The tenacity of the enemy is incomprehensible. The Yanks actually end up supplying them with discarded materials which they use to defeat the Yanks and us. If we had any brains we would join them not the Yanks. They are the best soldiers I've ever seen in action.'

Both the CO and his companion stand in shock, made speechless by the OC's comment. I can sense the tension. A knife could cut the thick tropical air.

The radio alongside me crackles into life. It's the Sioux helicopter pilot returning to pick up his two tourists. I answer the radio and grab a smoke grenade, pull the pin and roll it into the landing zone. With a pop, the orange smoke drifts up through the trees.

'I see orange. Over', the pilot calls.

'Roger that, on orange', I reply. I call over to the career man and his clean skin companion. 'Taxi service has arrived Sir.'

The rickety little Sioux Bell Bubble chopper descends onto the LZ. The two tourists squeeze in beside the pilot. The motor revs then the blades strain and lift them skyward. It looks like a lawn mower motor hanging off a Meccano set with a silly glass dome to sit in. These amazing machines first found favour in the Korean War. I have never flown in one. I grab my notebook…

> *What a buzz sitting in the Perspex dome with 180-degree vision all round. Would make tree surfing a better thrill than sex.*

I look around to see the OC giving a derogative finger to the chopper as it disappears over the treetops. The OC looks round and realises I am watching, there is an uncomfortable silence. I decide to ask the question, 'You don't like the CO all that much Sir?'

'He is a prick on two legs', the OC responds. 'Personality wise I'd rather talk to a piece of dog shit than share a conversation with that wanker.' Pausing a short moment, 'Look, don't misunderstand me on this point, the CO is the best thing that ever happened to this battalion. He looks after us like no other CO I have ever served with in my 15 years as an officer. He is not short of courage either. Trust me it isn't easy sitting up in a command chopper getting shot at from the ground.'

'So what is it between you two?'

'He's just an arrogant prick of a person that's all. He doesn't know how to communicate with his junior officers properly, let alone his troops. He is always on my back about lying low in contacts with the enemy, says I should let my junior officers do the dangerous work. Fuck him, I lead by example. I am no fucking coward who…. who… well never you mind. He calls you all 'his boys' like you were some sort of thing to play with rather than soldiers. I don't like the man but I'm glad he is our CO. He knows who's who in this man's army, all the right contacts, anything we want or need and he finds a way to get it to us.'

The OC decides to pass one final bit of wisdom to me, 'Listen son. You are in a privileged position as battalion signaller. You see and hear things most diggers don't ever know about and it's sometimes best they don't. I can't operate the Company HQ if I can't be myself. What you see and hear is not for sharing or you will incur my wrath, and Sandy's. Got that?'

'Yes Sir, I never assumed it was for sharing, that's why I'm a sig Sir.'

'I like that answer digger.' He stares at me with a strange smile on his face, 'You often tell officers to fuck off when on the radio son? That's the first time a private has told me to, and may I quote you, "Fucking wait out."'

I blush. 'When the situation calls for it I will tell anyone to fuck off Sir. We were on silence situation, listening for enemy movement.'

'Good, I like a man with balls', he replies with a smile, 'you are now my zero alpha sig. There is a certain someone needs lots of telling to fuck off and I don't have the time to do it myself. Stay buddied to Sandy though, he will teach you the ropes better than me.' The OC then calls to Wingnut, 'Take this AK rifle and damage it so it can't be re-used, then cocoon it with these dead soldiers inside the bunker when you blow the thing up. But make sure the bodies don't get blown to pieces, I want them buried in the bunker not splattered. Someone will come looking for them one day.'

Wingnut raises an eyebrow, the weapon should be returned to task force as 'captured', but who is he to question the Major's order. He picks up the weapon and wanders off to poke some C4 explosives into it.

'One thing I hate more than anything else is a souvenir collector', the OC almost spat out the words. 'Enemy or not, it is an undignified thing to do to a fellow warrior who has fallen. By the way, out here call me Skip.' He turns to Sandy, 'Go thank that Hun fella for his assistance, we sure need people like him to help us understand our enemy and his culture. And arrange a lift back to the fire support base for him and the assault pioneers.'

I suddenly feel a sense of shame. Only weeks ago I was urinating into a souvenir helmet taken from a dead soldier. I move back to my position and take up my pen and notebook.

> *I think I am being accepted by everyone, I hope so. Embarrassed that I puked in front of the OC. I was thinking about Robby's girl Emily. Jesus I am confused about what happened after the ambush. I think It was the right thing, fuck I just don't know! I guess Nunger is right and the others are okay about it, even Doc and Sandy. I watched the diggers place the*

dead enemy in the bunker, the bodies had gone stiff and rigid. Good God they just cut the back of that dead boy's tendons so they could straighten out his leg and they shoved him into the bunker then pushed his head underground with their boots. I almost puked again. I never imagined it would be like this!

OC and the big boss obviously don't get along. Not my problem. None of it is my problem, just do your job Bri, just do what you are told to do. Bit confused by OC or Skip as I am allowed to call him, he seems to actually like the Vietnamese. He was so patient with that Hun fella and really does insist on doing the right thing by the damn enemy dead blokes. I just don't know how I feel about them. They are my enemy. They will kill me if they get half a chance just like Nunger tells it. But they are also just people like me. I just have to stop thinking of them this way. I must see them as Gooks or Nogs or something. Maybe then I won't chuck up my guts every time I see a young dead boy.

Men and Monkeys

As PREDICTED, THE re-supply chopper is as exciting as Father Christmas dropping through the trees in his sled.

On board are the little luxuries that lift the morale of tense, weary soldiers. Clean dry clothing and fresh hot food are the main attractions. The company quartermaster sergeant and the Salvation Army's 'everyman' have flown in with the resup and are personally serving up hot food prepared by the cooks back at Nui Dat and placed in hot boxes for transport. There are two urns, one filled with cold milk chocolate and one with hot milk coffee. Each platoon takes turns coming in to the central area, using the buddy system within each section so that the outer defensive perimeter around the captured hospital and LZ remain well manned.

Smiles are apparent on all of the soldiers' faces with the exception of Doc, who finds himself as busy as ever. With clean jungle greens ready to change into, diggers become brave enough to remove their army boots. Once these boots come off, the extent of tinea and foot rot is discovered. More magic white antiseptic powder and boots back on before the itching drives the young men to pick and scratch the damaged skin, making it unbearable. Fresh kits and raised morale help prepare the soldiers for their next task.

Regardless of the noise the company created in the last eight hours, we will not be withdrawing from the patrolling area. Although probably deserted by now, we will continue to try to locate a base camp. The OC decides to follow his hunch and split the company into three patrolling forces moving in single file. Two platoons about 300 meters apart. With the Third Platoon and Company HQ moving 200 meters behind, as a ready reaction force in reserve should enemy contact occur. In this formation, the company will search the area along both sides of the creek line identified the previous night as the probable dry season source of water used by the enemy camp.

The OC also identifies a large clear region beyond the planned patrol area where the company can be picked up en masse and flown back to Nui Dat.

Three days patrolling, maybe only two and the company can take a break. My morale is particularly high as I've overheard the CO and OC talk about R and C which means two glorious days in Vung Tau. The thought of endless booze and girls is enough to keep me going for a couple more days. The going however is not really getting any easier. The wet season continues to dump buckets of water upon us. Clean new jungle greens soon become the same wet muddy rags we had gleefully discarded only hours earlier.

As we patrol further through the jungle the undergrowth is thinning into tropical forest. This makes movement easier, reducing the risk of a twisted ankle, knee or lower spine. But this is a landscape that's both abundant and forbidding. The wet season creates endless changes in the density of the oxygen dragged into the lungs of each soldier straining under the weight of his equipment. One moment it is benign and easy to breathe, another moment heavy and fearfully assaulting our strained lungs. Each soldier is sucking hard to fill the upper cavities. The topography always changing, ever restless with unidentified sounds and flickering movements of light.

Tree spiders are everywhere in this bit of jungle. Giant monsters that seem to deliberately set up their webs just at the right height to catch my radio whip aerial. I don't know how poisonous they are. At least the bird eaters are up a bit higher in the trees.

As the group patrol in single file formation, the soldiers to my immediate front are kind enough to point upward whenever a web is sighted. They then duck under or move around it. I need to pull down the whip aerial over my front shoulder while ducking each monster's trap. The extra weight on my back causes thigh muscles to ache from the constant squat-like walk that is required to avoid the webs.

Exhaustion envelopes me, I give up scanning my allocated arc of responsibility to search for enemy on the ground. Concentration is now only on the trees and branches overhead. The thought of one of those eight-legged arachnids getting pissed with me because that whip aerial has torn a web is enough to keep me vigilant about spiders and spiders only. I just don't want one of these beasts biting and munching its way down the back of my soggy sweaty shirt.

A second new threat to good health is also in abundance - red ants. These are meat-eating beasts with big nippers that can take a tiny piece of skin out of the back of a man's neck. They swarm up trees looking for unsuspecting bugs and small animals that they overpower in numbers and eat voraciously. Easily dislodged from low branches by a radio sets whip aerial. Just as easily as the monster tree spiders.

After what seems an eternity it is lunch break.

It's now day two since leaving the enemy hospital in a mess of destruction from well-placed C4 explosives. The dead enemy bodies are cocooned inside the imploded hospital area to save digging separate graves.

For me, the great advantage of finding the hospital was that the assault pioneers had brought with them plenty of plastic explosive. They brought in more than was needed so the left-over C4 was shared amongst the privileged few who got in first and grabbed it. The C4 can be lit and burnt like hexi to boil water. Its intense heat means a hot brew can be acquired in a moment instead of waiting for the hexi to slowly bring water to the boil. I was quick to grab some C4 and am now amongst the privileged few. My water boils in an instant and I now sit enjoying my hot mug of coffee while treating the ant bite on my neck with antiseptic and a small Band-Aid.

Lunch breaks on patrol are short stops which means Sandy doesn't cook lunches and I am blessed with cold meat straight from an American C ration tin. This is not the most luxurious meal but the missing Tabasco sauce means I can eat without a burning numb throat, I can also taste the coffee.

Wingnut and Doc are again having another one of their strange little disagreements.

'Ears, yeah I heard that furphy but it ain't real is it Wingnut? Another story from that Mick prick friend of yours?' Doc is saying.

'Yep, real alright! Seen it myself on last tour. I was with the ANZAC Battalion and I tell you the Kiwis collect the ears off the dead Gooks.'

'What a load of crap. You telling me all Kiwis cut the ears off dead enemy?'

'Well, not all of them but this one guy did. He had three of them strung on his dog tag chain, I seen it with my own eyes mate - all dried and shrivelled up.'

'That's sick.'

'No it ain't, not really. It's a warrior thing that the Kiwis have had for centuries. This bloke was collecting them to take back to his grandfather. Apparently he brought some Japanese ears home from Borneo and his great, great grandfather has some British ears from when the Kiwis tried to stop the Poms colonising New Zealand.'

'That's sick.'

'You bet it's sick if you're a Pommy bastard. That's your problem! Probably one of your relatives, aye Doc, was swinging off some Kiwi head piece?'

'Never mind my old relative's ears you little dip shit, you look after your own pointy little freak things. Some Kiwi would find it hard to resist those. Hell they're already dried out and shrivelled.'

Sandy moves close to Doc and Wingnut. 'Keep the feckin noise to a whisper you two or I'll cut the ears off both of you and eat them for breakfast, just like feckin corn flakes.'

'Is it true Sandy?' Doc asked.

'Who cares, just keep your noise down. In fact, just shut the feck up. I hear another sound from you two and I'll kick your arseholes 'til yer noses bleed.'

The two men fall silent. Sandy makes his way back to where the OC is briefing the platoon commander and the FO.

I smile and rest my head back against a tree, checking first that it is not a highway for red ants. Just for a moment life feels wonderful luxuriating in silence with a hot brew of bitter coffee. I reach for my notebook.

> *My socks have rotted inside my boots, shit this jungle is tough. Can't wear jocks out here, already got a sweat rash under my balls. Wish I had stayed back in the Dat. Fuck I am tired, always tired. What I wouldn't give for just one night when I didn't have to do a shift or worry about the shit spilling.*

The quiet of the late morning is disrupted by the sound of some quick shuffling and a muffled, 'fuck me dead' from nearby. Everyone falls flat on their stomachs, grabbing weapons and making ready to engage an unknown force.

Silence!

Suddenly Eleven Platoon's smiling sergeant slips past me. 'Stand-down, it's okay', he whispers as he passes on his way to let the OC know what is happening. I get up off my stomach and look around to see if my precious hot brew of coffee is still upright on the ground, I'm delighted I discover it's intact. Heaving a sigh of relief, I again go about enjoying this little Tabasco-free luxury, not caring what the fuss is.

Soon the Sergeant and Sandy pass by, heading to the location where the swearing came from. Shortly after, Sandy returns and squats next to me, 'Feckin krait slid right between the two diggers on gun watch and disappeared into the bush heading this way. Keep your eye out for the little fecker, short with coloured bands around it. Get bit by that little fecker and you're dead in 60 seconds, no anti-venom, no hope.'

'Oh great', I respond, 'spiders, carnivorous ants and now we get the deadliest snake in the world sliding around our arseholes.'

'Just one of those days son and don't forget about the tigers and scorpions', Sandy mused. 'Remember what I told you when you dropped your dumb arse into this jungle? Feckin Gooks are the least of our problem. Welcome to the real war!'

'How many types of snakes are there in this place?'

'I've been told there are about 100 types and 99 are deadly poisonous', Sandy answers, a cheeky grin forming under the camouflage cream.

'The other fecker is the giant python; he just strangles you to death.'

Lunch break over, patrolling continues into the afternoon. No enemy base camp found in these two days patrolling near and along the creek line. The OC has not picked Charlie's plans as well as he had thought.

I am thinking that by nightfall we will get close to the large clearing 500 meters ahead. Just one last night in this place and it's a chopper lift-out in the morning. As long as nothing happens between now and then. My mind is already contemplating a hot shower.

However, I am in the somewhat luxurious position of being a HQ waller on the patrol line. Up front, the soldiers are not thinking about anything but survival. They do not know, as I do, about plans for a lift-out. For them this is yet another day of tension and anticipated combat.

The Forward scout

Nowhere is that tension greater than at the front of the patrol line. Private Mick Fulkenstein is carefully moving through the undergrowth in his usual role of forward scout. A natural athlete, Mick has always been the platoon leader in fitness training and endurance tests. He is also the most popular digger in his platoon, if not the entire company. He is the man with a million jokes to tell at any bar he leans on. His mischievous smile always warning his fellow diggers that another practical joke is about to be played on some poor unsuspecting soldier. Above all, Mick has that rare ability to change everything difficult or tiresome into a funny or positive event. He likes to lead and be a leader amongst peers. This position of scout seemed quite natural to him back in Australia as the battalions trained for this tour of duty. He chose the job and always insisted he was the best scout in the platoon. Mick also chose to carry an SLR rather than an M16.

'When I shoot 'em with this pig gun they gunna stay shot', he boasted with the innocence of a man yet to be blooded by wars reality.

That however, was back in Australia, now he is in 'Nam and that early exuberance to be out front has become a curse to his nervous system. After a few short months in 'Nam he began to hate the job. Despite his increasing nervousness and dread, Mick has not been able to bring himself to ask for a change of role. That may indicate to his peers that he is not the man they assume him to be. Scared, yes, but coward he is not and a man of pride hides his fear. In Mick's case he hides it behind his humour. His pride is all that keeps him setting out as scout each time his rifle section is directed to take point.

On this day Mick is particularly nervous. He has never experienced such a sense of foreboding. Is it instinct or a gut reaction? Or is it his training sending a message to his subconscious, has his conscious mind overlooked a warning sign?

He stops just long enough to collect his thoughts, gather his mental courage and find the emotional strength to go forward. His nose sniffs at the tropical air seeking an unusual scent, anything that might warn him of enemy ahead, a cooking smell, a latrine dug near a bunker system or just an unusual body odor. Nothing!

His logic tells him all is well but his body is not interested in what his brain is saying. His body remains tense, sifting through other primitive thought processes hidden in the dark corridors of his brain. A brain re-tuned to the basic survival of a hunting beast, the predator who may also be the victim of another predator. Every nerve tingles with the anticipation of death or dismemberment.

The young scout wills his eyes to stop darting around nervously and carefully scans the jungle scene in front of him one square meter at a time. Slowly from right to left he carefully checks the tree line. Still his nerves are tingling uncontrollably. Something has to be wrong!

Mick scans the ground to his front for a trip wire or any sign of disturbed ground cover that may indicate a buried anti personnel mine. Nothing!

His heart is pounding in his chest. The hair on the back of his neck is tingling and his stomach churns as a million butterfly wings dance under his rib cage. There is something out there, something wrong but he just can't pick it. Wait! On the tree up ahead! A scuff mark on the bark! Why?

His spinal cord tingles with the sensation of a million ants crawling beneath the skin. His heart skips a beat then leaps upward into his desert dry throat. Mick's eyes snap upward to the treetop. An ominous shape is propped in a fork of branches amongst the leaves. The young soldier's legs turn to jelly, his arms like lead weights force his SLR rifle to swing quickly to his shoulder, its muzzle pointing skyward. Sighting along the barrel with both eyes he squeezes the trigger three times. Mick can hear himself screaming as the powerful weapon recoils into his shoulder.

'Contact front! Contact front! Contact front!'

The air expels from his lungs as he falls backwards and rolls to his left side. He is alive and unhurt, his mind races with a surge of adrenalin-driven exaltation as he hears a large form crash to the ground

The resounding boom, boom, boom of three rounds fired from a 7.62 rifle cuts through the jungle with deafening abruptness. Soldiers begin scurrying everywhere, screaming 'Contact front!' as they rapidly perform their well-oiled drills.

I close quickly up behind the OC, radio in hand, on the blower in seconds. 'zero alpha this is four, we are in contact. Wait. Out.'

Ahead the platoon commander is barking orders for some information on the enemy sighted. The scout yells back. 'Sniper, in the trees to our right, I got him, I heard him fall.'

Sniper! My heart leaps into my mouth. If a forward scout fears mines and booby traps, then a signaller fears snipers. Any enemy soldier worth his salt knows that if he can kill the radio operator and put a bullet through the radio, he will have cut the rest from artillery and air support.

Ants, snakes and spiders are now unimportant. I squeeze as close to the ground as possible and grasp the whip aerial in my hand, pull it over my shoulder and under my body to hide the tell-tale evidence that might entice a sniper's bullet. With wide eyes and a dry mouth, I look around for some protection against an enemy sniper in the trees above. I sight and crawl to a broad buttress tree and slip in between the wide fanning roots that protrude from the trunk. Hidden in there I know that an enemy round could easily penetrate the thin wide tree roots but they offer a better hide than just laying prone on the ground.

Radio barks in my ear, 'Four zero this is zero alpha, send contact report. Over.'

I roll onto my back, lock the M16 into my shoulder, push the safety catch to auto and rest my chin centrally over the rifle butt to scan and shoot. I scan the tree line, ignore the radio call and concentrate on possible sniper hides. Heart pounding but training enables me to scan right to left, checking each tree, each branch for any unusual shape or unnatural clump of leaves. Again, the radio handset comes to life.

'Four, call sign four, this is zero alpha. Give me a damn contact report. Over.'

I grab the handset and press the talk button. 'zero alpha, call sign four has contact with possible sniper situation. Things are pretty tense out here. I will get back shortly. Wait. Out.'

The forward platoon has sent out a section under the control of the platoon sergeant and they are now moving in a broad careful sweep around the right side of the patrol line. Searching and sweeping for a sniper is tense business. The potential victim in this hide and seek situation is the soldier on the ground. The sniper has the advantage of hiding in a camouflaged position from where he can pick off the troops as they search for him. All the diggers are now at the edge of their nerves. Is another sniper out there, is he aiming at me? The question dancing just on the edge of every soldier's stretched taut lips.

There is no new gunfire which gives me some comfort. I assume the vigilant digger has fortunately sighted and hit his target before the sniper was ready to engage. Possibly, there are no other snipers in the area.

Suddenly the sergeant yells out. 'Fucking snipers in the trees my arse, you dumb prick Mick. You shot a monkey, all I can find is one dead monkey.'

I look out from between the buttress roots at OC and Sandy. They all lie there motionless for a moment. Slowly Sandy's face forms into a smile and then the laughter starts as he realises what has actually happened. 'Just imagine what that poor feckin digger is going to have to live with for the rest of his life. Oh my lord I murdered an innocent monkey, I'm sooo feckin guilty.' Sandy quips, 'He will be seeing the God botherer when he gets home won't he? Forgive me father I have sinned, I shot a feckin innocent monkey who was unarmed and not very feckin dangerous.'

The OC is laughing now and responds, 'Never mind the priest. He'll have to put up with his mates taking the mickey out of him for the next six months. Let's take bets on young Mick's new nickname shall we? My guess is Mick-the-monkey-fucker', he calls out aloud.

Soldiers are laughing everywhere now, the tension released via Sandy and OCs humour. From a forward position comes, 'Hey Mick, get the monkey off your back.'

Another calls out, 'Mick, the monkey wrench.'

I am also laughing. 'Monkey spanker, yeah, Mick the monkey spanker', I call out to the OC who by this time has tears rolling down both cheeks.

Everyone was now cheering the 'Monkey Spanker'.

'Give it a spank for me will ya,' shouts Nunger, 'Think of a sexy little chimpanzee with its bright red arse pokin' in your nose.'

The radio set is crackling in my ear, 'four, four, this is zero alpha, niner speaking, what is happening? Over.'

Too busy laughing now. I look at the OC and call, 'Career man on the blower. Skipper, what will I tell him?'

The OC picks himself off the ground desperately trying to control his laughing fit. He walks over motioning for me to pass the handset. With every muscle in his face straining to stop himself laughing, he speaks to the CO, 'niner this is four, sunray. One of your boys just spanked his monkey. Over.'

The OC has lost his marbles. He falls to his knees laughing aloud. Everyone is now laughing aloud. Even poor Mick the unfortunate soldier who had shot before looking is now laughing at his own plight.

'Four this is niner, say again, I don't understand. Over', comes the CO's reply on the radio. The Major gives the handset back to me saying, 'You're the expert signal's man, you think of something that will explain what happened.'

'Maybe I need to explain to the man, what 'spanking the monkey' means.'

'No', says OC, 'the guy's a big wanker.'

I laugh back before pulling myself together enough to respond, 'Niner this is four, sunray not available at present. We had a false alarm, sweeping the area now. No enemy found. Out to you, zero alpha this is four, will send SITREP shortly. Out.'

The incident has broken days of tension and frustration but it has also driven home the realisation that we are on the edge of our endurance. Strained and a little trigger happy, our concentration is slowly falling away and a rest is needed.

After the situation settled, a militarily appropriate situation report is sent back to the fire support base. The Major sends word for all platoons to rendezvous at a grid reference some hundred meters from the northern edge of the large clearing identified on the map. We will reach the area with plenty of time to secure it and settle down for the night.

In the morning, D Company is going home to the Dat.

OC and CSM liked my Monkey Spanker joke. Broke the ice I think. We were all shit scared when Mick yelled out, he thought there were snipers. I sort of panicked but got my shit back together okay. I think I am going to be alright out here with the rifle company. Mick, or should I now say Monkey Spanker, will have it in for me, I am a dead cert for a payback practical joke before this war is over. Sandy has warned me that the man's a legend when it comes to practical jokes.

Hot Insertion

THE THREE PLATOONS gather at the rendezvous point as planned and next morning sweep around the large clearing to check for enemy before organising an airborne extraction.

Flushed with D Company's success in destroying the enemy hospital, the battalion's commanding officer is determined to find the enemy base camp. He orders Bravo Company to replace Delta Company. This means that each Huey flying in to retrieve the D Company soldiers is also dropping off fresh diggers to continue the hunt.

A slick of four choppers takes three runs to disembark B Company and load D Company. As company signaller, my duty is always to be amongst the first to land when going into a hostile area and last to leave. Propped on the edge of the jungle clearing I call each slick into land. I watch the organised chaos as fresh soldiers jump out and run for the jungle's edge to take up defences while tired soldiers walk and limp to the empty choppers. Finally, the last slick arrives and we remaining 24 D Company soldiers lift our backpacks for the last effort to climb on board the four Hueys to safety.

Corporal Steve Hinckle, a B Company signaller jogs up to me, his freshly camouflaged face beaming its usual smile. 'Can't you Delta boys hack it out here, leave the mopping up to real soldiers are you?' He calls over the noise of four choppers preparing to lift off as soon as all are aboard.

'Real soldiers hunt, boy soldiers mop up', I reply with the mocking jocularity and confidence of a now blooded veteran, raising an upturned index finger in a well-known gesture. 'Enjoy yourself, all I got to look forward to is a hot shower and two days in Vungers.'

Steve laughs and shakes his head, 'Get out of here you bastard, B Company will finish the hunt.'

I don't care about finishing any hunt. All I am thinking of now is my first trip to Vungers to see if all the old digger stories about the place are true.

I arrive home to the relative safety of Nui Dat and discover that in my absence the signal platoon storeman has moved my meagre belongings over with my new comrades in D Company. The D Company area in the Dat is below SAS hill on the opposite side of the airstrip to my former Support Company tent. This is my first visit to the D Company tent area in Nui Dat.

Amazed at how Spartan it is compared to the tents over at Support Company area. Here, there are just tents and beds, sand-bagged blast walls around each tent and no furniture. The Support Company and Administration Company areas have reaped the benefit of having soldiers permanently based at the Dat. When not performing duties, those diggers amuse themselves by constructing basic furniture from discarded artillery shell boxes. They also tend to have record players and reel to reel or cassette tape players sending out a constant stream of music to help drown out noise from the airstrip. I guess rifle companies spend little time in the Dat and diggers are usually too tired to play at 'nesting' on those rare occasions. Makes sense, I am too tired to care and I have only completed a half op.

Word has spread through D Company soldiers that R and C is being arranged. With that proposition comes the order that no man will go unless each and every soldiers' kit is squared away and each and every weapon stripped to their most basic parts; cleaned and inspected by the platoon sergeants or the CSM who now insists on being called Sir, not Sandy.

Bodies are scrubbed clean, bandages and ointments applied and fresh clothing issued. Now it is just a matter of waiting for transport. The diggers had been patrolling for almost four weeks before I joined them. We are truly in need of a break. Not just physically exhausted, our nerves are strung tight and need to be unwound a little. The planned solution is alcohol and sex!

Joy turns to anguish as word comes drifting down the gossip trail that ANZAC Battalion has hit a large enemy force in Long Khanh Province and are taking a beating.

The Australian Task Force brigadier and his intelligence officers are convinced that the hospital D Company destroyed was ready for the battles to come. Command has decided to deploy a second infantry battalion into neighbouring Long Khanh Province believing that the enemy is in that area training to launch a new offensive into the Australian controlled Phuc Tuy Province.

The ANZAC Battalion has both Australian and New Zealand soldiers and has been highly successful in engaging the Viet Cong cadres from the local villages, particularly in the Binh Bah rubber plantation area where on several occasions they've ambushed and killed large groups.

Their success has possibly provided them with a false sense of their ability to fight the enemy. They have now come up against well-trained regular soldiers, including North Vietnamese troops. Once in contact they literally charged forward expecting the enemy to be overpowered or retreat. Instead, well-armed and trained soldiers employed disciplined tactics and cut them to pieces. Now the ANZACs are licking their wounds and dragging to their rear areas: four dead, and six wounded soldiers.

Alpha Company, from my battalion, has been placed on standby to be lifted into the area and word is spreading that D Company will have their R and C cancelled in case more reinforcements are needed. The next lot of bad news soon follows, all officers and non-commissioned officers from D Company are ordered to report for briefing. The company's main sigs are also to attend. Now depressed I drag my body over to the mess area for briefing.

The OC speaks plainly at this briefing. Straight to the point, 'ANZACs are engaging a large, well-equipped enemy force. They will have armoured support shortly and we expect that will drive the enemy back over in this direction here.' He points to the large wall map before continuing, 'We are going in to cut them off, and by we, I mean A Company and D Company. We will be dropped at this clearing. We do not know what's waiting for us when we land in that buffalo grass so it is going to be a 'hot insertion'. Two Companies in one flight or about 35 choppers if we include our gunship support.'

The group in the briefing is now beginning to fidget with nervous excitement. The OC continues, 'I know the boys are exhausted, but this is a rare chance to break up this enemy group and do some damage to them before they get organised and retrained enough to come after us. Our company is going in with A Company to set up ambush positions across this area here', again pointing to his map in a broad sweep. 'We can expect to be there no more than four days before we are brought back for that rest we all need. A Company will do any further patrol work, or possibly C Company who are currently on R and C.'

The OC now pauses, a serious look on his face before finalising his general brief. 'Let's not underestimate what we are up against, it will be NVA and trained Viet Cong regulars, not the local stuff. Sandy, you and the NCO's get to work on the troops. Dutch and Brian, go set up the codes and give a short brief to the platoon sigs. The terrain is a little hilly and they will need to carry dipoles for comms. Make sure they know exactly how to string them up and advise them on what to do if we set up an aerial retransmission system. Platoon commanders remain with me for more chart details.'

D Company area is now a buzz with activity and tension. Diggers have quickly pushed aside their disappointment at missing the two-day break in Vung Tau and are now focused on the task ahead. Jesus, a hot insertion! As lead signaller I go in on the first run. First boots on the ground! My guts are churning over like hell. What if we land on top of a whole battalion of enemy soldiers? Hope nobody notices I am nervous.

Fresh clean ammunition is issued and new rations for a four-day patrol are packed away in our kits. As we move by truck to the task force kangaroo chopper pad, tension is growing into the adrenaline surging anticipation of the battle that may be upon us within the hour.

The sight of 30 to 40 Huey choppers lined up as a major slick only serves to raise the nervous energy amongst the diggers. I am as excited as any, the mixture of fear and excitement causes that strange taste in my mouth. I am aware of a small knot in my stomach. I had first felt this knot after the ambush and killing of the three enemies back at the underground hospital system. Although faded since our return to the Dat, it is now apparent again.

At the task force helipad, soldiers leap from the back of their trucks in platoon strength, formed into section slicks and move to our pre-determined boarding area where we squat or sit and wait for the word to climb aboard our allocated chopper.

Each chopper in the slick brings their rotors to full revs. All around dust is swirling, adding to the tension and surrealism of the moment. Soldiers poised ready, hands shield our eyes from the swirling dust as we watch for the door gunner to signal the boarding.

Suddenly the thumbs up comes from chopper after chopper and the diggers surge forward, quickly climbing into the aircraft. The first aboard slip on to the canvas seats along the rear bulkhead, the rest sit on the floor. Within a matter of seconds, two rifle companies are ready to be airborne and the entire slick of aircrafts is reaching full revs, each chopper visibly shaking on its landing skids ready to drag itself skyward.

Slowly they become airborne in groups of four, diamond formation. Climbing and starting a long broad circle over Nui Dat. The slick growing from four to eight to twelve until the entire slick forms like a swarm of wasps. As one, they bank gently and move in formation over the Australian base camp then out into an unknown reception in Long Khan Province.

Whop   Whop   Whop   Whop   Whop

The sight of 30 or more helicopters flying in formation is stirring at the best of times, to be in one of them is a remarkable sensation. The whole flight climbs to about 1500 feet in tight formation. From my position by the open door, I can see the faces of the diggers in the choppers closest to me, their hair buffeting in the wind and down draft. An infantry machine gunner in the chopper across from me sits with one leg over the side of the doorway, his M60 resting across his thigh. Next to him, the American door gunner is checking the twin machine guns mounted in front of him, making sure the belt feeds are unhindered. I glance to my side at the soldiers in my own Huey. Mine is the first chopper on the ground and Sandy and I have our own personal bodyguards. There sits Tiny from Support Section, his SLR rifle turned upside down with the muzzle facing the floor. The magazine is removed and held in his hand as per standard procedure. With his thumb Tiny keeps pushing the top round in his magazine up and down, up and down in nervous anticipation.

Nunger leans over and calls to Tiny, 'Forget the upturned rifle and mag off bullshit, we are in Yank choppers they ain't so fussy, we're about to drop into a fucking hell hole. Get the weapon ready.'

Tiny stares at the door gunner, pointing to his SLR. The door gunner nods, so Tiny pushes the magazine home and cocks the rifle sending a round into the chamber. He checks his safety catch and then shows the weapon to the door gunner who quickly glances at the safety catch before giving the thumbs up sign. Tiny now rests the SLR flash suppressor on the edge of the open door beside my feet. Realising the flight would soon be landing I drive home the magazine of my M16, pull back the cocking mechanism and allow it to slide forward delivering a round to its chamber. I check my safety catch then push shut the small dust cover before letting the flash suppressor rest on the edge of the doorway facing down toward the jungle below.

Whop   Whop   Whop   Whop   Whop

Three Australian UH1C gunships are circling around the main slick. These converted Hueys do not have the same firepower as the more sophisticated Cobra gunships, but they do carry Gatling guns and two rocket pods, which can be launched into the jungle edges as the fleet comes in to land.

Bushrangers 71, 72, and 74 are armed to the teeth and Bushranger 73 is back at Kangaroo pad ready as back-up so that the Australians will have constant air support by rotating fire power between the four gun ships with two engaging, one peeling off to re-arm while one is coming in ready from Kangaroo pad.

For that moment, I feel powerful and invincible, as though we are too many and too well-armed for defeat by any army. I convince myself that I am immortal, able to survive anything ahead, too young to die.

The door gunner is now pointing into the distance. I stare out the side of the chopper door and can see the clearing up ahead with artillery shells exploding within and around its edges. The whole formation of choppers is veering around and staying clear of the artillery fire.

Suddenly the explosions ahead cease and the formation turns as one and drops down lower to the tree line in a sweeping arc around the landing site. My own chopper is now heading directly toward the clearing. This is it. Why did I have to be a fucking sig operator? The gunships separate from the formation and fly alongside my chopper taking the direct path to the clearing. I feel the aircraft slow slightly as the gunships move ahead of my chopper. Once there, 71 and 72 roll in behind each other laying down fire along the jungle edges and trying to draw any enemy fire. As each gunship rolls out of its strike, I watch spell-bound as gutsy door gunners place one foot on top of the rocket pod, stand, and lean out of the chopper with both shoulders pressed into their twin machine guns, strafing the jungle. A keen sense of balance and a length of lifeline or monkey strap is all that keeps these men from falling to certain death.

Heart in mouth, I am on my haunches at the chopper door ready to step onto the landing skid and down onto the ground as the Huey comes into land. Behind my lead chopper the slick is waiting ready to swoop into the landing area. Eight choppers will land at a time as soon as Sandy and I can confirm the quality of the buffalo grass and swamp marsh. I squat, mesmerised by the noise and explosions along the jungle edges.

Whop   Whop   Whop   Whop   Whop

50 feet, 30, 20, now only 10 and I step down onto the landing skid with one leg. Suddenly the door machine gunner opens fire, strafing the jungle beside us and more diggers surge toward the door ready to decamp.

Partly from the fright of the door gunner triggering a long burst of fire and partly from a digger behind me surging forward, my leg slips from the skid. I feel myself tumble, spinning around the landing skid and falling to the ground headfirst, landing on my neck and shoulders with the heavy radio set crashing into the back of my skull. Blinding pain overwhelms me as my back twists over behind my chest and my body ploughs into the muddy buffalo grass. I think I hear a pop somewhere inside my body at the same time as the sig set smashes into my skull.

Semi-conscious, winded and dazed, I am aware of a sharp pain in my right wrist and worse still in my lower back. I lie trying to clear my head of the sharp ringing sound in my ears, wondering if I have broken my spine. My head is spinning. I lie still, afraid that if I move I will do myself great damage.

Suddenly a surge of pain as I am lifted by the straps on my backpack. I am being dragged through the mud and grass by two soldiers, one screaming loudly at me, 'Help us you prick you're too feckin heavy.' Its Sandy's voice. I am safe in Sandy's care and discover I am able to move my legs. I struggle to get them moving enough to push myself in the direction I am being dragged. Shrubs and branches scratch my face as I am dragged from the clearing to the jungle edge and dumped like a sack of potatoes onto the ground. Vision blurred I can hear Sandy calling out above the din of gunfire, 'Get his feckin M16 over here and find the feckin medic.' He grabs my radio handset yelling into the radio, 'Taking some small arms fire. Hot on the northern perimeter.

We need gunship to concentrate on the northern flank. Possible panji spikes in swamp. Got a digger stuck in a hole screaming in pain. Over.'

Pain and vision begin to fade as I slip into a black void. The sharp pain at the back of my skull help bring me back into consciousness.

'Steady, don't move just yet, I'm putting a couple of stitches into your scone', Doc is talking to me in a calm and caring voice. I lie still and feel the needle going through the skin again. 'You had old Sandy worried he had lost you', Doc continues. 'All the blood from this cut on the back of your head made it look like you had taken a bullet. But it's just a cut from the radio smacking into your skull. Head cuts always bleed colourfully. You're going to live a little longer.'

'That's nice to know', I reply, head pounding. As I move, I feel an even sharper pain in my right wrist. 'Jesus, I must have broken my wrist.'

'No, not so lucky, but it sure is swollen up. How's your back? You were mumbling something about your back before you started talking any sense to me.'

'Sore. A real bad ache type of sore.'

'The good news is that everything is in working order, so I guess you have just given it a very nasty twist. Look forward to back trouble in your old age my good man.'

Sandy now walks over to look at me, 'How is he Doc?'

'He will have concussion and probably vomit now and then. A few stitches, a bandaged wrist and a bad back. Apart from that, he is just dandy.'

Sandy looks at me, 'Feckin sore back aye, a likely story that one', he snorts. 'Suppose you want me to put you on a chopper home and arrange some warm milk and cookies be brought to your feckin bed, do ya son?'

I am flushed with anger and embarrassment. 'It's sore Sandy. I'm not trying to bludge my way out of this op.'

'You can't mister. You're our only battalion sig now.'

I am stunned by this statement. 'Where's Dutch, what happened to him?'

'Feckin panji', Sandy replies. 'Dutch came in on the second wave and stepped on a fecker straight up through his GP boot and through the other side. You think you got a problem, we had to cut him off the feckin thing and put him on a chopper squealing like a shot pig.' Sandy paused a while to watch my response, then continues, 'We got dropped into a shit-hole full of booby traps. That new digger from A we had on our chopper went into a panji pit too. Poor bastard, it didn't just go through his flat foot like old Dutch, went right up into his leg.' Sandy grimaces as he imagines the pain. 'Dutch will be back on his feet in a week or two, the other digger has big trouble, wakey for him I figure. So much for an extra soldier for Nunger's team. One week in country and he is back home with a leg that will be fucked for the rest of his life.'

Doc now entered the conversation, 'We also found two trip wire booby traps and the boss thinks there are more around here. You just slept through the whole thing you lazy bastard.'

'Fuck you', I respond. 'You want the pain in my head you can swap with me any time.'

'Don't get shitty with me and the Doc here son, just get up off your arse and join us in the real war for a change', Sandy replies before looking at Doc and asking, 'Can we get him moving for the next couple of days, remember we should be in stationary ambush sites for most of this trip?'

'I'm going to shoot some morph into him for now and we can pump him full of pills for the rest of the trip as long as he doesn't get shot. I'm short of the good stuff after those panji injuries and the aspirin in these spare pills will cause him to bleed badly if he does.'

'I'll do my best to avoid getting shot Doc', I reply caustically, as I feel the needle go in and the mild rush of the morphine begins its surge.

'Sorry mate', Doc says as he scrawls a large M on my forehead with his felt pen. 'Got to wear the sign in case I ain't here to tell some other med you are sailing.'

'I'll have his gear distributed amongst support section so he only has to carry the sig set and his rifle for the next day or two', Sandy announces, before looking me squarely in the eyes. 'Welcome back to the real war son. So get off your ass and earn yer pay.'

Sandy then turns and walks away. Later I would reflect and write…

Embarrassed again, fell out the bloody chopper door and knocked myself out, what a Wally. Poor bloody Dutch hope his foot heals okay. Extra responsibility now. I will make up for that stupid mistake at the LZ. Can't let the boys down, not ever. Fuck my back aches, when I straighten up it sends a sharp pain down both legs. My wrist is really sore. Hardly write with it.

Night Fight

The enemy logic is both simple and cunning. There are only a few possible locations where American or Australian forces can be delivered to the area by air in large numbers. These are booby-trapped.

Two Australian soldiers suffered injuries as a result of having a foot slip down a camouflaged, narrow hole in the ground. Sharp steel or bamboo spikes lay in waiting at the bottom to drive up through the unfortunate victim's foot leaving them impaled and trapped in agony.

The trip wire booby-traps are somewhat more sophisticated. These consist of a small green canister of explosives wrapped in serrated wire, complete with Soviet instructions for use stamped on the side. This is secured to a tree. A thin, high tensile wire is stretched from an anchor point on another tree back to a double trip spring system on top of the explosive device that causes it to explode should the wire trip be pulled or cut. The trip wire, barely seen in the jungle shadows, is suspended ankle to shin height above the ground. The enemy carefully place these traps in the most probable location that Australian or American troops would place machine gun positions when securing the area. The careful placement of the booby traps enables Australians to locate and disarm them quickly.

By good fortune, a machine gunner from Alpha Company extended his M60 bipod legs to lay the weapon on the ground. To his horror and relief, he noticed the weapon's flash suppressor had touched, but not tripped, one of the deadly devices. The Australians quickly realised the enemy's cunning and took immediate booby trap action. They concentrated their search on probable defensive positions and within minutes another three traps were located and disarmed.

This confirmed the Australian Commander's worst case scenario. These traps were not the work of village terrorists. These were set by experienced, well trained, North Vietnamese soldiers who knew basic Australian infantry tactics. Of equal concern, the enemy is well-armed with Chinese and Soviet weaponry.

I have little time or desire to worry about the enemy. The mix of concussion, pain, and tinnitus ringing in my ears, combined with the slightly euphoric sensation from the morphine injection, makes my immediate environment seem surreal.

Part of my brain is functioning at near full capacity, still able to decode messages sent to and from Battalion HQ. At another level of consciousness however, I have the sensation of just drifting. Walking along a green and grey tunnel, menacing vines and low branches brush past my face. The jungle and people around me appear as if in a dream. Any moment soon I will wake up from a deep sleep, I will be somewhere else, anywhere but here.

Even though I am carrying a lightened load, my back aches each time I bend or turn. As the company moves through the jungle in single file an occasional sharp pain shoots down my legs, right leg mostly.

A surge of heat envelopes my aching body, I bend toward the ground as vomit spills between my gritted teeth. I drop to one knee and vomit a second time. The hot flush passes so I grab my water bottle for a quick rinse then try to re-focus my eyes and attention on the job at hand. I need more morphine but I also need to do my job. I am in hell!

Suddenly I feel a tiny wisp of tropical breeze against my perspiring face. Almost immediately the thick undergrowth around me turns into a foreboding dim harbinger of evil and silence. Above, the upper jungle canopy grows eerily darker. Darker and darker, I am concussed and stoned on morphine but am also in awe of the world that is dramatically changing before my eyes. Later this day I write…

Birdlife began scurrying for protection as purple-black clouds massed overhead forcing the tropical sun into retreat. It may have been my concussed, drugged state but I was startled by a flash of lightening and what sounded like a deep V8 roar of thunder. This was followed immediately by an ever-increasing roar that sounded like a train rushing through the Sydney underground rail system, as a wall of water thundered across the treetops towards our patrol. The first drops were like bloody airborne puddles, they cascaded through the tree canopy smashing into branches and shattering into a thousand droplets. The airborne puddles gathered in numbers, a heavy shower, a wild storm, a torrent, like wild river rapids cascading on us poor bloody soldiers below.

Never have I experienced such an intense tropical storm. One foot in front of the other, I keep repeating. One foot in front of the other. The storm continues, ear splitting clashes of lightening. Thunder roars like an artillery barrage. The water saturates deep into the bones of all in its path, the very souls of the patrol members begin to drown in the misery of this saturated rotting Hades. Tough diggers can do little more than succumb to the mud and puddles that appear instantly beneath their feet. The patrol is forced to stop, to crouch or squat, trying to protect the working parts of our weapons as best we can and shelter our eyes from the stinging spray of shattered water droplets.

Almost as quickly as it came at us, it was gone, the walls of water turned to flying puddles again, then just droplets dancing from leaf to leaf as they made a final plunge to earth. Meagre rays of sun fought their way through small openings in the tree canopy. The jungle fell silent except for the drip, drip, dripping. Suddenly more sunlight snuck through the jungle canopy and it was over. WOW!

The patrol remains in disciplined silence. Each man props or squats, staring at the wonderland as though in a state of shock. The jungle stares back in undisciplined silence, taking its long breath to recover from the storm's onslaught. Gradually the noises return; the rustle of birds in the treetops, the buzzing and humming insect wings. At the head of the patrol, the forward scout glances back at his section commander. A check of the compass, a point in the directions of advance, a silent nod and the patrol moves on. Finally, the group goes into our night harbour.

Company HQ is travelling with Twelve Platoon, creating a combined force of 38 men. The night harbour consists of a forward ambush site manned by two rifle sections and twenty meters to the rear a HQ defensive position.

The OC believes the enemy will be driven away by the ANZAC Battalion's assault on the area and will be waiting until the cover of darkness to try to slip past any blocking force deployed to mop them up. He has arranged for the other two Delta Company platoons to be in ambush positions covering the most probable areas that could be traversed in darkness. It could be a long wet night for friend and foe. I am going to be okay; I just know it in my bones.

I go about setting up the Company HQ radio area, and despite the pain in my wrist and back, begin digging holes for the ANPRC sets, placing them below ground-level to protect them from the potential damage during a night fight. Next, I helped Jacko dig out a two person shell-scrape in which two soldiers could lie in safety and man the radio equipment if a battle occurred. Once finished, my back is aching too much for me to dig my own shallow trench but I am unconcerned. If a contact occurs tonight, I will be in the HQ pit.

With the increased pain in my wrist, head and back, I plead to Doc for more morphine.

'No!' Is the curt response and simple painkillers are provided instead.

'You've got to understand Brian, I only carry so much of the stuff. If any other diggers get shot up tonight, I might need it.'

'The damn pills won't stop this pain mate', I whine.

'Tough luck my good man, the pills will take the edge off it and if you get shot up tonight you will give thanks to Christ that I didn't waste any of this morphine.'

He was right and I knew it. Reluctantly, I swallow two pills and set up my night area ensuring the com cord is stretched tight directly between my sleeping area and the radio sets.

Stand-to is signalled at the same time as another monsoon downpour arrives. At the rear of the ambush site I can take some protection. Those lying by the ambush killing ground can do no more than call on mental self-discipline to steel themselves for yet another night of saturated sleeplessness. In the last-light of dusk, the rain attacks the soldiers, like thin steel spikes the water drives into their bodies, dancing off their weapons then spluttering and gurgling in puddles around each sodden soul.

After stand-down, I take the first shift on radio, lying silently for two hours before waking Jacko and then slipping off to my own sleeping area. There is no hammock tonight, regardless of the tropical downpour. Wet and for the first time shivering from cold, I wrap myself tightly in my spare hooch, rolled under the main one and wait for my own body heat to dry my clothes and warm me enough to enable some sleep. Eventually the shivering stops. I can feel my exhausted body and mind drift through the pain and into a light sleep.

Three Claymore mines exploding together jolt me upright. But the sound of the M60 machine gun firing off a hundred rounds in rapid succession has me lying flat to the ground in an instant. Infantry small arms fire pours into the ambush killing-field.

There is a different sound amongst the crescendo! For the first time I hear the distinctive sound of the enemy AK assault rifle.

Suddenly an almighty 'whoompah' as a rocket-propelled grenade is launched by the enemy into the trees over the Australian position. As it hits a tree, it explodes in a blinding flash causing my ears to ring with a high-pitched scream. Handheld flares are being fired by the Australians casting a white light over the killing field and illuminating the treetops. Now eerie shadows mix with tracer. Red streaks of hot shrapnel are all around me. I roll over to make my way to the HQ radio when suddenly another 'whoompah' seems to lift me from my prone position on the ground and I feel a sharp hot pain in my chest just below my left pectoral muscle.

'Oh fuck I'm hit', I scream. My voice lost in the crescendo of violence all around me.

I roll onto my back and stare incredulously skyward. The world above me is filled with tracer, red hot shrapnel and now the ripping sound and popping of artillery illumination shells. Small white parachutes wafting high above the trees and dancing in the hot tropical breeze like gigantic bright glow-worms. Their glow causing the jungle's canopy to paint a million shadows jumping and prancing amongst the flashes of tracer from small arms fire. The flares descend ever closer to the ground, their bright white glow becoming spotlights illuminating a drenched piece of mud and decay. In the flashing dancing light, I cannot help but think of the Asian enemy in those blackened trees and leaves. In my shell-shocked mind every shadow, every movement in every tree hides slanted eyes. A soldier's most dreaded enemy, the God of fear, wraps its talons around my innards, twisting intestines into a knot and snapping my sphincter muscle tight. My thoughts are in a state of temporary confusion.

I lie for a while summing up the courage to raise a hand and feel the wound in my chest, my mind is racing back to the young enemy soldier with the gaping hole and frothing blood. Slowly I slide a trembling hand toward the pain. Nothing! No gaping hole. But wait, I feel a hard and hot lump. I pull on it and feel a sharp pain in my chest. The metal is now between my fingers and I realise it is still hot enough to burn. Regardless of the burning, I hold it up to my eyes. A hot jagged piece of shrapnel, still glowing red between the brittle cast metal splinters. I am not going to die! Dead shrapnel has hit me. Not exactly dead, but its velocity was reduced dramatically before it struck me in the chest, maybe it passed through a thin tree or some other object. I didn't know or care. I was not badly wounded, barely touched at all. I roll back onto my stomach and crawl over to the command post to discover the OC and the artillery FO in his pit. I am above ground and exposed.

'Took your bloody time son', the OC calls above the din. He is smiling not frowning.

'Where is Sandy?' I call.

'Gone forward to organise ammunition', the OC replies, while grabbing a radio handset and passing it to me. 'You keep the CO informed about what is happening down here and no matter what the bastard says or threatens to do, I don't want to speak to him. I'm too busy to have a chat with him. Got that?'

I nod and put the handset to my ear, greeted with the CO calling from the other end. 'Four, call sign four, this is niner, fetch your sunray. Over.'

'This is four, my sunray is not available. Can I assist? Over', I reply.

'No, damn it! Get me your sunray', comes the Colonel's angry reply.

Shit, I've never had to deal with this sort of thing before. 'I'll get sunray as soon as possible, until then can I assist? Over.' The battle of delaying tactics has begun. After 20 minutes of abuse and counter statements, I look over at the OC.

'The boss is getting really pissed with me, Skipper', I plead.

'Fuck him', the OC replies.

Ten Platoon has also tripped an ambush some 300 meters away and two battles are now occupying the OC's mind. My nerves have settled enough to absorb the atmosphere around me.

Unimaginable violence. Small arms fire, grenades and now artillery high explosives are tearing at eardrums. To my front, soldiers are yelling to each other and pointing out movement in the suddenly dark jungle. I hear Sandy barking orders to get the diggers focused back on the actual killing ground and warn them that artillery will soon be coming in danger-close. A man somewhere in the darkness is screaming in agony and now distant violence as the other platoon kills the enemy as they walk past their ambush site.

The artillery FO has directed the big guns' shells to explode close to our position now. Shrapnel is ripping through the trees and branches are breaking free and falling around the men as they lie in battle. Each artillery shell causes a ripping sound through the air, followed by a moment's silence before the explosion. As the shells land closer, the silence before each explosion seems longer.

'It's when you hardly don't hear them at all, they're the ones to worry about', the FO calls out to me. 'And you won't hear the bastard that lands on top of you so no point in fretting over it young fella. Just keep your nose and your dick pointed at the mud.'

In time it becomes apparent the enemy is no longer returning fire. The artillery has driven them away. There will be many blood trails through the jungle tomorrow. The OC motions to me to hand over his radio handset. I pass it over like a hot coal.

'The CO is angry with me Skipper. If I get locked in the brig I hope you bring me some flowers.'

The OC smiles and begins talking to the commanding officer. I can make out the last part of the conversation. 'Roger niner not the young man's fault, he was unable to reach me and finally had to crawl through a wall of small arms fire to get to me. He deserves a medal not a kick in the bum.' The OC looks up at me and winks. I smile back, beginning to feel accepted by my company commander, a part of the team.

Sandy suddenly crawls up to the HQ area. 'I have redistributed all spare ammunition forward. I think we can get through the night without a resup, he calls. 'As long as they don't try a counterattack but I figure they're out of here. We cut a big hole in the bastards.'

'Any casualties? I could hear a man screaming before', the OC calls back to Sandy.

'Feckin Gook with his guts spread all over the place, not one of ours. We came out of this one without any casualties but Charlie is cut to pieces. The reason they put up such a fight was to try to get their wounded and dead away from us. We can still see bodies in the kill zone but they managed to drag quite a few away.'

The OC nods, 'I have arranged for illumination to be fired at regular intervals 'til first light, both here and over the other ambush site.' It's 0400 so it will cost the army a small fortune in shells but the CO somehow manages to get task force command to agree.

'Nice of the feckin Brigadier to spend a few dollars keeping his troops alive,' Sandy grunts. 'Must remember to thank him when we get back, raise some money through a chook raffle or somethin'. Buy him a little card.'

He just finishes the statement when another illumination round explodes over our position. The OC smiles, 'Wars cost money Sandy and the brig has to account for his pennies with the politicians back home. As for our own CO, he might be an arrogant prick but he looks after his boys. This is when I'm glad to have him as our battalion commander.'

OC looks at me, 'Dig out a bit of a hole in the corner of the pit here and put on a hot brew. Use hexi not C4, it's going to be a long night and a slight glow from the hexi won't make much difference with all this illumination going off.'

For a brief moment, I consider telling the HQ group about the shrapnel that hit my chest but feel embarrassed. Compared to what the diggers on the ambush line went through, I was lucky. I say nothing, pull my bayonet from its sheath and begin attacking the corner of the shell-scrape. A small hole dug and the water boils ready for the first of many hot bitter coffees before the first rays of morning sun signals the beginning of the day.

First light arrives without further incident at HQ or Ten Platoon's ambush site. A section-sized patrol is sent from each site to sweep the immediate area around the Australians. Both patrols return reporting no live enemy but blood trails indicate more bodies to find once the search begins in earnest.

The OC requests a dog tracker team to assist Ten Platoon. He will rely on Nunger to track the enemy from the HQ ambush area. Three enemy lay dead at HQ and another body lies twisted and broken in front of the Ten's Platoon's machine gun site. Soldiers strip-search then bury the corpses.

I don't go forward with OC to examine the carnage, I will see that gruesome sight soon enough. Instead, I return to my own hooch area to try and unravel what has hit me and how. I examine the destruction around me, amazed that no Australian was injured.

Trees have been stripped bare of all foliage, several literally cut in half by RPGs exploding against them. Masses of holes in the trunks indicate the ferocity of the enemy response. Well-armed they had fought back tenaciously.

I examine the holes three to four feet up from the base of the tree. I learned in training that in combat, soldiers tend to fire high and that the safest place in such a situation is as flat as possible to mother earth. 'Get so low to the ground that you look up at the worms, and when you return fire, deliberately try to point your weapon lower', a corporal instructor had told me. Here was the proof.

'Well you're a lucky little fecker, ain't ya?' I hear Sandy say. I look across and notice Sandy standing at my sleeping spot. I move closer to see why Sandy is commenting. A knot returns in my stomach. My hooch is peppered with holes, at least 10 maybe 15 shrapnel holes. But these are not holes from falling dead shrapnel that comes with artillery fire, the hooch is tattered from almost ground level. My backpack lies on the ground beside the hooch where I had placed it before dark the night before, twisted over to one side. I squat down and examine it, a gaping hole in its side.

Trembling I open the pack flap and discovered two ration tins are punctured, shrapnel has passed right through them both. A radio battery is also damaged, a deep rut gouged in its side and an exit hole torn through the other side of my pack. I examine the exit hole then look to where I lay when hit by the dead shrapnel and a cold chill runs down my spine. I look up at Sandy, tug loose the bottom of my shirt and lift it to show the CSM the now bruised and weeping flesh wound.

'Lucky little fecker indeed', I say, trying to imitate Sandy's unusual interpretation and over-use of the fuck word.

Sandy raises an eyebrow and bends down to examine the wound. His concerned facial expression changing. 'Nothing to worry about, you just joined a club of about 200 diggers that copped a light shrap hit since we came into this stinking war, just get Doc to treat it for infection', Sandy mumbles before standing and letting out a little giggle. 'I figger you've had the worst patrol of any bastard I met except the ones what got shot. You've been kicked out of a chopper, fecked wrist, twisted back and now this little gem.' He looks me square in the eye and smirks, 'You're not tough son, you're just something between lucky and feckin stupid. You don't belong in this war, you belong in a Donald Duck comic.'

'So get me out of this war Sandy', I reply dryly. 'And thanks for all your genuine concern for my health and well-being, ya stinkin' arsehole.'

'Now don't get all shitty son. Don't get all girly with me or you'll start cryin'. I'll make you a hot brew and let you clean your weapon in peace', Sandy replies as he pulls out a packet of cigarettes from his top pocket and throws them to me. 'Change ya feckin brand, these seem just right for you', he quips as he turns to get a brew ready.

I look at the packet and examine the brand name. Lucky Strike!

I tear open the top corner and tap the packet on my M16 butt until one comes clear. Pushing it into my mouth, I light and draw back hard, trying to get the harsh smoke to penetrate deep inside me and hit the knot in my stomach. It seems to help. I blow the smoke from my lungs and curl back my lips.

'It must be my imagination but this fag tastes like shredded dog shit wrapped in dunny paper', I grunt back at Sandy, who by now has prepared an instant hot brew with his C4 explosive. 'Tastes worse than your cooking Sandy'.

'Get this into you son, don't come up to HQ just yet, take a break from sigs for a while. You feckin earned it', Sandy says quietly before patting me on the shoulder. 'I'll tell Doc to come visit you with some antiseptic.' He turns and walks away.

I sit quietly, almost too exhausted to lift the hot steel mug to my lips. The slight wound on my chest is throbbing and itching at the same time. My back continues its dull ache and the injured wrist leaves me unable to hold a coffee mug without support from the other hand. Finally, I reach for my notebook.

I cannot recall a time in my life when I have felt so alone and miserable. Jesus I thought I was going to die last night. I did okay in the end, but I've got to stop myself from panicking. But it hurt like hell and I just thought I was hit really bad. Wish I hadn't thrown that bit of shrap away last night, good souvenir for my great grand kids.

Never imagined a fire fight could be so big and loud. Once I got over the panic, it was sort of exciting. I wonder if being shit scared and fucking revved up on adrenalin is similar. Main thing is, I didn't let anyone down. I think the OC trusts me and fart face Sandy almost cares about me in his own grumpy way. That dead body out in the killing field is just pumped up mincemeat. Claymore mine must have put all 700 ball bearings right through the bastard. Well it's them or us I suppose. We got out of this one scot free.

Program Performance Budgeting

'Just what in hell are you sprouting shit about now Wingnut?'

Wingnut smiles back at me through his insane little eyes.

I am beginning to understand Doc's irritation with the little sapper, always talking a lot of crap about one thing or another, with annoying little habits. Fidgeting and spitting, chewing food with his mouth open, slop slurp, slop. Wingnut's blond hair has been cut to an almost bald crew-cut which accentuates his flapper ears poking at right angles to the strange little smile and beady insane eyes.

'No bull! Mick told me back at the Dat and Mick ain't ever wrong. It's called 'Program Performance Budgeting' and that's why we are digging up these graves mate, PPB.'

I am looking back at Wingnut with curiosity. The little man is seducing my ever-inquisitive brain. Nothing makes any sense about this war, so why should Wingnut's theory be worse than any other.

We are trying to eat a meal while other diggers are exhuming freshly dug graves, discovered two days after the successful ambushes. Only two days, but the tropical heat and the unusual creatures that inhabit the jungle earth have started doing their worse to the bodies. Bodies hurriedly buried by an enemy army that has taken a beating and desperate to escape the encircling Australians.

The stench of death is overpowering. It creeps off each corpse and spreads its putrid tentacles over all who are near, penetrating their clothing and sticking to their skin, particularly those who have to handle the decomposing maggot-ridden flesh. Never had I imagined I would bear witness to this sight of wasted flesh. No longer human beings, not even corpses as I had known or imagined a corpse to be. No funeral parlour make up here, no clinically cleaned body drawn from a fridge for identification. These are pieces of rotting flesh, a head with the back split open, remnants of grey-blue brain material almost dripping from the cavity and covered with crawling black creatures. A torso with only one leg and no arms or head, its intestines half covered in pale green slime, adding further colour to the tangled mash of yellow, blue, black and grey innards flopping from the gaping hole that was once a stomach. There is no child of God in these pieces of flesh. No soul to go to heaven or Paradise. Or anywhere else. I am instantly and sickeningly aware that religion might simply be in the minds of people who fear ending up like these poor bloody creatures and want to convince themselves that there is a better life, an eternal life somewhere else. I know that from this day onward death will never have that sad but comforting innocence. Life will never be the same either. It is one thing to see death on a grand scale but knowing that we caused this mutilation of some mother's sons seems altogether horrifying.

Eventually hunger has driven me beyond the initial desire to vomit. I'm numbed by this experience. The smell is still there, but somehow it has pushed past my nostrils, back into some part of my brain that just doesn't want to register it. I finish chewing on a can of C ration turkey and beans and wash it down with hot coffee and a Lucky Strike.

'Tell me more Wingnut, about this numbers thing.'

'Mick says that the American President feller, Johnson, signed a thingo with the army based on performance. The more they can prove they are performing well, the more guns and stuff the President gives them.'

I cut in immediately. 'So what has that got to do with digging up bodies?'

'Simple', Wingnut replies. 'If we can prove we kill more of them than they kill of us, then we are winning the war, that's the performance thingo Mick is talking about.'

'Thingo! What crap is thingo? You mean contract not thingo you dumb dip-shit', I spit back at my sapper comrade.

'Whatever!' Wingnut replies. 'We don't win counter insurgency wars by capturing hills and stuff. So we got to win it by killing more Gooks than they kill us guys. Mick says the thingo, contract thing requires about three dead Gooks to one Yank. The Yanks are on about four-to-one so they get more war stuff from the President.'

'So why are we digging up bodies?' I ask. 'We aren't Yanks are we?'

Wingnut shrugs his shoulders. 'The Yanks probably use our numbers to boost their own. Besides, we have a higher kill ratio than any other mugs in this war, something like 14 of them to every one of ours.'

I am yet again depressed by this latest theory. 'I heard a rumour that the Yanks claim any dead body as a kill. If a sniper shoots at them from a village they call in the Napalm and wipe out the village and count them all as enemy. So why don't we just bullshit about how many bodies we claim? We don't have to do this shit for Christ's sake. The Yank President ain't going to come over here and personally collect their gold teeth, is he?'

Wingnut shrugs his shoulders. 'Our Brigadier likes to do it by the book, and then he can brag to the Yanks that we are the best in the business. Apart from that I bet ya the battalion commanders have a bet between themselves about which battalion gets the most kills.' He pauses to scratch his closely cropped head, 'I don't know everything do I? You ask Mick at the store when we get back to the Dat, he can explain it better than me.'

I shake my head. 'Maybe we dig 'em up to see if any info is buried with them, army intelligence likes bits of paper and stuff. Doc is right about your mate, Mick. He is a wanker, maybe you are too Wingnut. A wanker like this Mick bloke.'

At this moment, a dead enemy soldier's head rolls up to our feet as we are finishing our lunch. Bluish-black in colour, its top lip eaten away by maggots, one eye missing and the other rolled completely over to expose a decaying grey jelly-like substance. I look up to see the other Mick, known as Monkey Spanker, has a cheeky grin on his face.

'Thanks a lot, dick wipe. Can't you see we're trying to have a Sunday roast here?'

Wingnut stands to his feet and with a sharp jabbing motion, kicks the head back toward Monkey Spanker. The head rolls to the left of them, bounces off a tree root and wobbles back to Spanker's feet. He traps it under his right boot with the deft skill of a soccer player. As his boot slammed down on the head the blue-black nose breaks away and dangles by a piece of decaying skin. Spanker grimaces, looks up at me, 'I owe you that for putting the monkey handle on me Turkey.'

I ignore the reply and discard my near empty can of turkey and beans. 'OC sees you treating those dead Gooks like that and you're in very deep shit. You know how fussy he is about treating enemy with respect.' I look over at the grave site. 'How many?'

Spanker shrugs his shoulders, 'We are just putting some of the bits together. It's kind of hard to drag them out of the mud, sometimes they just fall apart, you know, bits of arm or leg just come off. Christ, some are all soggy like pea soup.' For the first time in his life Mick is unable to turn an experience into a joke. He screws his ashen grey face into an awkward contortion and looks at his hands before continuing, 'Artillery obviously got most of them. Still haven't found a body to match the head, but I figure about 15 in this hole. There are more buried just over behind that tree.'

I stared at the pile of bodies lined up as neatly as possible. Black-bluish-purple corpses with the soft fleshy parts already in decay or attacked by the bugs that live within the jungle dirt. The jungle bugs go for the soft flesh first, eyes and lips already half gone. I should feel something, I am numb. I have just watched a human head used as a soccer ball.

I visually recall one of the bodies left in the ambush killing ground two days ago. The fleeing enemy could not recover it. A claymore mine had exploded only feet from him and most of the 700 tiny steel ball bearings had literally passed straight through his body, turning him into instant jelly that had then turned to minced meat as the diggers tried to move him. To bury him they had simply dug a shallow hole where he fell and scraped him into it with the backs of their entrenching tools.

At least 20 enemy soldiers died in these few days and that does not count the damage done by the ANZAC Battalion who have lost four of their own and inflicted a yet to be determined number of casualties on the enemy. I was right beside the artillery FO when he called in the guns that turned most of those corpses into mangled pulp. I even took over for a few minutes and called them to repeat a salvo while he was crawling back to his hooch area for a spare battery. I was a part of this mayhem, a contributor to the destruction of some mothers' sons. Yet I do not care so much about those mangled pieces of flesh as I do about the stupidity of the tactics of war. Futile. Nothing captured, no ground gained, just body counts to say we killed more of them than they killed of us. So we win this time but there is no point in winning battles if you can't win the stupid war. What the fuck am I doing in this shit hole?

I have now reached a state of total disillusionment. I am scared of dying, of looking and smelling like the corpses in the pit. Scared of letting down my mates, scared of snakes and spiders, frightened by the thought that I may be disembowelled or have bits of my body blown off. What's more, I cannot get the young boy's death out of my mind. Did we do the right thing or was it murder by another name?

Worst of all, is the growing feeling that I have been betrayed by my country. Betrayed by my father for teaching me as a child that to serve your country is an honourable duty. There is no honour in what I am sitting in front of at this moment. I feel betrayed by the army, for telling me that this war was about the 'domino theory' and stopping communist aggression reaching Australia.

I look over at the bodies lying in the filth and mud and feel dirtier than they are. I need more than ever to talk to someone about it. What am I doing here? Was anyone else feeling as miserable as me? Do they get so scared sometimes at night that they have to curl up into a ball and scream under their breath? On the other hand, is it just me, am I the one who can't cut the mustard?

Wingnut is using his bayonet to scrape the decayed bits of flesh off his right boot which he used to kick the severed head. 'Don't touch decaying bodies with your fingers whatever you do mate', he says as he methodically scrapes away the last bit of flesh. 'The stink gets into your own skin and stays for days, even when you light a fag you can smell it on your fingers.'

'How do you cope?'

'With what?' Wingnut replies, before he notices me looking over at the dead bodies. 'Oh that stuff, well you just put it out of your mind that's all, you force yourself not to think about it and it goes away.'

'Jesus Wingnut, it can't just go away, it has to go somewhere and I think it's going into my guts here. I got this horrible knot that just won't unwind.'

Wingnut suddenly becomes fidgety. He stands up. 'Just forget about it, don't let it get to you or you're fucked man. You got to control this sort of shit or you're stuffed, I seen guys lose their balls thinking about that stuff. Shut it out or go crazy'. The pointy-eared soldier turns away to avoid further discussion.

Sitting alone, I reach for another Lucky Strike, push it into my mouth and light it, drawing back hard to get the smoke to hit that spot in my gut somewhere. As the cigarette comes to my lips a second time, my finger brushes against my mouth. For a moment, I think I can taste the decaying flesh of a dead enemy. Bile rises in my mouth but I force it back down, a shiver running down my spine.

Wingnut reckons I should just get on with it and soon it will go away like it must have with guys like him. This war is killing me a little bit at a time, inside I will be dead soon then the knot will go away. The smell will go away. Fuck I wish that smell would go away. It's all over me.

I throw out the leftover swill in the bottom of the mug, pick up my M16 and walk over to HQ.

OC is talking to Hun the Vietnamese interpreter who has landed by chopper to examine the few documents found in or near the graves.

'So this one was found wrapped in a plastic bag and pinned to a tree. What does it say?'

Hun reads the document slowly. 'It is a poem or a simple version of a poem by Nguyen Du a famous writer in my country. I will try to explain to you that there is a traditional belief that the souls of those who die violently such as these poor soldiers, are condemned to wandering lost in the after world. Vietnamese Taoist believe there must be what you Christian Australians call a prayer for their absolution. Nguyen Du wrote a poem for their absolution just as your priests have writings in a thing you call a missal. In English language you would call this poem maybe something like 'The wish for, or appeal to, the dead who wander'. These are the names of the dead here at the bottom.

OC raises his left eyebrow, 'Can you translate the words for me?'

'I will try, let me think for a moment.'

Quickly I grab my notebook and ready my pen to write down the interpreter's words.

Slowly Hun begins his English version of the poem for the dead soldiers.

'In the long or eternal dark or night time. There will come into sight, spirits in the flickering or early morning light. There is pity for the 24 creatures or soldiers, their drifting souls wandering in alien lands. For these 24 not a joss-stick has been or will be burnt. Alone they will wander night after night.'

He puts the poem back in its plastic wrapping, 'It is hard to translate in a way that truly explains our customs in poetic verse. Best I just translate that when the war is won and we will return for the bodies and wash their bones. We will take them back to their families so that their souls will wander no more.'

He breathes a slow sound from his lips, 'I beg you Major, please return these bodies to their graves and place this note back where it was found. It is a marker for the North Vietnamese to locate the bodies of the 24 who died in your recent battle. They are just soldiers like you their names will help trace family in the north when the war is over. I beg you not to stack the bodies on top of each other and leave them for the pigs to eat as the Americans often do.'

OC nods his head in agreement, 'These soldiers will be re-buried just as the three bodies you saw last time we met were. We may be their enemy but we are men of honour. I guess we now know how many of them are in that grave site, 24 mothers' sons.' He shakes his head slowly, '24, how many more before this madness ends?'

OC turns to Sandy, 'Have the boys stop digging and counting and return the bodies to the ground, then get Nunger to put this message back where he found it.'

He passes the package to Sandy who raised an eyebrow, 'It should be kept for records John.'

OC looked across at the Vietnamese interpreter then back to Sandy, 'Fuck the army records Sandy, what would you want the NVA to do if they found one of our boys dead in the jungle. We haven't lost any yet but if we do I hope they bury him and mark his grave so that we can return and get him when the war ends.'

OC then turns back to Hun, 'I have a record of all dead enemy soldiers and their approximate place of burial just in case some future humanitarians wish to find their bodies. It is an Australian tradition, just like the Vietnamese, that we give our dead a decent burial after the war. We have war graves all over the world thanks to our stupid government's willingness to fight other people's wars in strange and distant lands. All our boys killed in Vietnam are returned to their families nowadays. I hope that one day these 24 will find their way home to their families.'

Hun places his hands together and bows his head to OC, 'You are a good man Major. Sadly, there are not enough of you in any army fighting in my country, war turns good men into animals, I appreciate that you try where others do not.'

I feel my face turn scarlet red, only moments ago a dead soldier's head was thrown at my feet in total disregard for the body or the family of that body. Ashamed I put away my notebook and step over to the three sig sets. Jacko is on radio watch so I just sit beside him, 'Take an early break mate, I got nothing better to do so I'll squat here if you like.' Jacko doesn't need any prompting, he stands up and disappears to his harbour position. I look at the message book and read the last decoded SITREP from zero alpha.

I am amused to find that Bravo Company has finally found the enemy base camp that D Company failed to locate. The OC's guess was close, another couple of day's patrol would have put D Company in the right location. The message goes on to say that the enemy had built several small huts and used the place as a bit of a rest area for NVA moving along the route between Long Khanh and Phuc Tuoy Provinces. B Company was about to burn it to the ground but the CO flew in some Australian reporters to get a few pictures and tell the story of how we had beaten Charlie yet again. They got some great shots of the huts burning.

Big deal! I throw the notes on the ground beside the radio. Next, I examine an INTSUM. The 274 Regiment is reportedly assisting the D445 Viet Cong group in a variety of short sharp assaults on ARVN positions across a broad area from Long Binh in the Bien Hoa Province to Xuan Loc in the Long Khanh Province. Phuc Tuy Province is enjoying the fruits of Australian and New Zealand military involvement. Little enemy activity is occurring in Phuc Tuy for the moment but we can expect to engage NVA, probably the

3rd Battalion of 33 NVA in the Long Khan region we are patrolling. I muse on this information awhile. We got 24 of the 33 in that pit, tell us something we don't know for a change. Big fucking deal!

The OC soon joins me and scribbles a new message for coding. 'You're going to like this one', he beams. I take the notes and read them. I am smiling. The message to be encoded is the planned withdrawal of D Company from the area. We are going home to the Dat again and hopefully this time a trip to Vungers will occur. The evacuation will be by armoured personnel carriers, not choppers. A long, uncomfortable drive home but better than walking. It means a short patrol to a pick-up area some 300 meters away. I encode the message as quickly as I can, ignoring the pain in my wrist as I write down each piece of code.

SAIGON TEA

D Company has been awarded two days' Rest-in-Country and we arrive at Vungers early in the day. We receive a quick lecture by the company captain about morals and venereal diseases. Then a warning not to trade in military payment currency because it finds its way into the black market for the purchase of war material for the communist enemy. Next, a Military Police sergeant warns us diggers which bars not to frequent due to their poor hygiene standards and high rate of venereal disease.

Soldiers being soldiers, simply take the warning to mean that these black-listed bars must be the best places to go. Many make a mental note and are already discussing how best to get to these dens of iniquity.

After the formalities, it is time for a company barbeque on the beach. Sausages and chops are washed down with a trailer full of ice cold Victorian Bitter and Southwark Bitter beers in their distinctive metallic green cans. The American soldiers refer to these beers as 'green death' due to their alcohol content which is much higher than the American brews.

Gradually the mostly unmarried boys begin drifting off to catch a ride into the township of Vung Tau. While those with other commitments head for a tourist style bus ride to visit the large statue of Buddha.

Two other soldiers, Tiny, Brando, and I wander past the MP sentries at the gate of the Peter Badcoe Club, sitting behind their sand bagged wall with a

M60 machine gun propped on its tripod. Three or four Lambro three-wheel taxis are just beyond the gate waiting for business. The three of us jump in the back of the first one in line.

Brando yells, 'You go Flags, Diddy Mao, Diddy Mao.' The driver kicks the little machine into gear and turns the handle bar accelerator as far as it will go. Wind in our ears, foreign smells in our nostrils and sexual anticipation churning in our loins, we three young men swallow up the environment we are passing through. Bicycles, rickshaws, trucks and Lambretta tuk-tuk taxis do high-speed battle with an endless stream of step through scooters and motor bikes often with three people stretched across them. Horns blasting, people yelling and occasionally waving to each other amongst the frenzy. Road rules seem simple enough, he who is alive at the end of the journey is clearly using the right rules. The roadside gutter is the sewerage and waste disposal system on the outskirts of the city. As the Lambro speeds towards the city's centre the foul stench of the aged sewer system diminishes, giving way to more exotic smells.

Into the centre of Vungers we roar past the little sidewalk cookeries, their strange smells mingling with discarded waste, rotting foodstuffs and a never ending throng of pedestrians.

The Lambro slows as it commences a broad circle around the central square in the middle of which flag poles fly the colours of the various nations who have found themselves involved in this war. We decamp, Tiny argues with the driver before handing over an unknown amount of Dong.

We stand in the middle of the town square, amazed at the sight before us. Endless bars line the streets with girls standing in the doorways calling us to come over and have 'jiggy, jiggy' or 'sucky fucky'. For just that moment, we young men exposed to battle are now cowering at the thought of so many girls calling us to buy sex.

Tiny spots a bar called, Kangaroo Bar, 'At least the name is familiar, let's start there.'

The three of us cross the road and enter the dingy, smelly bar, the bar girls surround us yelling and pleading, 'You buy me Saigon Tea. Then we go jiggy jiggy.'

I order three beers and the barman pours the bottles of the locally made 33 Beer into badly cleaned glasses. I lift a glass to my mouth, swill and spit the contents out onto the floor. 'This is bloody hot', I yell at the barman, who reaches down under the bar and comes up with a handful of crushed ice that he slops into the glass.

'Cold beer soon, you wait', the barman says, then stands back far enough to avoid any swinging punch I may choose to throw.

I turn to Tiny, 'Where's Brando, the other digger who was with us a moment ago.'

'Cunt-struck!' Tiny replies. 'Some bitch started wanking him off against the bar and next thing I know he is going off with her for a fuck.'

'Jesus we got the rest of the day and all night to take a prostitute', I reply. 'You think the least he could do is look around and compare the quality. It's not as if there is only a couple to choose from.' I push away a girl and reach for my notebook.

> *I am unsure if all these prostitutes are an exciting experience or a somewhat degrading experience. My fellow soldiers and my participation seems to degrade men as much as it does the poor women who are, after all is said and done, simply trying to survive in a war.*

The pair of us are now feeling crushed by the girls surrounding us, all calling for Saigon Tea. We push our way free and out through the front door and commence the task of bar crawling along the street. Vung Tau is a throng of people, colour and smells that intoxicate me as I wander about with my friend. It is alive with energy and tension like no city in Australia. I love it. I can feel the bamboo growing in my veins, sending me instantly 'troppo'. I am beginning to laugh along with the many bar girls now rather than feel a mixture of intimidation and shame.

After visiting three more bars, Tiny also disappears with a young woman. I am left alone with the frustration of being harassed by prostitutes and a desire to grab any one of them and go off to their little room. I yell angrily for them to leave me alone and I sit at a small table in the corner of the bar and again produce my notebook. I must capture the moment, the feelings of this crazy foreign city.

Little stands on corners sell hot sweet smelling rice bread rolls which they fill with your meat of choice, be it pig, dog or monkey, and salad of your choice. Heppo rolls as they are known to the soldiers as they have been traced to the cause of hepatitis infections amongst soldiers on R and C. Other cheap little eateries are crammed into little sidewalks. I smell steamed rice and boiling chicken mixed with strong spices and pungent fish odours. The foul smell of durian mixes with the smells of oyster sauce and fish oil. Each scent explodes through little open doors as they are splashed into almost red hot woks. Locals gather in tight clusters around their food, eating with chopsticks, wooden spoons and hands. Children squeal on their parent's laps or play under the table, there is no personal space yet no local seems to mind. People are smoking, coughing, standing and squatting. I see strange little shops selling baskets and hats. A tailor shop with an Indian gentleman resplendent in a white cotton suit sitting calmly behind his counter beckoning me in.

'I will tailor-make a fine suit for you my friend, something to wear when you return to Australia.'

Do I love this place? I think I do!

I am now alone and walking along the street. Gangs of children aged between five and ten are surrounding me, grabbing my wrist and calling for money. I push them away knowing that as they grab at my wrist they are trying to undo and steal my watch. The grabbing has also rekindled the pain in my swollen wrist, the lingering reminder of that humiliating stumble from the door of the helicopter.

A street vendor sits propped against the wall on a stool, his wares on a tray in front of him. I walk over, more fascinated by the vendor than the wares for sale. One more entry in the notebook.

The man has both his legs missing. One below the knee and one high up his leg somewhere under his shorts. One hand severely damaged with only a single small finger attached to scar tissue. The man's face is scarred horribly by a long deep gash that starts under his cheekbone and rises up through what was once an eye socket, and is now just an ugly piece of flesh stitched together without concern for aesthetics.

I know straight away that he is obviously the victim of a land mine blast, either he has trodden on one or was right beside some other poor soul who had trod on one. I notice the tattered service ribbons on the man's shirt and realise that this poor soul was once an ARVN soldier.

'So this is how the South Vietnamese army pensions off its wounded is it?' I ask the man, who smiles back at me. 'You buy, you buy, and I eat.'

I look at the wares on offer. Rings, chains, watches and souvenir trinkets share the tray with knives and Zippo cigarette lighters. The engraving on one Zippo catches my eye. I pick it up and read it out aloud, 'Yeah though I walk through the valley of death I fear no evil. For I am the most evil son of a bitch in the whole Goddamn valley.'

I look up at the mess of a man in front of me, evil son of a bitch? No a poor victim of madness would be a better engraving! I put down the Zippo and look back at the flick knives on the tray. Picking one up and trying the spring-loaded action to check that the blade will spring out and lock into place.

'Good, very good flick knife', the trader offers. I put it in my pants pocket and look at another Zippo. Engraved on the front is a map of Vietnam, on the reverse side the writing, *'When I die I will go to heaven; I have done my time in hell'*. The deep engraving is rubbed with red paint to make it stand out.

Again, looking back at the broken scarred vendor, 'You a Christian my friend? You going to heaven when you die?'

The vendor just looks back at me through his good eye. 'You pay, you buy flick knife and lighter', he says rubbing his stomach with his mangled hand. 'You buy, me eat.'

I reach into my pocket and pull out a generous handful of Vietnamese paper currency which I leave on the tray. I will not barter with this poor wretch. I take out a packet of Lucky Strike cigarettes, light two with my new Zippo and put one in the vendor's mouth, then point to the lighter, 'see you in heaven', and walk off to find another bar.

I find a bar that quickly titillates my imagination. Loud Jimmy Hendrix guitar music blaring from within. Looking through the door I can see a room full of uniformed Black American soldiers, so I amble in to join them.

'Hey dude you got to be chasing trouble to come in here, this is out of bounds to white meat', one of the soldiers calls out to me.

'Don't give me that white meat bullshit. I get it all the time from my good mate Nunger.'

The group of soldiers look at me for a moment, realising I am Australian.

'Okay, we gonna make you an honorary black man for a while mister Australian man', one soldier replies, moving aside to find space on the bench for me to sit.

'Let me buy this white Nigger a drink, what will you have white Nigger?'

'Beer.'

'Oh no, you don't drink that local beer man, they put embalming fluid in it, it's bad shit', the soldier replies. 'Let me buy you some whisky.'

After four full glasses of whisky, I am getting to like my new-found American friends who have obviously adopted me into their little group. These men are into Hendrix and Malcolm X. I pull out the notebook.

> *Black Power is their bag and they see their drafting into the war as simple white oppression of blacks who then oppress Asians. I don't really understand or care about their politics. I just find them menacingly exciting. There is nothing like these characters in Australia, so intense, so*

much suppressed rage, and yet so willing to laugh and joke and so polished
in their street language. Cool has a new meaning

'What you penning white Nigger?'

'Nothin' man, well just notes about Vung Tau, you can read it if you want.'

'Hell no man, I don't read that good any ol' how, not that scribble stuff. You got to print it if you want me to read shit like that. Now we don't buy whisky so you can just ignore us man. Put the mudda fuckin' book down and tell us shit about your home.'

The conversation turns to Australia, to me and my world. With similar intensity, they ask endless questions about Australia, kangaroos and koalas.

I lie, almost convincing them that koalas are mightier and more ferocious than the piddly little grizzly bears in America. Full of whisky, I spin yarns about how my father had taught me to catch them with my bare hands by crawling down wind, sneaking up behind them with a handful of goanna poo and quickly rubbing it in their noses. I go to great pains to explain that despite their huge size, koalas are allergic to goanna poo and drop to the ground in a state of temporary paralysis.

The Afro-American soldiers are laughing and calling for more stories, 'You Australians tell the best damn lies I ever heard.'

'Another Aussie whitey told us them koalas was just like itty bitty teddy bears. He probably more full of bullshit than you is man', one of them then calls to his friends. 'Hey, let's buy the white Nigga a blow job for his damn good bull shitting.'

The group agree and one calls over a bargirl. 'Give Uck da Loi sucky fucky', he says to the girl as he pulls out a wad of military payment currency.

The girl looks around, 'Mama-san no like in this bar, you buy Saigon Tea, maybe we go my place for sucky fucky.'

The Afro-American yells out to the old woman behind the bar, 'Mama-san, MPC, good for black market. MPC for sucky fucky in bar?' The woman comes from behind the bar and grabs the wad of money.

'Okay, under table, not in open, give bar bad name otherwise', she says, motioning to the bar girl who is on her hands and knees and crawling under the table. She undoes my belt and unzips my fly. I feel her small hand and then her lips on my member now instantly hard. I later write…

I never imagined as a growing young boy that my first 'blow job' would be in an Asian bar cheered on by the Black American soldiers who had generously paid for the show. Paid with money that may one day be used by the VC to buy weapons or ammunition. Probably shouldn't write about this. Fuck, why not - who will read it anyway?

Thanking my new-found friends, I stagger out onto the street. The whisky is having the desired effect. The world is now swimming in front of me and it is a good feeling. Onward ever onward, I motion to my Black Power friends, who decide not to tag along just to watch the stupid Aussie get himself into trouble.

From that bar, a succession of bars.

I stagger on in an ever increasing alcoholic stupor until I meet up with Wingnut who leads me into a den of sin that provides grotesque live shows.

The thick heavy smoke is gradually choking me, my nostrils fill with the stench of 33 Beer spilt on sticky floors, blending with body odours and foul breath as too many drunken soldiers try to cram into too small a room. The noise of the live band is causing my ears to hum and a thumping set of vibrations attack my aching head.

I am drunk, too drunk to be feeling happy, what I feel at this moment is an urge to puke. This urge is increasing rapidly as I witness the live show on the low flat stage in the centre of the bar room around which the soldiers are sitting or standing.

The young woman has managed to discard all her clothing and perform a variety of body contortions that has everyone amused and fascinated for a while. But these crude acts have gradually become a little boring. Now, however, she is lying on her back, peeling a large banana and inserting it in her vagina until it disappears completely. By some miracle of the human condition, the young woman is now contracting her vaginal muscles and pushing the banana back out from the orifice, her legs wide apart, knees raised high. Suddenly, Wingnut cannot contain himself and dives head-first between her legs, biting off the protruding piece of banana. The room suddenly fills with the sound of cheering soldiers. Screaming obscenities, laughing, booing, some just gob smacked by what is happening in front of them.

It's all too much for my senses. I cannot help but wonder what else had been inserted or deposited inside that vagina this day?

As Wingnut turns to face me, his mouth full of the partially excreted banana, I call out over the noise, 'For Christ's sake, what diseases are you trying to catch?'

Wingnut chews a while then swallows, 'I think you're right, we don't know where that banana has been before', he screams back, ducking his head back between her legs to bite off some more newly exposed banana.

I shake my head and swallow the last drops of warm beer in the bottle of 33. I need to urinate and throw up at the same time, so I stand up and stagger toward the back door which I know will lead to the toilets.

Up a narrow hallway, I find the toilet, its door long ago ripped from its hinges. A low flat porcelain bowl with two feet stands in the middle confront me, designed so a person can stand on the feet stands and squat down to piss or crap.

The bowl is half blocked with newspaper and excrement. In the corner, two or three used sanitary napkins lie as they had landed when thrown. A mix of stale urine, faeces and vomit is now attacking my nostrils. In one quick stomach contraction the warm 33 Beer and the whisky I have been consuming in excess, gush from my mouth into the corner of the toilet. I undo my fly and lean forward placing one hand against the stained and smeared wall to steady myself, while the other takes charge of the penis to direct urine in the general direction of the bowl.

I am almost finished when a slender hand comes around from behind me, gently grasping my penis and holding it for a moment, before shaking the last drops free from its end. 'Uck da loi want jiggy jiggy', comes the voice from the young prostitute who has followed me into the toilet.

'Piss off bitch', I respond, pushing her away and depositing my member back into my pants.

'Uck da Loi number ten, number ten bad fucky', the girl yells.

I shove her against the wall and raise a hand to hit her before catching myself and realising what I am doing. I later write…

> *In all my short life I have never hit a woman or allowed a woman to be hit by another man, and yet I was only a moment away from beating this prostitute and I do not know why. Is it because she is Asian? Viet Cong are Asian. Or have I simply lost all respect for women such as this girl and failed to consider her desperate need to survive this terrible war?*

'What the hell is happening to me in this God-forsaken hole?' I yell before lowering my arm to walk away from the scared young woman, who pushes herself away from the wall, spitting in my general direction and screaming, 'Uck da Loi fuck dogs, go fucky home and fuck dogs.'

Passing straight through the bar and out into the hot tropical night air, I stand swaying in the dim lights of the Vung Tau back street. What am I doing here?

The bar Wingnut led me to is well away from the main streets of Vungers and I am walking through back alleys, quite lost and wondering if I might not get attacked while wandering alone in the dark. I appear to be in a deserted, open-air market place. The filth and rubbish left from the day's trading is scattered everywhere. The smell here is not exotic, it is sickening and I once again bend and vomit. It's just liquid now - bad whisky and hot beer. Wiping my chin I notice my face is slightly numb on one side. I don't care.

Up ahead I can see a skinny dog dragging a large fleshy bone backward across the street. Suddenly a little girl of no more than five years approaches the dog and tries to wrestle the bone from its mouth. The dog growls and bares its teeth so I run up and kick it in the ribs. The dog yelps and scurries off, tail between its legs.

I look down at the young child wearing nothing but a pair of tattered shorts many sizes too large and tied around the waist by string. The child is dark skinned yet Asian, the product of a Black American and a prostitute. She picks up the bone and holds it in spindle thin arms close to her chest. Big black eye sockets filled with hunger stare back at me defiantly, as if to say it was hers and I could not have it.

'Hey little one, where is your mum?' The girl stares straight back at me, clinging ever more tightly to the bone with her pencil-thin arms. A bedraggled old woman soon appears screaming at the girl and me. She runs forward and grabs the child by her wrist then pushes herself between the child and me as though protecting her. She begins yelling at me through betel-nut red broken teeth, flapping her right hand in my face while slowly moving backward toward another side alleyway.

I reel back in shock realising that the woman thought I was about to grab or molest the child. 'No, no, I just want to help', I call, reaching into my pocket to find some money. 'For food, here take it', holding out the money. The woman pays no attention to the money and spits in my face. Grabbing the child in her arms, she runs up the street leaving the fleshy bone on the ground. My God, I think the old hag thought I wanted to pay for the little girl!

Speechless and bewildered by this experience, I wipe the red spit from my cheek and stagger on to find somewhere for another glass of whisky. The vomiting has sobered me up and I want to be drunk. Just drunk and happy, this might be my last chance in life to have a good time. It was back to war in less than 48 hours. I could be dead or mutilated in just 40-fucking-8 hours. I could kick a mine and end up like that poor bloody street vendor!

I come upon a bright red building with a flashing light illuminating two signs, one reads 'Steam Bath – Massage' the other 'Jade Bar'. I enter the door and follow the sign to the steam baths.

Wrapped in a towel with my wallet and my newly acquired flick knife, I enter the steam area and find Nunger and Monkey Spanker sitting in there, both with bottles of 33.

'Hey there Turkey, welcome to the next best thing to sex', calls out Nunger. 'You know this man?

'The Spanker? How could I forget him, he ruined my Sunday roast by chucking a Gook's head at my feet.'

'You deserved it', Spanker responds. 'At least this steam bath might get the stink out of my body. Damn that was a god-awful job, wasn't it?'

'Hey', I respond, trying to get the conversation away from the gravesite. 'I ain't the one shooting innocent monkeys. You earned that name, I just happened to be the one who thought of it first.'

We sit in the steam room allowing the perspiration to drain the toxins from our body. Suddenly the door opens and four Americans enter the room. Nunger calls over to them, 'G'day cobbers!'

They stop and stare at the three naked Australians, fixing their eyes on Nunger.

'I didn't know you Aussies had Niggers', one American says.

'Call me a Black fella, or a Murri, do not call me a Nigger. It's in your best interest to just call me by my nick-name. It really is best you call me Nunger.'

The Americans look at each other and smirk, before one turns to Nunger and says, 'Murri, Nigger, what's the difference?'

Nunger smashes the bottle of 33 in his hand and grabs the American, pushing him against the wall and pressing the jagged edge of the broken bottle into the soldier's groin. The American stands frozen in fear, now naked, as the towel has fallen off. The other Americans stands up quickly but Spanker has also smashed his bottle and is standing ready to lunge. I reach into the towel and produce my flick knife, pressing the button and allowing the blade to spring out and lock.

Nunger is looking at the now extremely pale American straight in the eyes, 'I'll tell you the difference fuck-knuckle. Call me Nunger and I might let you buy me a replacement beer but call me Nigger again and I will twist this bottle and deposit your balls on the floor.'

One of the Americans bailed up in the corner says, 'Hey guys, we don't want any trouble, just joshing man.'

We three Australians stand silent, still ready with weapons.

'Come on guys', the American pleads, 'are you insane or something?'

'Oh, didn't they explain to you Americans about us Australian soldiers?' Nunger responds. 'We are all fucking insane. You see we don't have prisons or lunatic asylums in Australia, no death penalty or life in jail. Once the judge finds us guilty or once the shrink certifies us criminally insane, we get put in the army so we can go off and kill people in foreign countries. It's Australia's way of making the world a better place.'

The three Americans move slowly around the wall to the door.

'Don't leave your mate with us, you gutless scum', Nunger yells at them, before pushing the American in his grasp toward the others. 'Fuck off and disappear from my sight for the rest of the war', he yells as the four men scurry out of the steam bath.

Nunger sits back down. 'They're not all racist bastards you know, I met plenty of Yanks I like, but I hate that word Nigger', he explains. 'Even in Australia I never let any turkey call me Nigger, I'm a Murri and I'm proud of who I am.'

I close the flick knife, 'You're okay man, you're okay, long as you're on my side cause you ain't no Nigger but your one mean black bastard when you don't like people.'

Nunger laughs, 'Black and proud, don't you forget it you white bastard, I am black and I am proud of being black. So don't you forget.'

Spanker wraps his towel around himself and wanders out of the steam room to look for more alcohol, returning with three more bottles of 33. We sit quietly consuming the hot mix of alcohol and embalming fluid.

Too much steam and too much warm beer has left me again needing to move on. I leave the two Australians in the steam room, have a quick cold shower and bypass the massage rooms. After my under the table experience I do not need a massage with its 'happy ending' so I head into the noisy Jade Bar looking for whisky.

On the small stage in the corner is an Australian soldier sitting with the Vietnamese musicians playing one of their guitars. The bar is almost empty and I realise it is nearing curfew when all people have to be off the streets.

It is too late to seek a ride home to the Australian base at the Peter Badcoe Club, so I look around for an attractive prostitute to spend the night with. Two girls are sitting at a table near the band so I wander over and sit with them.

'You buy both Saigon Teas?' one asks.

'Yeah, then we three go jiggy jiggy for night.'

One of the girls smiles and replies, 'No three ways sandwich Uck da Loi. I with music man'. She points to the Australian soldier on the stage.

I look up and notice the baby-faced kid from anti-tank platoon playing the guitar with the Asian band. He is good, very good. He's playing the tune to 'Johnny be Good'. I produce my notebook.

I heard about this digger, 'Chucka' is his nickname, not because of his love for the American rock legend but because he threw a grenade at the enemy and forgot to flip back the safety bale. Apparently, the enemy made off with the unexploded grenade. Apart from that one mistake, he is regarded as a cool operator in the 'J'. Man he can do a lick on that axe.

This is about all I know of him except he is a bit of a loner. I look at the other girl. Classic French-Eurasian mix, probably the illegitimate daughter of a French soldier or ex-German soldier who joined the Foreign Legion. Stunning gold brown skin glows from under jet-black hair hanging loosely over her shoulders and emerald green eyes. 'You, me go jiggy jiggy?' I ask as anticipation of her delights swell in my loins.

'Uck da Loi no hurt My? No silly sick boom, boom.'

'Of course not, I reply indignantly. 'Is your name My?'

The Prostitute

My smiles and nods. She is actually older than the boy but has been blessed with a young looking face and body. It is all she has that she can use to survive in this world of war. This boy seems to look a little lost and lonely, she does not fear him as she might other drunken soldiers. What choice does she have? No sex, no food and no money to pay mama-san for access to the bar

My replies. 'You buy My two more Saigon Tea and we go home.'

A long narrow alleyway leads to a door in a large rendered building that looks like a left over from the previous French Colonial rule. Inside are several rooms filled with families of five or six packed in each room. Small kerosene cookers are burning, children swinging in hammocks somehow nailed or bolted into the walls, some mattresses on the floor. Up the stairs are more rooms but these are obviously occupied by prostitutes, smaller rooms with double beds covered in mosquito netting.

My leads me into one and points to the toilet at the end of the corridor, 'You go now.' I wander to the toilet and relieve myself. I turn on the old tap and scoop a mouth full of water into cupped hands, gargle and spit out the foul taste in my mouth. Aware I have no toothpaste, I use a finger trying to remove as much grime and stench from my teeth as possible.

I return to the room to find My naked and squatting in a tub of water washing her vagina with soap and water.

I look at the girl who is now without make up. Sixteen, seventeen maybe, or is she older. Twenty? I decide that she must be at least that age as she has a perfectly formed woman's body, adorned with fully formed breasts, not budding lumps. Despite my eagerness I quickly grab my notebook and scribble a few lines…

What the heck. Only 19 myself.

The young prostitute watches the boy soldier scribble into his book, she does not hate this boy, all men are bad to her ever since her mother gave her to the nuns because she could not raise a half-French girl child and hope to find a Vietnamese husband to feed her. My had been raped by four boys in the nuns' home when she was just 12. The nuns had abused her for tempting the boys with her flirting.

Poor My, all she wanted then was to make friends. Now all she wants is to survive and this Australian boy looks so young and safe compared to some of the horrible men who had paid for her. Why do some men have to be so cruel, why do they treat her so badly and do things to her that even an animal would not do? Why does war turn some men into animals? But this boy looks so sad and lost, just maybe he will treat her without pain and even pay her more if she is good to him.

My beckons me to put down the book, waves me over to the tub and undresses me. I stand in the tub and she washes my whole body with soap and water, stopping to examine my penis in detail. She runs her thumb along the length of it to see if any discharge occurs, indicating gonorrhoea. Satisfied I am clean she takes my penis in her mouth and I become instantly hard. My removes the penis from her mouth and smiles first at the proud strong member then up at my boyish face. 'Uck Da Loi is strong, yes, I make Uck Da Loi very happy.'

She dries me with a towel and leads me to the bed. I break free of her hands and grab my wallet and clothes. I carefully lay my pants and shirt on the floor in such a manner that I could leap out of bed and dress quickly in the dark. Next, I discreetly remove the flick knife from the pants pocket and slide it under the pillow where I can grab it quickly if needed to defend myself from an attack during the night. Finally, I lie back in the bed and wait for My to join me.

Above me, a rickety old ceiling fan turns slowly making a strange sound as it rotates on old bearings.

Whop   Whop   Click   Whop   Whop   Click   Whop   Whop   Click

There is a rap on the door frame and My quickly pulls a cotton robe over her body before pulling aside the hanging cotton door to reveal another young woman and an ARVN soldier. The soldier is armed with a M1 carbine and I become increasingly worried as he speaks to My in a raised angry voice, occasionally pointing to me in aggressive gestures. I reach under the pillow and feel for the knife, then press the release button and feel the blade flick out and lock into place, deciding that if the soldier raised the M1 rifle in my direction I would lunge quickly.

My looks over at me and notices the tension in my eyes. She comes back to the bed and speaks to me, 'It okay, he old friend looking for sister, he say she working as bar girl, very angry. We say she work in factory but he don't believe us.'

I relax slightly as My returns to talk to the soldier and the other girl. Finally, they leave the room and My removes her robe and slides up next to me, 'He goes now before he shot at curfew. He still think his sister bar girl.'

'Is she?' I close the knife blade and reposition it under the pillow.

My nods, 'No money in sewing factory, work very hard for food and room to sleep, bar girl make lots of money, better chance to marry American soldier and go to America.'

'You want to go to America?'

'No war in America. Always food, TV and Hollywood. Everybody is rich and happy.'

'What will happen when he finds her?' I ask, choosing not to destroy her misguided dream.

My shrugs her shoulders, 'He is only here one night before he go back to fight. His mother sent him looking for sister. Mother very sad, husband and one son killed in war, one son taken by army to fight again and now daughter in bar girl job.'

'And your mother?'

The young girl ignores this question, 'We make jiggy jiggy now.'

I lay beside the young girl, fondling her young breast, two supple lumps of caramel fromage topped with dark chocolate buds. I lean over and gently caress her left nipple with my lips and allow my tongue to trace around the firm bud protruding boldly upward. My hand moves down over her tight flat stomach to her trim dark black pubic area. My trembles momentarily. Revulsion or anticipation? I know it is probably the former but pretend it is the latter.

I caress her neck with my lips, noting the sensual sweet smell of a female body. A different smell to girls I knew back home. Pungent, yet very feminine. A memory of Australia and happier times floods back to me. Memories of my first school-boy sexual experience only some three years earlier. The memory of my girlfriend who had broken up our relationship before I went to Vietnam, saying she was unwilling to wait as I might be killed.

I slide on top of My and am about to enter her but am suddenly overcome with remorse and depression. I roll off onto my back, staring at the ceiling fan through the mosquito net.

Whop   Whop   Click   Whop   Whop   Click

What has happened to me and why am I here? My mind fills with images of the dying boy, a decapitated head being kicked like a soccer ball, the shattered, deformed man in the street, the young soldier desperately looking for his sister, the young child wrestling a bone from a dog and the old woman who spat in my face. Tears roll down my cheeks and more than ever I just want to curl up into a ball like a lonely frightened child seeking the comfort of his mother.

My looks over at me, 'You miss girlfriend, no can Butterfly with My?'

'No, I not play Madam Butterfly boy with you', I respond through tears. 'No girlfriend anymore, so no have you as Madam Butterfly.'

My gets out of bed and comes back with a wet cloth, she wipes away my tears, smiling for a moment then kissing my eyes. She lifts my head against her breasts and holds me tight. Rocking me back and forth, as she says quietly, 'Bad war for everyone, bad war.'

I lie like this for a while, floating in a child-like trance upon a mother's gentle breast, then look up at her face, she is crying quietly also.

She looks down at me. 'My scared and sad too.'

I pull my arm around her and hold her close to my chest. She tries to pull her body so close to me that she seems to want to be swallowed inside me. I hold her tight. We lie crying silently together before falling asleep.

Whop   Whop   Click   Whop   Whop   Click

GOD BLESS AMERICANS

'YOU'RE ALL AS weak as piss; the feckin lot of you', Delta Company Support Section and HQ hangers-on are standing in line receiving a tirade of abuse from the company sergeant major. He is fuming because the American Military Police arrested Nunger after a drunken brawl in Vunger and he's now in a prison cell awaiting his fate.

'You never let down your mate', Sandy yells at us. 'How many times have I got to tell you little worms that Nunger has a drink problem, and with the drink he has a fight problem? You should have taken turns looking after him.'

'He was okay when I left him Sandy', I respond.

'We're back at base you dumb assed sig operator, you call me Sir or Sergeant Major, not Sandy, or I will rip off one of your arms and beat you to death with the soggy bit on the end of it.'

'Yes Sir, but he was okay when I left him in the steam bath. Besides he was with Spanker, so someone was looking after him.'

'Spanker is just that, a monkey spanker', Sandy quips back at me. 'He ain't even in Support Section, he ain't responsible for Nunger. You little worms are responsible for Nunger, he is your mate, your section commander. So what do you all do about it? I'll tell you what. You chase pussy and leave your mate to get himself busted up and in a cell.'

The group stands in guilt-ridden silence. Sandy is now satisfied that the troops are sufficiently brow beaten.

'Well that's the Nunger for you, if he wasn't in some sort of mischief he'd die of feckin boredom', Sandy shakes his head, smiles then drills his eyes toward the six foot two-inch-tall soldier immediately in front of him.

'Tiny, you will be the acting section commander. I'll get you a stripe for your trouble. With any luck the Major will prevent Nunger copping a court martial and he will be busted back to private again and returned to us.' Sandy is pacing up and down the line of diggers. He stops and looks Tiny in the eyes. 'When Nunger returns he will take over as section commander, even if he is busted to private. You Tiny will do exactly what he tells you, got that?'

'Shit yeah San… Sir', Tiny replies. 'I never plan to tell Nunger how to do his job.'

'Good, now we are going to have us a whole week or more here in the Dat so it will be gun rosters on the perimeter and TAOR patrols.' Looking directly at me, Sandy continues, 'Not you, you dumb pogo, you get a slime job because of your wrist and back.'

'What do you mean Sir?'

'You're off to play with the Yanks for a couple of days. Some liaison officer in headquarters asked you to be his replacement signaller. But don't think you're out of this war son, it's only for a couple of days while the pogo bastard doing the job has some R and C in Vungers.'

'Asked for me?'

'That's right, by your name. You know this officer by any chance?'

'No Sir, don't know any officer from task force.'

'Well for some reason he knows you and as is often the case with these little snot nosed task force subbies, he pisses in the Brigadier's ear and gets whatever he wants.' The CSM gives me a wink, 'Lucky bastard, those Yank firebases got every luxury a poor bloody digger could ask for. Go on, grab your kit and get your arse down to Task Force HQ. Enjoy the break.'

I stand outside Task Force Headquarters, listening to laughter from inside the building. A mud-caked Land Rover is parked awkwardly under a rubber tree. The top is off and the windscreen removed. I can see old bits of paper and general rubbish strewn around the front seat area. In the back, I notice a box of M16 magazines,

> *Just thrown there with little thought for security. Bloody hell, what do these guys do down here at HQ? If one of our lot did that he would be knee deep in shit with the RSM kicking his butt 'til his nose bled.*

My attention turns to the sound of a fly screen door being shoved open. A young officer appears from the building. He wears American issue jungle greens, a black baseball cap on top of snow blond hair. Despite youthful looks his handsome face shows the signs of an Aussie surfer's eye wrinkles and a few laughter lines cut down the side of his cheeks, a shining gold Rolex watch adorns his left wrist. The officer notices me near the Land Rover, walks casually up to me, 'You're Johnno's replacement, Brian aren't you, old friend of his?'

'Yes Sir, I guess so', I respond, realising the officer has to be talking about a task force signals operator whom I had shared a few adventures with back in Australia.

'Drop the Sir bit unless some military-minded prick is within hearing distance. My name is Pete, Johnno usually calls me Skip', the young officer says. 'He tells me you are perfect for the little job ahead, so I asked for you.'

I shrug, 'I met John on an advanced sig course back in Aus. We spent about six weeks together in Sydney. We got on okay. Yeah he was a good guy.'

'Got on okay! From what Johnno tells me, you two spent many nights in Kings Cross smoking five paper joints and chasing women.'

I am taken aback by the young officer's statement. John had no right to tell anyone about the bit of dope shared on leave in Sydney, yet the young officer seems quite amused by the story.

'Chasing women maybe but not very successfully', I reply, careful to avoid any comment on the drug issue.

The young officer's next statement gives me quite a shock. 'Well Johnno taught me how to roll those five paper joints just like you taught him. Hope you don't mind if I smoke a joint or two out on ops, it gets me through the war.'

'Wouldn't smoke the shit in a war zone personally', I reply. 'Makes me paranoid, as if I ain't got enough to worry about already.'

Skip laughs, 'You only get paranoid if you run out of ganja. I got plenty enough for both of us. Now jump in the Rover, we are in for a long drive.'

The Land Rover makes its way out of Nui Dat and along the road to the village of Baria. We pass an old picture theatre standing as a monument to war, shell holes and 50 cal bullet marks scarring its exterior. Villagers go about their daily tasks barely noticing the two Australians. We drive straight through the village then turn left along a dirt road.

I am distinctly uncomfortable with my current situation. I had no briefing on what I was to be doing. I am trying to guess where the vehicle is heading. Surely not toward Binh Ba? That damn rubber plantation is full of enemy activity and we don't even have APC support. My mind tries to align the lone vehicle's direction with my memory of the landscape as seen from both the air and maps. My throat is dry and my eyes begin the nervous darting movement searching for potential trouble. I can make out the distinctive landform of Nui Nghe in the distance and decide we are heading in the general direction toward Binh Gia village. This gives me some comfort, as Binh Gia has not popped up in any of the INTSUM reports I decode almost daily. Not a hot village, but no reason for us to go there either.

I am also concerned about enemy mines on the dirt road we are travelling on. The Land Rover is heavy enough to trip an anti-tank and offer no protection at all to the young officer or me. Unprotected from mines and unprotected from ambush, I'm aware we are driving unprotected by anyone. I scan my memory. The last time I had seen a military intelligence map of this area no roads were marked as red or potentially hot, but it has been a long time since I checked such maps. I can only assume the young officer driving the vehicle has the benefit of up-dated intelligence reports.

'You ever worry about ambush or mines on these roads?'

'Only when I run out of dope and get paranoid.'

As the vehicle rolls along, Skip gives me an update on the war. Apparently, the enemy base camp the media filmed burning to the ground has become a major drama back in Australia. The media ran a story about suffering local villagers and showed the film of the Australians burning the base camp. For most Australians watching the story on TV, it looked like the Aussies were burning a local village full of peasants. The task force commander was furious with my battalion CO and banned any cooperation with the media from that point on.

'How's this for a laugh,' Skip continues. 'Some reporter and his camera guy wanted to go bush, so the task force commander sends them over to our local ARVN commander with instructions to distract the buggers. You know the drill, just take the journos for a ride in an APC and pop off a few belts of ammo. So the ARVN commander shoves them in the back of an APC and sends them on a ARVN live fire training run. You know the stuff, the APC troop and the infantry attack a bit of shit scrub blazing away with every weapon at their disposal. Ha, Ha, Ha!' The young liaison officer is laughing uncontrollably.

'So? I don't get the giggle', I remark.

Skip continues the story, 'These media blokes actually thought they were in a real attack, they were all excited that they were getting award winning footage, but their camera runs out of film or breaks down or something. So they ask the ARVN commander to stop the attack while they fix it. Ha. Ha. Sure thing says the Gook commander and he halts the whole pretend war so these wankers can get their camera rolling again, then he tells his troops to continue the exercise'. Skip continues to chortle and laugh, 'What a crazy war we are having! The camera footage gets plastered all over Australian TV as an eye witness account of a battle in 'Nam and these media blokes think they are fucking heroes. No digger back at HQ had the heart to tell them the truth. Let them be heroes the Brigadier says, at least it kept the bastards out of the Australian unit's hair.'

Skip regains his composure and explains that the battles fought in Long Khanh are still causing some excitement and the Americans have set up a fire support base in the area to give the Australians good artillery support from their long-range mobile 155 guns. Our job is to act as liaison between the Americans and Australians. Nothing fancy, just answer any questions on slightly different tactics and communication issues.

I gradually ease my tight grip on the M16, allowing it to rest comfortably across my lap. I begin to relax out on the road despite the vehicle travelling along without armed escort.

The young officer explains he fell into the job after he was conscripted. Having a university arts degree, he went to officer training school for national servicemen. When the army learned he spoke fluent Chinese, they sent him on a crash course to learn basic Vietnamese and made him a liaison officer and then straight to Vietnam and into the war. He finds the whole thing a bit of a joke really. Before he was conscripted, he had been a protester for the anti-war movement in Sydney. Now he is knee deep in the war and thinks both sides of the argument are full of holes.

'Who gives a damn', he laughs. 'I'd only be stuck back in my old man's office block learning the family business and I'm not ready to become Snoage and Son Pty Ltd just yet. This is much more fun.'

'Up until now I never thought of war as fun', I reply, my smile leaving the young officer unsure if I am expressing agreement or contempt.

We turn off the road and make our way down a rough track gouged out by tank tracks. I can see the firebase ahead, surrounded by barbed wire and filled with mobile 155s. Behind the wire is little more than a thick carpet of dark red mud, torn and gouged by tank tracks and four-wheel drive vehicles. Horrible mud! It covers tents, sandbags and any human being that attempts to negotiate his way across it. In places, timber pallets have been thrown down to form random walk-ways on which soldiers try to negotiate their way through the quagmire. But like the American army itself, the pallets are slowly losing their battle with Vietnam, sinking deeper into a sticky reddish-brown slime created by the abuse and misuse of American technology. Their military hardware kills jungle and green pasture as easily as it kills people.

I immediately notice many men walking around with their shirts off, their skin shining in the sun, begging a sniper to take aim from the tree line. Armoured personnel carriers are propped almost haphazardly within the wire perimeter. As we approach, the sound of Creedence Clearwater Revival bangs out its rhythm through loud speakers propped on the side of an armoured command vehicle, drowning out the noise of Huey choppers coming in to land within the base area.

Our vehicle drives through the open gate unchallenged, the soldiers simply look up from whatever tasks they are doing and watch with general disinterest. Skip drives up to the rear of an APC command vehicle, climbs from the Rover and points, 'Welcome to your home for the next day or two.'

'RPG target's not a home', I reply, as I stare at the overly large box shaped object propped on tank tracks.

Skip laughs, 'You sure you don't smoke lots of shit, you're more paranoid than a junky on dry out.'

Inside the command vehicle are two bunk beds and a bank of radios. John had left his mementos behind for me to read. There's a dozen or more Playboy magazines on one shelf, an ashtray and remnants of brown-green tobacco on the bunk itself. I allow my nose to adjust to the stale smell of the sweat, tobacco and ganja trapped within the compartment.

'So what do I do now?' I ask Skip, who is already lying on his bunk.

'Blow a joint and wait 'til supper. They have a mess style tent about 20 meters from here and cooks serve the meals.'

'Tough war these blokes are having', I remark caustically.

Skip laughs, 'No kidding. Fresh cold chocolate milk and would you believe Mr Whippy soft serve ice cream. I tell you what Brian, if you got to have a case of the munchies then this is the place to have it.'

I have just spent the last two hours wandering around the firebase, meeting and chatting to soldiers, mostly Black Americans, all of whom greeted me with a smile and occasional handshake, usually trying to imitate the Australian drawl. 'G'day mate', they would say, and I would respond with 'G'day'. I am fascinated by the casualness of these soldiers. I asked questions about their defensive perimeter and patrolling tactics. Mostly they responded with a shrug of their shoulders. 'We just go where the man tells us to go and do what the man says', being the standard answer.

I find a picture book comic and to my amusement, a busty young blonde-haired woman as its hero, called Sweet Sixteen. It is her job to teach the soldiers how to look after their M16 rifles. 'Comics for shit's sake', I say to two Black American soldiers playing Black Jack with a well-worn deck of cards. 'I suppose Superman and Batman teach you guys how to fly choppers do they?'

One soldier looks up from his card game, 'He's got a point there Frank, why don't Superman come over and win this war for us. I'm going to complain to those white dudes who write them picture books when I get home.'

'Yeah, goddammit, and what about Green Lantern and that other new creepy dude we been reading about, Spiderman, yeah, Spider dude, that's the one. They should get their fancy arses and pretty blue tights down here also', the soldier named Frank replies dryly. 'Man I tell you I hate spiders but I figure that the freak in them comic books could come out here and win this goddamn war for us. I wouldn't be so damn hateful of spiders after that. No Sir!'

I smile, 'Yeah we could use some extra help to kill these Gooks.'
The man named Frank stands to his feet and stares coldly into my eyes.

'Who you callin' a Gook mister? You call them Gooks just like you call us Nigger, I ain't no Nigger, I'm a Black American, they ain't no Gooks, they's Asians.'

'Take it easy man I didn't call you a Nigger, I was just saying we could use some help to beat these Viet Cong that's all', I reply defensively.

Frank sits back down. 'Their country', he responds caustically. 'Their country not ours, I got no quarrel with no Asian. I ain't here by choice man, I just here as cannon fodder for a white president who hates my black arse. That Green Lantern and Spider dude, they's pure white heroes, let them come over and win this mother fucking war, and let us Black Americans go home to our filth and squalor in the ghettos of New York.' He throws his cards on the make shift table, 'Let us Niggers go home to good ol' boy country where some whitey with a goddamn bed sheet over his head can whop our black arses and hang us from some damn tree.'

It takes me a couple of seconds to absorb what I have just been confronted with. I turn and walk away embarrassed, ashamed that I had made such a racist remark without realising what I had done. Despite this awakening I remain confused, apathy and racial tension is one thing, but so is profession-alism. Frank may have good reason to be against this war but right at this moment he is here like it or not, and bad attitude can lead to an early grave. Awkwardly I move on.

I come across an older 'Top Kick', a professional American senior sergeant with a worn marine emblem displayed on his shirt sleeve. He gives me some details between his incessant chewing and spitting of tobacco. 'Sweet Sixteen! Well I have to tell you some of these here Nigger draftees can't read nor write that good but they pay attention to a picture of a white blonde gal with big boobies. Many of these boys are just doing their 'Project Hundred Thousand' that's all. No-good Nigger draftees who don't give a damn about this war and don't want to think about it too much. Besides we don't have a real war down south here, not like the goddamn DMZ up north. Don't judge our army on what you see here. These boys are mostly made up from what we call the

Moron Squad. We got crack units up north, professionals every man of them, not like these black sons o' bitches.'

I wince as I absorb the gunny's racist remark.

'Moron Squad? Project Hundred Thousand? ' I ask.

The gunny looks across his nose toward me, 'You Aussies don't have no Moron Squad?'

'No. What the hell are you talking about?'

'Goddam! You Aussies damn lucky not to have McNamara as your boss', The gunny remarks. 'A moron squad is part of our army these days, back in 1966 Rob McNamara set up a system where any dumb arse Nigger who don't pass the IQ test to get conscripted can still be shoved in the war. They only need about one third the pass mark of any other soldier. It's called 'Project One Hundred Thousand' son, cannon fodder for unimportant bits of 'Nam so the Marines and Air Cav can fight the real enemy.'

'I've seen real enemy soldiers down here in the south', I reply. 'Some of them would be licking their lips to get a crack at these guys, lambs to the slaughter. Surely your army should train and support these guys with a bit more than damn comic books.'

The gunny spits out a mouthful of dark brown slime, 'Well they ain't getting a chance at me son. I wouldn't go out of the wire with this bunch of junkies. No Sir, all I want is to finish this tour of duty and go home upright instead of in a box.' The old-lifer pulls out a packet of chewing tobacco, tears away the top and bites another mouthful, poking it to one side of his gums so he can continue the discussion, 'I'll tell you somethin' else son, iff'n I tried to whip them Niggers into some sort of soldiers I'd probably find a grenade in my bed one night. Getting that way a mans more scared of Niggers than he is of Gooks.' He runs his hand through his short cropped grey hair, chews hard on the tobacco in his mouth then pokes it back to one side of his gums, 'Shi-oot son, I been in this man's army since Korea, probably fought alongside your daddy at the battle of Kapyong. This is my last goddamn war that's for sure. Make sure it's your last war son.' Again he pauses to spit out more tobacco-coloured phlegm, 'Go home find a good woman who'll forgive your failin's and have a few littlens. Make 'em grow up as book-keepers or goddamn fiddle players, not soldiers.'

He looks around the muddy fire base, a deep, desperately sad expression carved across his face, 'Don't let your own young'uns become soldiers' son. No pride in bein' a goddamn soldier no more'. With his right hand he wipes some tobacco slime from the corner of his mouth, 'Maybe's that your army is still proud but there ain't no goddamn pride in this army no more.'

That said, the gunny walks away leaving me standing alone propped on top of a wood pallet which had sunk some four inches into the red mud. I take a long deep breath and let the air out slowly through my teeth. I jot down a few short notes…

> *I remember old war movies I grew up with; John Wayne, Henry Fonda, Jimmy Stewart. The TV show Combat with Vic Morrow gallantly saving Europe. American heroes on the screen. This is no movie or TV show, this is reality and it makes me sick in the stomach.*

I step off the pallet and slosh my way back to the command vehicle.

At dusk, I instinctively leave the APC command vehicle to prepare for stand-to. I watch as the Americans move into fire positions on the perimeter. Then to my surprise the soldiers fire their weapons, emptying a mag or two before sitting back and casually chatting to each other again. Some light up a cigarette, others turn on their small radios and tune in to Radio Vietnam.

'That's their stand-to procedure in this dump', Skip calls from inside the smoke filled command vehicle. 'Lets the Gooks know we are well armed if they want to try and attack us and it also burns off old ammo.'

I am speechless. I shake my head and climb into the back of the command vehicle. Outside, the loud speakers attached to an APC blare out 'Jingle Bell Rock', reminding me that it is Christmas today, or is it tomorrow? I do not care really, Christmas in Vietnam seems somewhat out of place with its songs of peace on earth and good will to fellow man. I pick up my notebook but struggle to put on paper what I am experiencing, Finally I find two words to describe what I have witnessed …

Fucking circus!

I push the notebook back into my pocket and strip and clean my weapon, then reassemble it ready for action.

A new song on the loud speakers. Bing Crosby's 'White Christmas'.

I pick up my sweat rag and wipe the sticky perspiration from my brow and neck. I call to Skip, 'You ever heard of this project thing, a Moron Squad for Black Americans?'

'Not just Black Americans', Skip responds from a cloud of ganja smoke. 'Any so-called disadvantaged American boy. I heard in uni back home that they lowered the IQ assessment down from 90 plus to somewhere around 60. You probably don't know much about that IQ stuff but a 60 score is pretty sad stuff Bri.' He takes another long toke on his joint, expels the smoke and continues, 'But it keeps the sons of politicians and the Yankee equivalent of rich kids like me from doing hard time in 'Nam. They shove the rich ones in the National Guard or the Air Corps and make up the shortfall by dumping low IQ boys into the vacant slots. It's supposed to help them by making them good citizens.'

'Make them dead citizens from what I been looking at, and mostly black,' I snort.

'Yeah, mostly black but always underclass. IQ tests measure lack of nutrition and education as much as they measure so called intelligence. Don't let it bother you Bri, it's the American way'. Skip sucks in more smoke, holds his breath a moment then exhales, further corrupting the hot stale air in the command vehicle, 'Who gives a squat anyway, their democracy, their vote. They deserve the government they elect.'

I drive home the M16 magazine and check the safety catch, 'We also vote Skip. We also deserve what we get. For the first time in my life I'm beginning to think about that simple fact.'

It is night time, I break my own rule and share a couple of joints with Skip and another American officer. I am shaken into some form of reality by the crescendo of gunfire on the perimeter. The two officers climb up through the observation turret and sit on the roof of the command vehicle yelling and yahooing in their drugged up state. I grab the radio handset and poke my head up for a look.

The whole perimeter is alive with gunfire. Some soldiers are running down to the edge, loading weapons as they run and let rip when they get close. Soldiers are firing madly into the surrounding area and I cannot see what they are shooting at. I squeeze the button on the handset and speak to the Australian command centre, 'zero alpha this is lima, oscar one, we are in contact, movement on the perimeter. Over.'

'Roger that', comes the reply. 'Sounds like more than a probe, is it a frontal assault? Over. The base command post can obviously hear the massive waste of ammunition through my handset.

I am stoned enough to have the giggles myself. In the white light of parachute flares, I can see what all the shooting is about. Some poor Vietnamese peasant has tried to sneak into the rubbish tip just outside the wire. He's been spotted by a sentry, who opened fire. That in turn started the debacle I am now witnessing.

American soldiers are firing their weapons in any direction aiming outside of the firebase. There appears to be no discipline, no orders, just soldiers shooting. The most amazing thing of all is that the man running from the rubbish tip was not hit by small arms fire and finally managed to disappear into the tree line.

Above the din I call back to zero alpha, 'Just a shoot-out with an attempt to penetrate our defences. We appear to be able to repel the assault. I am confident this will be over soon. I will send detailed SITREP once things settle down. Out.'

I then drop the handset, letting it fall to the bottom of the APC turret and climb up onto the top of the command vehicle beside Skip and the American officer. I lie on my back looking up at the constant stream of parachute flares fired off at random by soldiers without any idea of what they are doing.

Skip passes me his already half-smoked five papers joint. I suck in the smoke from this cigar sized joint and hold it as long as I can but have to expel the smoke as I start laughing.

Skip flops down beside me, 'God bless the Americans!' he calls aloud. 'Ain't this better than bunger night back home?'

'God bless America', I reply, laughing uncontrollably.

Two days later a chopper lands delivering Johnno back to his position as LO signaller.

'Have a tough war while I was away?' he asks with a cheeky grin on his face. 'Apparently you really impressed the Brigadier back at base, says he could hear you on the radio above the noise of battle. He said you were cool as a cucumber under fire. "That young infantry man who replaced you", he said to me, "under heavy attack and he casually states, 'We appear to be able to repel the assault.' Cool as a cucumber".'

'Stoned as a fucking maggot more likely', I reply. 'What a crazy war we are having.'

Skip walks over to greet Johnno, 'Welcome back old buddy. Hope you picked up some more grass from that prick in Vungers.'

Johnno pats both shirt top pockets which are bulging with packages, 'Pity Brian has to fly out on that chopper when it's loaded, otherwise we could have a great time.'

I shake my head, 'No, I think you can do it without me.' I grab my kit and start toward the chopper.

Skip calls out after me, 'You won't breath a word about this little perk will you? 'Cos Johnno has still got his R and R for seven days and I will need a replacement who understands our business.'

I stop and look around me. What I am seeing is a piece of insanity in action but something about it all appeals to my now completely corrupted brain.

Despite the appeal, there is also a certain foreboding. A gut reaction to stay away from this man. I feel like he will take me on a sort of headlong rush into some horrible event. A premonition maybe? Stuff the gut feeling. 'Give me a call when Johnno is going on R and R, I'll be only too happy to help you with the war effort.'

The Huey is restarting its engine. The rotor blade slowly turns and gathers speed, the slow whine gradually turns to the rhythmic beat of modern warfare.

Whooo   Whooo   Whop   Whop   Whop   Whop

I do not wait to obey any safety instructions. I just bend over slightly and walk under the rotors. Climbing on board, I throw my kit on the floor and relax as the Huey gives its familiar rock and shudder then becomes airborne. I grab my notebook.

> *Looking down on the firebase below I could see Johnno and Skip walking back toward the command vehicle. Two little children enjoying their adventure into madness.*

Whop   Whop   Whop   Whop   Whop

The chopper heads back to the real war.

Whop   Whop   Whop   Whop   Whop

The Other Sides of the War

'Circus, a fucking circus I tell you Sir', I provide details of my visit to the American firebase, minus the drug taking.

Sandy snorts then replies, 'Yeah they got some bad ones but don't paint them all with the same brush. The damn Marines and Special Forces boys are tough and mean. I don't mind having them fight alongside me.'

'Special Forces, you mean Green Beret?'.

'Apart from a song and a dumb stupid John Wayne movie I don't know much about them Green Berets. But there are a bunch of Yanks working the Mekong Delta that you and me would feel good working alongside, navy bods. I think they call them Seals.'

'Never heard of them', I respond. 'But trust the Yanks to come up with silly names. Maybe we should call our SAS boys Platypuses or Wally Wombats or some stupid thing just so we could be more like our American masters.'

Sandy detects the contempt in my voice but chooses to ignore the sarcastic comment for the moment.

'Nah the Seals ain't spoken about much, but they are a sort of cross between us grunts and our SAS diggers. Small patrols of about 15 men, silent movement, lots of ambush tactics. They're pretty good if my mail is correct.'

'Well they'd want to be an improvement on what I saw', I reply. 'Some of them can barely think straight they're so doped up on weed. They have comics for training manuals. No crap Sandy, their own gunny calls them Moron Niggers.'

'Tell you what, young fella', Sandy responds, 'I seen some Yanks in combat last tour and they got more guts in their little fingers than some of our boys have in their whole feckin backbone. I think it's all that rah-rah training they do. Spend more time training them to think they are invincible and less time training them on jungle warfare. Believe it or not, some of them Yanks think we are a pretty gutless lot.'

'How's that?' I ask.

'What we call cunning they think is just plain chicken. We sneak around the jungle, they make noise. Let the bastards come they say, let 'em find us and we will give 'em a fight.' Then they look at us and say, 'You Aussies hiding from Charlie are you?'

'Hiding! We don't hide. We hunt and we hunt properly.' I feel affronted by what Sandy has just told me.

Sandy laughs, 'Don't get personal about it son. Those Yanks won two world wars for the Poms and us. Don't ever think they didn't. We could not have beaten Germany without them and certainly not the Japanese. Trouble is, the Yanks are into technology not cunning. They put too much faith in modern weapons and equipment. Just great for limited warfare or tank and air battles but no real help against terrorist or any counter insurgency warfare.'

'They also die in large numbers', I muse aloud. 'Hell, if we took the sort of casualties they did we would need a lot more than national service to fill our ranks, we would need women and kids as well.'

'Yeah, I agree with you on that one, they sure take heavy casualties and some of the carnage could be avoided if they just used more cunning than guts. That's America for you ain't it? Their history is full of massive loss of life in war starting with their own Civil War. Somehow, the damn nation accepts it. Buggered if I know why. After World War I in them damn French trenches, us Australians started to get smart. But the Yanks still do the up the guts and plenty of smoke shit.' Sandy looks squarely in my eyes and responds to my earlier caustic contempt for our allies. 'That old Yank Top Kick or Gunny, who told you that the real war is up north on the DMZ, he wasn't telling bullshit son. Full-on battles all the time up there, we don't do it so tough. Occasionally we get caught in a big stoush, but the Yanks are in major contacts every feckin day. Show them some respect when you meet them. That's a feckin order son.' He stands up and walks back to his tent.

I sit silently for a while thinking about what Sandy has just said.

Sandy is a fair judge of character and he reckons I should respect the Yanks then that's what I'll do. Besides, the stories of American chopper pilots taking chances to lift out wounded soldiers is legendary, and true.

The Americans were yesterday. Today I am back with Australian cobbers and about to go on yet another op. My experience at the American base is soon a distant memory, now back with D Company and the 'real war'.

Occasional moments of adrenalin rush as new tracks are found or unusual sounds push the grunts into combat mode, but actual contact with the enemy is rare. We diggers simply call this war, 'The Odd Angry Shot'.

I learn the hard way that it is not the actual combat that drains the nerves and spirit of soldiers, it is the constant possibility of contact. It's the knowledge that at any moment the world around you could erupt into death and destruction.

There are no front lines, no rear echelons and no safe areas in the thick jungle and sweeping paddy fields. Nor are there any barbed wire defences to offer some protection when the day's patrolling ends. I just can't quite switch off and take a mental break. Even at night I seem to sleep with one eye open. I get tired.

With Sandy's coaching, I have come to respect the environment as a help not a hindrance. Jungles and scrub keep us hidden. This is always important to signal operators as the aerial swinging above our backpacks is a dead give-away to the enemy who would immediately target the person carrying the radio. On the rare occasion the patrol has to cross a clearing or a paddy bun, I grab the whip aerial and pull it down over my shoulder to make me less of a sniper target. No Australian soldier likes crossing a clearing. Signals operators hate it with a vengeance.

Possibly the most disconcerting thing of all is that the enemy are not signatories to the Geneva Convention. They do not mark their minefields, just place deadly mines wherever they feel they can do the most damage. Only they and their supporters know where mines are planted. For the enemy, the role of anti-personnel mines is not as a blocking weapon to stop enemy movement, but as a damaging weapon, a morale-shattering weapon and as a terrorist weapon. To the enemy it is preferable to badly wound their opponent rather than kill him. They know this will slow down their opponents and place massive pressure on the medical infrastructure. They also know there is nothing more devastating to a soldier's morale than to see a close friend with legs blown to shattered bone, damaged genitals and agonizing pain.

The enemy also uses booby traps, some of which are capable of terrible damage to human flesh. Even their simple panji pits are usually covered with human excrement to ensure any soldier who falls into one not only had spikes driven up through his foot but will also get a guaranteed infection or blood poisoning.

Days become weeks, which then become months.

The Delta Company diggers are now seasoned soldiers. Bright shining eyes that once belonged to boys replaced with a hard edged stare. We have learned to live with nagging fears tucked just behind our conscious reasoning.

I take this environment for granted now. Little sleep, ever-aching back, endless snip, snip, snipping of the vines and bushes that cling to equipment as we move silently through the jungle. Eyes darting back and forth, up, across and down. Searching for the next violent moment of truth, the next enemy contact that may or may not happen, but will eventually occur in all its violence and fury.

Thumbs on rifle safety catches, fingers on trigger guards, twitching, waiting for that moment. When would it happen? When?

Apart from my initial experiences, there has been little actual combat since I joined the company. A mine has wounded two soldiers from Eleven Platoon, one had lost half a left leg and his right foot, the other digger, a section commander suffered severe abdominal wounds and lost one eye. Twelve Platoon has been in a brief skirmish which appeared to cause no casualties for either side and Ten Platoon has tripped a successful ambush, killing four local Viet Cong who were slipping out of Xuan Loc after curfew. I want to go home. I want out of this place. How does that song go? Show me the way to go home, I'm tired and I want to go to bed.

Still the daily grind continues with no let up on the tension. Just the odd three or four-day break in the Dat before setting out once again in the pursuit of the elusive enemy. All that matters is getting through each day or getting from one coffee break to another. Right now the patrol has stopped for a coffee, smoke and leech check. Like the others, I am adjusting to the lifestyle but as always, ever curious about my foe.

What drives these people and why do they continue with such human carnage when the eventual result could only be one of two things. Remain a peasant to the wealthy and corrupt or become a peasant to the powerful and corrupt.

'What do you reckon Wingnut?' I ask my companion over a hasty brew and smoke. 'It's your second tour in this shit hole. What do you know about these people, what makes them tick?'

Wingnut looks back at me with a blank emotionless expression, 'I reckon all that counts is we stop the little fuckers ticking mate that's what I reckon. Who cares what they think or why, we kill them or they kill us.'

I am listening but am momentarily distracted by the large bloated leech I have discovered while doing a body check. It has attached itself to my inner thigh only inches from my scrotum. 'Glad you decided to stop there mate.' I place the hot end of my smoke onto the bloated beast which drops to the ground. After finishing a check of legs, I pull my pants back up and secure them before returning to the discussion with Wingnut.

'What do you think of them as soldiers?'

'Depends, local Cong are pretty piss poor as fighters, they're badly equipped with mostly old weapons and little ammo and they don't know much about combat training. What they do know is their patch of ground. They put in the booby traps and shit. It's their damn traps I hate the most because they are cunning and unethical. Not like the NVA who tend to use Chinese or Russian equipment to set up their traps.' As he speaks, Wingnut is using his bayonet, continually stabbing the leech dropped from my leg, 'I remember this one trap I came across last tour. At first it looked straight forward, a spring loaded trip system which set off a bag full of explosives, mixed with bits of nails and broken glass. Just as I was about to pin it I saw a second vine that just didn't look right.' He shakes his head as his memory takes him back to that moment of truth, 'It was set up so that the person disarming the first trap would trigger the second one. A bamboo spring-loaded sapling with great big razor sharp spikes on the end of it. Would have swung across and hit me right in the face. No eyes left after that finished with me that's for sure.' He looks up at me, 'I ain't scared of no jumping jack mine or no anti-lift grenade stuck under it. If one of those goes off in my face while I'm trying to disarm it I'm cactus. Dead! Dead ain't painful. But those booby traps that leave you blind or paralysed or some other shit. That's what I have the odd nightmare about mate.'

Wingnut finishes his destruction of the leech and stares at the blood soaked end of his bayonet before continuing, 'The regular Cong, good old D445 and even the 274 NVA regiments are better but not as well trained and armed as the real NVA who travel down from way up north. They are good because they have been at it for so many years. We must have killed hundreds of the bastards but they keep re-forming as a fighting unit, keep recruiting or forcefully conscripting new boys for cannon fodder. Then there are the hard-core propaganda Viet Cong. They are brain washed with Ho bullshit and don't ever give up. They are the bad bastards that don't mind a bit of terrorism with any locals who support the South or the Yanks and Anzacs.' Wingnut's face contorts as he spits out the next sentence, 'Kill as many of those bastards as you can mate, they are not nice people. Been known to booby trap little kids and send them in to mingle with ARVN soldiers before detonating the device. Kill the kid as well as the soldiers, they don't care, it's just a war to them mate. Some little Nog kid is expendable as far as they are concerned.'

I have reasonable knowledge of D445 simply because I am a sig operator and often decode intelligence summaries from HQ. I have heard my share of stories about VC terrorism but not seen any official report when decoding messages. Still I have no reason to doubt that the enemy is capable of acts of terror.

'What about the other NVA, 33rd?'

'You sure know when you come up against those bastards. Shit, we ambushed some on that big op, remember?' Wingnut replies. 'Well-armed with Chinese and Russian equipment and usually plenty of ammo to throw at you. Well trained by Chinese and sometimes Russian advisers they travel light out of their base camps so they can carry extra ammo. Usually you only find a bit of rice and dry fish on their bodies. What they can do is rely on the local Cong as guides and to feed them extra bits of meat and vegetables.'

'So how do you tell VC from NVA, apart from the basic uniform and boots? I mean when the shit spills, how do you know if you are up against NVA or locals?'

'Trust me mate, you always know. For one thing, the NVA will close up on you as quick as they can. They know we will use our artillery. They move in close so we can't fire the damn guns onto ourselves unless we got a good FO like this bloke with us. They also have a very definite amount of extra fire-power than the local Cong and they fight tactically as we do only they don't use radios as much in combat because they only have one or two for broader network stuff. So what you will hear is things like bugles or whistles which they blow like a sort of Morse code, you know, two blasts mean form on the left four blasts means some other thing. I don't know the code but they sure do. They are bloody good soldiers' mate. Bloody good.'

I make an observation to Wingnut, 'The intelligence reports I read say that Three Battalion of the Thirty Third Regiment NVA are our main opponents in this area. I have read a bit about them being on the ball so to speak. A whole battalion of them would be hard to knock over if we hit the main force. Particularly if they get back up from the 274 regiment that is also active in the Long Khan Province.'

Wingnut smiles, 'A battalion of NVA ain't like a battalion of us guys. You know how we are often short because people are sick or on R and R, well they take a while to get reinforcements down from the north, so whenever we kill a bunch of them they take a couple of months to get back up to strength. That's why they do hit-and-run shit or spend a lot of time hiding out. They ain't any different to us in the way they like to make sure the odds are stacked in their favour before they get seriously aggressive.' Wingnut finishes the tea in the bottom of his mug, 'We got a bunch of the little bastards when we sprung those two ambushes in that big night fight. They haven't been seen since so my guess is they are hiding out in the thickest bit of jungle they can find, waiting for more ammo and reinforcements to come down the Ho Chi Minh Trail. But we will meet them again. They don't ever go away completely.'

I look around me and notice there is no stirring to indicate the patrol is about to resume, possibly the OC just wants a long break. Sometimes this happens. Even the OC becomes fed up with non-stop patrolling and just wants to sit on his bum for a while. I don't care. As long as I can get the weight of my pack and sig set off my back, I do not need to concern myself with what is going through the boss's mind. I look back at my strange little companion.

'So that's the bad guys, what about you mate, why are you back here on a second tour? I mean you must be crazy doing this job, mines and booby traps, crawling down tunnels. You must be plain dumb crazy to do it a second time.'

Wingnut smiles his insane little smile but there is a tinge of sadness in his expression. 'I have been home mate and it ain't home anymore. My girlfriend was screwing some other bastard while I was fighting in a war. I was a national serviceman and supposed to get my old job back, by law. But you know how it is, they give the job to some other jerk and then don't want to sack them to take on a bloke just back from war with a shit load of personal problems. So the boss takes me back because the law says he has to, but I get shit jobs and lots of suggestions that I might be happier somewhere else. My old friends didn't want to know me. My dear old mum died just after I got back and I just didn't belong to any thing or any one.' He shuffles nervously for a moment then looks me in the eyes, 'Over here you belong to something and over here you are part of a team. It's like everyones in the same boat so we all belong to each other. I trust you with my life and you trust me. You don't get that back home mate. All you get is shallow ignorant bastards that will knife you in the back if it means a job promotion. They will screw your wife as soon as you leave town and not give a damn squat about you. But here mate you are surrounded by real mates, people who you trust with your life.'

He looks around him at the diggers scattered amongst the undergrowth. 'So I signed up for three more years army and requested a posting back to Viet Nam. I been home mate and it ain't home anymore, this is my home now.'

Wingnut grins, 'I am sort of honorary grunt ain't I? We drink from the same cup us grunts.'

'What cup?'

'Well grunts know a certain mateship that pogos don't know about. On patrol, life gets right down to basics, animal necessity and the instincts of a hunter. Kill or be killed. After a few months of war the basic instinct is like a drug all of its own. Grunts are just like any heroin junkie wandering the streets of Kings Cross, desperately looking for their next fix. The junky hates himself but has to keep looking for that fix. Scared the next needle in the arm will deliver a fatal dose but seeks it out anyway. Desperately wanting to get it over with! Grunts drink their war drug from the same cup, every day they patrol this donga. Only those who have sipped from that cup know what mateship is all about.'

I feel overwhelmed with a deep sense of sadness for my strange little companion. I felt a slight chill run down my spine. How many Wingnuts would this war produce before it was over? What will happen to them when they no longer had a war to fight, a team to belong to?

Sudden movement to my right. It is Doc lifting his backpack onto his shoulders and adjusting the straps to their most comfortable position. Doc glances over to me. He gives no hand signal just that look of painful resignation then a nod in the direction of advance.

'Here we go again', I whisper to Wingnut, who looks up then slips his bayonet back into its sheath.

I lift and strain to get my pack and radio onto my shoulders but it is just too heavy. I rest it against a tree, sit down and slip my arms through the straps then roll onto my stomach. With the weight distributed across my back, I now struggle onto hands and knees, then using my M16 as a lever, drag myself onto my feet. The 40 or 50 kilos dig deep into my under-nourished but war-toughened shoulders.

Next, I slip my map from its leg pants pocket and pull my compass from the left hand shirt pocket. A quick check of the bearing confirms the patrol is moving toward the approximate area that the OC plans to reach by last light. I glance down at my Mickey Mouse watch and guess it will be an hour of patrolling before we go into night harbour.

Jesus, a whole hour! My only comfort is that every other digger is in the same predicament. I look up and notice the patrol is on the move again. Resigned to my fate, I take up my position on the patrol line.

It's a Drag

'Curse you Wingnut, you know I don't take six million sugars in my coffee.'

I cannot help but overhear the whispered banter between Doc and his buddy.

'Six million my arse Doc I just put a few in there. Anyway, what about you chucking away all the Vegemite and leaving us with only jam. You know I like Vegemite', Wingnut responds.

'You don't chuck out Vegemite, you flush it down a dunny like any other shit', Doc replies. 'We agreed to split some of our rations and share the weight. I don't mind carrying extra food, but black toe jam ain't food its black shit on a stick mate.'

'Pommy bastard go back to your chip butties and Liverpool swill. Vegemite is the food of the Gods mate', Wingnut pauses a moment. 'It's why Australians beat Pommies at cricket and rugby and any other sport you want to think of.'

'You will live a lot longer if you could keep your hand off your dick you little pointy eared abomination', Doc snaps back. 'I never knew a man who could masturbate with his brain before. But you are a medical marvel, a medical freak. Or, let me put it to you in simple terms Wingnut - you're a fucking wanker!'

'Shuddup the feckin pair of you or I'll come over there and bend you over, pull your scrotum's back through your legs and over your head then make you spend the rest of this war walking around like red back spiders!' Sandy has had enough of the banter and notices the noise level has risen from whisper to agitated argument. Silence in the jungle is paramount. Personal differences are pushed aside.

I look at my CSM, 'You got a real subtle way with words Sandy, a real gentleman you are. I'm sure a lot of mums would be happy knowing that you are teaching their little boys the art of good English and good manners.'

'Bah!' Sandy retorts as he splashes yet another quantity of Tabasco sauce into the dehydrated scrambled egg packet slowly boiling over the hexi stove. 'Talk about sharing rations. What's with this dehydrated ration shit you carry anyway?'

'Weight, Sandy, weight. I got to carry a 25 sig set and spare batteries in addition to ammo and stuff. Weight is what I gotta think about. Food is a luxury only a bastard like you can afford.'

'Well it ain't normal', Sandy replies. 'The dehydrated eggs make the Tabasco sauce taste funny.'

I roll my eyes, 'Perhaps, just perhaps we could do something different like eating the stuff the way it says you should on the cooking instructions.'

'Damn tucka fuckas do things by the instructions. Me, well I like real food', Sandy responds. 'I got this theory that the reason the Slopes and Gooks all over the world can live on shit food is because they use lots of chilli peppers and curries and stuff. Now this Tabasco sauce is all of that in a feckin bottle, my man. Guaranteed you will have a long healthy life no matter what shit you eat', Sandy pauses to concentrate on stirring up the now red eggs in their packet. 'I ought to know about how to survive shit for food sonny boy, 'cos I been in the army more years that you been alive.'

The company is in an early night harbour and making the most of having extra time to cook a hot meal and clean weapons before the night descends. Sandy is cooking the meal while I completely strip my M16 and give it a thorough clean. Once assembled, I reach over and take Sandy's SLR, 'Looks pretty clean, mate.'

Sandy looks up from his witch's concoction, 'Yeah, it got the good goin' over this morning. Just give it a 'pull-through' and check the mag for grime on the top rounds.'

I remove the magazine and slowly draw back the cocking lever quietly removing the round in the SLR chamber. Locking the breech open, I drop the pull-through cord down through the dust cover's ejection aperture and into the breech, its weighted end allows it to slip down the bore to the flash suppressor and beyond. I drag the lightly oiled piece of cloth through the bore then inspect the cloth for signs of grime or rust. Clean as a whistle. I am not surprised. Next I peer into the ejection aperture and inspect the face of the bolt and firing pin. It remains clean and lightly oiled. Sandy is a true professional soldier, his weapon is his true love and he treats it with great respect. Next I check the magazine for any grime on the top rounds. I press them in to test the spring and get the response expected. I slide the loose round back into the chamber and quietly allow the bolt to drive home. The magazine is locked back in place and I check that the safety catch is on. I remove the gas plug and piston, as expected find both clean and lightly oiled. Finally, I check the gas setting. I need to ensure the setting is correct. I know from experience that Sandy's SLR is set on four.

It is on five.

Had Sandy accidentally knocked it, or was he testing his buddy?

I reassemble the piston and plug then re-set the gas to four and present the weapon to Sandy, 'Round in the spout and safety catch on Sandy.'

Sandy takes the weapon, double checks the safety, glances quickly at the gas setting before allowing his lips to turn upward in a smile. He nods before returning to his meal preparation.

We two men have established a standard routine. Each morning Sandy completely strips and thoroughly cleans his weapon while mine remains ready to use. Once done Sandy takes my M16 and gives the weapon a quick 'short cut clean'. Each evening the reverse procedure occurs, both comfortable in the knowledge that each would do a professional inspection before declaring the weapon ready for any possible combat situation. This is part of Sandy's trust building regime which he imposes on all diggers in the company. 'Each man will learn to trust his buddy and his buddy must at all times be trustworthy', he drums into his diggers at every opportunity.

'Get this into you boy, put hairs on your back', Sandy says, as he passes the menacing meal to me.

'Girls don't like hairy backs Sandy', I reply, as I contemplate the best method of attacking the red concoction before me.

'Hey Cherry Boy, I know what girls like and it's got more to do with the lead in your pencil than the hair on your body. My food is full of pencil lead young fella. Guaranteed 'hard on' material, that keeps on working 'til the early hours of the morning. And speaking of early hours, you got the death shift tonight, so you better check your gear and your com cord.'

I nod and take a first attempt at Tabasco eggs.

'Jesus Sandy I ain't sure I will live 'til my radio shift, this shit you feed me is eating a hole right through my gut.'

'Another satisfied customer', Sandy replies. 'When I retire from the army I might open a restaurant, "Sandy's Fine Food House" I might call it.'

I swallow the hot mess and hold my breath 'til the burning subsides.

'One way to ensure none of your old war mates bothers you in later life I suppose.'

In the distance, the muffled sounds of battle catch our attention.

'Someone's found Charlie by the sounds of that', Sandy whispers as he rises to his feet and moves over to the CHQ area. I stay away from CHQ as I know there are enough inquisitive soldiers hanging around the radio. Besides, I will know soon enough what is happening in the jungle some two klicks away. The number of explosions and small arms fire tells me that the distant battle is obviously a big one. My mind flashes back to the night in the boozer, the night Robby died. Ray's words ring in my ears, 'It's not a game Brian, people die out there'.

Ten minutes later Sandy returns, 'The other company has found a bunker and the Gooks are staying put, could be a long night tonight and by the sounds of it we might just find ourselves over there tomorrow. The CO is talking about a major assault with tanks.'

'Sounds a long way for us to move in the morning.'

'There is a squadron of APC not too far from us. My bet is that we will be picked up in the morning and sent over to do the assault sonny boy', Sandy replies as he picks up a small stick and crushes it in his left hand. 'You are going to find out about real shit hitting the fan my young man, so if you and I are on different jobs tomorrow just remember one thing, keep the feckin head down and no hero bullshit.'

I feel a sudden chill run down my spine. This is not the usual cheeky but cheery banter coming from Sandy. He is deadly serious.

'Could be pretty bad you think Sandy?'

'Real bad son. Bunker assaults are bad news', he looks drawn and almost sad as though he was grieving a lost love one.

'My guess is the OC will want you with him and me on ammo and casualty. If I ain't with you tomorrow 'cos you're with the boss, I want you to promise me no hero crap. Just keep ya feckin head down, okay?'

'Sure', I reply feeling the tension of the moment, 'I ain't a hero, just a dumb arse pogo sig.'

'I've kinda grown accustomed to your face son, I don't know why and I should know better, but I like you too much to see you hurt that's all, besides you remind me of someone's son.'

I have never seen Sandy express emotion like this and it unnerves me even more.

'I promise Sandy, no hero shit. Whose son?'

Sandy smiles, stares at me through watery eyes and puts his hand on my shoulder for a fleeting moment, 'The one I never got to know.' He gives a little shiver and puts back his usual stern face.

'Enough of this girly emotional shit, I just think you'd look feckin ugly in a body bag that's all. I got better things to do than shove pogo sigs in body bags', he quietly clears his throat of phlegm, stands up, turns and walks back to HQ.

I am sitting silently, trying to make sense of Sandy's behaviour. A son? He never mentioned this son stuff before.

Of most concern to me is Sandy's worried face. The man had been in some big battles with the enemy on his last tour of duty, he was at Coral during the Tet offensive. If anyone knew about bad bunker assaults, it was Sandy.

I am now experiencing a new type of fear.

In the patrolling monotony of 'Search and Destroy' operations, contact with the enemy is always in the back of my mind. The fear sort of suppressed and forced just behind my conscious thought. But to have to sit awake all night knowing that tomorrow we will be attacking a heavily defended position the next morning….knowing that tomorrow people will die!

Not 'might' die. - Will die! - Knowing that I might be one of those people. Jesus I just can't write about what is happening to my guts at the moment. Is this what a prisoner feels like on death row? Is this how it feels knowing that tomorrow he will hang?

Suddenly I feel a thousand butterflies careening through my chest cavity.

I don't want to die, not now, not here. It's not fair.

I run a line through the last entry, take three long deep breaths and blow the air out slowly.

Get a grip, get a grip. A calm soldier is a live soldier, I repeat three times to myself. I take three more long deep breaths.

I move past the panic attack. I'm no longer talking to myself aloud but thinking calmly. Stay low, head down, stay calm. Besides, I'm a damn signaller not a platoonie. I'll be safe behind any main assault line.

I move to my night position and check all is in place. I will be on the 0300-radio shift but that doesn't matter. I will not get any sleep regardless of what shift I have.

I pull a Lucky Strike from its packet and push it between my lips. The Zippo lighter flips open and the flame placed to the smoke tip. I'll have one last fag before last light.

My thumb runs across the deep engraving on the side. I stare at the words. *'When I die I will go to heaven; I have done my time in hell!'*

I thought the statement was amusing when I first purchased the Zippo. It isn't funny now.

INTO THE BREACH

Perched on top of the armoured personnel carrier, I am hanging on for dear life as it moves and twists its way through the scrub and bushes, avoiding the larger objects and careening over the small, creating a path of minor destruction.

A helo gunship circles overhead as extra protection, from time to time the commanding officer's Bell chopper appears to check the company's progress.

We are moving to undertake an assault on an enemy bunker system.

Charlie Company located the large fortified position in the late afternoon and engaged the enemy, only to find themselves up against a well-armed force not prepared to retreat. Heavy artillery has not shifted them. The Colonel decided that C Company would continue to engage the enemy from its current position and D Company will assault the bunker system from the eastern flank with tank support from the aging but dependable Centurion tanks, which are slowly moving into position ready for the assault.

I sit like most soldiers when riding the APC. I'm not in the armoured box but on top of it. I'm more afraid of being inside if the APC strikes a mine than being shot at as I sit perched on top. Inside is a metal box that jerks wildly as the vehicle manoeuvres in sharp sudden motions caused by the bulldozer tracks beneath it. It's a death box if an RPG rocket is fired at it. All diggers know that the armour is designed to deflect rounds fired at it, but its square flat sides mean that a heavy calibre round could penetrate the aluminium armour if it hits 'square on'.

To be one of the lucky ones sitting on top gives me the opportunity to jump clear if the vehicles are ambushed.

There is a deathly silence among the soldiers, no new orders or general banter above the roar and hum of the powerful engines thrusting us toward the battle ahead. Each soldier is pale and introverted, sucking in the stench of the engine fumes and contemplating his chance of survival.

This is not an 'if or maybe' operation, we are heading directly to a battle to attack a heavily fortified bunker system. In the next few hours, some amongst us will be dead or wounded, this is an inescapable fact. Each one of us tries to convince himself it will be someone else who takes a bullet.

'Don't worry too much', Wingnut had told me. 'I done this before on my last tour, not with tanks, but I bet it will be the same. The Gooks will leave a small force to keep the bunker active, a sort of suicide force if you like, but the rest of the little buggers will have pissed off during the night. You and I just stay back from the front assault and we will be fine.'

Don't worry! A suicide force means fight to the death stuff, even if there are only a few of them there.

'How will the Gooks bug out?' I had asked Wingnut.

'Escape tunnels mate. The little bastards are like Welsh miners, dig, dig and dig. They will have a tunnel that pops up a hundred yards away somewhere.'

The sounds of battle are now audible above the roar of the APC engines. Diggers are fidgeting and re-checking their weapons and web equipment. I am desperately trying to remember protocol when working with tanks. I am now experienced enough to realise that the battle ahead will be filled with chaos and confusion. The sound of combat will be too loud for me to be able to talk calmly on the radio. This is going to be screaming and shaking all the way. I am glad to be a signaller following the tank assault rather than one of the grunts pushing the charge from the front.

The APCs slow, then stop short and form into three small harbour positions at the rear of the battle area. Their doors drop and the troops dismount, immediately forming into sections and platoon positions.

I attach myself to the OC who is moving around the company, reassuring his soldiers while at the same time talking into the radio I carry. This means wherever the OC moves I must follow.

Within minutes of dismounting the APCs, the well-trained diggers are forming into assault formation. This is yet another drill rehearsed so many times back in Australia and carried out with robotic precision. All soldiers are ready and primed, squatting on their haunches and knees looking around nervously. Behind the assault lines, Sandy and Jacko begin organising dump points for the heavy backpacks which are not carried into the assault. Sandy briefs two lucky soldiers from each platoon positioned to guard the dumped packs. Nearby, Doc is on his knees preparing his medical kit for the inevitable casualties.

Still the pangs of fear are not quite settling in my stomach. My task is to stick by the OC no matter what and work the company frequency, but I am too experienced to leave it there. As soon as the OC stops moving, I swing the sig set from my back and quickly unscrew the small wingnuts at the top of the frequency dials, I then pre-set them so that the lugs will lock onto the battalion's frequency with a simple flick of the wrist. I tighten the wingnuts finger tight and test the dials to ensure they respond as designed. This allows me to flick between the two frequencies without removing the radio from my back.

The radio set is heaved back over my shoulders and I re-join the OC now moving to speak personally with one of the platoon commanders. That done, he moves on again. I have little time to think or get my bearings, too occupied with just trying to keep up with the Major who is now talking to the tank commander by radio and becoming increasingly frustrated by the regular interruptions from the CO in his chopper above the firefight. Dutch has the zero alpha frequency and the OC yells at him, 'Get that prick of a CO off my back. Tell him I am not available right now. Earn your damn pay Dutch, I don't need Brian on that task at this moment.'

Finally, the OC squats down beside the company medic, 'Nearly ready Doc?'

Doc is laying out field dressings and extra morphine, his right hand is trembling as he hurriedly threads the morph bubble syringes on a piece of string which he hangs around his neck to dangle alongside his dog tags. He packs the dressings into his small bum pack, large ones to the left side, and smaller ones on the right. 'Left for guts and chest, right for arms and legs', he repeats several times to himself in the hope that in the confusion of battle he will instinctively grab the right bandage when required.

He looks up at the OC, the strain already cutting lines through his white forehead, 'Ready as I'll ever be I suppose.'

The OC smiles through lips drawn tight like two steel bars, 'You'll be okay Doc but let me give you a tip; you will need a sharp knife or scalpel to open up those bandages as they wrap the damn things tight to protect them from the elements.'

Doc unsheathes a razor sharp knife strapped to the shoulder strap of his web equipment. 'Cuts through anything', he replies dispassionately. 'The serrated edge on the back of the blade can even cut through bone just in case I have to get rid of smashed bits in a hurry.' The OC turns slightly pale at the thought of his medic cutting away a digger's smashed leg or arm.

The Company Commander

Above the tree canopy, the sun has climbed high into a tropical sky, its bold red glow rapidly turning to a bright white fire slowly burning the morning mist. The sun and fear parch the Major's dry throat. He has been here before as a platoon commander. Three years earlier he led his men in an attack on an enemy position, had ordered four of Australia's finest to their deaths. Now as a Major he was about to commit three platoons to battle. How many today?

OC pulls his water bottle from its holster and draws down a long swallow of fluid then offers a drink to his medic who shakes his head and smiles from grey lips set between pasty white cheeks. He straps his bum bag full of shell dressings to his back. The veteran officer nods calmly, looks at me and draws a deep breath blowing it out through his mouth loudly, 'Tell them to move now.'

I raise the handset to my mouth, but for a moment my voice has disappeared, replaced by a large lump the size of a golf ball. I swallow hard and speak into the handset.

As one, the company rises to its feet and moves slowly through the undergrowth toward the sounds of battle.

No enemy rounds are passing through us as we start our controlled walk. I am looking for the Centurion tanks which I can hear grinding their heavy tracks through the scrub ahead. The sounds are increasingly close and loud. My heart is thundering within its rib cage, beating back the demon butterflies that threaten to leap from my stomach. I can see the mighty steel monsters positioned ready in front and wonder how an enemy could withstand the desire to run from such steel beasts of war.

The Major's plan is simple. Three tanks in a line moving up with two platoons of soldiers, each platoon in two assault lines one behind the other. One tank and one platoon in reserve. Company HQ positioned behind the centre tank to guide the battle as we climb over the bunker system.

OC and I move ourselves behind the centre tank and the OC motions to me to pick up the phone handset at the back of the tank, which allows infantry troops to talk directly to the tank commander. I pick up the handset, suddenly realising how short the attachment cord is. This means I must be standing to talk, exposing myself to small arms fire. 'Just checking the comms', I call into the set.

'Yeah, yeah I hear you, no need to yell, the bloody thing is wired into my headset', the reply comes from the tank commander.

The OC is talking directly to the tanks by radio. The phone is a backup and I am now wondering how the OC can keep talking and dragging me with him through the battle. Furthermore, I am unable to understand what orders are being given. I wish the OC would just ask me to relay the messages but this is obviously not going to be the case.

We are moving forward again and now the enemy is firing at us. The soldiers drop to the ground and begin the leapfrog style of assault on hands and knees, even crawling to avoid enemy gunfire. Tanks unleash their power, firing deadly canister rounds into the bush in front of them. Thousands of metal darts spray from each canister into the area to their front, clearing the scrub of any leaves and undergrowth.

Enemy small arms fire hits the tank which OC and I walk behind in a crouched position. The AK 47 rounds ratta-tat-tatting off the metal structure. I wince each time a burst clangs against the steel shell. The tank suddenly jerks hard to the left and then swings its turret, gun pointing down to a possible bunker slit. A mighty roar deafens me as the tank fires a solid 20-pound shell into the enemy position at point blank range. I feel the ground beneath my feet heave upward and settle again. The tank then jerks back around to its original course. As I regain my composure, I notice infantry soldiers from my company quickly rolling out of the tank's way as it lurches through the chaos. The air suddenly fills with acrid smoke and the smell of hot gun oil.

I'm sure I will die today.

Through the smoke, I imagine I see a black-cloaked ghost with a reaper's sickle. My sphincter muscle shuts tight and I feel a sensation of cramping fear drive upward from my lower abdomen to my chest. One leg buckles and I stumble but quickly regain my footing. The legs begin working again, Grim Reaper or not, I have one task and one task only, to stick with OC.

To my left I see Doc kneeling over a soldier trying to wrap a large gunshot bandage around the digger's waist and back. I can see the streaks of enemy tracer rounds scudding inches from Doc's exposed body but the man is fixated on his medical task. Doc stops wrapping for a moment and then picks up a handful of the man's intestines, which are spilling from the wound, and pushes them in under the bandage. The digger is screaming in agony but his screams are barely heard above the roar of cannon and small arms fire.

The OC falls to the ground beside me and for a moment I think my hero's been hit. To my relief the OC waves me on, yelling at me to pick up the handset. The OC crawls over to the Doc and the wounded soldier to see how bad his injuries are.

I press the handset to my ear, instantly picking up the situation as the right-hand tank commander yells to the platoon commander of Ten Platoon to get his soldiers clear of a bunker ahead.

The platoon commander screams back, 'We are pinned down by a machine gun to our left.' My own tank then comes on the air.

'I've got it, I've got it, and I'm going to crush the bastards.' The tank lurches forward quickly and I struggle to keep up but my legs just won't respond as they should. Like gangly lengths of rubber, they somehow keep me moving forward in slow motion. My heart is now pounding so hard I feel that at any moment I will have an actual heart attack.

Suddenly the tank crashes over the top of a bunker system crushing the timber and earth supports under its mighty weight. Breathless I follow and trip into an enemy crawl trench.

Amidst the sounds of splintering wood, I hear a scream above the grinding metal and gunfire. I look down the crawl trench to my left side and see an arm protruding between two crushed logs. I fall quickly over to my right side and raise my weapon to fire before realising there's a man crushed inside the bunker that the tank has just rolled over.

I am somewhere in the middle of a bunker system which is still manned by enemy soldiers. Panic grips me as my eyes dart left and right looking for enemy. I hesitate, confused, wondering if I should stay with the tank or return to the OC.

The tank begins reversing back over the crushed bunker. 'No no', I scream in fear. I scurry from the crawl trench and run clear before I too am crushed by the metal beast. I am now more afraid of the metal monster than the enemy.

In my short life as a soldier I expected I would be a brave man in battle, imagined myself not as a hero but as a good dependable soldier. Now confronted with the reality of weak legs and gut wrenching fear, my mind is struggling to cope with the smells and sounds of chaos. Military training gives way to a mind swallowed up in a world of death. That Grim Reaper is swinging his blade. It screams and snaps as it cuts through the air around me. The reaper's laughter is a high-pitched shrill. The gates of hell have flung open and I have danced through those gates, dancing to the sounds of the Grim Reaper's rock band. High-pitched electric guitars screeching, bass drums thumping and the squeals of the harmony girls screeching out of tune.

As I fall to the ground again in a moment of panic, the OC dives down beside me, 'What's happening?' The OC yells.

'I don't fucking know', I yell back as another cannon shell streaks from the tank to our front. I do not know, I am totally confused and scared, just doing whatever I am doing. Chaos and confusion, mixed with a screaming cacophony of snapping rounds, splintering logs, explosions and grinding tank tracks. I desperately want to grab the OC and scream for it all to stop.

Oblivious to my terror the OC grabs the handset and calls his forward platoon commanders for a report. I suck in a deep breath, somehow I regain my composure, once again a soldier. The Grim Reaper slides into the fog of battle to terrify another poor soul. I cannot hear the OC's discussion above the sounds of battle but can tell by the officer's behaviour that he is planning to bring up the Third Platoon. The Major hands the handset back to me, yelling in my ear, 'Twelve Platoon is coming through us and pushing through the bunker, we are almost there. You let the tanks know what's happening as soon as they stop talking to each other.' The OC then scurries off toward the right flank where Ten Platoon is leading that side of the assault.

The Platoon Commander

In the reserve platoon, Lt Robby Dowelment received his orders with a rush of excitement. This was his moment. Afraid? Of course he was, but the adrenalin surging through his body overpowered any doubt about his own courage. He screams orders to his platoon sergeant as he passes the radio handset back to his young platoon signaller. The young officer hears a burst of AK fire. For a split second his eyes fix upon the shocked pained expression on the face of the soldier who reaches to take the hand set.

I wait for the tank commanders to stop talking, but to no avail as the over-excited chatter between the tank commanders dominates the air waves. I stand up and grab the phone set at the back of the tank. A burst of AK 47 rounds ratta-tat-tat on the metal armour and snap by my right ear causing my stomach to leap into my parched throat. I swallow it back down and scream into the tank phone handset, 'Get off the fucking air we are trying to talk to you'. The radio goes quiet, so I drop back to the ground and speak to them, telling them that the forward platoons will hold and Twelve Platoon will advance through them. The tanks stop and prop, ready for the next platoon to pass through.

The diggers from Twelve Platoon pass me on their haunches, faces white with fear, eyes darting back and forth. They move through the tanks and into the breach of battle. Twelve Platoon's sergeant squats beside me behind the stationary tank.

'Where is the OC?' He yells.

'Over with Ten.'

The sergeant looks at me and calls out over the din, 'Platoon Commander and sig are down, hit by a burst of AK. I will push the platoon through but I need a signaller.'

Not me mate! I think to myself. 'I'll find the boss and get back to you', I scream at the sergeant and scurry off on all fours in the direction where the OC had disappeared.

Rounds are still snapping around my ears. Are they enemy or friendly? It's all too confusing. I drop to all fours crawling like a baby. I can hear myself screaming, just yelling aloud in rage, as I had been taught in bayonet training. I pass a wounded soldier lying on his side holding a bullet shattered broken arm. Again, I have the sensation of the snapping rounds passing close by my ears but they seem to be coming from the direction of friendly forces not the bunkers.

I stop but the digger waves me on. 'I'm okay, you go get the bastards', he yells at me. I seem transfixed in fear and confusion. Help or go on, what do I do? I instinctively turn to help the wounded man.

'Medic, medic where are you?' I scream as I try to pull the shell dressing taped to the digger's rifle butt, finally ripping it free from the weapon but then unable to tear away the tightly sewn protective cover. My mind races back to the OC's comment to Doc and I reach down and draw my bayonet from its sheath under his M16 hand grip and cut away the stitching enough to get sufficient grip to tear the wrap open. Quickly I open out the dressing and place it over the wound. I can feel the shattered bones grinding. The wounded digger stares at me without expression of pain or fear. The man is slipping into shock.

'Hold it tight 'til a medic gets to you', I scream before looking around to find my company commander. The wounded soldier looks back at me then down to his shattered arm, 'It's my bowling arm'.

I grab the digger's left hand and wrap his fingers around the bandage, 'Hold it tight mate, real tight! You will be okay.'

Ahead I can make out the OC talking to Ten Platoon Commander and dart across as fast as my rubber legs can take me.

'Twelve Platoon Commander and signaller is down, we need a signaller to go with the Sarge. Do you want me to go?' my eyes begging and pleading the OC to say no.

'Fuck it, not young Robby', the OC screams before pausing to think. 'No, you get on the battalion frequency and keep the bloody CO off my back', he screams, then looks at the Ten Platoon signaller, 'You're it son.'

The young soldier swallows hard and replied, 'Where the hell are they?'

'Follow me', the OC replies, as he reaches out and drags me back in the direction I had come from.

I scamper at a low crouch behind the OC, somehow feeling braver following the Major. If he can, so can I.

Dutch the other signals operator, somehow appears alongside me, eyes bulging through their sockets, face drawn tight and white skin showing through the cam cream. I realise that Dutch has been there all along but trailing just behind the OC and me, which is exactly as he should be doing. Dutch calls to take the company frequency so that I can take the battalion's frequency.

The platoon sergeant has moved forward slightly to give orders to his troops when he sees Dutch, the OC and me returning with the new signaller. He moves close to the OC and yells, 'I figure it was a tree sniper after the sig set, Robby didn't know what hit him, head shot. The sig took a bullet in the leg. Doc is organizing a Dustoff with Sandy and Jacko.'

The OC nods and points to the tanks, 'We are almost there, just push the boys forward a few more meters, 20 at the most and we will have run right over the bastards.'

The veteran sergeant nods and moves forward with his platoon. I now take the handset and call the tank commander to move forward with the new platoon. I stop and wait to hear Dutch talking to the tanks too. Both OC and the platoon have new signallers and I am relieved it is my turn to keep low. I reach back to the dials on my sig set and flick them to the pre-set battalion's frequency.

Why the OC wants me on this frequency becomes immediately obvious. My job is to find excuses to stop the commanding officer annoying the OC so that he can get on with his task of leadership from the front.

I bury my face into the churned up ground in front of me and take three deep breaths. It is Dutch 's turn to try to keep up with the OC now and I can lag behind a little, take that little extra care to stay alive.

I lift my face from the dirt, get onto my haunches and crawl forward on all fours, occasionally dropping to my stomach as another snapping sound comes perilously close to my ears. Occasionally I stop to reply to the commanding officer's incessant requests for more information.

'Niner this is four, sunray not available, get off the air, we are almost over the bunker. I will advise when we are there. Wait. Out. Wait! Out!' I scream into the handset again before crawling onward, ever onward. For some reason Dutch could not bring himself to stall the CO and the Major has had enough so he has given the job back to me. As always, I will be the bad guy, rebel enough, or gutsy enough to delay my commanding officer. I crawl on. Surely, it will be over soon.

BOOTS GP

I CANNOT RECALL a time when I felt so physically exhausted, as though every part of this body had been wrung dry of energy. Nothing left in the tank, just sheer exhaustion. The adrenalin has pumped me up so high and I am now paying the price for abusing this self-created body drug. Deep in the back of my parched throat, the taste of burnt cordite and hot gun oil smoke.

The battle is over. Two soldiers dead, including the young platoon commander from Twelve Platoon. Five wounded, one critically and any amount of cuts, bruises and swollen joints.

As another rifle company secures the bunker, the Delta Company soldiers return to their packs and equipment stashed before the assault. We emerge through the after-battle haze and stench of cordite, faces gaunt and eyes drawn deep into their sockets. With our black and green facial camouflage cream smeared and running from sweat and tears, each man looks like one of the living dead from an old Boris Karloff horror movie.

Each man is in a state of shock.

Fatigue now battles with our desire to celebrate victory, not the victory over the enemy, victory over death itself. We collect our equipment and form into a loose company harbour defensive position and sit or lie staring into the surrounding bushland. Staring into our own shell shocked souls.

I take up my place in the Company HQ area right where the dead diggers are. Sitting on my backpack I look at the two dead bodies in front of me wrapped in their hooches.

I imagine I can hear a mother wailing in anguish.

Dutch limps up and sits beside me, still experiencing discomfort when he walks, a reminder of the injury he incurred during the hot insertion.

A long silent pause. No words spoken between we two exhausted young men. Dutch has Catholic rosary beads in his hands. He is staring at the two dead Australians wrapped in their hooches. Army issue 'Boots, General Purpose' attached to their feet protruding from one end. No one has packed the proper body bag and the sight of the dead men's feet somehow makes the picture all the more gruesome.

Finally, Dutch speaks, 'One of the tanks deliberately drove over the top of a dead enemy just a moment ago for no reason at all, just crushed the body into the ground then backed over it again.' He pauses to move the beads through his fingers, 'The boys watching the tank just laughed and said, "Well we won't have to bury that one, just sprinkle some leaves on him".' Again, Dutch moves the beads, 'I can hear God crying mate, I can hear God crying.'

I look at my fellow sig operator coldly and dispassionately, 'No God here mate, just four dead feet poking out of those two hooches and I don't give a squat about some flattened out Nog… flatter the fucking better!'

Dutch stares at me a moment, a single tear rolling down his right cheek. He stands and limps away.

Delta Company is a spent force but victorious with the help of tanks. Enemy dead are yet to be totalled but no one is interested in trying to dig up the crushed and destroyed bunkers.

'Stuff the head count', the OC says to Sandy. 'We'll just say we killed 25.'

'Come off it John, apart from the four enemy bodies we can count there wouldn't be more than eight or nine of the bastards buried in that bunker. You know they would have bugged out last night. Why 25?'

'Why not, that was young Robby's age wasn't it?'

Sandy looks over at the OC, sympathetic but angry. 'Permission to speak, Sir?' Sandy spits out. Sandy's tone stuns the OC.

'What's this permission to speak shit Sandy, what's up with you?'

'I know Rob was an officer and a friend Sir, but we lost a feckin good digger also, do we add his lousy 19 feckin years to the total? I suggest you get your shit together and visit the platoons, they are hurting just as much as you feckin are.'

Stunned by Sandy's comment the OC sits a while then replies, 'You're right Sandy, but just for a short moment I don't want to be a company commander, I just want to be a digger whose friend was killed.'

'Well you are a feckin company commander and there are a lot of diggers who think the sun shines out of your feckin arse. They know you will be hurting, but they look up to you and need you to walk amongst them right now, so get off your feckin arse and earn your feckin pay. Now Sir!'

The OC looks up at Sandy, 'You'll come with me?'

'Of course I'll come with you, they're not just your diggers, they're mine also.' His voice calming down from its cutting edge, 'Including young Rob. I wet-nursed him from a snotty-nosed officer into a damn good leader and I don't want him dead anymore than you do John.'

The two professional soldiers stand up together and walk amongst the exhausted young soldiers, patting shoulders, examining cuts and bruises and taking the time to listen or talk.

I take a pencil in my still trembling hand…

Why had they chosen their careers? Did they ever imagine war would be like this, and why do they keep soldiering on year after year after year? I have survived what I consider to be a major battle against a hardened enemy, yet I am still confused as to what actually happened. How had they known when we had completed the assault? How did they manage to be so organised amongst the chaos?

All I know is that I was so scared I went numb at some stage. The noise and explosions of this battle were louder than I had imagined. I have seen a digger, young like me, lie screaming in agony, another in shock wondering if he would ever play cricket again.

Above all else, I know I am alive and unharmed. Elated with life, yet deeply ashamed of my lack of bravery I stare at the four dead feet. With trembling hand I scrawl…

Why them, why not me? Horrible, yet somehow addictive, I cannot put a finger on it. It is as if I almost enjoy what I am feeling, even though I still tremble uncontrollably from time to time.

I attempt to draw back smoke from my Lucky Strike cigarette and instead get a mouthful of my own spit. Adrenalin running out of control again it has dribbled out of my mouth, the smoke acting as a wick, absorbing the fluid until it actually extinguishes the fire at its end. I recall Doc telling the boys about some shrink with a dog that could salivate when a bell was rung. What is ringing my bell right now? Don't know or care.

I stare, thinking about the young officer and his even younger signaller. Behind the main battle and in reserve they had been cut down, one killed by distant bullets from an AK 47 while soldiers only metres from the enemy, survive without injury. Another shiver in my chest, I grab water and wash the foul metallic taste from my mouth with a swill, spit on the ground, a dirty green brown gollop of spit from somewhere deep in my lungs. I can feel the heavy knot deep within my guts. With trembling hand, I reach for another Lucky Strike and pull out my Zippo lighter. *'When I die I will go to heaven; I have done my time in hell.'*

I strike the lighter wheel with my thumb and place the flame to my cigarette, drawing back hard to get the hot feeling right down to that knot deep inside, easing the pressure somehow.

Anyhow, I do not care.

Wingnut squats down beside me, 'Hear about Henry?'

'Yeah, gut shot I think, but word is he will pull through okay. I saw Doc with him during the assault. Almost got killed himself.'

Wingnut takes a long drag on his smoke, 'Back shot, not gut shot, one of our own diggers hit him by mistake.'

'Jesus! how did that happen?'

Wingnut is about to speak when Doc walks up suddenly, grabs Wingnut by the collar and drags him up onto his feet before head butting him on the nose causing blood to spurt over both of them. I leap to my feet and push the two apart, stepping between them, 'What the hell is going on?'

Doc hisses out his reply, 'As if we haven't got enough on our plate, now this little prick is going around telling everyone we shot our own man.'

'We did and you know it for a fact you fucking saw it happen', Wingnut replies, as he tries to stem the blood flow from his nose.

I look Doc in the eyes, 'So, is Wingnut telling the truth?'

Doc let go of Wingnut's shirt and sits down on the ground, his legs crossed like a young child at a picnic. 'What do you expect, tanks going crazy and not holding a straight line of attack? Diggers trying to crawl forward between enemy bursts of fire, some get in front of others, accidents happen.' He pauses for a while, 'Jesus Brian I saw you running right in front of some Ten Platoon boys who were trying to keep a bunker slit quiet. How you managed not to get shot by a friendly is beyond me.'

I sit down on my pack again, legs suddenly wobbling like a baby learning to walk. Speechless! I know the confusion that occurred and remember not knowing quite where I was going, the rounds snapping around my ears.

A hot flush consumes my body, I feel sick. How close to death was I? Deep breath! And another. The hot flush passes.

Wingnut has managed to slow the bleeding, 'So what's with the fucking head butt then?'

Doc looks at him, 'Can't you just accept that things like this happen, it's best not to go round telling everyone and get them wondering if it might happen to them next time, This is a war mate. When the shit spills it happens in a very big, bad, way.' He pauses before continuing, 'I saw it because I was back behind the assault checking a wounded digger. You saw it because you were back behind the assault looking after your own sorry arse, Wingnut. So don't be a fucking coward AND an expert on who fucked up.'

'Don't call me a fucking coward mate', Wingnut retorts. 'I don't recall you ever volunteering to slide down an enemy tunnel with me or step up to disarm a bloody booby trap.'

I am too exhausted to care anymore, 'Why don't you both just get out of my face and go punch the shit out of each other somewhere else. Right now, I'm glad I ain't poor old Henry and you know what else, I'm even gladder I ain't the poor bastard that shot him by mistake. How do you think he must feel right now? Spare a thought for him instead of fighting each other over who and what went wrong.'

Sandy and the OC had seen the commotion from a distance and both wander over to us.

'Please explain why killing enemy is not enough excitement in one day and why you have to try punching up friends as well?', the OC enquires of Doc.

'It's nothin' Sir', Doc replies. 'Nerves are a bit jittery I suppose.'

The OC stares at the three of us, 'I know about Henry and I know who shot him. Henry advanced faster than his rifle group. He ran too far forward and one of the gun group from the section beside his own hit him by mistake. Let's just thank God he is going to pull through thanks to some quick work by you Doc.'

The OC looks across to Sandy, then back toward us three young soldiers, 'My report will show that he was wounded in action while assaulting this bunker. It won't say that he stuffed up by running too fast and too far, nor will it say that another digger was too busy firing to aim properly. All it will say is my company took this bunker and the men in my company are the best damn soldiers I ever served with. I am proud of every one of them', he pauses and looks at Wingnut. 'Every single one of them!'

Sandy now speaks, 'God help any feckin soldier that says otherwise or passes judgment on any digger who did his job as best he could in a feckin tight situation.' Sandy then walks up to Wingnut staring him eyeball to eyeball. 'Get the message Sapper, or you will have more than a broken nose. This is grunt business.'

'Yeah', replies Wingnut who then looks at the OC. 'Yes Sir. Loud and clear!'

Sandy then looks over to Doc again, 'I figure I saw you expose yourself to enemy fire on five occasions to treat some of the boys. I spoke to John here and we are putting in a commendation for you soldier. You did a fine job today, you deserve a gong.'

Doc's sudden response shocks all of us.

'Don't!' Doc snaps back at Sandy. 'Don't recommend me for any fucking medals. Just get me out of this fucking shit hole and let me go home.' His hands are trembling violently now, 'I don't want a bloody medal to remind me of this fuckin' mess. I want to quit, resign and hand in my stripes, I want out of this senseless war.' He punches his leg hard, 'You hear me Sir? I fucking quit, I can't do this anymore.'

The OC looks at his medic, who sits on the ground trembling and fighting back tears, 'Okay son I understand, no commendation.' He pauses, trying to think of an appropriate response to his medic's outburst, 'Just get yourself a hot brew and take it easy for a bit.'

The man is an infantry Major not a psychologist. He is obviously awkward with the situation confronting him. The man he wants decorated for bravery is begging to be relieved of duty.

'You're going to be okay son. Have a chat with your mates before you make any final comments about quitting. You don't want that on your military record.' Completely stuck for words he looks at Wingnut, 'He's your partner son, broken nose or not, your buddy, look after him. Make him a brew.'

The OC and Sandy turn and walk toward another group of diggers. Sandy stops for a moment, looks back at Doc, then returns to touch him on the shoulder. He says nothing, just touches the young man's trembling shoulder for a moment. Doc's shoulder stops trembling, he wipes away the tears in his eyes and looks up at his CSM.

'You're alright Doc', Sandy says in a quiet, calm voice. 'Best damn medic I ever served with that's for sure, nobody is going to know about this moment except us and we are your mates.' Sandy turns and walks away to re-join the OC.

Wingnut has managed to stop his nosebleed. He produces a steel mug and some C4 and goes about making a hot brew of coffee. Once done, he hands the steel mug of black brine to Doc, 'Here you are mate, get this in you.'

Doc looks at Wingnut, takes the mug of coffee, 'Thanks mate, sorry about the head butt. I can straighten up that nose in a minute when my hands stop shaking.' He pauses to look at his trembling hands holding the mug, 'I ain't quitting. I just lost it a bit.' He takes a deep breath, raises his eyes skyward, 'I'll be back in control in a minute. I've got a pain killer for you and I can fix the nose. Okay?'

'Forget it. I deserved it!' Wingnut replies, as he put his hand on Doc's shoulder. 'We are buddies you and I, we're in this together, like the boss said, get a brew into you and you will be okay. The nose will mend.'

I dig into my web pouch and find a C ration chocolate Hershey bar. I break it into three pieces and share with my companions.

Like the others, I simply did not know what to say. I wanted to hold Doc, to cry with him. But I couldn't. Real men don't... are not allowed to cuddle and cry, so we just shared coffee and Hershey bars. I hate this fucking war.

We three young men sit quietly staring at the two bodies in front of us. Four diggers appear and awkwardly lift the corpses onto an armoured personnel carrier.

The APC's engine roars into life and the dead Australians are deliberately 'disappeared'. They are whisked away as though they never existed.

I swear to God I saw the Grim Reaper as we went into that bunker, I can see his skull-like face, his hysterical eyes. Why can't I remember the faces of those two poor diggers, their second names, if they were married, some of their habits, anything about those dead men? I try and try, but all I see are four dead feet. Each in army issue, 'Boots GP'.

SKY PILOT

'Wank, wank, wank. That's all it is, just wank', I am looking up from my bunk at Dutch who stares back indignantly. 'There ain't a God in Vietnam mate, but if there is he sure is a mean pig of a God for what he allows us all to do to each other.'

Dutch stands speechless for a moment before responding, 'Show some respect you prick, if not for me, then for the poor bastards we are having the memorial service for.'

'So we gather on the hill while the 'sky pilot' does his God bothering shit. It's too late now ain't it, he should have prayed for them before they got killed. At the very least we could have had a service before their bodies were sent back home, don't you think?' I respond angrily.

Dutch just shakes his head, 'I feel sorry for you Brian, you're a sad little prick if ever I met one.'

'You telling me you actually believe that God crap?'

Dutch looks at me for a long slow moment before shrugging his shoulders and replies, 'I got to believe in something Brian and God makes more sense than your bottle of whisky. I'd go mad if I didn't have religion, I'd end up like you.' He then turns and walks out the tent.

Wingnut stands and starts toward the tent exit.

'What, you too?' I ask.

Wingnut turns, talks through a swollen nose filled with some cloth Doc stuffed in there the day before, 'Have an each-way bet mate, just in case there really is a God, don't get him pissed with you.' He moves toward the sandbagged entrance, turns again, 'It's like old Dutch said, it's not for me, it's the poor blokes who copped it. Maybe their families back home would like to think we had a prayer for them.'

I sit silent for a moment, reflecting on my dead friend's parents and girlfriend.

'Wait for me Wingnut, I suppose you're right about the family stuff.' I slide the half empty bottle of whisky under my mattress and grab my M16. Together we wander to the assembly point where the army chaplain is holding his memorial service.

I was surprised at the number of diggers who had made their way to the bottom of the hill. All there for different reasons, few practising Christians among them, some just rekindling the childhood teachings they had pushed aside long ago. But all came out of respect for the dead people's families. They gathered in unmilitary clusters, some nodding to others, a few 'good to see ya' comments and all with green giggle hats removed. Almost to a man, they stand awkwardly, shuffling their feet or trying to do something appropriate with the weapons in their hands. Most aware of the irony of praying for fallen soldiers to a God of mercy while holding a weapon of destruction.

The preacher wants to give a service for the two dead diggers from D Company calling out their names and age, their home towns and their religion. One digger was a Presbyterian the other a Catholic. He also asks all present to pray for a machine gunner from the ANZAC Battalion who had fallen off the back of a Land Rover when drunk in Vung Tau. Finally he offers a prayer for a sapper who died of wounds he received trying to disarm a booby trap three days before the bunker assault.

No one in the company had heard about the sapper or knows anything about the man. It happened on some task force op with ARVN, but we bow our heads when the preacher starts.

It is the right thing to do.

The Army Chaplain

Standing quietly the young man of God watches as soldiers slowly gather for his service. Just boys even younger than himself. He never imagined that being an army chaplain would cause him such emotional turmoil. He knows most of these boys haven't been inside a church for years, that they openly call him the sky pilot or worse, the God botherer. Is he just bothering God? And now after six months in this war he has even asked himself whether there is a God at all? There must be! He must hold his faith closer than ever. He must persist and find a way to ease the stress of these young boys in uniform. If not as a priest, at least he could offer friendship and counselling. The boys are gathered and ready for his sermon. His bothering of his God.

The chaplain commences his sermon. At the back of the gathering, I stand silently trying to hear the words above the constant ringing in my ears which has not gone away since the bunker attack. I do not know the preacher, have never spoken to him. I wonder if he is a Catholic or Protestant. Finally deciding he is a Catholic because Dutch appears to understand what happens with the hands. As for me? I had very little exposure to religion as a child. In the back of my mind, I can hear words from the hit song 'Sky Pilot' - how high can you fly, you'll never, never reach the sky.

At the end of the service the soldiers scatter.

Dutch is standing with the chaplain and Wingnut has wandered off to the PX to buy some trinkets. I make my way back to the tent, grab the bottle of whisky and take a swig. The knot in my guts responds favourably so I put the lid on the bottle and slip it into my steel trunk. I grab a Playboy magazine and actually read the articles. The pictures had been examined in minute detail many times and are now old hat.

'Mind if I come in?' I look up and see the chaplain standing at the entrance to the tent.

'Free world Sir. That's what we are supposed to be fighting for, or so they tell me.'

The chaplain sits on the bed across from me, 'I was speaking to your mate and he is very worried about you.'

I look up from the stick book and examine the man sitting across from me. The good looking and solidly built man could easily be a rugby centre with his broad shoulders. The sort of young man who would have little trouble attracting female attention. I move the Playboy magazine in such a way the blonde centrefold is exposed for the preacher to look at but this fails to raise any response. The guy is probably gay I suppose.

'What mate is that Sir? Dutch? He's worried because I'm not a good Christian is he?'

'No! Because you are drinking too much and calling out in your sleep.'

I have no answer to that response. Just sit there speechless. I was not aware I had been calling out. Sure, I had jumped up out of bed a few times since getting safe behind the wire, but that's not so unusual, I am not alone at that little caper.

'You are having a hard time of this war son, aren't you?'

'No, I like it here, best paid holiday a man could wish for. The natives are real friendly.'

The chaplain sits quietly for a while. He then speaks, 'I've seen young men like you before son, trying to be tough and brave. You can fool those around you but you can't fool yourself, it's catching up with you son.'

He sits on the bunk opposite. 'Some diggers are not that well-educated or raised in an environment of social equity. They don't think much about right or wrong, good and evil and if they do it is simple black and white thoughts.

They do not explore the many shades of grey. Men like that do their time and go home. You think too much, ask too many questions and the answers frighten you, they don't reconcile with your real inner self. I know your type better than you do son and I know the answer to your struggle is not at the bottom of that whisky bottle you hide in your trunk.'

I am now angry. Dutch has even dobbed about the whisky. Half the company has booze in their steel trunks but what if the preacher tells the fucking RSM?

'Oh I see, it's in God is it?' He will make this all seem perfectly normal will he? Killing is easy with God helping you to squeeze the trigger, is that what your trying to tell me? Ain't no shades of grey in that belief are there?'

'Forget I'm a God botherer or whatever you fellows call me. I'm not here to talk about religion, I'm here to be your counsel. Talk to me for God's sake, don't drive it inside. It will come back to haunt you years from now if you do.'

I sit quietly for a moment then look up at the man in front of me. A small voice inside calls out: try, just try and explain it to this man.

'I try to talk, to find someone who understands but they won't talk either. They just say, forget about it, push it out of your mind and stuff like that. They say you got to stay in control of your feelings and shit. They won't talk and they won't even listen.'

'I'm listening son, if you want to talk.'

I now feel embarrassed because I have let down my guard, I can feel my eyes filling with tears.

'You may be listening but you don't understand Sir. You sit here in base and say prayers and shit. But you don't dig up bodies and kick their heads like soccer balls. You don't live in fear that one day the world under you is going to blow your legs and balls off. I need to talk to someone who knows what I know, not because he heard about it, but because he lived it, smelt it and fucking did it. You don't understand, and the grunts that do are just like me, we don't talk about it.'

I regain my composure by turning tears into anger, 'You do what you gotta do, you try not to think about it too much and if you do think about it, well it's better to tell a few black jokes. Laugh it off rather than get all emotional and stuff.'

'I can listen. But you need to talk about feelings, emotions, not just what happened.'

'What do you mean by that?'

The chaplain sits back a little on the bunk, 'You were there when the bunker was taken, the lads killed. Tell me what you remember about it. Tell me what you were feeling during the actual assault.'

I think for a moment and respond, 'Smoke. Not just the smell, you can taste it on the back of your throat.' I let out a deep, sad sigh, 'Most of all I remember big feet. I see them in my sleep now.'

The preacher is surprised by the answer, 'Go on, what about the big feet?'

I suck in a deep breath before speaking, 'It was the dead platoon commander. He had great big feet. His boots were poking out the back of the hooch we wrapped him in and I kept thinking, jeez they are big feet. Now I can't remember his face, just big fucking feet. Sorry for swearing! But... well I can't get his feet off my brain.'

The chaplain nods, 'Yes you're right, young Robert did have large feet. He was a big man, six feet four I believe. I have a recent photo from an officer's mess function which shows his face clearly. I'll get it for you to look at if you wish. You should try and put a face to the boots. It will help if you remember the face instead of the boots.'

'I don't need another dead face to look at, thanks just the same.'

'That's the second soldier named Robert we have lost isn't it? The priest asks. 'The other lad was a Signals Operator, just like you.'

'Yeah, I was a close friend. We grew up together back in Cronulla.'

'So what was it like during the battle? What were you feeling?'

'I don't know, really scared I guess, shit scared. I just did what I had to do then it was over.'

'Just stop for a moment and think beyond that. What you're saying is what most diggers say, but when you look beyond that, get to the actual feelings and sensations it's much, much more. Concentrate and think back, it might be uncomfortable but it helps to run through the actual event from that perspective. You said you could taste gun smoke, what did that feel like.'

I let my mind go back to the assault on the bunker, allowing time to put the pieces into place, 'You ever had a bad accident in a car or something where you were sure you were going to die?'

The chaplain nods, 'A car accident with my father when I was young. The car rolled over at least twice. I remember the thought that I was going to die, and later the blood all over my father. He lived thank God, but yes I think I know the feeling.'

I nod, 'Attacking that bunker was like that car accident only it wasn't over in one or two rolls. I found out later it took 40 minutes for us to cross that bunker system under heavy fire. 40 minutes not 40 seconds. Every miniscule moment of those 40 minutes I believed I was going to die. A round was going to rip my head open or grenades blow my body into bits of mincemeat.' I stop as a shiver runs along my spine and back up to the base of my skull.

'I had no real concept of time. It seemed to take forever but when it was over it seemed to happen in a flash. All the time those rounds bouncing off the tank, just snapping so close to my ears, some of the actual snaps were so close they hurt my inner ear. The ringing is still there. Those bloody tanks were frightening, grinding metal only feet away from me and turning every which way. Their guns were deafening up that close, they were firing 20-pound solid shells into bunkers just feet in front of us. I swear the ground under me lifted with the impact, picked my body inches off the ground. Jesus I'm glad they were on our side. I was so scared of them crushing me. Imagine what the Gooks must have felt.'

'Yes it must have been horrific for the enemy. I am pleased to hear a soldier considering that his enemy is human just as we are. That's part of your problem son, but it's a good problem, it makes you a good man in a bad war.'

I shake my head slowly, then continue, 'Guys screaming, a man with his arm just hanging by a bit of flesh and when I put a shell dressing on it I could feel bits of bone rubbing against each other.'

'You stopped to help a wounded digger?' The preacher asks. 'You must be proud of that.'

'Nah! I just did what had to be done then moved on. The medic, good old Doc, he was the real hero out there. I saw him trying to stuff a digger's intestines back into a gaping hole in his stomach, enemy rounds dancing off the dirt all around him. That's guts, real guts. He should get a gong for what he did. Me, I just crawled around in a state of shit-scared confusion, doing whatever needed to be done and getting that wrong. I almost got shot by the boys in Ten Platoon.'

I reach for a smoke and hold it between trembling fingers but do not light it, throwing it on the ground instead.

'You said you remember the blood all over your father but that was after the car accident not during those four seconds you actually thought you were going to die. The blood and guts I was dealing with was happening at the same time as my 40 minutes'. A second shiver runs up the back of my spine, 'I never imagined I would be alone in a battle, surrounded by a whole company of soldiers and four monster tanks, but all alone. Fighting a desire to crawl up close to the Major, just crawl up and lay close beside the brave bastard, look him in the eye and say, "We're going to be okay, we are going to make it. Please tell me we are going to make it okay." I couldn't do that, I had a job to do, but even when I was screaming into that sig set I felt so lonely, like the people on the other end were a million miles away. It seems unreal but it was real and yes, I was so fucking scared.' I let out a long sigh, 'Believe it or not, scared or not, I was committed to getting over that bunker, something inside me, or maybe just a part of my training kept me going. No way was I going to let my mates down, no Sir, no matter how shit scared I was. I am ashamed of how scared I was. Yet, sort of brave at the same time I suppose.

Damned if I really know what that means. In the end it doesn't matter what it means.' I shake my head. I feel tears welling up inside, 'Two good men dead so we could capture a bit of ground then walk away and let the enemy take it back again.' A tear trickles down my cheek 'Then there were those big feet. I can't get those damn feet out of my brain.'

The preacher leans over and places his hand on my knee, 'It's hard I know but you will be better able to deal with these things if you can get them clear in your mind. I would like to talk more about this with you, I think I can understand what it must be like.'

I am suddenly angry with the preacher. He has drawn out my emotions and it is too damn uncomfortable; I am vulnerable and not in control. I look straight at the preacher with cold hard eyes.

'Sure you can. That's like saying that because your sister told you about childbirth you can understand how it feels. Bullshit Sir, only a woman who has had a baby can understand. Did Dutch tell you about the Gook the 'turret heads' ran over in their tank, not just once or twice? Backed up and did it three times. Looked like a dead cat in the middle of a highway back home. Everybody cheered that one Sir. We didn't have to bury the little Slope. The bush pigs will clean up that lot in no time.'

I watch as the preacher tries to hide his disgust. I continue, 'Another Nog got crushed in the bunker, just his right arm sticking out between the smashed logs with one finger pointing. His trigger finger I guess. Some of the boys got quite creative and made a sign and hung it by string from the pointing hand. The sign said 'Saigon 30 miles'. Get the joke Sir? The dead Nog is pointing to Saigon. That had us all laughing for a while. Least until the CSM and OC got wind of it and put a verbal rocket up our arses.'

The preacher looks down at the floor, 'You can tell me how you really felt rather than how you pretended to feel.'

'You can leave me alone. If you want to do me a favour, just leave me alone.'

The chaplain stares awhile before standing and walking out of the tent. Once outside he turns, 'I am always trying to understand, trying to help you boys even if I'm not a soldier, I try to help. But you have to want my help.'

I ignore him. I hate him and don't know why. The chaplain walks away.

Fucking sky pilot, what would he know? I stand up suddenly overwhelmed with emotion, tears run freely down my face. I grab my towel and wipe my face, take a deep breath and reach for a Lucky Strike. The harsh smoke burns the back of my throat but it isn't enough. I open my trunk and grab the whisky bottle. Two full swigs get the burning sensation down into the gut, feeding the knot, easing the tension.

I return to my Playboy magazine and read the article on the new Ford Mustang. Escaping into the American dream is a less painful experience than confronting Vietnam's reality.

Wish I had one of those.

Choose Your Poison

THE WET SEASON has passed. Constant damp gives way to dry heat.

Slowly I manage to adjust to the heavier weights of the extra water bottles I now carry on patrol. In reality, all I have managed is to leave behind more and more basic items to lighten the load on my back. My back has adjusted to the constant dull ache, the remnant of my fall from the chopper almost two months earlier. Like most soldiers, I am eating less food.

A soldier can live a long time without food but he must have water. The stomach contracts and he will not get hunger pangs after a while. We've got no choice. They didn't tell me this stuff at the recruiting office that's for sure.

As time passes we all grow thinner, living on just enough food to maintain strength but sacrificing the weight of food to accommodate the extra weight of water.

The lack of rain-saturated army greens has highlighted the amount of perspiration draining from each body as we go about the daily grind of search and destroy patrols. Shirts and crutch lines are now wet with sweat and salty white marks appear where the previous day's sweat has dried overnight.

The heat, without the constant watering down of the body, also brings on a new set of variables. Ear and eye infections are increasing amongst the soldiers. Rashes from prickly heat are turning into festering yellow pus sores under backpacks, and leeches are becoming more desperate to latch onto any living creature that passes their way. In the still moist areas of the rain forest and along creek lines, the leeches are in their most damaging numbers.

Soldiers give up removing any sighted leeches on their body and let them fill and gorge themselves with blood knowing they will drop off once mealtime is over. Each stop for a break in patrolling is a time to carry out a leech check of more vital body parts. A cigarette is lit and shared by diggers to burn the leeches until they let go and drop to the ground.

This patrol is proving to be a disaster for the company. Conjunctivitis is spreading rapidly through Eleven Platoon. They are becoming a useless patrol force and the OC has been forced to arrange for almost half to be evacuated back to the Dat. The problem will not end there, all diggers know how contagious this eye disease is. It lies dormant among the remaining soldiers ready to fester again.

The remnants of Eleven Platoon and the tattered remains of Company HQ are in a semi-ambush harbour along the edge of a tributary of the Sonhg Rhy River. They place guns and claymore mines facing down over the water in the most likely positions that an enemy group would use to refill their water supplies.

HQ is positioned back from the planned killing ground, set up ready to organise further evacuations of sick soldiers.

The OC has in truth chosen this spot more as a rest area than a serious ambush site. Not far from the river is a clearing large enough to land two or more choppers and the OC is of the opinion that we will need that clearing to lift out more diggers shortly, if not the entire remnants of the company.

It is my birthday. 20 years old. I feel 60.

I have told no one of my birthday but have packed a small tin of pound cake from the American rations which I warm gently before opening.

The smell of the warm cake in the little green tin seems a luxury beyond comparison at this moment. No Sandy and no Tabasco sauce.

I dig the spoon-like end of my little Aussie issue can opener into the cake and remove a bite sized chunk. Happy birthday to me.

Sandy is not with the company on this trip. He has managed to get his R and R and is enjoying himself in Singapore somewhere. The company quartermaster affectionately known as Staff is his replacement. This means no Tabasco sauce for a whole two weeks. Staff is not a bad sort of character at all, not as mean and evil with his cussing words as Sandy, but then again, not as fatherly and protective either.

The OC is tolerating Staff but missing Sandy's extensive bushman skills and combat experience. Staff had not been in the field since promoted from sergeant back in the post-Malaya days. He fumbles his way through the scrub rather than slipping through it. He treats the jungle as an enemy that is trying to break his spirit and places him at risk of an unseen Viet Cong. Sandy taught me that the jungle is a friend that can hide us and give us the advantage. Sandy told me to help old Staffy. I'll do what I can.

At Sandy's request, I have taken the role of wet nurse to the company quartermaster. I help him understand the routines and set up night shifts for the sig sets. All these things just happened when Sandy was around and I now understand how hard Sandy worked to make it all look so simple.

'We will fill up our water bottles tomorrow morning after stand-down and clearing patrol', the OC says to Staff. 'I'd hate to have boys ambushed refilling water at the very same time as we are trying to ambush Charlie.'

Doc, sitting within hearing range shakes his head, 'We should get a chopper to drop water Sir. I don't recommend drinking water from that damn river - ever.'

The OC looks at Doc a moment, realising he is serious, 'The water looks reasonable and we got chlorine tablets Doc, that should do the trick.'

Doc reaches over, takes the OC's map and spreads it in front of him, 'For a start those chlorine tablets that the army claim are the safe maximum amount of chlorine useable, are about three times stronger than anything we can legally put in water back home, remember that chlorine is a poison.'

He then points to the map, following the river to its source, 'There is a heap of chemical spraying going on up there. I don't know what it is but we flew over it that time we were heading to the Nui May Tau mountain area. You can see that it is killing the jungle faster than any poison I have ever known, killing everything. These chemicals don't go away after they kill stuff, they can stay in the ground and on the trees and stones for 50 years or more. It's got to find its way into the water system and down here where we are drinking the shit.'

'They have been spraying the jungle for some years now Doc and we have been drinking the water for years. Every damn platoon takes water direct from the damn creeks and rivers, we couldn't complete our patrols other-wise', the OC replies. 'I don't see any soldiers dropping over dead, do you?'

'Not yet', Doc responds. 'Not yet. But I didn't spend two years in med school for nothing. Like radiation from a nuke bomb, chemicals are bad news. They get at you over the years not when you first absorb them.'

'You dropped out of med school Doc, so you can't call yourself an expert'.

'I got kicked out of med school for having drugs on campus. I didn't drop out', Doc responds. 'I can't tell you your job Sir, and we need water bad, but drink this water and we all pay for it in years to come.'

The OC sits quietly thinking, suddenly he answers. 'Then we will pay Doc. I can't jeopardise the ambush site by getting water flown in. Besides, if what you are telling me is true, it's too fucking late anyway. God only knows where the water back at base comes from', he pauses, 'and don't go talking this up amongst the diggers, we got enough morale problems with the pus eyes as it is.'

I sit drinking my coffee which suddenly tastes different. In my notebook I write in large bold letters...

BIRTHDAY ON TRIBUTARY OF SOGHN RHY. MIGHT BE DRINKING CONTAMINATED WATER. DOC THINKS IT IS SOME SORT OF CHEMICAL POISON. HAPPY BIRTHDAY! YEAH, REAL HAPPY!

Doc squats down beside me, 'How's the book coming Bri? What's the big issue today?'

I look up at Doc, 'Thanks for spoiling my perfect birthday with the water story mate.'

'Birthday, how old?'

'Twenty.' Doc looks at me, surprised by the age, 'I had you figured at about 24 or 25'.

'I had you at 65 you Pommy arsehole. It's the low-stress lifestyle and healthy diet that keeps us looking like this.'

'And the poisoned water my good fellow. Happy birthday anyway, you couldn't ask for a better place to turn 20 could you? Here in a tropical paradise filled with friendly natives.'

'I never knew you went to med school?' A question more than a statement.

Doc smiles, 'Yeah, in a different life long, long ago Brian but I stuffed up big time. Ruined my future and broke me mum and dad's heart.'

'So, why the army Doc?'

'Don't really know for sure, it seemed a good idea at the time. I figured I would become a medical orderly in some base somewhere. Then I find myself in Vietnam. But when it's all over, I'm going back to university. It's still a long way off but I reckon that Whitlam bloke is a shoe-in next election or one after. That means free tertiary education for adults like us. Probably can't ever get back into medicine but I could study law.'

'A Pom in an Australian war, not wise mate, but a Pom with an Australian law degree! Fucking scary.'

'I'm an Aussie with a Pommy accent', Doc replies. He then smiles at me, 'Once I become a lawyer I might even go into politics, the Labor Party. That my young man would be really scary.'

He looks again at my book. 'Can I read some more?'

'It gets a bit personal in places Doc.'

'Sure I understand, but you let me read that bit where you described the tropical thunderstorm, remember, after the 'hot insert', it was bloody good writing Bri! You should write a book.'

He smiles again, 'A real book Brian, the truth about boys and war, tell them how I cried and wanted to quit, I don't mind, young boys need to hear that stuff. No John Wayne heroes out here just young boys who didn't know what the fuck they are really getting into.' Doc stands and wanders back to his night position ready for stand-to.

The shortage of fit and healthy diggers has forced the command group to place the radios on the perimeter along with one of the machine gun locations, this allows soldiers to combine radio and gun watch. I am sharing the 0200 watch with a platoon digger. The night is pitch black with no visibility at all. A hand held to the nose cannot be seen by the naked eye.

The digger's watch has ended and he taps me to let me know he is crawling off to wake the next sentry before heading back to his own hooch to get some shut-eye. He grabs the com cord and slides off into the blackness.

Time passes, too much time. I realise the digger has woken his replacement and then gone straight off to his hooch without ensuring the replacement was properly awake to start his turn on watch. This has placed me in an impossible predicament. I am alone and unable to leave the gun or the radio to wake anybody. I will have to see out the night alone.

Alone and on the perimeter in a hostile jungle.

Anger gradually gives way to fear as each night sound becomes louder and harder to define. Is that rustling a nocturnal jungle rat or a Viet Cong assassin sneaking into the company harbour? That strange smell, is it a jungle cat or the body odour of an Asian enemy living on different food and excreting different smells from his sweat glands?

Suddenly, a distinct sound! It's a movement of bushes from out of the blackness and a grunting sound. Is it a wild boar, a bush pig foraging in the dark? My heart is pounding so loud that I worry an enemy out beyond the perimeter might hear it. The thought of the pig reminds me of the grave we stumbled on when patrolling some weeks back. Pigs had dug up the body of a dead enemy and devoured half of it leaving the rest to decay in the tropical heat. My memory is flooded with the stench of rotting flesh and the amazing sight of the remnants covered in little butterflies. Were they eating it or depositing their eggs in the fertile waste of a human body?

Fear is slowly overtaking logic, testing self-discipline and training.

I peer into the blackness and make out two or three enemy soldiers crawling slowly toward the gun position. Impossible! Imagination running wild that's all. And yet?

Get a grip, get a grip. I keep repeating to myself under my breath, eyes straining to make sense of the blackness in front of me. There is no one to support me, to back up my judgement. If two soldiers are on watch, they calm each other or at least both sense impending danger but this is my call. Alone and scared.

I reach for the claymore clacka. If the Viet Cong are there all I have to do is fire the mine and empty 50 rounds into the jungle. That would bring the rest of the diggers into action and I would not be alone anymore.

Is it just imagination and fear playing tricks on me? I strain my eyes to peer into the blackness at what I think is enemy soldiers crawling slowly toward me. I see something now. Do they have knives clenched in their teeth? Not quite sure.

Suddenly the image becomes clear and I reel back in horror, a gasp escaping my lips. Dead enemy soldiers are crawling toward me, their eyes eaten by animals, maggots devouring their lips and rotten flesh hanging from their arms and shoulders. We had dug up these same bodies earlier. On the left the headless body seems to be searching for its head, the same head that Monkey Spanker had thrown at my feet.

I must not scream and press the claymore clacka. Logic battling with terror.

This is not real, it is a nightmare I tell myself repeatedly but I am wide-awake. How can I have a nightmare when I am not asleep?

I am fucking insane. I have cracked, that's what is happening to me. I cup my trembling hands over my mouth and let out a long silent scream under my breath and look back to where the images were. They have disappeared.

I quietly curl up into the foetal position and repeat the silent scream several times before trying again to gain composure. Discipline, self-discipline and training that's what will get me through this, I whisper angrily. I must control my emotions and feelings or I will go stark raving troppo.

I resume my position behind the machine gun and stoically wait out the darkness. In the morning, I will find out who has stuffed up and left me out here alone. There will be a black eye or broken nose when I find this man. As the first rays of morning cut their way through the canopy, I am no longer fighting my demons and have regained my fascination for the jungle. I have survived the night and am confident there is no enemy out in front of me. I recall Doc's praise for the written description of the storm. I relax my grip on the M60 and take up my pencil. A new entry in my notebook.

Morning light sneaks into the jungle a fraction at a time. Pitch black reluctantly turns to dark grey. Ever so slowly the jungle regains its personality, tree forms appear in silhouette, their detailed gnarly trunks and leaves become more apparent as dark grey sneaks into a misty pale. Sunlight begins its sojourn finding a path through the jungle canopy, dancing off the reflective side of deep green foliage and splintering into chandelier brilliance as it cascades over giant spider webs hanging ready to entrap the sudden buzzing of insects as they awaken for another day's survival. It is a living thing this jungle, I swear it has a personality. I just can't decide if it is a good personality or an evil one.

I allow my eyes to adjust and push back the deep sense of exhaustion from an extended gun watch. I can sense the machine gunner stirring from his light sleep, in a few minutes I will hand over the gun watch for stand-to routine, once the order to stand-down is given. I will seek out the diggers who let me down.

I am relieved on watch and return to my position.

The stand-to is all but completed and the morning clearing patrol is just leaving when the chaos of combat engulfs us. The clearing patrol has walked into an enemy force that is obviously moving to the river to refill their water supplies. A large enemy force.

The remnants of Eleven Platoon and HQ are outnumbered and possibly out-gunned for the first time.

Two soldiers are down and wounded. A wall of automatic fire from the enemy cuts through the foliage around us Australian diggers. Whistles are shrilling amongst orders screamed in a high-pitched Vietnamese voice as the enemy commander swings his forces around to the higher ground and forms an assault line to attack.

'They are using our tactics, high ground to lay on fire and sweep from the right', the OC is yelling. 'Get me some big guns and do it fucking quickly', he screams to the Artillery FO. 'Danger close. As quick as you can get it here. We got NVA.'

Realising what the enemy is planning, the OC quickly screams out to Tiny and Nunger to get the support section onto the flank perimeter. Their extra automatic weapons will help stop the enemy assault.

Although stunned by the sudden violence and deafening crescendo of such a heavy gunfight, I somehow manage to get my act together. Sandy is not here and Staff is probably in a state of shock after having a long break from any combat experience. The extra sense of responsibility keeps my head and heart acting sensibly. I throw one of my bandoliers of M16 magazines over to Nunger, 'You will need these.' I then look for Staff and scream to him, 'Get on with your job and organise the weapons and ammo, I'm on the fucking blower from here on.'

I notice Staff lying still for a moment and wonder if he can do his job. Quickly Staff collects his courage and springs into action, old habits once taught last a lifetime and nobody doubts that Staff was a damn good soldier in his day.

Crawling along the ground remembering the bullet marks left on trees after the night contact months before. Stay low, stay low I tell myself as I scurry across to the two other signallers and grab the zero alpha radio set.

'Four this is niner, what is happening? Over'. I hear the CO calling on the battalion's frequency.

'Niner this is four, wait out to you, zero alpha this is four, contact report. We are in contact with a large enemy force November Victor Alpha. I say again November Victor Alpha, well-armed. Alert Dustoff! We have two down and more could be likely. Over.' I am in charge of my fears now, too busy and too scared to be frightened.

'Four this is zero alpha, that's a copy. Are the friendlies Whisky or Kilo over', came back at him on the radio.

'Whisky you prick, that's why we want Dustoff.'

Artillery rounds are now ripping the air above us and the FO is skilfully guiding them in quickly. There is no time for caution as the enemy is now launching an actual assault on our position. Through the ground cover I can fleetingly see the black shadowy figures standing, running and dropping in a line as they advance on the Australian position. Nunger and the boys are waiting for them. Two machine guns and the extra automatic weapons from support section are cutting down the enemy as they rise to advance.

Nunger is screaming almost hysterically to his support section, 'Short bursts, aim low, short bursts.'

The disciplined soldiers respond as ordered as each automatic weapon only squeezes out two to three rounds at a time. The enemy advance and stunned by the extra fire power, begin to falter. Again Nunger's voice screams out above the gunfire, 'Okay boys M16's to semi, one round one kill, aim your weapon. One round one kill! So help me I will personally shoot the first digger to waste his ammo.'

'Four this is niner, I'm in the air and heading toward you, fill me in. Over', Career Man is calling on the radio. I grab my handset, 'Niner, four, we are taking a direct assault on our flank. The artillery is not getting close enough to break them up. Are there gunships in the area? We need bushranger and fucking quickly. Over.'

'Where is your sunray?' the CO asks.

'On the flank being assaulted. We are stopping their assault but need gunships to get in close enough. Over.'

'Roger, I copy that and am organizing 74 and 73 on the other frequency. 'Your Dustoff is in the air. Have you a pick up Lima Zulu? Over.'

'Roger. We have a clearing four zero meters behind the contact zone but insufficient reserve to secure it. Over'.

'Niner, do your best and try and get sunray to me, no shenanigans son, I want your sunray. Over'.

'Four, out.' I let the handset drop to the ground and looked around for OC. I sight Staff, Doc and two diggers dragging the two wounded soldiers to the rear of the contact. I wave him over. 'We need to use the clearing back there for Dustoff and might need to steal some diggers to secure the area', I scream above the din of gunfire.

Staff yells back, 'No hope of that Brian, too many bad guys out there. I've pulled two out from the actual ambush site to help move the wounded, it's all that we can spare safely.' Staff is staring wild-eyed at me, fear furrowed deep into his facial expression, 'We are outnumbered two to one up front. Can I use you as sig? I've never done a hot Dustoff in my fucking life.'

'I need the OC before I do anything', I yell back, still searching for my company commander.

I can hear Nunger screaming abuse at his machine gunner, 'Short bursts you fucking dick head! Don't melt your barrel or so help me I will shove it up your shit shoot like a hot poker!'

OC suddenly appears beside me screaming and yahooing, half-insane with an adrenalin overdose, 'Nunger and the lads cut the bastards to pieces. Shot the living stuffing out of them as they ran into a wall of automatic fire. I need 10 Nungers, I could win this fucking war with just 10 Nungers.'

I hear loud shrilling whistles in the jungle beyond our perimeter. The enemy commander is clearly rallying his troops for a second assault.

'Sounds like they ain't finished yet', I scream back at OC, who nods.

'Yeah but I know what they are up to, read 'em like a fucking book, simple infantry tactics and I got their metal, we need gunships in close.'

'CO has bushranger on the way, I've also got The Man asking after you.'

The OC is laughing hysterically, 'You're my main man Brian, got the gunships happening already have you? Thanks mate, now you can tell the CO to fuck off, I've got a war to fight.'

I was not doing that again. I picked up the handset and threw it at the OC, 'Fuck you Sir, you tell him. I got a Dustoff coming in.'

The OC stops laughing, 'How bad are they?'

Doc replies, 'One leg wound and one chest wound. The lung ain't punctured but he has lost a shit load of blood'. He licks his lips, says calmly, 'They will live skipper, they will live if we get them out in time.'

The OC looks around again, 'Okay Staff, I got the CO and the gunships, take Brian and a radio to the clearing with some protection from the ambush group and take Doc with his rifle too. Watch out these little bastards don't get on to what we are doing, they might circle around and shoot you up as the Dustoff comes in.'

'We are organised to do just that', Staff replies and motions to me. I grab another sig set and crawl off behind Staff toward the diggers' protecting Doc and the two wounded.

Our small group crawls to the edge of the clearing. I lead and the other four able-bodied diggers carefully drag the two wounded. Two to three-foot-high buffalo grass confront us. My heart sinks at the vista before me, the long grass and surrounding tree-line could be hiding a battalion of NVA. There is no way our small group can clear the area. I flick the radio to the company frequency. I know that an unsecured and indefensible clearing places us in a no-win situation. An enormous weight of responsibility crashes down upon me, its pressure pushing my stomach up into my chest. I depress the talk switch and call for the Dustoff. My voice is slightly squeaky as it passes through trembling lips. As I wait for the pilot's reply, a shiver runs up my spine.

'Hello four bravo, this is Dustoff. Inbound and in a hurry. What is your situation? Over.'

'We have a Lima Zulu but it's very hot'. I respond. 'Are you with bushranger?'

'Roger that, bushranger is on four alpha's push', the pilot replies. 'We are waiting for the artillery to lift and then we are coming in together. Over.'

The artillery bombardment ceases abruptly. For a moment, the world stands still in a strange silence and then small arms fire continues. Suddenly the CO flies overhead in his Bell Bubble, before a call comes through from Dustoff for the dropping of smoke.

I hesitate, there are no gunships to back up the Dustoff. The gunships are going straight for the enemy flank directed by the OC on the other frequency. It is wrong!

Or is it? I look to Staff. 'This is wrong', I scream.

Staff stares skyward then back at the two wounded men. 'Fuck I don't know', he calls back. 'I'm a bloody storeman damn it. I'm not Sandy. I don't know. What do you think?'

Hesitation, uncertainty. Fuck it! I rip a smoke grenade from my web strap, pull the pin and throw it into the clearing. Nothing happens.

'Fucking dick head, I'm just a dick head', I pull the second smoke grenade free, this time taking the tape from the lever before pulling the pin and throwing.

Bright yellow smoke blooms up.

'This is Dustoff, I have yellow. Over'.

'Roger on yellow, but Victor Charlie may be crawling around. To the south of the clearing.' I pause, 'Dustoff be advised it's tricky. Over.'

Again, the gut gnawing feeling of foreboding is upon me. The gunships are swooping down on the other side of the Australian perimeter obviously still under the direction of the OC.

I gather my strength and try as much as I can to speak calmly into the handset. 'Dustoff this is four bravo, I say again the area is hot and unsecured. Your call. Over.'

'Dustoff. Roger.' The pilot responds 'How bad are your boys? Over.'

Clenching my teeth, I suck back on dry lips to stop them trembling. Fuck I wish Sandy was here to call this one. I stare at the pain-riddled wounded digger on the ground beside me, his face pressed into his trembling hands. The other wounded digger is lying on his side curled into a ball, his shirt and trousers covered in claret red blood. Doc is using a blood-soaked finger to draw a large M on the man's cheek.

'Four bravo. Ah… he… ah… they… ah… they need a hospital soon, but ah… oh fuck.' I try to swallow some phlegm down a sand-papered parched throat. 'Ah, Dustoff this Lima Zulu is full of what-ifs and fucking maybes, your call on my warnings. I need these boys in Viper but will back your choice if you go the other way. Over.'

At the control of his chopper Surf has moved beyond a chest full of butter-flies and can feel the sphincter muscle snap tight with fear. The digger on the ground is giving him a clear warning and an honourable exit if he chooses. He hits the intercom button, 'We got a tricky situation boys, fucking tricky, a shit load of trouble down there, but some bad-hurt diggers. Do we go for it?'

After a short pause Beaver answers for the whole crew, 'Your call Surf, we back you all the way. What about you med, you realise what we are flying into?' Surf inquires. The young medical orderly is on his first flight and has no real idea of war, he is scared but probably more excited than gut rotten fearful, he pushes across the talk switch on his headset. 'I'm a medic not a pilot, my job is to look after wounded diggers, you call the flight.'

Surf tries to push some saliva past the dried up knot in his throat, his trembling hand pushes aside his talk piece then reaches for the small water bottle trapped between his thighs and swallows its entire contents in three large gulps. Talk piece back in place he speaks to his crew, 'Well med, you can't look after those boys if we are up here and they are down there.' He eases forward the cyclic, 'bend over and kiss your arses goodbye boys just in case, then hold tight and pray. We got some wounded diggers to look after.'

Whop   Whop   Whop   Whop   Whop

The Huey is coming in over the clearing, still some 50 feet from the ground. Suddenly I see the front cockpit window shatter as a spray of enemy gunfire hits it.

With Surf killed instantly the aircraft tilts suddenly to the left side and flings Beaver into space. His long monkey strap safety line causes him to swing underneath the chopper skid. The co-pilot has no time to regain control of the lurching aircraft which drops like a stone on top of the hapless crewman.

As it smashes to the ground, crazed rotors wobble drunkenly, spinning and slashing at the buffalo grass just a few feet to my front, threatening to fly loose and careen in my direction.

'Dustoff down! Dustoff down!' I call on the radio as I run to the stricken aircraft. The co-pilot is crawling free from the front of the machine. The dazed medic and second crew member are trying to free Beaver from under the broken machine. Suddenly the whole machine bursts into flames. Lapping flames at first but we all know what is about to happen. Three survivors run clear before a mighty 'whoompa' as the avgas explodes. I turn my head and wrap my arm over my face as the heat momentarily envelopes me, my short fringe and eyebrows disappear in a sizzling stench.

Looking up after the explosive heat has passed over me I see the dead pilot still strapped in his seat, already blackened, then I hear the screams and look down at the man trapped under the aircraft. He is on fire and madly flailing his arms around. Suddenly the screams stop and he seems to lie in a ghastly position, arms raised high covered in flames from the avgas.

I cannot imagine a more horrific death. I stagger back from the horror unconcerned about my upright standing position and the rounds snapping around my ears. I fall first to my knees, then realising my vulnerability, fall to my face. I can smell my blackened eyebrows and singed hair. I can smell the burning flesh of the trapped aircrew which adds a sweet smell to the avgas fumes. I have an image of the pig roasted on a spit by some Kiwi's back at the Dat. Everyone had got drunk and forgot to keep turning the pig. The smell of that burning pig seemed inviting at the time. Now I smell burning human beings. Burning because I had called the chopper into a hot LZ without protection.

'Four bravo this is nine where are you? Over.'

The CO is calling for me but somehow I am frozen, cannot speak or even reach for the handset button.

'Four bravo for fuck's sake where are you? Over. Give me a SITREP.'

I fumble the handset to my mouth. 'It's down, the chopper's down, pilot and door man are dead. I killed them.'

There is a long pause before the CO speaks calmly into the radio.

'Four bravo this is niner, your sunray, you did not kill anybody, the enemy did.' There is another long pause, 'Pull yourself together son we need you and we need you now, just take a long deep breath and get a grip on your nerves. Don't let me down soldier. I'll talk you through what we need to do. Over.'

The small Bell chopper flies over the crash site where I lie frozen with fear and horror.

Chudda   Chudda   Chudda   Chudda   Chudda

The loss of the Dustoff chopper causes an amazing reaction in the skies above the D Company battle. Choppers appear from nowhere as if by magic. An American Cobra gunship that has been listening to the battle some distance away immediately diverts from its original mission and comes to assist without orders.

The ammunitions resup chopper buzzes around angrily, as are two other Hueys from God knows where, seeking revenge. One of theirs was down and they want their pound of flesh. Like a swarm of angry wasps, they dart above calling on the radio for a piece of the action. I have lost my cool after witnessing the door gunner's fiery death. I need someone to tell me what to do.

In the sky above, the commanding officer, the career-man, has somehow managed to get things organised again. Giving me orders to get more smoke ready and organising for the ammunition resup chopper to come in with the two spare Hueys covering each flank and spraying the jungle along the clearings edge with their side door guns.

As the ammunition is thrown off, the wounded diggers and the mildly burned Dustoff survivors are thrown or climb on board. I assist the surviving pilot.

'Sorry mate. I'm sorry you boys got hit', I scream to the airman.

'Not your fault, our call. Poor bloody Surf would have landed in there even if you told him not to. It's our job to get you boys back to Viper. So don't feel bad about it.'

My heart leaps back up into my throat, 'That is Surf back in that burnt chopper, Surf Marshall? Oh fuck please don't tell me it is Surf.'

The pilot nods, 'You know him'?

'Yeah.'

The flyer just nods, he understands my pain. He climbs into the chopper. I drop down onto all fours and crawl back to the Delta Command area where I lie flat on the ground as the OC continues with final mop up orders for his platoon commander. Once done he stares at me. 'You look like you just seen a ghost son.'

Tears are forming in my flash burnt eyes, 'Much worse than that skipper, much worse than that.'

MISERY

I SIT BOLT upright, pulse racing. Heart thumping, breathing shallow and fast. I struggle to identify where I am, disorientated by the feeling of a hooch on my head as I sit up. Confused that only one eye will open.

Gradually, I reorientate myself to the surroundings. I am still in the jungles of Vietnam, lying under my one-man hooch in the shallow shell-scrape I had dug to sleep in. I'm no longer able to sling a hammock for fear that I will be hit again by shrapnel from an enemy rocket-propelled grenade.

Since the battle with the NVA the company has gathered its platoon remnants into one fighting force which means I am no longer required to sleep on the perimeter and do gun watch as well as radio watch.

I feel safer. Just a little safer!

I lie back onto my side and reach in the dark for the water bottle I had placed beside me. Feeling for my sweat rag, I pour some water onto it to make it moist and try to wipe the sticky pus from around my eye. The pus has dried hard and glued the left eye shut, wiping is not helping. The sting of burnt eyelids finally forces me to give up. I need a hot water solution to get the sticky slime loose and that will have to wait until morning. My other eye is not so bad. A wipe removes most of the pus material around it. I gently touch my cheeks, still red and sore from the heat of the chopper's avgas explosion, like bad sunburn. A picture of the screaming airman flashes before my eyes and I push back the urge to vomit. My mind slips back to the farm area above Voodoo reef at Cronulla, watching one of my heroes careening down a dangerously sharp wave on an eight foot board. A tear slides from my open eye. My hero is dead and it is my responsibility!

I lie on my back and stare into the blackness with the one eye open. Now I can feel the stinging in my right foot. I am sleeping with GP army boots on, as always, and can almost imagine the tinea eating away at my toes, all five of them, particularly the little toe which has been eaten around and under by the foot rotting disease.

The rough peeling skin on my legs will also start itching soon. As soon as I think of one ailment, the others start playing on my mind, driving me crazy with frustration. The legs are the worst because I can reach down and scratch, the more I scratch, the worse it becomes, the hard lumps then start to break and bleed, soon they will fester.

I will myself not to scream in frustration and anger. Or is it anguish? Control Brian, get a fucking grip. Control. I keep telling myself repeatedly until I seem to somehow pull it all together into one miserable feeling deep inside me.

What has wakened me from fitful sleep is the nightmare of being in a crashing helicopter. The same nightmare for three nights now. This has replaced the horror of dead enemy soldiers crawling through the dark to get me.

Struggling with my sanity now. On the edge of total madness. The recurrent nightmare is dragging me closer and closer to the great abyss from which there will be no return to any form of sanity.

A confusing dream of being trapped, yet also a person trying to free the trapped soldier. Flames slowly covering me and burning me alive. A horrible nightmare which has already visited me too many times.

I mentally revisit the tragedy of five days ago. What could I have done differently? What should I have done? Sandy would not have allowed that Dustoff to come in unprotected and be destroyed. I failed Sandy and failed the two dead airmen. I failed Surf, my adolescent hero. The OC told me and Staff to watch out that the enemy did not try to sneak around to get a shot at the chopper. I had failed the OC also. It was not Staff's fault. He had not let the wounded diggers down. I took the initiative and called the Dustoff in.

Repeatedly I replay the mental tape of what happened. Yes, I did warn them it was hot. Yes, I did warn them that the area was not secure. However, I should have done more. I saw the gunships spraying the enemy in the actual combat site. Sandy would have insisted the gunships spray along the edge of the clearing before the Dustoff tried to land.

Oh God. My guts are tight with the hard knot that is now a daily and nightly part of my life. I pull my spare hooch over my head to block out any glare from the flash of my Zippo lighter and light a Lucky Strike and suck back the smoke. Cupping the cigarette in my hand to hide the glow, I lie on my stomach drawing in the smoke until the last bits burn my fingers. I butt it out in the bottom of my shallow pit.

The pitched battle ended with two D Company soldiers wounded but not critical, and two dead airmen. I am burnt slightly, not unlike bad sunburn, and have no eyebrows or a fringe.

Enemy casualties' numbers are much higher. Eleven bodies were found and many blood trails to indicate more wounded or dead enemy were dragged away.

I have no doubt that the OC has earned himself a medal, probably the Military Cross. No one would argue that the OC was the decisive factor in the battle. He picked the enemy strength and tactics and organised his forces accordingly. He also demonstrated amazing courage under fire, leading from the front as bold men do.

The OC is one of those strange men, who can continually convince himself he will not be killed in battle. Is it fearlessness or insanity? I am inclined to consider it is the second. The OC is often half-crazed and laughing in moments of combat. Yet! If he is crazy, his company is glad he is.

I do not understand how the OC made his decisions in all that chaos, how he knew where to move his support section. But then again I do not know much about the bunker assault we had done earlier. It all seemed a tangle of noise, fear and screaming people and then suddenly it was over.

I bite down hard on my bottom lip to help fight back tears. I can't get it right. I'm no good at this stuff. I just can't keep it together.

Somehow, the OC kept it all together. Wide, wild eyes, crazy screaming and laughter, yet he always got it right, always led from the front.

'He's one of us now', Sandy told me once. 'Sure he was a Duntroon 'two pipper' on his first tour, but he has become one of us. He has got the digger's fever, he is an adrenalin junky and his career is as good as fecked. He won't even make lieutenant colonel I'll bet. They won't like him once he gets shoved in a job back in Canberra somewhere, 'cos he's feckin mad. He's one of us.'

Lying in the blackness, I am also assuming that Surf will get a gong posthumously, giving his life while trying to save others. The poor door gunner will probably get nothing, just a horrible death and half a cremation.

What I do understand is that I am a spent force, scared, exhausted and miserable beyond comprehension. I want out of the war, out of the country and out of the army. How can I look the OC in the face tomorrow and say, 'No more Sir, no more killing and no more pus in my eyes and no more rashes on my legs and back. No more strange dark red lines across my body, no more fucking madness. I quit Sir, I quit right here and now.' After the bunker attack, Doc said this but changed his mind. What will I do?

Tears are now flooding from my open eye. The other eye is glued shut, bulging and now pulsing along with my heartbeat.

The first seminal rays of morning light make it possible for me to see enough with my good eye. I take up the notebook…

> *I want so desperately to quit but know I cannot do that. It takes more courage to be a coward than to just hold it all in and be a conformist digger. I do not have enough courage to confess publicly I am a coward.*

I curl up into the foetal position and scream silently under my breath. Twice, three times, four, I take a deep breath and blow out slowly. Get a grip and get this under control. You will be out of here soon.

I lie silently in my misery until I hear Staff slide along the com cord and gently touch my boots, 'You're on Brian', Staff whispers, and waits to see that I respond before sliding back to HQ in the half dark.

Quietly I rise from my shallow grave, take my M16 and feel for the com cord then slide my hand along the cord as I crawl to my turn on radio picket.

'Nothing. All quiet', whispers Staff.

'Okay', I whisper back.

Staff slides along the cord that leads back to his own night hooch. I am alone now on radio shift. One hour until morning stand-to.

The morning stand-down and health check show there is little left of the once proud fighting force of D Company. The battle has done minimal damage in terms of numbers on the ground. The conjunctivitis has wiped out most of the platoon and the HQ group itself. Even the OC is showing the first signs of the lurgy. The other two platoons are war-weary and covered in prickly heat rashes.

We are defeated this time, not by the North Vietnamese soldiers or Viet Cong. The jungle has beaten us, it sure has beaten me. I feel like a dead man, a pus corpse.

The OC passes the request for evacuation to Jacko and me for encrypting. I try for a while but am almost blind, continually blinking to get the thick pus from my eyes. I give up and just look helplessly at Jacko. I am all but a broken man, no fight or self-discipline left in me.

'Sorry Mate.'

Jacko looks sympathetically back at me, 'Get Doc to put more solution in them eyes before you do some permanent damage Bri', I'll get this done.'

As soon as he finishes the coding, Jacko takes the handset, 'zero alpha this is call sign four, crypto message, zero bravo to copy. Over.'

The misery is too great to bear. It is time to withdraw and lick the wounds.

Grow up Sonny Boy

Thwack   *Thwack*   *Thwack*   *Thwack*   *Thwack*

The monstrous Sikorsky Skycrane passes overhead carrying its load underneath. A huge connex container filled with items of war.

It is heading toward the task force chopper pad which is more like a mini airstrip than a pad. A huge expanse of clear ground large enough to lift half a battalion's troops in one giant slick of Hueys. It is from that pad that Alpha and Delta Company's flew en masse for the hot insertion.

Story of my tour I fuck up everything I do in this man's army.

'Get a feckin load of that', Sandy says to me, watching the Skycrane manoeuvre in the distance. 'Everything the Yanks do is big, ain't it.'

I snap out of my thoughts and look at Sandy, cold beer in hand and looking relaxed after his Rest and Recreation break. I take a cold beer in my own hand and raise it to my mouth.

The cold bitter fluid barely touches the sides of my throat as I swig it straight from the chilled green can. I reach for the second oversized monster beer, which Sandy has already opened for consumption and is holding it out ready for me to take. We sit on the grass, or what is left of the green plant life under foot, on the side of the hill in Delta Company area back at the Dat. This is the same area where the chaplain held his service for the two diggers killed in the bunker assault. Near enough to the Delta boozer and its supply of green death, but far enough away for Sandy and me to have a father and son type chat.

Seasons change in Vietnam just as in any part of the world but somehow I missed the progressions from wet to dry. There seemed to be no spring or autumn, no gradual increase or decrease in daylight hours. I long for home and the Australian landscape, the rugged bushland and suburban gardens of New South Wales. Orange and red grevilleas and yellow wattles blending comfortably with a spattering of introduced European trees and shrubs. Where is the callistemon and the smell of lemon myrtle? Not here. Where are the leaves turning to gold and crimson? Or flowers stretching their petals, enticing butterflies to rest amongst their blooms. Their gentle colours adding to the flashes of reds and greens as flocks of Rosellas soar above over-active honeybirds. Where is the frenzy of nest building activity and the warble of magpies wooing a new mate?

The birds and plants are different to home but the seasonal changes had of course happened here, I guess I just didn't notice. This morning I made an entry in my notebook.

> *Somewhere in the past months, somehow in the grind of war I have lost my sense of wonder, my love of nature and my curiosity about new creatures. I no longer believe in the dignity of man. I have lost my innocent child-like soul. I grieve that loss as one would grieve the loss of a twin brother.*

I have lost self-confidence, I'm a shell of the boy who came to war. I glance at my mentor, 'I let you down Sir. I really stuffed up didn't I?'

Sandy takes a long swig from his own chilled can, lets out a prolonged, 'Ahh', then wipes his lips before responding, 'I suppose ya feel feckin guilty too about the feckin fly boys.'

'You could say that.'

'Feck me dead', Sandy spits out the words. 'I go on some R and R and the feckin lot o'yas jest feckin fall to pieces.' He shakes his head, takes another swig of beer and continues. 'I got the OC crying in his rum because he took the gunships off you and Staffy and let you try and bring in the Dustoff without support. He thinks he is to feckin blame. Next thing it's feckin Staff pissing in my ear about how he failed in his duties and left you to organise the chopper because he was too chicken shit scared and didn't know what to do. So he thinks he is to feckin blame. Finally, I got to put up with your bull-shit.' He pauses, takes a quick swig of beer and continues, 'By the sounds of it, seems to me that between the three of you, you managed to wipe out the entire Australian Air Force.'

Sandy now looks at me with his steel hard eyes, 'Ever stopped to think the pilot knew what risk he was taking? It's war son, we take big risks and sometimes it just turns out shit. Whoever he was, that pilot is a bloody hero. And you son are not to blame for his courage. Him and his crew chose to try and get our boys out, they are bloody heroes son, probably won't get any feckin medals but heroes just the same.'

'Yeah, I keep tellin' myself that, but I reckon you would have handled it differently.'

'Who feckin knows what I woulda done son. You gotta be there at the time. Ya gotta call it as you see it. In a combat situation it is all about instant choices. Ya sum up the surrounds and ya make a call. Even a bad decision is better than no decision.'

'Not funny Sandy, not funny. I froze out there after the chopper went down. I couldn't make any decisions.'

Sandy looks at me for a moment, 'Not funny, you want to hear a good one, a real funny story ya little pip squeak, do ya?' Continuing before I could say yes or no, 'First tour I'm backin' up the Nunger, me scout at the time. We gets hit from the front by God almighty his-self, feck they was even throwing sticks and stones at us, kitchen feckin sinks and all. Me and Nunger manage to crawl behind a brute of a log and I just put me head down and froze solid.' He takes another swig of beer, 'Me gunner cops a round through his feckin face and blows off the back of his head. Half me section is on the ground screamin' at me "whadda we do now Sandy?" I just lay there shitting me pants. Nunger beside me, we're absolutely fecked and shittin' ourselves we are.'

I sit staring at my mentor, my hero. I can't imagine this larger than life soldier hiding behind a log, 'What happened?'

'Platoon sergeant crawls up out of nowhere, shoves his SLR right in me feckin nose and says, pull ya shit t'gether boy or I'll blow the feck out of ya sinuses.'

We sit silently for a while. I can see Sandy reliving the moment in his mind.

'So I snapped out of it and I somehow got the job done, but for that moment I was fecked son. Just like you probably was when the chopper burned. It happens to most of us, that's why we back each other up. We are in this thing together. Someone always backs you up, helps ya to snap out of it.' He coughs to clear his throat, 'That very same contact saw the sergeant get killed and they gave me a Mention In Dispatches for feckin bravery, feckin bravery on the day I froze shit scared, even put me in his job for the rest of our tour. Yeah, we all got bad shit we have to live with son. So snap out of it.' Sandy takes a quick swig on his can, 'I snapped out of it and so will you.'

I recall that the CO had told me to take a deep breath. He had called me on the radio and had said, 'We need you son and we need you now'.

'I suppose the CO snapped me out of it a bit, but I had to be told what to do after that. I just couldn't make any decisions on my own Sandy. I lost it, I ain't sure I can get it back.'

'Grow up sonny boy. Too many of them bullshit John Wayne movies that's your feckin problem. You aren't barely old enough to be feckin potty trained, can't even wipe yer feckin arse properly and yer upset because you don't act and think like a 20 year vet.' He pauses for breath, 'Staffy is singing your praises. The OC says he could not have managed the show without ya. He wants to talk to the Support Company OC to get ya a couple a stripes for ya troubles.'

The wily old CSM takes yet another swig of beer, 'What about you ya feckin dick wipe, ya sits here sayin', "I let me feckin mates down". Why don't you let them be the judge of that, because they sure think the sun shines right out of your tight little shit shoot. You know the Major thinks you were bloody marvellous in that bunker attack, running through a wall of AK rounds to get him and stopping to help a wounded digger. Damn preacher tells me you think you let the Major down. You didn't boy. You are a damn good soldier.'

He shakes his head from side to side, 'Grow up sonny boy, jest grow up. This is war, not feckin John Wayne bullshit. We all just do the feckin best we can with what we got left in our tanks. The main thing is we stick together no matter what, and we never let our mates down, no matter what.'

We sit silently staring over the dust-ridden scenery that the Dat has become.

'This tour of duty ain't over yet so learn from what happened. Not just about how the chopper met with disaster. Think about how you can respond and what little piece of special something you got deep inside ya that you can draw on. Tell yourself now that if there is a next time you will draw on your deep strength and finish the job no matter what. That's what I did. It helps me live with myself! Yeah you heard it right, it helps me live with my feckin self and that feckin oak leaf pinned on my service ribbon. I ain't no hero son but from that day on I took an oath to never let my old sergeant down. Never.'

Sandy stares straight into my eyes, 'Look at me boy, look at me and make a commitment right now that you can draw on your inner reserve when and if you have to. I know that you can but that isn't good enough. You gotta know it, you gotta believe it.'

'I won't let you down Sandy, you or anyone else.'

'Again son, say it again, loud and clear and let it sink into your very guts and soul.'

'I WON'T LET YOU DOWN SANDY!'

'Sir, not Sandy ya dumb pogo, we're in feckin base now ain't we?', the CSM responds sharply, a hint of a smile caressing the corner of his lips.

The conversation is brought to an abrupt halt as Sandy finds a way to rearrange the emotions of the moment. 'Get a load of that will ya', he's looking over toward the task force chopper pad as the Skycrane shoots almost vertically upwards, as no other helicopter could possibly do. 'Feckin Yanks have got a machine for everything ain't they?'

Later that day I scribble a short entry in my notebook.

> *As I stared straight back into Sandy's eyes, I suddenly felt a great weight fall from my psyche. If Sandy believes in me then I can believe in myself.*

> *That giant helicopter became magnificently silhouetted as the tropical sunset ignited the dusty sky. Below it, deep red earth clashed against the rich greens of the nearby vegetation. We watched in silence as the monster flew off, back to Da Nang. I will never forget that moment. Never forget how much I owe Sandy. I will never let him down as long as I live. Never! Never! NEVER will I let him down.*

PART TWO

Bloodshed is the primary tool of war
inflicted upon the guilty and the innocent
With utmost violence

We bathe in its brutality
We worship each victory by counting the dead

Bloodshed the ultimate decision maker
The deity of our cult
The supreme ruler over every warrior

AND POWER CORRUPTS

THE DUST MIXES surreally with the heat haze and the hot dry wind, creating a less than welcome vista for a young visitor to the military compound. It is built on the slight rise outside the ramshackle little village and apart from the small hill this is flat and open country, rice country. Around the village are the remnants of an earthen wall. There appears to be four openings in the old wall, north, south, east and west. The age and dilapidation of the wall indicates that it was probably used for village defence maybe 100 years ago. Inside the western part of the wall grows a thick patch of bamboo which the villagers obviously grow to use as building material and firewood.

Dry paddy buns stretch to one side of the road. On the other, behind the village, heavy machinery from the Australian task force army engineers are destroying natural vegetation in the name of progress.

What fascinates me at first is not the village or the land clearing beside it. It is the actual military compound. More like a prison compound, reminiscent of an old William Holden movie about a German prisoner of war camp. Surely, this is not to be my base for the next nine days as LO sig?

Inside a perimeter of a barbed wire concertina is chain mesh fencing which forms an inner wire of the compound. There is a look-out tower constructed from scaffolding which stands five or six meters high. At the top an ARVN soldier sits behind a stack of sandbags and looks over the surrounding area.

The chain mesh fence is obviously there to detonate any enemy rockets fired toward the compound. A rocket striking the chain mesh would explode on the perimeter rather than allow the rocket to strike any of the not-so-carefully protected buildings.

'It's a great view from up there', Skip says noticing me staring upward. 'You can see right over the village and the land clearing. Why don't you climb up and see for yourself?'

I shake my head, 'Sniper's bait, Skip. If I was a Gook out on that tree line, I could pick off the sentry with the bloody aperture sights on a standard SLR. If I had a decent sniper weapon, I could choose which eyeball to shoot out. Fucked if you will get me up there mate.'

Skip shakes his head laughing, 'Still paranoid and you aren't using dope. I can't get over you Brian. Shake loose, you're with me now, not playing grunt with the battalion you come from.' He points to the pre-fabricated shed on my right. That's home, drop your kit and I will show you around, introduce you to who you want to know.'

I slip my gear onto the empty bunk in the small-prefabricated shed. I take out my notebook and enter my initial observation.

My new temporary home consists of two bunks and three chairs, a folding table with a sig set attached to an outside aerial poled up about 25 feet high. Electric lighting from a nearby generator and a ceiling fan to move the air enough to make life bearable. Empty 105 howitzer ammo boxes are stacked sideways on top of each other to make simple shelving on which Skip has placed a few home luxuries. Shaving cream and talcum powder from his mum back in Sydney, a gold plated biro from his old man and several pages of Salvo note paper for letters to the folks, two green towels, a spare Zippo lighter and about 20 Playboy magazines. I think Skip and Johnno give their right hands a good work out. Playboy magazines seem to be part of their military kit.

Whop   Whop   Whop   Whop   Whop

The ceiling fan spins out its endless tune.

'Luxury, just luxury compared to where I've been lately', I comment to Skip. My mind slips back to yesterday. I was in the jungle with my company only hours ago.

'We need him with us', Sandy had argued angrily with the OC. The OC was somewhat more philosophical. 'The boy did a good job last time and so the task force command want him back. It's only for nine or ten days.'

Sandy looked at me. 'Yer just a lucky bastard that's all', he cussed.

I looked back at Sandy, 'It's the Lucky Strike fags Sandy.'

The OC acknowledged the message from Battalion HQ. He then turned to Sandy, 'They are going to drop in another company sig to replace Brian for the rest of this op.'

Sandy rolled his eyes. 'Another wet nurse job for me I suppose. Took long enough to potty train this bastard', he replied pointing to me. I smiled back at him. I didn't care, I was getting out of the jungle and off to have fun with Skip the young liaison officer with a kit full of dope.

And now here I am, a real bed to sleep in at night and probably the odd joint to share with some cheap whisky. I look at the soldiers in and around the compound. Normally, locally trained militia guard their own villages but these are definitely regular South Vietnamese troops, ARVN.

As I look around the inner perimeter, I can see soldiers manning, or at least sitting in, crudely constructed fire pits. They are not reinforced fighting trenches but sand bagged walls with a bit of a tin or canvas roof slung above to keep the sun off. They clearly need the chainmesh to pre-explode any rockets as a direct hit on the sand bagged defences would blow them apart.

There is casualness about the whole place, it's very different from the insanity of the three days I spent in the American firebase as LO Sig.

The ARVN seem to let it all hang out. This is their country, their life. Born into a war, grew up in it and would most likely die in it. They are not here for a 12 month tour of duty and it shows in a thousand ways.

The centre of the compound is an open space. I can tell from the tyre and track marks that this is where the heavy engineering machinery park each night.

A chopper pad is positioned to one side of an elaborate building with slightly improved sand bagged defences around it. I assume it is the command centre or at least the ARVN commander's hut.

'The engineers, the 'ginger-beers', park the machinery each night and fly home to the Dat. They come out again the next morning with a bunch of diggers from your battalion's anti-tank platoon to provide protection', Skip explains. 'The plan was to build more rice fields for the village to work, but I think they are now clearing it ready for some other type of crop.' He points toward a newly constructed galvanised iron shed, 'The plan includes building a diesel power plant and improving the water storage and pumping facility. I figure the village will be dragged out of the fucking Ming Dynasty and into the 1960s.'

I am impressed, 'Why the whole company-sized ARVN unit?'

'Protect the villagers from reprisal. You can't agree to get all this help without pissing off the Viet Cong, can you? The compound backs up as a safe haven if the Viet Cong attack. The villagers can piss off up here', he sweeps his arm at the ARVN soldiers, 'and they can protect them.'

I look at the defensive set up, 'Protect the villagers, they don't look capable of protecting themselves. I assume they've got TAOR patrols out each day and a few ambush sites going on at night time.'

'Hey, we are talking ARVN not Australian.'

'And our job, you and me?'

'Same as always! Not much less than sweet fuck all, a twice daily SITREP and a MAINTDEM each night to look after what the ginger-beers want. Order in the gear that sort of general bullshit.' He pats me on the shoulder, 'Enjoy the ride, mix with the natives and blow the odd joint. Tomorrow I'll take you for a walk in the village, meet the head honcho.'

The next day finds us wandering casually around the village, carrying M16s by the handgrip. We also wear a simple web belt with a Browning handgun on the right hip and a separate pouch attached over the left hip to hold a few spare magazines of 9 mm and 5.56 ammunition. We are generally acting like tourists.

The huts and buildings are a mix. Some of the older buildings show immaculate detail in their construction, even beautiful carving and engraving in the main wood beams and door surrounds. Others, slightly make-shift but not the scrambled together tin shanties of a refugee or relocation village. This village appears, on the face of it, more like I had imagined a Vietnamese Village to be.

Most huts are the thatched type on posts, a couple of feet above the ground as insurance against the monsoon rains. Some are of solid construction in the old Portuguese or French style, cement or whitewashed mud and straw construction. Once proudly washed walls are now grey and dirty with traces of pink and white. Faded remains of rusty red and blue decorations remain over some doors and windows. Inside buildings, I could see hammocks with children swinging in them like play pens, the smell of little chip fires, the burping noise of kero stoves and the smell of food cooking wafts from some. My nostrils catch a mix of jasmine, fish oils and occasional sweeter smells like frangipani find their way into my senses when I pass by these doors. Strange as it might seem, these aromas add an almost bearable fragrance to the more common stench of pig swill and the kerosene drums which stand in their own puddles of spill. I am captivated by an elderly woman sitting in the doorway eating a bowl of steamed rice with her fingers, occasionally pushing small amounts into the mouth of a tiny child perched on her lap. She doesn't care who I am and seems quite disinterested in why I am here. I get the same reaction from a wrinkled old man. Ugly! His lips and teeth are red with the stains of a lifetime of chewing betel nuts. He squats beside a hut with a pushbike disassembled and scattered in pieces on canvas spread flat on the dirt in front of him. With great care, he is cleaning and oiling every moving part before re-assembling the bicycle that I would say is older than the ancient looking man. Not many young men and woman can be seen. I assume they are in the paddy or possibly out with the Viet Cong. It's a bit freaky not knowing whose side these people are on.

A road to 'somewhere' on one side of the main buildings, and behind the main buildings narrow lanes lead to other buildings, scattered amongst low foliage and the odd banana tree.

Pigs are penned in odd places, their stench is quite strong and chickens seem to wander freely along the narrow lanes or scrape away under the huts. Dogs are everywhere, skinny runt animals that all look overdue for worming. Word is, amongst soldiers back in the Dat, that the locals eat their dogs, particularly at Vietnamese New Year called 'Tet'. These dogs are no sight for hungry eyes and unlikely to be stolen for food by hungry Viet Cong and there are too many for them to be a regular table dish. I pass a sort of box filled with pre-burnt incense or joss sticks and a little statue of Buddha. It must be like a village prayer box or something. I like that idea, it's simple and it sort of fits with the people I am walking amongst.

At one end of the village is a French colonial church with its bell tower damaged and the bell long since missing. Its walls are dirty grey but it still stands solid and proud. It is now used as a meeting room and village school. In front of the church is a water well which seems to be the general meeting place for the older women and men.

'Apparently the last nun left the place years ago after her fellow nuns were raped and murdered on their way to another village to spread the word of God. The Viet Cong don't like the Catholics, can't have two types of brain-washing in any one village', Skip comments. 'Catholics got a foothold back when a Froggy Jesuit missionary arrived in the Asian area. I think his name was de Rhodes. Yeah Alexander de Rhodes, he pushed in around 1620 or 1630. About a hundred years later the boss of what is now Vietnam signed a deal with old King Louis of France. Big mistake that was. The old Froggies were into empire building so a treaty to them was as good as an invitation to take over completely.'

'You seem to know a bit about the history of this country Skip.'

Skip shrugs his shoulders, 'It gets boring out in these jobs, so I read old history books, it kills the time between joints. Anyway, when the French got control, they gave the missionaries the big go-ahead and it spread like wildfire, but the communists are out to piss it off if they can. The nuns cop the blame for French imperialism.'

I am not religious and not a great fan of missionary attitudes about foreign beliefs but neither do I see a need to rape and shoot the messengers. 'You telling me these people have been beat up by colonising nations since the 17th Century?' I quip, 'No wonder old Ho has had a gut-full.'

Skip laughs, 'Ho's ancestors were originally Chinese, they invaded the area way back in time, the Bronze Age. Some tough little Nog name of Trieu Da shoved the locals into the mountains and named the area Nam Viet or land of the Viet people of the south. Trieu of course became the emperor of the country he created. The Chinese have invaded several times over the centuries to claim the land as their own. They even had control of the country for a couple of generations but the descendants of the Nam Viets are a tough little bunch, they just keep coming back at whoever invades them. A hundred years or a thousand, it doesn't seem to matter. It's theirs and they intend to keep it or take it back from any nation who steals it off them.'

'Including us and the Yanks I suppose', I respond as I push open the rusty old gate beside the church and enter an old graveyard. We wander amongst the head stones. Names I cannot read because they are written in Vietnamese, Chinese or French. A large headstone stands prominently at one end.

'Priest', Skip comments. 'Died here back in the thirties. Doesn't say, but you can bet it was malaria. Who would want to be buried in this shit hole?'

I look around me, a hint of past beauty remains, 'It must have been close to paradise back then, before the Japs and the civil war.'

Skip ignores my observation of paradise ruined.

'I suppose you had to do the odd cordon and search of villages with your grunt mates?' He asks.

'No, I ain't had to do a cordon and search. Not yet. I don't think any of us grunts want to really. It usually involves sneaking into the area at night, sitting up with stuff-all sleep and then bolting in on the poor bastards the next morning at first light. Hopefully catch them out with a Viet Cong sprung in bed with his girlfriend or with some arms not yet stashed away.' I shake my head, 'Shit of a job if you ask me. You never know who is Cong and who is just a local trying to mind his own business. I'd rather hack it in thick jungle and believe me Skip, I hate that too.' I pause and look around at the locals, 'At least in the scrub you can shoot any bastard that you come across and assume he's a Cong but in these villages you just can't tell. Smile at you by day, set booby traps by night.'

A small bus trundles down the road and stops where villagers are gathered. A few women alight with dried or smoked fish in baskets and exchange them for red peppers and strange vegetables that I do not recognise. The people then reclaim their position on the bus and a few locals squeeze aboard before it slowly rocks its way down the dusty little road.

'Barter and exchange is the only economy that keeps them alive out here, any main crop or money goes out in tax, if not to the landlords, then the Viet Cong claim their share to help the war effort', Skip comments as he watches the bus disappear.

A young woman walks past us, she lowers her head, eyes hidden under her broad Asian thatched hat. 'Chao anh', Skip calls to the woman. 'Xin chao Uc Dai Loi', she replies in a singing voice as she scurries off. Skip looks at me, 'It's like saying G'day.'

I smile, 'While I am here you can teach me a few words. I don't see many young men, maybe I might have a chance with one of these girls.'

Skip looks around, 'Young men are mostly dead, or conscripted into the ARVN, or the Viet Cong for that matter. Their idea of conscription is to come into a village and take the young boys by force, then brainwash them with Uncle Ho's bullshit out there in the jungle. You won't see too many young women either, they keep off the streets when soldiers are around. Any soldier, any army, any nationality. Rape is still rape regardless of the colour of the soldier's dick.'

I refuse to respond to Skip's last comment and look instead out to the rice paddy, 'Is that a grave headstone out there on one of the buns?'

Skip nods, 'You will see more of them in strange places around the village. The Nogs bury their dead in one place and wait for the corpse to rot down to bones, then they dig the bones up and have a sort of washing ceremony. Then they take the bones to a special place that the family believes is sacred. They build a little mini-temple thing and Bob's your uncle. This is largely a Christian village but there will always be Confucianism, Taoism and Buddhism for the Vietnamese people.'

We walk to a make-shift restaurant. Capitalism is at work in this village and an enterprising villager had realised the Australian ginger-beers enjoy sitting at tables eating home cooked food, even if it is mostly bland.

'Hey Nguyen good to see you today', Skip says in clear English to the uniformed man sitting at a table. 'Meet Brian, he is taking Johnno's place while he has an R and R break.'

Nguyen stands immediately to his feet and holds out his hand for me to shake. 'Pleased to meet you Brian', he says in perfect English. I shake his hand and pull back a chair to sit at the table. Skip does the same and calls out to the villager, come capitalist-restaurant-owner in Vietnamese to bring drinks. 'Hai cam da, Hai cam da.'

The small frail man scurries off and returns with two glasses of orange juice filled with crushed ice. Skip holds up two fingers, 'Hai sup rau', he says, and the man scurries off again. 'Just bland vegetable soup but at least you don't have to worry what meat is in it', Skip comments, before looking across to Nguyen.

'Nguyen here is Hoa, or Chinese-Vietnamese. He went to school in Paris and London. A fucking lawyer would you believe?' I raise an eyebrow. 'Didn't think there was much need for a lawyer in this place', I reply while looking at the Asian man in front of me.

'There isn't. I'm just here in much the same way as you, a liaison officer, but for the Army of the Republic or ARVN as you usually call it. Yes, your friend is partially correct to say that I am Chinese-Vietnamese but what he does not seem to understand is that my family have been in Vietnam since China invaded and ruled the country for nearly a thousand years. China was finally driven out again but my ancestors stayed. And', he says with a cheeky grin on his face, 'Nguyen should be used as my last name not first. My first name is Duc but your Australian friend does not understand our culture as much as he thinks.'

Skip laughs and replies, 'Arrogant son of a bitch ain't he Brian?'

'It is better to be an arrogant son of a bitch than an ignorant son of a bitch my dumb Australian friend', Nguyen responds with a false smile on his lips.

The two men stare across the table at each other. The smiles are those of mutual contempt but both know they have to work together as all soldiers must, therefore soldiers learn tolerance of each other's failings.

I decide to break the ice, 'You speak excellent English.'

Nguyen smiles, 'Did you expect me to talk like - velly solly masta?' He mimics the western idea of Asians unable to pronounce the letter R. 'I speak five languages if you count Mandarin and Cantonese, all properly. My French is possibly much better than my English.'

I raise an eyebrow and dig into my pocket for the trusty notebook. Seeing that I was not pursuing his sarcastic reply the ARVN officer converses with Skip.

I smile and put pen to paper.

> *This educated ARVN officer is early thirties and well bred, it shows in how he carries himself. His shoulders are narrow which accentuates his long slender neck. His face is slightly chubbier than most ARVN soldiers*

indicating greater access to good food and spirits. A somewhat arrogant stare emanates from shining eyes beneath an almost wrinkle free forehead. I do not understand what a man of his breeding is doing in such a basic job within the ARVN.

I snap shut the notebook.

'I'm a bit surprised to meet a Chinese-Vietnamese lawyer in a village. You lot normally run the show as higher ranking officers or own the big hotels and stuff.'

The Asian smiles, 'My family did just that but unfortunately we were on the wrong side of the notorious DMZ when the country was divided north and south. My family had to flee for their lives for fear of reprisal. We took much of our wealth with us, or at least hold most of it in Europe and Hong Kong.' He shakes his head, 'My father assumed the south would win once the Americans became involved and insisted I return from Paris to build an economic empire once America created another South Korea.' Nguyen stares along the road, 'The family wealth can only do so much. We are not connected in the south and have not been in a position of privilege. Therefore, I am now a mere officer, a lieutenant not a colonel.'

'As I said, they have conscription too Brian', Skip cuts in. 'Bit different to ours but they get you just the same.'

'And what do you think of all this 'Vietnamization' stuff we are doing in the village, the "hearts and minds" bullshit?' I ask Nguyen.

'I think I would rather be somewhere else.'

'Paris?'

The Asian looks around him, 'Anywhere but this village. It is not a good place my friend. I worry about these poor people.'

'Looks like they are doing just fine compared to other villages.'

Nguyen looks around at the back of the makeshift restaurant to see who might be listening. He turns back to me, 'These people are not benefiting from your help, the village mayor as you might call him will gain a small benefit. His second cousin the regional commander of this ARVN detachment will gain great benefit through bribery and other local corruption but most is destined for Saigon. This land we sit on is owned by interests in Saigon.'

'What's new?' Skip interrupts. 'You think Australians don't get ripped off by capitalist pigs back home? I should know my old man is one of them, he is living proof that capitalism is another way of describing greed and selfishness. Free enterprise means freedom to plunder from the poor and uneducated. It happens in Australia. It happens all over the world. After my tour of duty, I am going to go home and join the old man, I can live with greed. I like it!'

'No, you don't understand what I am saying, listen to what I am trying to tell you. I don't care who gets rich, it is the way of my family to seek wealth through others labour', The Asian replies. 'These villagers have survived by having what you call a bet each way. They help the Viet Cong when they need to, pay their tax to both the Viet Cong and the South Vietnamese Government. They provide shelter and food to the young men who sneak out at night to try to kill you people. They help the Americans and Australians when they have to. They do not care about communism or capitalism. Many can't read or write, certainly not the English language which is after all, the language of capitalism and wealth. They live a simple life and want to be left to tend their fields.'

I am instantly intrigued by what Nguyen is saying and listen intently as the man continues.

'The village head has done a deal and tells our authorities who are Viet Cong sympathisers in this village. In return, the government puts it on the Australian list for hearts and minds. The village head gets what Americans call a kick back from Saigon, as does his cousin who brings in a company of soldiers to protect the family interest.'

He stops to pick up his teacup and sips the green tea. He then continues with my education.

'Viet Cong will understand villagers not hindering the capitalist forces. They will tolerate some villagers helping or working with the capitalist forces as long as there is compensation in the form of food and tax. However, to betray the local members of the communist party, to send them to their deaths, this will not be tolerated. Eventually, and I think soon, there will be reprisals. These villagers know this and they are afraid, they have to be nice to you Australians and us ARVN because we are in control for now, but they live in fear. These poor souls cannot win no matter what they do. Both sides will punish them.'

Skip looks at the Asian officer, 'They won't take us on mate, too many of us. They would need to launch an all-out assault and this village isn't worth that kind of effort. They won't risk marshalling all their forces to make such an attack. A couple of companies of Brian's grunt mates would be out here in choppers in no time and get at them in one foul swoop. We can rest easy.'

I smile, 'Yeah we could deploy out here pretty quickly and we would catch them in one big op rather than chase the little bastards through the boonies.'

Nguyen smiles at we two Australians, 'We can rest easy, you and me, it is not us who will be punished by the Viet Cong, it is the people in this village. If the Viet Cong let this village go unpunished then other village power brokers will get a similar idea. Power corrupts and absolute power corrupts absolutely. This is a western saying is it not?' He shakes his head, 'These people will pay my friend, and soon, the longer the Viet Cong take to teach this village a lesson the greater the risk that other villages will do the same.'

Still considering Nguyen's words, I notice yet another unusual sight, a finely dressed woman carrying a beautiful little girl in her arms. Of more interest is the little boy waddling along beside her. 'I've never seen that since coming to this country', I say to Skip, while staring at the boy.

'Seen what?'

'A fat child in Vietnam, they are usually all skin and bone.'

'Wife and kids of the village head, or some of them, he has another two boys, both fat.'

'And power corrupts', adds the Chinese-Vietnamese officer, nodding in the direction of the two men following some distance behind the woman with the children. 'You are about to meet the "family", our version of Mafia.'

I have to assert a considerable amount of self-discipline not to burst out laughing at what I see approaching. To laugh at them would be offensive. Two fat men, one of them walking as though he is the emperor with no clothes, oblivious to the fact that he looks ridiculous in the eyes of all who stare. I later write…

> *I could not believe my eyes at first. The ARVN commander is a round lumpy little man with Elvis Presley style chrome rimmed sunglasses propped on a somewhat upturned nose complete with flaring nostrils, a paper-thin moustache and double or triple chin depending upon which angle he holds his head. On top of that pudgy head is a US Marine style peak cap. Under the various chins is a bright yellow scarf, silk probably, neatly arranged to flair out of his open necked shirt as a big golden reminder that he is cock of the roost. His military greens are not just pressed but starched and in his hands, a riding whip. Not a horse for a million miles but obviously he feels the riding whip is a status symbol of some sort.*
>
> *Around his fat waist is a broad belt joined by a large silver buckle, with pistols suspended on each side. On the right side is what appears to be a Colt 45, chromed and with bone handles, slung low in gunslinger fashion and on the left a smaller automatic. I could not identify its origin but it too is chromed. On its handle is a polished pearl shell.*

'Mafia', I whisper back to Nguyen. 'More like a cross between Hop-a-Long Cassidy and Jacky Gleeson.'

Nguyen manages to keep a straight face as the two men approach. He stands to attention and speaks quickly in Vietnamese to the two men, gesturing toward me. Skip has also stood, more casually but as a sign of respect, his eyes darting to me to do the same.

I stand and nod toward the two peacocks. Skip says a few words in Chinese. The officer nods back to Skip who then looks at me, before speaking in a mixture of Chinese and Vietnamese himself.

'The commander wishes to thank you for joining us in the village', Skip now relays to me.

I look at the fat man and nod. Skip continues his interpreter role, 'He requests that we join him and his cousin at his cousin's home for meals as often as we would wish, they have a fine choice of spirits and their cook prepares French food.'

Again, I nod trying hard not to burst into laughter, 'Thank you.'

The fat peacock smiles at me and tips his cap with the riding crop in a gesture better suited to an old British movie. He then speaks to his cousin and they walk off in the same direction as the woman with the children. They all but ignore Nguyen.

Skip leans over and says to me, 'When I arrived here with Johnno last month I told them John was an officer like me, they think you are also. Go along with it and enjoy the ride.' He points in the direction the peacock is walking.

'They live in the big house off to the side over there. Good food, trust me. The commander returns to his troops in the compound each night. We should always strive to make the most of this war Bri', he finishes with a cheeky smile.

We three sit back down. I look at my new friend Nguyen, 'Now you blokes aren't all like that, surely?'

Nguyen smiles, 'I think what you see is similar to what the English call new money. It is an aberration and an insult to the finer class of Vietnam's gentry.'

'So we get a few meals with a French flair, what say we three make the most of that tonight?'

Nguyen looks at me and smiles his calm cultured smile again, 'The two of you, I am not welcome and nor do I wish to be. The soup here is bland and there are the odd exotic meats my friends, but the pho in that house is poisoned with corruption.' He looks around again, 'I do not want any Maoist communist sympathiser in this village to see me enjoying their company. If I must die I would prefer it were quick and painless.'

I look at Nguyen, 'I'm not quite sure if you don't almost like the VC Commies?'

'No. As a member of a wealthy family they are my enemies more than yours. It has nothing to do with liking them. I received my tertiary education in Paris, the birthplace of Marx's Communist Manifesto just as Ho Chi Minh did many years before me. In those days Ho had two different names. He was first Nguyen Tat Thanh and later as a member of the French Communist Party he became Nguyen Ai Quoc wich translates to Nguyen the Patriot. I read some of his early essays under that pseudonym. His actual birth name Is Nguyen Sinh Cung.'

'So you got the same first name as Ho have you?'

'I shall forgive you your ignorance', Nguyen responds. 'It would be too hard to explain the rights to naming and our family lineage system to such an innocently ignorant youth from a distant land. I am Nguyen Van Dong Duc, distantly related to former Prime Minister Pham. He was a friend of Vo Nguyen Giap, the great military leader of North Vietnam's Army. So I am aware of the communist ideals. I studied Marx as all legal and political students in France and England chose to. In fact, I also sat and studied in the great British library where Marx researched and wrote his incomplete Das Kapital but these communists under Ho and Giap are not Marxist they are uneducated poor peasants. Ho uses communism to unite them. He preys upon their ignorance to achieve his nationalist ambitions.' The ARVN officer sits back and stares at the few workers toiling in the paddy. 'I understand the desire of illiterate peasants but I am unwilling to let them follow their cause. It is not the cause of Marx. He was just a philosopher with ideas and concepts. The Viet Cong are following a cause much like Stalin and Mao. Marx would not agree with these despots.' He pauses, and points to the old men and the women toiling in the dry paddy, 'You see my friend, I do not need to be a Marxist to encourage capitalism to mature into a wealth sharing society as my family is already wealthy and privileged. But if I were one of those souls suffering in those fields, then I might be easily tempted to believe the mistruths of Mao's communist doctrine. They are puppets to a more powerful cause than Marxist communism. Let me assure you my friends, this war is not about communism sweeping the world'. He shakes his head, 'There is no silly plot to tumble countries like dominoes until you are fighting Asians in the suburbs of Australia, that is simple propaganda by the Americans and you. Australians believe it because of the Japanese reaching New Guinea in the last big war. This war is about betrayal by the British and Americans after the Japanese were defeated. Ho voluntarily disarmed his soldiers because the Americans and British assured him that Vietnam would be self-ruled.'

The Asian sighs and shakes his head slowly, 'Then they gave the country back to the French. You must understand that the defeated French became Vichy servants of Japan. No greater insult could the Americans and British bestow upon Ho's proud soldiers who fought the Japanese and the Vichy French for all those years. To feed the Japanese army as it marched across Asia the Japanese and Vichy French decimated Vietnams crops and caused a great famine in 1944. More than a million Vietnamese starved to death so that Japan could continue its invasion of Asia.'

The liaison officer sits back and reaches for his cup, takes a slow sip of green tea as he watches my facial reactions. 'Didn't the French catch him once' Skip asks. 'Yes he was arrested by the British in Hong Kong as Nguyen Ai Quoc and the French went there to bring him back here for execution, but he escaped from Hong Kong to China'. 'Escaped?' I ask, 'yes escaped, you see a British lawyer appealed his extradition order and won a retrial on the basis of an administrative error. Ho had to be released. However, a retrial was ordered in three weeks. To gain permanent freedom he tried to escape to Singapore but they sent him straight back to Hong Kong, so he managed to escape on a boat to China. I'm told he used an official British motor launch to get out onto the harbour and wave down a ship headed for China. The French were not happy with the British as you can imagine, had he been returned to

Hanoi and publicly executed, France may have kept control of Vietnam'. He takes another sip of tea, then continues with the original discussion, 'Now the Americans want to create a puppet government here in the south. That is just a new type of imperialism. These people want freedom from imperialism. Communism is not their goal, it is their tool, and it enables them to use China and Russia for arms. Their desire is nationalism not communism. You and your Americans cannot kill that desire, you can only kill some of those who have it. You cannot bomb desire, you can only destroy villages and breed a stronger desire to fight you.'

'What about Ho?' Skip asks in his disinterested manner. 'Kill that son of a bitch and we all go home. We can get him, that's where the Frogs missed out'.

'Ho is old and tired he will be dead soon anyway' Nguyen replied. 'As for Giap, too many wars for too long, he only thinks of winning, not the damage done to his country and its people. Ho is no longer the living, driving force in this war of independence, he is simply the torch light that cannot be extinguished with your bombs. The Name Ho Chi Minh Translates into English as 'Bringer of Light'. This war belongs to his general now, and a new breed of political leadership, not Ho. Generals love power and power corrupts the politics. Communist power, capitalist power, and yes even nationalist power. There is little difference in its ability to corrupt.'

I retrieve the notebook and add a final observation about this new acquaintance...

> *He is an arrogant little prick this Nguyen bloke, but he seems to be the first person I have met who has a handle on this war. Not sure I trust him. But I like the man.*

Hearts and Minds

Whop   Whop   Whop   Whop   Whop

The fan goes round and round. I stare almost in a trance as I imagine a helicopter blade ready to lift me out of this hot hell hole. I try to absorb Skip's latest piece of information.

'Bananas?'

'Yeah, bananas, that's what the ginger-beer said.'

Skip is responding to my somewhat amazed response when he told me that the fields are being cleared to create a banana plantation.

'Apparently, they reckon there is a big future for bananas in this country. The soil is good for the damn things and there is a need to diversify from rice and rubber.'

I sit up in bed and look across at Skip lying on the bed opposite me in the tiny room. The young officer is rolling yet another joint to help him pass the day. Skip's constant habit of smoking dope and wandering around wasting every day in a daze is getting on my nerves. Is it that I am now a little more battle worn and have been forced to a higher level of maturity, or is it that Skip has gradually become a victim of this war in ways not previously considered?

'Have you ever thought of going a whole day without a joint?'

'What for? I might as well cruise through my tour of duty. What's got into you Brian? You used to be a fun guy, that's why I specifically requested

Task Force HQ to get you back when Johnno went on R and R. Now you get serious about everything, even on the odd time you do share a smoke.'

'Last time we met, it was just dope, now I see a pipe. Opium ain't it?'

'Come on Brian. Just giving it a try that's all, I wouldn't get into the shit big time. I'm just trying it in a pipe, that's all. You have me pegged as a future heroin junkie don't you? Well I'm not and I won't be. I'm just giving it a try that's all.'

'Your life mate but I don't want to be around you when you use that shit. A joint now and then is fine. I'll have one with you some nights but not that other shit. Not in front of me. Okay?'

'Okay, okay, don't get your balls in a knot.'

I shake my head and smile back at Skip, 'I'm going down to the restaurant, you coming? I can't spend all my time lying on a bed looking at that fan going around.'

'Nah.'

I grab my M16 and wander out of the building. It is midday, hot and dusty. I have developed a liking for warm green tea and hopefully an enlightening conversation with my new friend Nguyen. I stop halfway down the slope to the village and make a quick entry.

> *I am worried about Skip. He is older than me in years but not life experience. He has grown up with a silver spoon in his mouth. His father is a wealthy business executive who allowed his mother free spending on their only child. He thinks this war is a joke. I have seen enough to know it is no joke at all.*

Skip spent the first 12 years of his life in Hong Kong before returning to Australia to live in a palatial home somewhere on the North Shore of Sydney Harbour. A mummy's boy. Private schooling and an irresponsible attitude that comes when everything is handed to you on a silver platter. He went to university more for fun than career plans. Daddy would look after his career. University was an arts degree, girls and dope, a march in the odd protest rally and a deferment of his national service. Once the army got their hands on him and discovered he spoke Chinese, it was 90 days' officer training and off to Vietnam as an intelligence officer.

What the army seems not to understand is that Skip has never been responsible for anything in his life. The worst thing they could have done to him was send him out as a liaison officer where he is alone, mostly without support and supervision from old hands. Letting a mere boy loose in a country with every corruption and sin readily available is no different to letting a child loose in a toy store.

Ah well, none of my business if the army gets it wrong, at least he can't do much damage in a place like this.

Nguyen is at his usual table on the outdoor restaurant verandah. He smiles as he sees me enter, our friendship is mutual. The last four days we have bonded in conversations about the meaning of life. I find Nguyen arrogant but honest in his values. He is also insightful and the people of this country are increasingly fascinating to me. These peasants are just that, peasants, no different to the serfs of pre- democratic England. I had not imagined what a peasant was until now.

These are the real victims of war. No matter who wins this war they will still be the losers. They toil every day in the field and keep just enough to maintain their existence while the profit goes to unseen faces somewhere in Saigon. However, I am under no illusion as to how things would be under communist rule. They would toil all day and the state would get the spoils instead of the business owners. There would still be unseen faces plundering the wealth of these people's labour. No peasant was better off in communist ruled nations. Chinese and Russian peasants are not exactly enjoying the power of their political masters. Eventually some form of capitalism will take shape, some mix of socialist control and capitalist greed.

My friendship with Nguyen is suddenly tested when the soup he orders for me arrives complete with chicken feet in the bowl.

'Delicious', Nguyen comments. A cheeky smile spreading across his face.

'I keep connecting chicken's feet with chicken shit, they usually go together', I respond, before picking up the hand carved wooden spoon and giving the broth a try. 'Taste is okay.'

The Asian smiles as he chews the flesh from the chicken feet in his own bowl, 'Trust me, my good Australian friend. Have I not introduced you to wonderful exotic foods, each one delicious? Tomorrow I will have them prepare durian as you have never tasted it before.'

'Never tasted it at all. Stinks, that fruit, just stinks like vomit. I can't imagine eating it myself.'

Nguyen's smile disappears, replaced by a mischievous grin and a waving index finger.

'Durian is a special fruit. It is sensual my friend. Its taste has the sweetness of custard. The texture on the tongue is far more tantalizing than the texture of wet flesh between a woman's thighs. Ahh, yes that is durian, tantalizing and one must wait for the fruit to ripen just as one must wait for a woman to reach fullness of body. It is the anticipation that excites the senses. In the mountain villages they watch the fruit grow on the tree but they never pluck it down. Instead they wait and wonder as it fills with juice and flavour. Only when it drops of its own accord do they taste its delight.'

He leans back in his chair and stares skyward, 'The mountain women know and appreciate this anticipation with the same joy as the men. Aha, I tell you my friend, in the mountain villages there is a belief that for every durian that drops a woman's knees are parted.'

I smile, tantalised with this new description of the tropical fruit, 'Okay, okay I'll give it a try, but no more of the weird and wonderful food you are testing me with. That white and black wiggly thing they cooked the other day was almost enough to make me puke.' The banter is jovial and friendly. I had asked Nguyen to introduce me to new tastes and explain a little about the 60 or more different groups who live in the Vietnam region.

'A tree grub my friend, a favoured food in the mountain country and up north where my family had business dealings. And not wiggling as you say, they cooked it before you ate it did they not? Crisp fried, served on a bed of healthy green leaves and a side dish of boiled rice. Don't your indigenous Australians eat grubs? I heard they swallow them alive.'

'Witchetty grubs mainly, or a similar grub from the river gums in the Flinders Ranges down in the south of Australia. Sometimes they eat them raw but usually roasted in hot ashes, or, so I'm told. You see I never ate them. Hell, I never even had an Aboriginal friend until I joined the army. Like most white Australians I never took any interest.'

'You are a poorer person for ignoring them', The Asian responds. 'We also ignore the six or more indigenous groups in what is now called Vietnam. Racism is not exclusively a white-Anglo trait. I am Chinese, twelfth generation in Vietnam but still I am Chinese. My parents insist I am Chinese. Many Vietnamese also insist I am Chinese. I sometimes think that some in this country look upon Chinese as many European cultures look upon Jews.'

'And what do you think, are you Chinese or Vietnamese?'

Nguyen's green eyes suddenly turned steely grey. He stares at me, his face showing no emotion, 'I am a survivor, whatever it takes, whatever I have to be.'

This response leaves me struggling to continue the conversation. Nguyen is skilled at giving answers that do not directly address the question. My thoughts are now diverted to the movement past our table. The same young woman I had seen on arrival is walking past our table so I decide to try a new pick up line taught to me by Skip the night before.

'Dem nay Ban lam gi?'

The young woman stops and looks first at Nguyen, then at me before replying, 'Xin Loi, toi khong di duoc.' She then turns to Nguyen, 'UK Dai Loi chua nhu cut meo', before turning and briskly walking away.

'So what did she say?' I ask Nguyen who is trying desperately not to laugh.

'You said in a somewhat simple way that you want to be with her tonight.'

'Yeah, I guess that is what I said. Skip told me what to say.'

'She said, no!'

'Just no! Seems like many words for just no. What else did she say?'

Nguyen smiles, 'Basically she said you smell like cat shit. I suggest you not bother her again. I don't think your success rate will improve.'

The Asian pauses, then reaches out with his hand to pat me on the knee, 'Don't be too offended my friend, it is as much the food you eat as it is her dislike for foreign soldiers. You Australian and New Zealanders do smell quite different to us, almost as bad as the Americans. Their fatty foods cause a sickly body odour.'

'So we don't exactly smell like durian?'

'Nor do you understand or appreciate the anticipation of waiting for a fruit to truly ripen and fall on its own accord. Always in a hurry you Australians. Depriving yourselves of so much delight.'

The conversation comes to an abrupt halt as we look toward the sound of an approaching motorcycle. A Honda 125, with a young European man at its controls rides past.

'Freelance journalist', Nguyen comments. 'That is bad for this village.'

I ignore the second part of Nguyen's comment and respond to the first, Don't those guys ever get killed riding around the countryside unprotected?

Only occasionally, usually by accident. The Viet Cong want them alive not dead.'

'I thought the European face was enough to make anyone a target.'

Nguyen again smiled his arrogant smile, 'You American and Australian people think the history of this war will be the stories of the helicopter don't you. It will not. It will be the story of the newspaper and the camera.' He sips from his china teacup and continues, 'Ho cannot beat you for air supremacy so he does not try. He lets Chinese pilots fly Russian jets over Hanoi to give his followers some strength to carry the fight, but he knows he cannot beat you that way. He can, and I am sure he will, beat you in the newspapers and on the televisions of the world. These journalists are his friends, not his enemy. He wants them to wander freely around the country. He does not care what they print, say, or photograph. In the final picture the world will see little Vietnam and big America. In Europe already, Ho is winning his war against the Americans. He does not need helicopters. He needs men with cameras.'

I consider this statement, aware of the growing moratorium movement in Australia, 'How come he lets us off the hook? I mean Skip drives around this country in an army Land Rover and never gets shot.'

'The Viet Cong do not need to destroy your friend. He is destroying himself quickly enough', Nguyen replies, while imitating Skip smoking a joint. 'Unlike your childish friend most Australians are good soldiers but you do not understand your enemy. You can fight him and win almost every time but you cannot beat him with weapons.'

'I don't get your drift. Is this more of that desire stuff you talked about, it doesn't wash with me. Sooner or later the Viet Cong will realise we will not go and they will have no choice.'

'You think war is about finding unfriendly faces and killing them before they kill you. That if you kill enough of them they will finally say enough is enough and you can go home the victors.'

'Basically, that's about it.'

Nguyen continues, 'The Viet Cong does not want to fight you. He spends all his time trying to avoid you. It's just that you hunt him down, chase him all over the jungle. If you left him alone he would not bother you. He knows you are just American puppets. Do not be so aggressive in fighting him, just pretend you are America's friend while you avoid too many casualties of your own. When America quits you can then go home with less dead boys breaking their mothers' hearts.'

'Tell that to the boys who died at the battle of Long Tan. Charlie sure wanted to fight us then and got his arse kicked for his troubles but he was the one doing the attacking. You think we like wandering around that jungle, do you? No my friend we hate it but if we leave Charlie alone he trains up and re-supplies his weapons and ammunition and plans his next big attack on us. We like to be the ones who call the shots, that's why we hunt him down and that's why he avoids us. We know what we are doing and I also learned the hard way that we do it better than any other bastards in this war.'

'And what good is that?' The Asian snaps. 'How will one tiny little province in Vietnam change the course of this war. Australia is not fighting this war, it is annoying the Viet Cong in one tiny province. What about the 50 other provinces the Americans can't control. Your friends patrol for nothing. They die for nothing.' Nguyen shakes his head, 'Now you chase him over the provincial borders into Long Kahn and Bien Hoa provinces. Leave him alone, have your agents talk to the Viet Cong and strike a secret deal. He will let you have your Phuc Toi with only a pretence of combat. There is no need for your friends to die in out of control American provinces.'

I can feel the anger welling up inside me. I am not angry with this arrogant Chinese friend. This Asian companion is probably telling the truth. Nguyen looks across at me, his words are softer now, 'My friend, the enemy chooses its targets. He does not try to fight a battle unless he is sure he can win. Yes, he has made mistakes, he foolishly thought he could destroy your Nui Dat base but you found him getting ready in Long Tan. He discovered you have far superior training not just superior weapons. But unlike the Americans he learns from his mistakes. No one is killed without a reason in this war unless by accident, misfortune or by being in the wrong place at the wrong time. Every landmine on a road is there for a specific target. Every bomb exploded in a market or bar has a purpose. It is not random killing. It is calculated murder, terrorist tactics. How many times must I tell you that one cannot beat a terrorist regime with an army. The Japanese did not defeat Ho, they defeated England and France for a short while but not Ho. The French did not defeat Ho. For that matter the Nazis did not defeat France they simply over ran the country but the French continued to fight. The French called them the resistance. Freedom fighters for their nation! That is exactly what the Viet Cong believe they are.' He stops and stares at the people preparing their fields, 'The Americans will not defeat Ho. He is not simply an old man.

Ho has a deep-seated passion, a fanatical passion that cannot be beaten with weapons. Ten years, a hundred years, it does not matter, Ho is timeless a light that burns in the people's soul. His followers will out-last you because they are willing to out-die you. Kill as many as you can, it makes no difference, others will take the place of those you kill.'

'So why are you still here, on our side?'

'Conscription in South Vietnam is a permanent matter, no short affair like your friend Skip', Nguyen responds. 'All my family has slowly disappeared to Hong Kong. They are trying to arrange for me to be smuggled out but they must be careful, if I am caught, I am a deserter. I will be executed.'

We sit silently without further conversation. My mind struggling with the obvious truth just handed brutally to me across the table. They will outlast us because they are willing to out-die us. Participants on both sides of this war are fools.

A little further up the road a helicopter is now lowering into place the large diesel powered generator that came as a gift from the Australians to provide limited electricity to the village. To win their hearts and minds.

I watch as the army engineers skilfully move it into place within the newly constructed generator building. The European journalist is taking photos and talking to an army engineer. I also see Skip standing with them. He must have come out of his hut for a walk. He looks like he is still off his face on ganja.

'A bit of good PR for a change', I say, breaking the silence.

Nguyen looks toward the journalist, 'That is not why he is here my friend, sleep close to your rifle and don't expect to see me in this restaurant from now on. I shall be staying in the compound.'

I stare at Nguyen, 'You think the guy knows something we don't?'

'It is not uncommon for these young European journalists to have contacts within the Viet Cong. I do not know anything my friend but I stay alive by taking no chances and watching for any sign of trouble.'

Nguyen stands, smiles and walks toward the compound. I sit and stare from the verandah, watching the locals go about their tasks. My hand once more reaches for the notebook.

> *I can't help but appreciate a certain elegance in their movements, a certain dignity in their hardship. At another time I would love this place and its smells and sounds, even the unusual foods that Nguyen is introducing me to. I wonder how Australian families would cope with such a life of civil war, poverty and hardship. I am amazed at the resilience of these Vietnamese people. They just endure and keep on enduring. Maybe like Nguyen says, ten years, a hundred, who knows?*
>
> *They will outlast us because they are willing to out-die us.*

More than ever I am glad of my birthright, to be Australian is to be lucky. Australia has made its own luck, sometimes paying dearly for it by playing a secondary role to Great Britain and America.

I remember what the OC told me about this war way back when we stood inside the hospital bunker. We are not here to win a war we are here to protect Australian trade interests, to maintain the Australian capacity to be a lucky country.

As I take one more glance around this village, I wonder if there are more important things than keeping Australia lucky. What about keeping Australia neutral.

I stand and wander back to the compound. Skip and I need to make up the nightly SITREP to radio back to Task Force HQ. The same old lazy daily routine of the liaison officer and his signals operator. A bit of bull about the success of the hearts and minds project, more fuel for the bulldozer and a few trinkets and goodies for the locals.

Tonight we are eating with the village head and his family again. I want to clean up a bit, have a shave and wash under my armpits, some clean greens to wear.

I dislike the fat little cousins who seem to own this village but the chief's wife is so dignified and charming. It is a dignity and charm that overcomes the language barrier. She reminds me of my elder cousin back home in some ways.

The fat little boys are clearly being trained in the art of arrogance but the little china doll has melted my heart, often hiding behind her mother's dress, or peeking around doorways, then giggling and hiding again once I cast my eyes on her. I hope I have a baby daughter one day. Maybe I am just a softy but girls seem so much more fun than boys. It's like comparing fairy floss to mud pies. Besides, I know about boys, I used to be one. Children are children the world over. Even in this horrible war innocence prevails amongst the very young. This sweet little child melts my heart. How I wish one day to have my own china doll to love when I get home. Sugar and fairy floss are much better than skinned knees and footballs.

These visits to the mayor's home are the one true joy of this little posting. They are the only positive experience since arriving in the war. Before leaving for dinner, however, I have time for a catnap so I can sleep off the meal with Nyugen. I strip off my shirt and lay on my bunk looking up at the ceiling fan.

Whop   Whop   Whop   Whop   Whop

And the Dogs were Howling

Two DAYS HAVE passed since the arrival of the young European freelance journalist and the self-imposed restriction to the military compound by Nguyen. I am advised that Johnno will not return to his LO sig position for another three days due to treatment for venereal disease picked up while on R and R.

I met the journalist once at the restaurant. Once was enough. I found the young German to be brash, rude, arrogant and secretive.

On the other hand, his tales of war as seen through the eyes of an impartial observer mesmerised Skip who willingly shared our ganja. The young German has travelled the length of the country of South Vietnam and spent most of his time further north, particularly along the so called demilitarised zone from where most military hostility emanates. He travels back to Europe regularly but makes most of his money selling his photos and stories to mainstream journalists who tend to laze around Saigon. These people discovered it was easier and less risky to buy a story than go out and get it for themselves. Change a few words, put their name on it and they are instant heroes back in Europe, the United States and probably Australia.

'I don't see why you hate the guy', Skip says to me as we sit in our hut preparing the daily SITREP for task force consumption.

'He is a war monger, that's why. The man makes a living out of photographing human misery. He travels around looking for death and destruction just so he can make a buck. If that bastard saw someone bleeding to death he would not render assistance would he? No mate he would try to get a picture of the actual moment the poor bastard died from blood loss. A war monger of the worse kind.'

'What does that make us soldiers then?'

'National servicemen. Or like me, young men serving the democratically elected government of Australia. Even the Viet Cong are fighting for what they believe is their birthright, and the south and the north, it's their civil war damn it. That Kraut is just here to make money. He is a mercenary, a vulture, scavenging on other people's misery. He ain't bringing truth to the world like some official journo, he is selling misery for money. The more horror, the more money.'

I am increasingly frustrated with the young officer with whom I share this job. I had wanted to come out as the LO sig and looked forward to being with the young man with whom I had spent three days back in the American firebase. A break from the endless patrolling with a rifle company and yes, even a few joints of an evening. I expected nothing like this. There are two more days, maybe three, before Johnno, the substantive signal's operator, returns. He can have it.

I am relieved that Nguyen was obviously wrong about the reason the German was in the village. The man stayed two days then moved out that afternoon. Just rode off on his Honda to the next village down the dusty dirt road.

Skip too is feeling the tension that has gradually risen between the two of us. But Skip has only one simple solution to the problem, 'Cool it a little will you Brian, we got a couple more days together. Let's just cool it. I got some good bourbon and lots of ganja. What say we both let our hair down tonight?'

I look at Skip, the little boy in uniform. 'Please play with me', is written in his naive eyes. The tension I feel recedes.

'Sure, why not. Let's get these messages out of the way, later we can wander down for some fresh salad at the chief's house and when we get back I could go a five paper joint. What the fuck, it's a stupid war anyway.'

I sit at the folding table and pick up an encoded message that neither Skip nor I had bothered to decode. Another INTSUM. The damn things come out with regular monotony and rarely hold any useful information but I want to pass the time of day. I grab the codebook and start the task. Above me the fan turns slowly.

Whop   Whop   Whop   Whop   Whop

Darkness is descending over the village so I reach over the table and switch on the light. Decoding is quick when I'm on the job, almost a second language after my time as a command post signaller.

A quick read of the decoded message confirms my view that the intelligence summaries are not much value to me or Skip. One road near Saigon upgraded from blue to red. Enemy movement out of the Long Green area but nothing in this region.

The yellow tobacco tin packed full of ganja sits on the table beside the radio. What the hell. A three-paper joint. One before we go eat French. I pull it open and start slipping Tally Ho papers from their sheath, lick one and stick it to the next, then turn the papers sideways and stick a third across the bottom. Next, I pack a good quantity of resinous brown-green in the middle and roll a thick joint. Twisting the end tight, I stick the other end in my mouth and produce my Zippo. The first joint is gone within a minute or two.

Maybe Skip has the right idea after all. I roll two more, toss one of them to Skip and then layback on my own bunk.

'Pass the booze Skip', I draw back on my next joint, sucking the ganja deep into my lungs and holding my breath for as long as I can before spilling the smoke through my nostrils. A swig of alcohol and I lay my head back on the dirty pillow looking up at the ceiling fan. The ganja is almost pure resinous head, very strong. I am already feeling stoned. The fan mesmerises me. Like a giant rotor blade on a chopper, it draws me into a deep trance.

Whip   Whip   Whop   Whip   Whop
Whoop   Whooop   Whoooop   Whooooop   Whooooooooooo

I snap straight upright in my bed, this is no dream. I am sure I heard two distinct sounds. I had heard them before in Nui Dat. Mortar tubes?

But these are too far away to have been fired from the compound. Suddenly the explosions ring in my ears. We are under attack.

'Get under the bed', I scream to Skip who is now wide awake but dazed. Skip rolls out of bed, still stoned from the dope we had been smoking. He squats on his haunches, feels for the floor with his hands then sinks down slowly on his bottom and finally onto his back. Skip obviously had another joint after I drifted off to sleep. I can see it in his eyes. See it! I realise we had left the light on in our shed.

I'm a dumb prick. I scramble out from under the bed and flick the light off. More distant 'poinks' as two more mortar rounds are fired from beyond the tree line outside the compound.

'More in-coming Skip', I scream out as I dive for my web belt and M16 before sliding back under my bed. I have only a few magazines in the one pouch on the belt. I am trying to clear my head from the residual effects of the two joints I had smoked and the alcohol I drank.

The two mortar rounds explode, closer this time. I scramble out from under the bunk again, grab the radio handset and call the contact to task force. I then fumble around in the dark through my kit to find a bandolier of magazines.

'Skip let's get out of this building for Christ's sake', I call and push the door open as two more distinct 'poinks' can be heard.

I crawl out into the open. There is a poorly constructed fire pit some 20 meters to my front. That will have to do damn it. The next mortar rounds explode. I know from experience that a mortar will take about 15 to 20 seconds to strike after it has been launched from its tube. I look around and realise that no mortar has yet exploded within the compound. The enemy is not as skilled at this game as the Australians are.

'For God's sake Skip get out of the damn building.'

The ARVN soldiers are at last reacting to the attack. The generator that provides electrical lighting has shut down and at last tracer rounds from a 50 cal machine gun are snaking their way to the approximate area of the enemy mortar tubes. Firing from a tripod, the 50 cal can create an enfilade beaten zone over the general area at this range. This will hopefully cause the enemy mortar men to take cover.

I am slightly more confident now that I can see what is happening. The enemy mortars are small, probably only World War II, three-inch tubes maybe, light weight and mobile, able to be carried into position on the backs of troops.

Suddenly an RPG rocket screams out of the tree line and detonates as it hits the chain wire fence on the inner perimeter.

Skip crawls up beside me, 'Where is your weapon?' Skip lies there stoned and confused. I hand him my M16 and point to the fire pit in the distance with its poorly constructed sand bagged walls.

'Crawl over there, on your guts and keep your dumb dick of a head down', I yell to the young officer before turning and crawling back into the building.

Once inside, I fumble in the dark and find Skip's M16. I cannot find any web belt or ammunition; I give up and turn for the radio sitting on the table. Outside another RPG is launched at the compound and again the chain mesh does its job and explodes the heat warhead. I reach up and detach the fitting to the radio aerial, grab the ten-foot aerial from my kit and drag the radio, Skip's M16 and myself clear of the building as I hear two new 'poinks' in the distance. I bury my face in the ground. This one will be close if not right on top of me. The mortar rounds explode. One inside the compound this time near the helipad. Now I make my move, as two more 'poinks' sound in the distance. I have about 20 seconds. With my arms filled with equipment I scramble to my feet and dash for the fire pit, jump in and stare Skip right in the face. Eyeball to eyeball.

'Head down, do what I say', I yell at Skip, who just stares back at me through the semi darkness of the night. He is off his face stoned. I realise he's had a pipe full of opium on top of the joint I passed him. He is confused and bewildered.

Small arms fire is now coming from the tree line and I peer carefully over the sandbags in front of me. The enemy seems to be launching an assault, yet there are not enough of them, I am confused. Amazingly calm but confused just the same. This just isn't right, there's no logic in what is happening.

ARVN mortars are now sending illumination shells into the night sky, lighting up the clear ground between the compound and the tree line. Organised at last, two machine guns are now spraying the area in a pincer and crossfire method. The clearing is now a killing field to any enemy assault.

I am impressed. They are doing a better job of this than the crazy Americans had done back at their firebase. The ARVN are obviously under some decent command and are now responding with controlled fire.

Enemy mortar rounds stop and the battle reduces to small arms fire across the clearing. I squat down and flip out the ten-foot aerial for the 25 set, connect it and try Task Force HQ. Without the extra height of the base aerial I fail to get a response so I flick the dials to the pre-set frequency of the Horse Shoe Fire Support Base and call them. They respond loud and clear.

I now relay through them what is happening. Confirming that ARVN are now in control and the enemy attack on the compound is unlikely to succeed.

I sit back in the small fire pit, still slightly stoned and drunk but okay. I look across at Skip who is still sitting in a daze.

'You're not scared are you? You son of a rich prick. You're stoned off your tits.'

The two of us look at each other for a moment then in unison get the giggles. The giggles turned to laughter, tears running from our eyes and down our cheeks.

'Oh fuck me dead man, I have never been in this shit before', Skip calls out through his tears of laughter. 'Big spook that's for sure, but what a rush.'

Maybe Skip has a point, was it the leftover from the joint that has calmed me? All I know is that throughout the whole experience, for the first time in combat, I was not scared.

The small arms fire has reduced to the odd sporadic shot. ARVN mortars are still providing illumination but it is careful and considered firing now, no waste of ammunition. Again, I am impressed with the ARVN soldiers. These men remained in control of the situation, their NCOs and platoon commanders had organised a solid defence. The enemy would have quickly realised the impossibility of over-running the compound.

'I'm going back to the shack to get this radio hooked back to the base aerial', I call to Skip, then crawl out of the fire pit and move in a crouch position toward the shack. Suddenly my attention is drawn to the village just down the gentle slope from the compound. A building is on fire. The village chief's home.

I now realise what has happened tonight. The enemy assault on the compound was simply a distraction. The real target was exactly what Nguyen had predicted it would be days ago.

I push the 25 set through the door, wrap my bandolier of M16 mags around my shoulder and join the ARVN soldiers moving from the compound toward the village. I know the enemy will not be there. I know they had done what they had come to do and would now be disappearing into the blackness of night.

The village dogs are barking and howling in fear because of the commotion of battle. Each dog's howl sets another dog into action causing a chill to run down my spine. Dogs of war.

There are no villagers in sight, they are cowering in their huts and buildings.

The flickering flames of the building mix with the glow of the parachute flares fired from the mortar tubes to create a surreal, dreamlike world of changing shadows. Each shadow dances around me as I stand staring at the sight on the road by the burning home.

The village chief was brutally murdered. His stomach was cut open and his entrails dragged across the dirt. Beside him lies his wife, her head blown apart by a high velocity round at close range. The young boys, the fat little boys, lie dead on the road also. Each with their head crushed by a rifle butt.

I cannot see the tiny girl. I look around and can only make out a lump of something just away from the bodies, I walk closer.

My body is now tingling all over, my hair alive with electricity, heart thumping heavily against the wall of my chest. A strange crackling sound is rebounding between my ears. The sound seems to be becoming from within my head, not caused by an external source.

In front of me a headless little child, crumpled where she had fallen, as though she has dropped to her feet and just flopped down in a heap. I am screaming to myself under my breath, I do not know what I am saying to myself. My legs are moving me toward the object just on the side of the road. I know what it is and do not want to look but I cannot stop my legs carrying me toward it. I can see my own hand reach out in front of me and touch the tiny head. I seem to be watching myself now as both hands lift the little head and stare at its tiny face. One eye partially open, the little china doll mouth curled back revealing broken teeth on one side.

I feel the sticky blood oozing between my fingers and look down to see a long flap of skin running from the neck toward what was once a shoulder. I realise that the child had been held off the ground by her hair in one hand while the other used a machete. The body cut away from her head has fallen in a crumpled heap on the ground. The head, thrown to the side of the road.

I later write…

The crackling sound inside my head became a high pitch screaming, like a child screaming in pain. Was it this little girl's ghost? I realise it was my own silent screams, probably my own two-year-old child deep within me screaming in horror.

How often is the word 'horror' misused in the English language? How many times have I used the word without understanding its true meaning? The screaming in my ears disappeared and I seemed to float out of my body, above the scene, staring down on myself from outside like a ghostly spirit observing rather than feeling. I watch myself carry the child's head back to its torso, place it down and step back. To one side I can see Skip, crouching down and supporting himself with one hand, vomiting on the dirt. I can see soldiers standing around and hear people yelling in Vietnamese. And the dogs are howling. Oh Jesus, as I write this I can still hear the dogs howling. The dogs of war.

Vengeance, Bitter not Sweet

FIRST LIGHT AND I'm still awake, unable to close my eyes for fear of what I might see in the darkness of my mind. I have discarded my blood stained clothes and twice during the night tried to scrub my hands clean of the child's blood but the sticky sensation will not go away. Now, I resort to using petrol from the ARVN fuel supply, scrubbing until my hands feel raw. Eventually I give up, I might actually be going insane, I try writing something in my notebook.

I am now realising that the sticky sensation is between my ears not my stupid fingers.

Two troops of APCs parked in the village and extra ARVN soldiers move into the area to hunt down the enemy. A small blood trail found on the tree line had the ARVN soldiers chasing the trail on foot while the remainder of the force prepared to climb aboard the APCs.

The bodies were moved to the church-come-schoolhouse. The villagers are not prepared to attend this funeral.

The local carpenter has been press ganged by the ARVN to create simple wooden caskets. Holes are dug suitably deep enough to remove all trace of the atrocity before the tropical heat and flies claim the corpses.

Their grave pits are dug in the old cemetery, alongside the grave of the mysterious French Catholic priest buried back in 1938.

I will not attend the funeral. I cannot face it, nor can I go anywhere near the German photographer who has reappeared in town in the early morning. Photographing the bodies as they lie in the street, then again as they are placed in the makeshift coffins. The girl child's tiny little body placed on top of her mother.

I do not feel simple anger toward the German. It is cold hatred. That and suspicion that he knew what was going to happen all along.

For the first time in my life I want to kill another human being. Being close to the German with a rifle in my hand would be tempting fate. I am seething with a raw cold hatred that is screaming for revenge. How could this happen? The Viet Cong were deliberate in what they had done. Cold blooded calculated butchery. They had acted in revenge against the village head dobbing-in the VC sympathisers.

This was a calculated act of terror. Its purpose is not to punish all in this village. It is to tell all the villagers in the region that this is what will happen if you break your silence. This is the Viet Cong's version of hearts and minds.

In my mind they are not soldiers or even terrorists, they are less than animals. They are scum that need removing from the face of the earth. The young man I had witnessed die in Doc's hands was no longer a young boy. He was scum that had no place on this earth. I want to squeeze a trigger, I want to kill.

The ARVN troops are ready to move out on the APCs. I watch from a distance as the German runs over and talks to an officer. He then climbs into the back of an APC and pokes his head out of the central hatch. His camera at the ready with a large lens attached.

I spit on the ground, turn and walk to the shack. HQ wants hourly SITREPS now. No engineers will be flown back into the area until HQ is satisfied the area is clear of enemy.

Inside the shack I find Skip, pipe in hand. I calmly walk over to him and swing my outstretched hand at the pipe knocking it to the floor then walk over and crush it under my boot. Skip stares back at me. He looks scared. Is he scared of me or scared of the war that has now come to meet him in its dreadful reality? I hope he is scared of both.

I look at Skip's M16 resting against the wall in the corner of the shack. I move over and remove the magazine then cock the weapon. A 5.56 mm round flies clear of the breach, spinning across the room and landing on the duckboard floor. We share the tension and silence which is broken only by the sound of the round rolling under the small table, which supports the signals set, and other military items.

I stare daggers at Skip, shaking my head. This man was walking around stoned with a round in the breach, safety catch on thank God, but dangerous just the same.

The weapon is filthy. I am in the habit of cleaning mine twice daily while in the compound, partly from disciplined training, partly to ease the daily boredom. But Skip has not cleaned his for days.

I sit on my bed and begin disassembling the M16 deciding to fully strip the weapon. I pull down the spring loaded ring holding the two halves of the hand grip and remove them to find thick grime and rust. Fuck! I reach for my kit. I grab my small bottle of gun oil and then assemble the pull-through rod and screw a small wire brush at its end. I do not need to look, the bore will have rust within.

During the night contact, I had thrown Skip my own well serviced M16 and gone back to get Skips. A cold shudder runs down my spine as I realise I had been holding a weapon that would probably have failed me in battle had the enemy actually breached the wire. How could I have allowed myself to be so unprofessional?

Angrily I throw the M16 magazine at the young officer, 'Empty the mag and clean every round one by one. Check the spring before you reload the thing.'

Skip sits silently doing what he is told, stoned yes, but able to follow instructions. His training is in there somewhere!

'You're a fool Skip. Any time now a bit of brass could fly in here to have a poke around and you're stoned', I spit out at the young officer.

'I'm writing your SITREPS and doing your bloody job for you. Now I've got to clean your Gat and I'm pissed off mate, pissed off big time. Officer or not, one wrong word from you and you lose all your fucking teeth.'

Skip starts crying like a child.

I reassemble the M16 and pass it back to the emotionally broken man. 'Mag on and don't put a round up the spout this time', I snap, feeling more like an angry father berating a naughty son than a private telling his officer what to do.

I remembered what Nguyen had said about Skip, 'He will destroy himself soon enough.'

The bastard was right about everything and I hate him too. I move over to the table and scribble an update for HQ then begin encoding the message for sending in the next half hour. Part bullshit, part fact. HQ will never know. The main thing is to keep them away from the place while Skip is in this condition. I am angry and sick in the stomach.

I grab my M16 and walk from the building. I want to find Nguyen. I want to punch him in the face. I want to strike out at something, anything.

I walk to the restaurant looking for Nguyen but there is no one there. The place is shut down and the occupants are hiding behind their simple flapping plastic door. There are no army engineers to spend their MPC illegally.

I sit alone, looking down the road waiting for the little trader and passenger bus to pass as it always does. The little bus moves along the road but does not stop this time. I stare at the occupants peering out from the bus window looking for evidence of what happened the night before. Like drivers passing a road accident back in Australia.

They knew what had happened here last night and by now half the villages in South Vietnam would know.

'Bastards!' I scream. 'Look what we have done to your country and you just sit back and let us do it'. I am convulsing with guilt but blaming the poor innocent civilians. 'How can you let this happen to your country?' I leap from the restaurant, find a stone and throw it at the bus, 'How could you let us destroy your country like this?' My legs feel like jelly so I squat then sit in the middle of the road staring at the back of the bus as it disappears in the distance. 'How could you let us do this to you?'

The street is empty but I can feel eyes peering through doors and windows at me. Me the strange Australian soldier sitting in the middle of the road.

I regain my composure, stand and walk up the street and turn up the short path to the burnt down home that once housed the village chief and his family. Black charred timber and smoke stained walls. I had sat in this building eating meals with these people. I did not particularly like the bastard of a mayor but I would not wish this on any soul.

I walk through the doorway, wander through the ruins looking at each damaged space and finally sit on the floor of the little girl's room. Taking in the surrounds I make the following observations…

Smoke still rising from charred remnants of the family member's lives. No attempt was made to douse the fire and it has burnt itself out. Much of the roof has collapsed inward but the main walls stand firm. The little Confucian prayer area in the corner has been deliberately smashed by the Viet Cong. Ancestors memories are scattered amongst the carnage. I move toward the kitchen area, the bedrooms are beside that. I look into the room where the little girl, the little china doll was put down to rest each night. A cast metal cot, its white paint burnt away, is against the wall, its mattress blackened. I sit down in the little room resting my back against the blackened wall.

I failed these people. I failed the beautiful little china doll. I took my mind off the job. I should have realised immediately the attack on the compound was a diversion. Just maybe I could have collected some ARVN soldiers and got down here in time to protect the children.

So now I just sit in the china doll's room and bawl my eyes out. I am so ashamed.

The day passes slowly. I return to the shack to find Skip missing. I do not care. I could not find Nguyen either. Perhaps Nguyen has gone out with the APCs.

I send one hourly SITREP after another. Only on one occasion has HQ requested to speak to the liaison officer. I respond stating that he is helping to calm the villagers. More lies, who cares? HQ seems satisfied that Skip is doing his country proud.

As I look out through the shack window, I notice the ARVN commander emerge from the ARVN command hut, dressed in his peacock finery as always, but this time heading toward the village with a purpose. Nguyen is with him.

So that's where you've been hiding you smug little bastard. I wonder if that fat-arsed commanding officer would want you near him if he knew that you knew the proverbial crap was going to hit the fan.

In all my time here I have not gone near the ARVN command post, so I have no idea what is happening with the soldiers in the field. I wonder about this ARVN commander. It was his cousin and family that were brutally murdered. What is he thinking right now?

I look down toward the village and notice that Nguyen has gathered at some ARVN troops and they are going door-to-door ordering the terrified villagers onto the streets. The commander is standing in the area where the family had been butchered. In the distance I now see a troop of APCs returning to the village so I grab my M16 and hurry down to the village.

The APCs roar to a halt, their back doors drop and out spills a half platoon of ARVN soldiers. With them are two young men dressed in the traditional black pyjamas, arms tied at the elbows behind their backs and blindfolds over their eyes.

One wounded in the stomach, possibly shrapnel wound, as a gunshot wound would not allow him to walk. They are pushed into the centre of the street, the wounded one falls to his knees then bends forward, resting his head on the ground. He is in great pain. The other stands defiantly, staring blindly through the black rag around his eyes toward the sounds of the crowd that Nguyen has forcefully gathered to witness the occasion.

I feel hatred surging through my body again, fingers tingling, hair electric. These are Viet Cong. They had a role in last night's atrocity.

The ARVN soldiers are milling around me and I am stuck in amongst them staring daggers at the captured enemy. Some are spitting at the prisoners, others yelling their anger in Vietnamese.

The commander is now yelling out to the villagers gathered at the scene. I do not understand the language but I understand clearly what is about to happen. The fat little officer has removed his huge chromed 45 pistol from its holster. The villagers are about to bear witness to an execution.

I do not care, I want these men dead. I want revenge for the poor little girl.

The ARVN commander is yelling frantically now. Suddenly he turns to the standing prisoner and pistol whips him across the face. The man falls to his knees, head facing down, staring through the blind fold in a daze at the ground in front of him. The officer pushes the chromed handgun against the back of the soldier's head and squeezes the trigger.

I flinch as the explosion sends a 45 round from the back of his skull to the front. Obviously a dumb round, it literally blows the man's face off. He falls dead to the ground.

Still I feel only hatred. The soldiers around me are yelling abuse at the dead body. I feel a strange exhilaration, caught up in the moment of crowd madness I scream hysterically, 'That's for the girl you scum! That's for the girl!' My scream mixes with the frenzied screams of the soldiers. I feel almost euphoric, in a daze.

The commanding officer walks over to the wounded man and kicks him in the stomach. The man rolls onto his side screaming in pain. The officer's kick further opens the stomach wound. The crowd of soldiers cheer their commander. Again yelling in what I can only assume is abuse toward the man. We are like a pack of savage dogs egging each other into a maddened frenzy.

The officer spits on the screaming man. The ARVN soldiers are hurling abuse at the wounded man now and the officer again kicks him in the stomach wound. I am now completely absorbed in the frenzy, a mad dog in this pack, I too am screaming abuse.

The officer returns his handgun to its holster, walks up to an ARVN soldier and snatches a M1 Carbine rifle from his hands. He strides over to the wounded enemy prisoner. I wait for the explosion. The execution. Instead, to my amazement, the officer pushes the muzzle of the weapon deep into the stomach wound, twists the rifle and pulls it back out swiftly, carrying half the man's intestines with it. He is disembowelling the man as the Viet Cong had disembowelled his cousin.

Suddenly I sweep back to my senses, my stomach knots, I cannot accept this. Revenge, hatred, an eye for an eye but not this. I consider lifting my weapon to fire a single round into the poor creature to stop the agonizing screams. Nunger's words were ringing in my ears, 'Even a mangy sheep-killing dog deserves to be put out of its pain.' I cannot raise my weapon. I'm transfixed in horror my head screaming inside. What have I become a part of?

I again experience the sensation of floating outside my body, looking down on the scene in front of me. I seem to be staring over at Nguyen shouting at the villagers, doing whatever he was told to do, or whatever he felt he had to do to stay alive long enough to escape this country.

The villagers are standing silently, some trembling with fear. This was the soldier's vengeance not theirs. I am a part of this atrocity. I feel dirty. Vengeance, bitter not sweet. Yet I also feel numb, a comforting sensation of numbness engulfs my body and mind, a cold emotionless sensation. As though nothing matters anymore.

I ease my grip on the M16, push through the crowd of ARVN soldiers and stand over the dying man. Watching coldly as he slips into shock then unconsciousness.

Satisfied the man is at last dead, I step across the corpse and wander back to the signal's hut. I am sitting quietly with pen in hand. A hand that no longer trembles with rage or despair. I feel calm, emotionless and calm, a robot without feeling.

By bearing witness to this atrocity, I have lowered my values to that of the men I hate. It seems I am no better than my enemy is. I am scum. And yet! I don't care.

Technology Insanity

THE TERRAIN IS a mixture of open country and bush. It's what most Australians describe as scrub country. In this terrain, the armies on both sides of the conflict choose to move within the cover of the bush land. The enemy avoids being spotted by air surveillance while at the same time Australian soldiers lurk in the scrub attempting to ambush or capture the enemy as he skirts the open fields.

Tropical heat in this terrain differs from thick jungle. Under the layers of the jungle's canopy, the humidity clings to me like a desperate lover clinging to the person who no longer wants them. In this scrub the sun's rays force their way through the treetops and attack me. I'm burdened with my heavy back pack, radio and weapon. Perspiration evaporates quickly and my body struggles to ward off heat stroke. I'm trying to ration my water. Each hour is a battle between my self-discipline and the relentless fireball above me.

Along with the young liaison officer and the army engineers, I was extracted from the village two days after the terrorist attack. The matter is now completely with the ARVN military. I am happy to be back with my mates. Back to some sort of sanity. Yet I am a changed man, bitter and angry, innocence destroyed, a cold heart pumps within my chest. I like this coldness, this lack of caring, it is a safe place for my soul to hide. If I don't feel,

I can't be hurt, I can't feel guilt, I can't feel shame. I have found a safe place to live with myself. A new strength is surging through my soul.

The company has been patrolling the area for the last nine days, setting ambushes and generally wearing themselves out looking for the elusive enemy. My group are now stationary in a defensive harbour. I am sitting beside a digger from Twelve Platoon, sharing a gun picket while the Delta Company Command Group squat for an extended lunch break and medical check. The whole afternoon is given to Doc to see if he can stem the spread of dysentery that is sweeping through the combined Twelve Platoon and command group. Magic pills and a mixture of a thick white substance that tastes like plaster-of-paris is Doc's main weapon in a battle he is barely winning.

The Bushman Scout

Tran Vo Binh wipes the sweat from his brow, pulls down his Australian army issue trousers and squats over the hole. He feels his stomach contract and the toilet task begins. He opens his picture book for a short read. Tran loves his books, particularly poetry. It reminds him of an earlier time, an innocent time as a boy. Raised in Hue by wealthy civil servants, his father was educated in the same school where history teacher Giap had lectured on the military tactics of Napoleon's early wars. This was long before he moved to Hanoi and disappeared into China to meet with Ho Chi Minh. Tran's beloved father had been an inspired nationalist not a communist, but the many different nationalist organisations in Vietnam at that time were unable to form any cohesive plan or operation against the Vichy French and their Japanese masters. After Trans father's betrayal by a fellow civil servant, the family fled south to Baria hoping to hide with fellow nationalists. The Vichy French police however were able to hunt them down. His father was tortured and executed before Trans very eyes. His two sisters and mother were dragged screaming into the back of a vehicle where they became objects of pleasure for the French. Their naked bodies thrown from the vehicle and shot. Left in their own blood puddles. His young sister Ahn was just 12 years old. Ten year old Tran was dragged away to three years of brutal enslavement as a slop boy in the French barracks. A sexual object to a perverted officer. The beatings he received and the many brutal penetrations with foreign objects damaged his sexual capacity. He could not gain an erection or ejaculate but he could read his poetry and he often took the picture books carried by Australian soldiers. These picture books were not his beloved poetry, these books showed naked American women lying on their backs, legs spread apart waiting for a man to enter them. He loved to look at these American women with their milky white skin. He could not gain an erection but his mind longed for such a milky white skinned woman to lie with him, a gentle woman who would stroke his hair and press his face to her milky white breast. That would never happen for him, no woman, not even a Vietnamese woman could love him because he was a beast. A murderer who could not even satisfy himself as some men do let alone meet a woman's need to produce children. Regardless, Tran is content with his current circumstances and serves with the Australian soldiers as a bushman scout.

The fall of the Japanese gave a brief window of opportunity for Tran to be released from his prison farm before the Americans and British betrayed Ho and handed the country back to the French Government. Tran found his way to the jungle camps of Ho's Viet Minh where Ho refused to accept the return of the French.

Filled with hatred and still just a boy, Tran easily converted to the cause of liberation at any cost, by any method. Tran agreed to be a part of a regional assassination squad. For 10 long years he faithfully moved into villages at night to murder those who opposed the Viet Minh. As squad commander in later years, he began the task of killing those who supported the Americans.

Time wearies even the most bitter hatred and need for vengeance. Tran tired of death and butchery at such close quarters. He tired of hiding in the jungle living on a mix of native bush food and what little stores the local villagers might supply. He questioned his new masters. Were they any better than the French, the Japanese or the Americans? Had he not become as brutal and cruel as those French soldiers who destroyed his family? Tran knew his was a journey to self-destruction. Eventually he would die in this endless war and his death would achieve no more than the many deaths of those he assassinated through those endless years. Tran thought that if he must die he should at least have some luxury along the way.

The piece of paper he held in his belongings for two years was his hope of some comforts before his inevitable death. Dropped in their thousands by American aircraft, the paper had a simple message. Simple words Chou Hoi, Hoi Chan.

If Tran willingly surrendered to the Americans or their friends the Australians. If he agreed to help them fight the Viet Cong as a bushman scout he would be fed, armed, and treated as a hero. Tran was old, very old for his years, tired to the inner core of his soul. He'd had enough of killing. All he wished for was a sudden and painless death and a few comforts beforehand.

Tran understood that the Australians were his best bet. He had heard that many Vietnamese had tried to surrender to the Americans only to be shot while walking in with their hands held high clutching this piece of paper. The Australians he believed were more disciplined and better trained than the Americans. He chose well. After several months of reasonable interrogation and so called re-training, Tran was placed with an Australian rifle company. His role would be to use local knowledge and advise the Australians. Tran often smirked quietly to himself. He would deceive his new masters and only use his local knowledge to avoid any contact with the Viet Cong. He was sick of killing and wished only to live well for as long as possible. Three years later, he is still serving with rifle companies from different Australian battalions.

Tran knows that these foreigners cannot win this war. He knows they will eventually go as the Chinese, French and Japanese invaders have gone. He silently smirks at their feeble attempts to create democracy in a country with thousands of years of village politics and regional masters answering to feudal power structures. His is a nation of many religions and different races, all desperately independent. Above all else, Tran knows that the people of his country are fiercely independent and bend to no other nation. Theirs is a thousand-year history of struggle. These Americans and their Australian puppets a mere 200 years old. They may have many weapons but they do not have patience. They are mere infants at war against experienced elders. No these invading children will not last 15 years of war while the Viet Cong will last 100.

Still, thinks Tran, they feed me well, I am able to enjoy some comforts before my inevitable death, and above all else I am able to access many good picture books to read.

As he flicks through the pages of his picture book of American women, he glances back toward the machine gun position, noticing the signals operator is sitting with the machine gunner. Tran feels uncomfortable with this young boy called Brian. He has that same look in his eyes that Tran had seen in his own as a young boy seeking vengeance. The radio boy is cold and possibly cruel and Tran can sense that this boy hates all Vietnamese just as Tran had hated all French. He is dangerous just as Tran was all those years ago.

I have offered to take over the gun shift while the Twelve Platoon digger strides to the inner circle of the make-shift defensive harbour to seek Doc's magic potion.

I sit with my M16 ready as an automatic weapon while the section gunner nick-named 'Pillows' strips and thoroughly cleans the M60 before reassembling it. As Pillows goes about this most important task, I use a shaving brush to clean dust and grime out of the belt of ammunition. It would not matter how clean the working parts of the machine gun are, if the belt has grime or foreign objects caught in the links the gun would jam just as quickly.

'Where the hell did you get a name like Pillows?' I whisper to the gunner.

'Oh, you ain't heard? You must be the only bloke in the battalion', Pillows responds. 'Back in recruit training at Puckapunyal me and another bloke named Phil got caught in bed together. Normally they bust gays out of the army but the RSM says, "Not you two little wimps, you just staged that bloody bedroom act so you could get out of doing your bloody nasho time. Piss off back to your training and don't try that again". The bastard sent me back to purgatory'. The gunner shakes his head, 'The boys back in the platoon started calling Phil by the name Baxta, you know, backs-ta-the wall or he'll shove his dick up your arse. As for me, well because of the somewhat compromising position I was in when we got sprung, I got called Pillow Biter, Pillows for short.'

I chuckle quietly, 'Serves you right for trying to dodge your national service I suppose.'

'Nah, I wasn't trying to dodge nothing my friend, I really am homosexual, so is bloody Phil. The lads all know the truth, even Sandy and the OC, but you don't have to worry mate I only chase fellow gay guys. You red neck soldier types turn me off sexually so concentrate on cleaning the ammo belt for me. Mind you, I wish Jacko was on my team.'

'He ain't gay like you?'

'Nah, just pretty. You get men like that sometimes. They're just straight men in perfect gay bodies.'

I am no longer interested in Pillows sexual preferences or the belt. My eyes and mind are fixed on Tran, the bushman scout. I do not trust Tran. I decided after the village incident that 'once a Charlie, always a Charlie'.

I have seen first-hand what years of war can do to a man's ethics and values. The Viet Cong have been fighting under one name or another since the Japanese invasion. Death and murder are an unpleasant fact and survival is the driving force. Survival at any cost!

As far as I am concerned, Tran is a murderer, a criminal terrorist just like the animals who butchered the family back in the village. Changing sides does not change values. I wipe my hands on my trousers, trying to remove the sticky sensation that has stayed with me since the child's blood covered my hands back in the village.

Since re-joining the company and finding that Tran is now attached to the HQ group I have become obsessively fixated on the man. I want to kill him. I'm planning his death in cold unfeeling detail, waiting for the possibility of an enemy contact and turning my M16 on the man and squeezing off a short burst. In the heat of battle, no one will notice and the world will be rid of one more murdering terrorist.

I need to wait until an actual contact to carry out this plan, for now, all I can do is watch the man and await my chance.

Tran has just moved beyond the perimeter to use the hastily dug latrine. No shit pit is ever dug within the perimeter, always just out in front of one of the gun positions. Diggers are used to squatting and shitting in full view of the gun watch. It is a safety blanket just in case Charlie wanders along. The digger can retreat, pants around ankles, while the machine gun gives covering fire.

There are no sentries out beyond the three perimeter gun positions, a dangerous decision not to have these forward listening posts but the patrol is short of healthy men. Instead, electronic sensors have been placed about 70 meters to the front of each gun. These devices are sometimes used on tracks leading into ambush sites as early warning that someone, or something, is approaching. They're rarely used as forward sentry warning devices simply because their beeping alarm can be set off by animals walking close by, or even bugs crawling over them.

I am staring at Tran intensely. The bushman scout is squatting down crapping with a stick book in his hands, he's not affected by the trots as we Aussies are, he's just having an afternoon crap, stick book and all.

Between Tran and the machine gun is a claymore mine, its cord snaking back to the detonating clakka resting beside the M60 machine gun. I pick it up and look at Tran. One click and ya a dead Gook, I'm thinking to myself as I peer with an unhealthy hatred toward Tran. A simple squeezing of the clakka would send an electrical charge down the wire to the detonator screwed into the mine. Anything within 50 meters is dead. Seven hundred steel ball bearings would explode outwards in the direction of Tran, many smashing through his body and turning him into liquefied mince meat. One less murdering bastard in the world.

Tran looks up from his book, sensing that I am staring right through him. He smiles at me. I lift the detonating device and point to the claymore mine. Tran looks at the mine and smiles back thinking I am just having a bit of fun. My idea of fun is a little more cruel than a simple gesture. I remove the cord from the clakka to prevent the electrical charge speeding toward the detonator. I know that at this distance Tran will not see the wire is unattached. I smile at Tran, holding the clakka in my right hand and waving with my left, while mouthing silently the words 'bye bye'. With an overly obvious hand motion I press the clakka shut. Click!

Tran leaps skyward in fear, backwards, bum first into the shallow shit pit, legs flailing in the air.

'You low bastard', Pillows says to me in the usual jungle whisper. 'Must have frightened the shit out of the poor bloke'.

'Yeah, that's exactly what it musta done aye?' I respond coldly.

Tran is on his feet, faeces all over his lower body and his pants up around his waist. He's heading toward me with vengeance in his eyes. I stand to my feet, fist ready but hidden behind my hip. Tran moves in to hit but finds himself flying backwards as my hidden fist lashes out, catching the man square on his chin. As he falls to the ground I kick his stomach and grab him by his shirt collar. I pull him to his feet and spit directly into his face.

Stunned, confused and in pain Tran stares at me. He thinks he is staring at a psychopathic killer. Maybe he is, I don't care. Tran is frozen in fear. I feel powerful and calm. Our faces are inches apart, the emotions of hatred and fear confronting each other across a tiny space. Finally I break the spell, letting go of Tran's shirt collar. The Asian scout slinks back to his perimeter position to clean up his mess.

Tran is humiliated, he wants revenge, but he is too old, too tired of war and killings. Tran knows from his own youth that this angry Australian will kill him eventually. He wipes the faeces from his shirt tail. His mind struggling with the simple fact that to survive he has but two choices. Fight or flight.

I sit back down beside the gun and whisper to Pillows, 'Once a Cong, always a Cong.' Pillows looks back at me, 'You got it bad mate, you're one cold evil man if ever I saw one. You make an enemy of that little Nog then expect to be fragged by him if he gets a chance during a fire fight.'

'Not if I frag the bastard first.'

The Machine Gunner

Pillows returns his attention to his weapon, he like all diggers is wary of people like Tran. What he has just witnessed is beyond simple wariness or racism. It was frightening. The digger beside him is a potential psychopath. He makes a mental note to tell Nunger and the CSM in confidence about what happened when he comes off gun shift.

My attention is suddenly focused on more immediate matters as the digger I was replacing returns to the gun position in a hurry and drops beside us on his stomach. 'Stand-to, stand-to', he whispers. Pillows calmly pats the butt of the reassembled M60 and lifts it to his shoulder. Thumb feeling for the safety catch, I quickly reattach the clakka to the claymore cord and scuttle quietly back to the company command area. I drop beside the radio sets, run a quick eye over their frequency settings and ensure each is set to 'squelch'.

'What's the word?' I whisper to Sandy.

'Feckin technology insanity. Got a sensor going bonkers off the number two gun. If it's tellin' us the truth there is a whole feckin battalion out there.'

I raise my eyebrows and reply in a whisper, 'Last night's intelligence report said that about 100 Gooks from Three Battalion and Thirty Three NVA Regiment are in the area.'

Sandy shakes his head, 'Those intelligence wankers don't know shit from sugar.'

'Not an agent report Sandy a bloody SAS intelligence report', I whisper back.

Sandy now raises an eyebrow, 'SAS report, that's a bit feckin different. Now we can worry some. SAS oughta know, they would have personally counted the bastards.'

We lie in silence at stand-to for 20 minutes. The warning beepers have stopped but no chances are taken with such a large number of beeps. If the warning sensor is telling the truth, the enemy force is too large to tackle with this group of sick and sorry diggers.

Finally, the OC decides to take a look. He turns to Sandy, 'Get Nunger and the support section to check it out and send Brian with them for artillery back up.'

I reach over and tug loose the quick release straps on my backpack which is propped ready in the command area. I undo the dipole aerial from the set and let it swing loose, motioning to the other sig operator to bring it down from the trees above. Next, I screw on the whip aerial and look over at the FO's chart. The FO points to the company position then the eight figure grid reference about 1000 meters out from the number two gun. 'Same routine', he whispers to me. I nod back before quickly placing the grid references on my own personal map.

My pulse has increased slightly, the metallic taste of the rush reappears in my dry mouth. I'm scared but ready. I tie the extra bandolier of magazines around my waist and wait for Nunger to give me the sign to move with the section.

Nunger waves to me so I pull the 25 set onto my back, visually check my M16 to make sure the safety catch is on and move in behind the section as we slip silently out of the defensive harbour.

Nunger knows where the sensors are. He also carries a receiver that will tell him when he is getting close to them. He is leading the patrol and Tiny, the acting section commander since Nunger's trouble in Vungers, is right behind him. The gunner is next, another digger, then me. A small patrol, under these circumstances, too small for my comfort but I know that Nunger prefers small numbers in these situations, less people, less noise. More chance of seeing Victor Charlie before he sees us.

Movement is slow, the scrub offers cover but we need to space out quite a bit, placing greater distance between Nunger, the scout and me acting as tail-end Charlie. Despite this lack of thick cover Nunger is not moving from fire position to fire position, tending instead to walk carefully through the scrub with his M16 over-and-under tucked into his shoulder ready to raise and fire. Both of Nunger's eyes are ready to sight along the weapon instead of through the aperture sight, a technique regularly practised on live fire training back in Australia.

Finally, his hand signals a stop. I can just make him out in the distance as he moves to collect the sensor device. He signals for me to come up with the radio. As I slowly move forward, I notice Nunger waving me to the ground, left thumb down.

I am only meters away from Nunger now, so I quickly take up a position in a small piece of dead ground, squeezing into a deep rut caused by some large animal digging many months ago.

Ahead I can see Nunger slowly opening his under-and-over grenade launcher and removing the gold top from its breach. He is slipping in a shotgun canister, slowly, not making any noise. I understand that Nunger is not able to sight and fire while changing his M79 shell so I flick my safety catch to auto and pull my M16 into my shoulder to cover the area in front of Nunger. He looks back at me and nods a quick thanks.

Nunger is now raising a clenched fist in his left hand and tapping his head, signalling for the gun to close up behind him. He has obviously found tracks and is rearranging the patrol into his preferred tracking formation. He looks at me, imitates he has a radio handset in his hand, runs his finger across his throat then stands slowly and moves carefully forward. I understand the hand signal, no radio report at this stage. I am to keep off the air. My thumb returns the safety catch to semi, then safe.

The tension is at full intensity now. Nunger is moving slowly, his left hand gripping the trigger of the under-and-over and his right hand on the M16 trigger. He is picking out his next fire position, moving, propping and searching his arc carefully, then again searching the ground in front for more signs.

The gunner is following. He has already dropped his bipod legs ready to hit the ground firing. I am not at the rear but behind Tiny. Nunger wants my M16 close to the front to maximise automatic gun fire if needed. Last of all comes a rifleman.

The hunt is on, the fear, the excitement. I have developed a love/hate relationship with the rush of adrenalin surging through my veins.

'Four minor this is four, what's happening out there? Over.' The radio handset barks loudly in my ear. I prop and hit the talk button, whispering quietly to the company call sign. 'Four, this is four minor, we are tracking, request radio silence. Out.'

The patrol moves down into a slight gully filled with clusters of bamboo amongst tropical undergrowth and a slight jungle canopy. The heightened awareness caused by the adrenalin surge allows the gully's musky stench to assault my nostrils. The death and decay of damp rotting leaves and fallen branches reminds my sub-conscious that I too am treading perilously close to my own mortality.

Ten minutes turns to twenty.

We have followed the sign for some distance now and I am beginning to worry about the OC and Sandy back at the harbour. It is not good to hold radio silence this long, not under current circumstances. The OC will be imagining all sorts of things could be happening to the small patrol. Finally, Nunger calls off the track. He leads us back some 50 meters in the direction we had come from and signals us to set up a mini defensive position.

I move in close, 'What is going on?'

Nunger looks back at me, 'I made six of them, carrying heavy loads, probably porters bringing ammunition and supplies in to the NVA unit.'

'NVA?' I respond. 'SAS boys say there are about 100 of the fuckers in this bit of jungle.'

'Judging by some old sign, the place has had a large group of NVA in the area, you can tell by the footprint left by their issue boots. Those prints are a couple or three days old. The porters are fresh. Not 100 just six little Nogs with heavy weights to carry, they must have set the sensors off. Main thing is they are moving in almost the opposite direction to the company's general line of advance.'

I look at Nunger, 'So let's get after the little scum. I'll get the OC to prime the boys.'

'Like hell you will', Nunger replies in his jungle whisper. 'The last thing I want to do today is chase up some Noggy porters. I got a bad gut feelin' about this one mate. I'm alive because I listen to my guts tellin' me to back off. I intend to let it lie.'

Nunger's response surprises, if not shocks me!

'Those porters are carrying ammo that will probably be chucked at us in the near future. Let's get the scum before they get us.'

Nunger looks agitated, 'No, stuff you. Damn Turkey, we have only half a company left out here that's fit enough for a firefight. Most of us have shit ourselves empty, we ain't in no condition to be chasing these bastards. Have you already forgotten what happened last time we hit NVA?' Nunger looks drawn and scared, 'Shit man they were charging right at us. I saw my rounds cutting through some of them, saw bits of flesh and blood getting ripped off their bodies but they still kept coming, like they were on some sort of pain killer drug or something. You were with that chopper that got itself shot down but I was there right in front of the little buggers. They ain't natural, they got special drugs, maybe they just got evil spirits. You can't mess with no evil spirits man.' Nunger looks nervously around the group, 'We let 'em go and we don't say jack shit to the OC.'

I lift the handset to my ear, 'Four, this is four minor. Over.' I look back at Nunger.

'No drugs Nunger, no spirits, just evil and I want that scum dead mate, as dead as I can make 'em.'

Nunger is staring daggers at me, 'I don't know what happened to you Turkey but you sure have turned mean since you went off for that two-week trip. But I got a bad gut feelin' mate', Nunger continues. 'Whatever poison you got in your head needs to be balanced against my bad gut feelin'. You are thinking like a mad man. I am thinking like a digger on his second tour of this fucking war. Trust me! We need to let this one go by us.'

The radio barks back me, 'Four minor this is four, what tracks have you found? Over.'

Nunger was now sneering at me, 'You think killin' six Gooks is goin' to change the war?' He pleads, 'We kill them six and we get a whole battalion of NVA coming down on us. Them old tracks say big numbers of NVA and my gut feelin' tells me this is true.'

I pause to think about Nunger's statement. Think about what the OC had said way back at the underground hospital and remember what Nguyen had said to me over chicken feet and broth. What is happening to me? Does Nunger think my mind is poison? Am I becoming a callous killing machine?

I press the talk switch, 'Pigs, I say again, pigs. We followed up a bunch of pigs. Over.'

There is a long pause before the radio crackles back into life, 'Four minor this is four, roger that. You had us worried after the sensor readings. Over.' It is Sandy talking on the radio now.

I stare at Nunger and raise my handset to respond to Sandy's call. Sandy knows Nunger well enough to know he wouldn't be fooled into tracking pig sign. Yet Sandy is not letting on. The wise old owl is allowing us a second chance to think about our story. I know that Sandy will protect Nunger. So will I. I press the talk button, 'This is four minor. You know how it is with these things. Technology insanity and human failings. Just pigs. Out.'

Apart from Sandy, I see Nunger as my supportive mentor. Later that day I make a short entry in my notebook …

Nunger is somehow lesser in my eyes after today's incident. Yet somehow, he is also more real as a human being. Scared and superstitious, tired and mentally exhausted just as I am. Just as we all are.

Safe Behind a Wire

Two more days have passed and I am very aware that the company is patrolling in almost the opposite direction to that of the enemy.

For most it is the same routine and tension, for Nunger's support section and me the threat of contact is reduced. Sandy has said nothing to Nunger or me. No questions mean no answers and Sandy obviously feels it's better left that way.

The Company Commander

The OC is concerning himself with the state of his fighting force. Yes, they are still on their feet but any major confrontation with a large NVA force will find them wanting. Too many of his soldiers have suffered bowel problems, it is possibly food poisoning from foul rations or just bad luck. He wonders about what Doc said concerning the use the water captured from streams and creeks in this country. That is a military risk management decision as far as he is concerned, he has a job to do, orders to follow. Now, however, his soldiers are barely fit enough to maintain the search patrol. To drop packs and enter into a combat situation would sap what little fitness is left in them. Military intelligence reports suggested NVA are in the area in large numbers and the OC is becoming increasingly concerned about his company's defence capability, not aggression. He calls Jacko to him and gives new patrol orders to his platoon commanders.

To better equip the force to withstand any significant contact with the enemy, the OC has split the company into two fighting units. Ten and Twelve Platoon join and the Company Command Group is travelling with Eleven Platoon. Both forces patrol only 200 meters apart on the same line of advance. During a short break, I make a quick entry in his notebook.

The country we are traversing is more open which has allowed the front section of the group I have been travelling with to move in arrow head formation, with the two remaining sections two abreast. The command group behind is also two abreast. I have only seen this patrol formation on one other occasion since I joined the rifle company and that was when patrolling through the Courtney rubber plantation. The formation allows greater coverage of an area and immediate section strength firepower to the front if there is enemy contact, but exposes the flanking soldiers in the forward section to greater risk and tensions not dissimilar to the forward scout. Concentration is intense. We also have to get the navigation spot-on. No fuck ups. So the sigs and me better not make any mistakes decoding the grid references. That could cause a fatal clash of patrols.

The closeness of the company's two large fighting units means great care with navigation is necessary to ensure we do not accidentally patrol off-bearing and bump into each other. While Dutch takes over the zero alpha network, Jacko and I keep busy relaying messages in code from each group, continually exchanging information on progress and terrain. A regular stop to exchange pace counts and location estimates with platoon commanders and section commanders is now the standard procedure.

Each NCO and officer now reports their opinion on where they are by six figure reference. These are averaged and compared with the OC and FO's average. This painfully slow process ensures both patrol groups do not clash and shoot at each other, mistakenly thinking they are in contact with the enemy.

The OC developed this fastidiousness early in the battalion's tour of duty. He insists on its use after about day four on any operation. No one small group is responsible for navigation. Men get tired, men make mistakes. Professionals also make allowances for men's fallibility. The OC is a professional.

The day's routine is ending and I feel relieved to see the hand signal coming along the line indicating a reconnaissance or 'recce'. The forward section will now move out with the platoon commander and identify a night harbour.

The rest of the group squats, no smokes allowed. The harbour drill is like all the drills grunts practise endlessly. Section, platoon, company or anything in between. Once the harbour signal comes, soldiers respond with robot-like action. No different to drilling a Trooping of the Colours on a parade ground in that everyone knows exactly what to do and in what order. Soon the group will re-form into a single file and make a deceptive patrolling manoeuvre that will bring us in an arc to face back toward the direction we have come from. We form our initial harbour position with a machine gun placed to cover back along our former patrol line in case enemy is following our trail.

Next, the long silence, listening for enemy who may be in the area before commencing sentry and general harbour routine, ready for the last light stand-to. The perimeter tightened, with more careful strategic placement of the machine guns and the soldiers, buddy system commences, as weapons are cleaned, light meals prepared and the shallow fighting pits are dug.

This routine is performed this afternoon with its regular drill-like precision and I am now busy decoding a message from battalion operations at the fire support base. I pass the message to the OC and smile. The OC looks back at me, reads the message then raises his eyebrows before smiling back and taking his pen to scribble a response for me to encode and relay back to HQ.

First-hand information is one of the many privileges I have as a company signals operator. I know it and often feel humbled by my fellow grunts out here in the sharp end. From my position on the ground, I can just see to the outer perimeter area through the foliage. Not more than 15 meters away are the riflemen, scouts and gunners who form a protective circle around those of us in the command group. These few meters may as well be 20 kilometres in terms of the war they are involved in, compared to my war.

For them it is a daily grind of patrolling and tension, while I follow in comparative safety.

The enemy have cut down two signal operators. One, my friend, is dead and the other, a platoon signaller was wounded while squatting beside his platoon commander to allow him to talk on the radio. Both cases were sheer bad luck. The game of chance had gone against all odds for them. To the grunts in the field, the odds of death and injury are much greater than mine and I am in quiet awe of these men, particularly the scouts and gunners.

The additional risk is compounded by additional tasks. Perimeter gun shift at night is more intense than the radio watch and in extreme circumstance is doubled up with two soldiers, whereas usually only one soldier does radio shift in the centre. This means more rest for the HQ group. In all my time with the company I have not been called on to do an all-night ambush or a morning clearing patrol. I have not fired a single round from my weapon in combat. I have not at any time during my few contact experiences been directly targeted by an enemy. I have not had to perform the ghastly task of exhuming graves. I have watched in silent horror but have not had to handle the decomposing corpses.

My short patrols with Nunger and the support section are tense but are for a specific short purpose such as LZ recce's or water resups. The most dangerous short patrols for me are the follow-up tracker jobs to look for new signs or verify if an animal and not a human has caused the tracks. These are short and so far safe, with the one exception of the ambush on my first-ever section patrol. Very different to the half day slog that rifle sections endure up front day in and day out.

Other privileges are bestowed on me and the HQ group, we can talk more freely from within the inner perimeter, quiet whispering that carries only a few meters is acceptable inside the circle. But for those on the outer perimeter that few short meters of sound carries outward into the unknown. Their discussions are fewer and barely more than a tiny whisper. Each and every one of them falls into an introverted world of semi-silence for the endless days of patrolling. It's like a self-imposed and self-disciplined autism. Their minds concentrate only on the immediate surroundings and its potential for danger. I wonder what impact it will have on their behaviour after a year of living this way. How will they cope with the everyday simple banter and gossip back home in Australia?

For the grunts in the field, the company commander and the company sergeant major are mystery men, sometimes disliked or feared but always regarded with a certain respect. For me they are the OC and Sandy. I know them as people, I have buddied up with them, shared coffee and rations, am privy to their strengths and weaknesses, likes and dislikes, family worries, attitudes toward this war and all who fight in it.

I often carry personal knowledge that cannot be shared. My view of the war, of each day's patrols and every decision made by the company commander, differs greatly from those men just 15 meters away. I know which orders emanate from the OC and which orders come from HQ. I am privy at times to the logic and discussions about those decisions. The boys, the grunts, only know what little is told by hushed whisper or hand signal yet they carry on regardless and this is what I respect most in these men. There are many forms of trust and courage.

Darkness has descended on the night harbour but my task is incomplete. Huddled over a small penlight torch at the bottom of the command shell-scrape, I encode the OC's response to the message received earlier. I am a happy man at this time. I quickly scribble a few short words in my notebook...

The company is to be collected by APC's the following morning and will be transported to the battalion fire support base. We will spend three weeks guarding the base while Support Company gathers its assault pioneers, trackers and some of its signallers and mortar men into a makeshift rifle company. They will then head off on a patrolling operation to earn their Infantry Combat Badge.

The following day the company moves into the fire support base and wave good-bye to the Support Company diggers as they pass out of the wire to play soldier. Compared to the silence of patrol harbours, fire support bases are loud, noisy and very dusty places, which most rifle company diggers find hard to get accustomed to. A fire support base is in essence a mini Nui Dat.

I feel safe in this dust bowl. Rows of barbed wire stretch around the perimeter with claymore mines strategically placed to repel any enemy assault. Within the wire are artillery howitzers and mortar tubes, tucked behind earth buns for added protection. APCs move constantly in and around the base kicking up dust and mixing it with black engine fumes. The dusty helipad is kept busy most of the day. The command chopper goes on regular runs. Hueys deliver mail, stores and odd bods. The twin rotor Chinooks hover over the area from time to time delivering large water bladders suspended under their airframes. In addition to the commanding officer's personal bunker, two command centres are dug into the ground 'bunker style' and are able to withstand all but a direct hit from a heavy mortar shell. In one bunker, the operations centre, in the other, the administration centre. Placed strategically around the perimeter inside the wire barricades are fighting pits. These are mini two-man bunkers each manned by soldiers who sleep underground in the section protected by overhead sand bagging. Main gun pits connect to the command centre by phone.

No attempt is made to hide noise. It is impossible. Helos are constantly coming and going. APCs move out to pick up or deliver soldiers from one part of the country to another. From time to time, artillery or the two active mortar tubes, perform fire missions.

This Australian firebase is so different in its professionalism to the American base I had visited for three days . TAOR patrols are constantly moving through the nearby areas to prevent enemy from getting close enough to form up for an attack. Night ambush patrols go out each afternoon and the routines of stand-to are still carried out. Lights used in the command posts are not visible above ground, no enemy could use them as marker guides for zeroing in mortars. Machine guns are always manned and alcohol is strictly controlled to one can of beer per man. Unlike the safe haven of the Dat, the control on alcohol is self-imposed. No digger would risk letting his mates down if the proverbial shit hits the fan. Drugs are non-existent. The firebase is a fortress manned by professionals.

During the Tet Offensive, the enemy made the mistake of attacking two Australian fire support bases and paid dearly with hundreds of dead. There is little chance they would make that mistake again.

I have managed to score the best job on the base.

As it will not be the main firebase for three or more weeks, no admin command post is necessary, other than the standard resups for the Artillery and Delta Company troops. Each night, batteries are needed to power lighting. My job is to maintain the KVA generator all day and charge batteries. Aside from basic resup messages to Nui Dat, my day is filled with lazy moments and at night I can bunk down in the admin bunker. I do lots of reading and writing and only one turn on radio shift at the operation command post.

Even Sandy does not have such privileged comforts, but he doesn't complain. My zero bravo bunker has become the off roster hang out for Sandy and the three platoon sergeants. The air inside the bunker is rapidly turning blue-grey with cigarette smoke. The sand-bagged reinforced walls absorb the foul language, the boasts and insults as the old hands play cards and tell tales of female conquests and past battles. I am now privy to many a tall story and find the whole thing amusing until that time each and every night when I wish to go to sleep and they wish to keep talking.

'Get in ya feckin hammock and stop bitchin' ya feckin sheila', Sandy would say to me before spinning another tall tale of times in Singapore, Penang, Saigon, Port Moresby or just plain old Sydney town. These men were lifers so their stories were mostly about their military service in many parts of Australia or South East Asia. Between these old hands, a lifetime of army had taken them to many locations and filled their memoirs with endless tales of various levels in truthfulness.

Always the talk came back to Vietnam. Three of the four senior NCOs had served here before and all had tales of bar girls and drunken brawls along with the odd bit of humour about an incident some digger had been through. Sandy's latest favourite is still the monkey being shot out of a tree and the nick-name, Monkey Spanker, being bestowed upon the poor soul with the itchy trigger finger.

'And the boss is tellin' the feckin CO that one of his boys has spanked his monkey, ain't that right Brian?' He calls out to me as I lie in my hammock.

'Yep', I reply each night. The old hands nod and Spanker's sergeant shakes his head. 'Look at what I gotta put up with out there', he says every time the story is told before recounting his version of what actually happened up front. I always listen, quietly smiling to myself as I notice the story gradually rearranging its truths to make it just that bit more humorous. The story thus far has the clearing patrol tripping over snakes, the platoon commander hiding inside a hollow log frightened by a scorpion and finally, the monkey lying dead, with a smile on its face.

By the time the battalion returns to Australia this little monkey story will be first-class Keystone Cops material.

Eventually they tire, ready to wander back to their night pits. Invariably one of the sergeants decides to check his boys are on the ball on gun picket and Sandy always ends all conversations with the same well-worn statement,

'Ya can take the feckin soldier out of Vietnam, but ya can't take feckin Vietnam out of the soldier.'

Once the senior NCOs manage to leave me in peace, I grab my pen and notebook.

> *More and more I wish I had stayed in my safe little job back at the Dat. The battalion's tour of duty is more than halfway through and I have become well aware of my own mortality. I have seen too much of this war, much less than most riflemen, yet because of the village incident, so much more.*

I want to request a transfer back to command post duties. I want to be that naive young man I used to be when I first came to this land. But I cannot leave Sandy, not now, I have come to respect my fellow diggers in Delta Company and will hang in until the big wakey. I'll keep my promise to Sandy and not let anyone down no matter what.

> **Why can't we all be safe behind a wire, just 'til the end of tour?**

I write in bold letters before I flick off the light and lie back in my string hammock, enjoying the darkness, comfortable and content. Safe behind a wire. Drifting off to another night of fitful nightmares.

Photos and Trinkets

The twin engine, twin rotor Chinook helicopter climbs almost vertically skyward after delivering the huge water bladder. It had been slung below the Chinook on a cable and released automatically once the bladder was positioned neatly in the centre of the firebase. Dust is yet again rising off the ground swirling around and finding its way into every tent and bunker.

As the Chinook disappears, the rotor blade noise is replaced by the little KVA generator which I have been putt-putting along nicely. I've been charging up the bank of batteries that power the 12 volt lights which provide illumination in the command bunkers each night.

I am not alone at this time. I am squatting down with the company quartermaster and Doug, one of the platoon sergeants.

'This is what he found Staff, in the trench near the chopper pad. One of the Support Company wallers must have left it behind. Confirms what I had been told.'

The tough platoon sergeant is squatting next to the company quartermaster. They are examining a photo of some of the boys in Eleven Platoon standing beside a dead enemy soldier.

Staff gives a long sad sigh, 'No other way it could have got there. I mean one of your boys left it by mistake.'

'Nah!' Comes Doug's usual gruff reply. 'When I got wind of the two little shits sellin' photos to the pogos I put a rifle butt to any camera in the platoon, except the one I carry for company history files. Those two boys get the shit watch every night until wakey mate. Now what are you goin' ta do about your slimy little corporal storeman? Mick the fuckin' know-all.'

Staff looks around the firebase, he now understands why Doug has asked him to fly out with the resupply chopper.

'What corporal storeman? He'll be scrubbin' latrines for the rest of this tour', Staff responds.

'Hang on mate', Doug replies. 'The OC and Sandy don't know about this, you know how they feel about souvenirs and shit. For fuck sake, the company storeman buyin' photos and collectin' souvenirs from the boys and sellin' them to pogos so they can write home with bullshit stories about the war.' Doug shakes his head imagining the uproar, 'Sandy gets word of this and he will turn the company upside down. We got to get that bastard Mick on the quiet.'

Staff looks at me, 'The story from the Sarge here is that Mick sold photos to some pricks in signals platoon and mortar platoon, Dat pogos, any idea who?'

I shake my head, part of me realises that when I was in the Dat the lads always talked crap, including myself, and I had managed to pick up an NVA pith helmet from a Yank. It had been ruined after several nights of drunken humour filling it with beer and urine. This is a bit different, 'No Staff, no idea. For that matter, I don't want to know', I reply.

'Okay', Staff responds. 'RSM and I are old mates, we go back to Malaya together. I'll have a quiet word with him. Not a day goes by when you can't find some trumped up charge to ping diggers with, consider Mick a toilet scrubber.'

The platoon sergeant nods, 'Thanks mate, I can't stand that know-it-all bastard anyway. Thinks he knows what this war is all about 'cos he's been to uni-fuckin-versity. He don't know shit if it gets stuffed up his nose with a sharp stick.'

The Platoon Sergeant

Doug is not a well-educated man, not in terms of tertiary education. But in life education he holds the equivalent of a master's degree in hard knocks. Army life suited him when he was amongst the first group of young men conscripted. He rapidly forgot any plans to return to civilian life as a brickies' labourer and signed up for six more years. This was his second tour of 'Nam and he quite liked the war environment. He knows that diggers in his platoon hold a gruff respect for him but he is by no means popular because he dispenses military justice with enthusiasm upon any poor soul who falls foul of his personal view of the world. As far as he is concerned, he is doing the right thing by the men under his command. 'Toughening the bastard up, making real soldiers out of young punks.' But worse than young punks are the snooty educated twerps. He considers any poor soul who has the benefit of university training an instant enemy. He usually classifies all of them as, 'fucking know-it-all wankers'.

Of the three platoon sergeants in Delta Company, Doug is least liked by me, but on this occasion, I have to agree with the man's vitriol.

As Doug stands and walks toward his platoon perimeter area, I look around the fire support base that has been our home for the last two weeks. It has been a great rest from the usual patrolling but now it seems a bit stale. I am sick and tired of the dust and engine fumes. Endless dust kicked up by the choppers coming and going almost non-stop all day. Not to mention the APC movements in and out of the wire, dragging half the dust in Vietnam back in with them. In the field on patrol, the dust and heat takes second place in a soldier's world of worries but when you're stuck in a fire base in the middle of a man-made clearing it becomes an oppressive enemy of a different kind. This morning I made an entry in my notebook to remind me in future years of the hardship experienced in these hell holes.

Each morning a red ball signals the start of another torturous day, as the sun rises it turns from red to malaria yellow and burns the tops of any metal machine or weapon, making them too hot to handle without gloves. By midday the sun burns almost white hot. No breeze to be had and all things human come to a standstill in the fire base. Local peasants and their beasts of burden in nearby fields take shelter wherever it can be found. Machine gun sentries sit in puddles of their own sweat and peer out of their bunkers at a brown dusty land, shimmering, like a mirage and above all else oppressive. Temperature has no meaningful measurement in these hell holes, it is either very hot or fucking hot depending on what task is being endured within the wired compound. Digging a new latrine is as dangerous as going on a patrol, heat stroke as great a danger as a Viet Cong bullet.

As the day nears its end the sun again turns the same sickly yellow, a hot wind then blows off the distant mountains lifting the red dust into a swirling haze powdering and discolouring soldiers and machinery. Finally, the yellow ball turns deep red and drowns in the distant landscape. Relief from the heat is replaced with night mosquitoes and enemy movement around the perimeter as they try to identify weaknesses in our defence.

That is of no concern to me, there is no weakness in these defences!

Soon night will happen and I can once again crawl into my hole and slip into my hammock while Sandy and the senior NCOs play cards and allow their exaggerated stories to grow and evolve even more.

I look at Staff, whom I have become fond of after we did bush time together while Sandy was on R and R.

'Don't quite know what to say Staff. Don't know what to think. I suppose I might grab some little trinket to keep but sellin' photos to pogos is a bit off the line.'

Staff smiles, 'I'm a pogo son', he replies. 'Don't sound so nasty when you refer to diggers as pogos.'

'You know what I mean Staff. You have done more than your bit mate', I reply. 'Like Ray back in sig platoon. He's okay can't blame him.'

'You know what shits me Brian?' Staff asks, then answers automatically. 'For every digger in the sharp end, actually doin' the hard grind, there are about 25 pogos behind the scenes. Tucka fuckas, bottle washer, clerical wallers, storemen like me or that dick head Mick, you name it, they're all not actually doin' real time. Not at the sharp end.'

'So?' I respond. 'I'm beginning to wish I was one of them.'

'So. I'll tell you why', Staff continues. 'Every ANZAC day back in Aus you can watch the RSL bastards march and wank on about the war, "Double ya Double ya Two". They tell you back home in the RSL clubs, "Oh yes but we fought in the REAL war, not like you lads in Vietnam".' Staff shakes his head, 'Only one in every 25 of them did mate, but the other 24 keep the bullshit flowing like verbal diarrhoea running out of their mouths. Ever wonder where they got their trinkets from?' Staff shook his head. 'I used to look at all my old man's war souvenirs, old shell casings and stuff. Thought he was a hero I did, never actually asked him what he did before he died.'

'Who knows mate? Who knows? Just because he had trinkets don't mean he was a pogo, real diggers keep the odd trinket mate.'

'What did your old man do in World War II?' Staff asks.

'Navy, Ships Engineer I think.'

'Didn't talk to you much about it?'

'When I was a kid, I hardly saw him, he worked his guts out trying to build a business. When he wasn't working he was drinking. When I got a bit older, we didn't see eye to eye. I pissed off from home as a teenager. Now I am older we just don't seem to talk to each other much.'

'Pity he didn't talk more. I wish my old man talked more before he died. I was just an ankle biter of a kid during the war against the Japs. Not much older when my old man died. Wish he had told me before he died mate, I might have learned the truth about war from him instead of finding out the hard way. You keep those notes in your book Bri, tell your son if you have one.

Tell him that war is shit', Staff looks again at the photo. 'Turns my guts that diggers could actually sell this shit.'

'Or buy it mate', I reply, remembering the young German freelance journalist selling photos and stories to the mainstream reporters who hang around Saigon. The Kraut had taken photos of the little headless girl. Would they end up on the front cover of Time Magazine? 'Or buy the damn things', I repeat. A chill running down my spine as I instinctively wipe my hands on my trouser legs. It seems that sticky blood sensation just won't go away.

Staff let his eyes scan the inner sections of the firebase.

'Not fair on you boys having to go back out on ops tomorrow. Damn CO figures this is the equivalent to a rest in the Dat, so you lot are back in the boonies without even a decent night's booze-up let alone some more R and C.'

'Well at least the company gets out of this dust bowl', I respond. 'Never thought I'd see the day when I'd rather be bush than safe behind a wire but this place is driving me mad. As for the CO, well shit happens don't it?'

Staff smiled. 'You sound more and more like Sandy every time I see you.'

'Ya feckin reckon does ya', I goad with a grin from ear to ear. 'S'pose I'll be packin' me bottle of Tabasco in me kit and gettin' back to the real feckin war, aye?'

'Don't let Sandy catch you taking the mickey out of his language or his culinary skill', Staff replies before pausing, a serious grimace now covering his face. 'You won't have the OC with you this time, the Captains in charge while the OC takes a rest. It's not good changing teams like this. Like when I replaced Sandy. I'll never forget that day the chopper went down. Sorry I let you down, left you to handle the whole mess. I ain't no Sandy I'm afraid.'

'You didn't let me down Staff', I say awkwardly. 'I'm the one who made the wrong call.'

'No you didn't son, the pilot knew it was hot and unsecured. His call. You've got to admire those fly boys, they got guts.'

Staff looks at the deep red sun sliding westward and rises to his feet. 'Speaking of fly boys it's time to get a ride back to the Dat. The flight is leaving at last light. I got young Mick to sort out. Maybe I should get him transferred to a rifle platoon as a scout or gunner, he can take his own photos. I should put him in Doug's platoon.'

I smile, 'Nah, leave him back at the Dat Staff, get him to scrub out the dunnies and stuff, we'll all live longer with pricks like him safe behind a wire.'

Once alone again I reach for the notebook and pen then jot down in large letters…

> *PHOTOS, WHY WOULD YOU WANT TO KEEP FUCKING PHOTOS, SURF'S DEATH, NOT STAFF'S FAULT. MINE, ALL MINE.*

I read the words aloud and suddenly feel bile rising in my stomach. Why was I writing at all? I made one last entry…

> *Is this any better than taking photos? FUCK IT!!!*

'More notes for the memories I see Bri', Doc's sudden appearance beside me causes an embarrassing startle. I slam shut the notebook.

'Somehow I just lost interest in this fucking notebook Doc. And you! So mind your own fuckin' business and piss off and leave me alone.'

To my right is a water bladder with a hose pipe attached, the valve is faulty and a regular drip, drip, dripping has created a brown muddy puddle. I stare silently at the mud.

'It's dirt, just wet fucking dirt. This whole fucking war is just dirt and mud. And so is this fucking notebook. Put the dirt where the dirt belongs. I curse the day I started it. My old man was right. Ray was right. Fuck the war and fuck the book of fucking memories and you Doc can fuck off and leave me alone.'

I flick the book into the mud, stand and walk away leaving Doc shocked by my rudeness. His young friend is a very different man since he had taken that job in the village.

'Get back here and pick up that notebook soldier! And don't you ever turn your back on a good friend again.'

Sandy's voice snapped out with its usual air of authority. He had been watching from a few meters away.

I turn and pick up the notebook. 'Sorry Sir'

'AND?' Sandy barks.

I look across at Doc, 'Sorry Doc, I had a bad moment. Sorry.'

Doc smiles, 'That's okay Bri, we all have those, particularly in this place. Please keep writing. It's more important than you realise right now.'

I nod and tuck the now mud covered notebook into my pocket.

'That notebook of yours belongs to all of us son, like it or not you will protect it and keep writing for all of us, don't throw it away. Don't let us down. That is a feckin order son!' Sandy says in an authoritative tone, then scratches his nose a moment. 'Don't let me down son, fecked if I know why really, but your little book is important to me. No one else I know can tell it like you do, ya got the guts to admit when you're tired and fucked and scared, ya never read that stuff in most books.'

Sandy then asks me, 'Have you seen Tran that bushman scout? He seems to have shot through, gone A.W.O.L.'

'No Sandy', I reply. 'I don't want to see the little cunt either.'

'You sure son? I just want to know that you haven't had him in your area since we got here. Rumour has it you don't particularly like that man.'

'Hate him, hate all fucking Gooks, they are all fucking murderers as far as I am concerned.'

Sandy looks at me in a strange way, 'They are not all bad son, you need to think about that some. They are not all bad.'

He turns and walks away.

The Bushman Scout

Squatting alone in a thicket of trees and bamboo Tran stares at his picture book, a naked girl on the glossy front cover under the word PLAYBOY.

He opens the magazine to the centrefold and runs his fingers across the picture of the naked American woman. Vietnamese girls are much more beautiful with their lovely moon shaped faces and gentle smiles. Their elegant walk as they promenade along the streets. But the American women have milky white skin not golden brown. How he longed to touch that milky white body. He would never touch such a body. Tran knew that his time had come. If he stayed with the Australians, he would be killed by the mad boy with the radio set or he would have to kill the Australian boy first and he would be executed for that crime by the Quon Chan police. Even if he chose to kill the Australian boy what would that matter in his miserable existence. How many had he killed as a VC assassin. He was just a boy when he slipped into a hut and slit the throats of a man and his wife who had betrayed the liberators. At first it all seemed right and for a greater cause, but years of death, years of hatred had eventually destroyed any belief he had followed. He always knew that as a bushman scout he must one day meet his death. Kill or be killed. He could kill no more.

So he ran away and was now facing another even worse reality. He had betrayed the Viet Cong by going over to the Australians. They would soon find him and he would die a horrible death. Tran felt so tired of his world, he only wanted a life of happiness yet his was a life of pain, brutality and suffering. He would never have children, never lay with a woman whose skin was milky white. He would eventually be killed, next week, or next year. He felt so tired, and yet somehow at peace.

Tran closes the picture book and sits back on the ground. He places the muzzle of his M1 carbine in his mouth and with his left foot pushes his big toe into the trigger guard.

He remembers his father, his gentle mother and his beautiful sisters happy and smiling. A time long ago. A time when all that mattered was to laugh with his sisters as they watched their mother and father kissing in the garden of their home. A happy memory. His only happy memory. A tear slides down his cheek and he pushes down on his left foot.

THIRSTY WORK

THE UNBEARABLE WEIGHT on my back, the heat attacking my mind and body. Draining my soul of the mental energy to keep pushing one foot in front of the other. Pure self-discipline is all that keeps my eyes scanning my arc of responsibility as I move with the Company HQ in single file behind Twelve Platoon.

It has been three days since we left the firebase and I am reconsidering my opinion of how lousy that base was. Dust and noise – yes, but endless supplies of water.

The patrol stops moving forward. I push the M16 flash suppressor onto the end of my GP boot and allow myself to lean forward over the rifle butt to ease the weight of the backpack and sig set. I glance up into the thick tree cover, too damn thick and not helpful for getting good communication with zero alpha.

The company is patrolling the Dinh Hills with the notorious Nui Thi Vai and Nui Toc Tien peaks dominating the area some six to seven klicks west of Nui Dat. The company will not attempt to patrol the actual peaks of Thi Vai or Toc Tien, too damn difficult with giant rocks forming mini cliffs and a labyrinth of caves, and dominant fire positions from which the enemy could create havoc. They are like mini Long Hai fortresses. The peaks will be left to the SAS. Delta's job is to clear and secure the hills and re-entrants surrounding them. If the SAS finds anything on the peaks, the air force and artillery will drive the enemy down to be engaged by grunts.

Hills are more like mountains when you traverse them with 40 kilos on your back, and another 10 or more kilos of weapons and ammunition.

Be they hills or mountains, they create additional problems for signals operators. The ANPRC sig sets are VHF and require line of sight to get communications. Patrolling in gullies, re-entrants and behind hillsides creates blind spots.

From where I am, bent over my M16, I can look through the tree line and make out one of the two peaks that I guess is Nui Toc Tien. It has been a while since I have examined my own map and I am trying to remember which of the two peaks has an old ruin or ancient temple propped on top. I use this type of information as a memory jogger. The Thi Vai ruins locks in my mind. From this memory jog, a visual map springs into my mind showing each peak as it relates to magnetic north. I make a calculated guess on distance and compass bearing travelled in the last hour, it seems that the patrol should be able to sight Toc Tien peak, not Thi Vai.

Most signals operators don't carry maps, but I decided after my first op with Delta to never be without them. If called to do any reconnaissance with Nunger, I want to know exactly my position on the ground so that artillery can be directed immediately if the patrol hits an enemy force.

Nunger only likes small patrol groups and if the shit spilled out there, he would be very busy directing his section. It would be up to me to get guns firing as quickly as possible. I check the sheep counter taped to the front of my M16 handgrip. Each time my left foot touches the ground I push the lever with my left thumb, clicking up every second step I take forward. A quick glance at the total steps, multiply it by two and bingo, about 130 paces to every 100 meters in this hilly terrain. A check of the compass bearing as the patrol moves along, mark off the distance and I have a reasonably close LOCSTAT. Close enough for the first sighting rounds if I call them to land a thousand meters away. I take out the notebook …

Knowing approximately where I am helps me plan my signals requirements. If that mountain peak I am observing is Nui Toc Tien then I would get line of sight from my current location to the Dat, providing I can get an aerial elevated into the trees. This bloody captain ain't no OC that's for sure, not once on this patrol has he checked with me about comms. The bastard won't even call me up and get an opinion, just talks into Jacko's head set and wonders why no bastard can hear him. We got to get into a night harbour soon. What the hell is Sandy doing?

I more than anyone understand, it is communications that force the company to extend its patrol time to the edge of last light. The acting company commander wants good comms and the company lost direct contact with base an hour ago. He hoped that by pushing on, we may get a better line of sight for the VHF radio sets but orders the patrol in the wrong direction. Twenty minutes ago, the company could at least relay messages through Alpha Company who are in the area on the other side of the hills. Now we have lost radio contact with Alpha also.

This is the time of no return, if the patrol does not take up a night position now they will be forced to set up in the dark. I examine the types of trees around me. Not for snipers. I have formed the habit of always examining my options as a sig operator. Just as the scout and platoonies up front constantly check for good fire positions and safe hides, I check for ideal trees to sling an elevated aerial. In battle, it would be my fellow signallers and me that enable artillery, gunships and medevacs to support us in battle. It is my job to be as professional about these possibilities as it is the machine gunner's job to ensure his weapon is so clean it could never jam in battle.

The trees are high enough for a dipole aerial to work if I get lucky. But I decide that once the patrol sets up its night harbour, the best option will be to connect a length of claymore cable to my ten-foot rod and hoist that up into the treetops. By tying com cord in a series of hitches one third of the way from the base then looping the cord over a tree limb near the canopy top, I can slowly elevate the aerial in such a way that its tip will protrude through the canopy. Theoretically, this is not supposed to get good comms. However, theory and practice do not always sleep together. Other sig operators and I have used the technique successfully regularly.

To the right of the patrol line a tall tree shoots skyward and near the top a branch juts out at almost 90 degrees. I hope I find a tree like that when we get into the night harbour.

As I guessed, the signal came back that the forward platoon will send out a small recce patrol and decide on a night harbour position. I let out a sigh of relief. I had earlier cursed myself for my poor management of water rations causing me to run out of easily accessible water an hour ago. I only have a small amount of water left tucked inside my backpack where I cannot reach it.

It should only be another 20 minutes until we set up camp for night harbour. I might still have time for a hot brew if I heat it with C4. I remove the strip of cam cloth that I tied around my forehead to stop the sweat from dripping into my eyes. It is dry. I am dehydrated. I will be a walking tragedy in about 30 minutes if I am not able to get water.

It should only be 20 minutes if the boys up front are as keen as I am and don't fuss too much about the best spot to set up camp. I decide not to delay the patrol while I take off my backpack and dig out the last bottle.

The Forward Scout

At the front of the patrol line, fuss is the last thing on Spanker's mind as he leads the harbour recce. He is also keen for enough daylight to cook a hot brew. The young scout takes a quick glance behind to ensure that Fletch his section commander is ready. A quick nod from Fletch and he moves off slowly. Just two short paces.

Spanker feels it, he knows instantly in that moment what is about to happen. A sort of click as his right foot touched the ground. He has 1-2-3 seconds. The blinding flash and jarring as his right leg flings upwards, followed by a dull ache in his left leg and excruciating pain in his stomach.

I felt the blast even back on the patrol line. I know instantly that one of ours is dead or injured.

The Section Commander

Fletch feels a sudden pain in his chest and something seems to hit him in the neck. He knows instantly that his scout has tripped an anti-personnel mine and he responds as trained. Fletch turns to the machine gunner behind him and tries to yell, 'Mine freeze!' but no words come out of his mouth. He can hear a gargling sound coming from his own throat and he can see bright red blood spurting straight out in front of him. His hand reaches up to his throat and he can feel the pressure of the blood spurting. His jugular is ripped open.

He realises that he is about to die.

As Fletch falls to the ground, Pillows, the section machine gunner screams out the warning, 'MINE FREEZE! MINE FREEZE!' His right knee buckles beneath the weight of the backpack and gun and a sharp pain surges up his thigh. Pillows drops to his knees and flicks out the M60 bipod legs which he rests on a fallen log ready to return fire if any enemy are nearby. He glances down at his left leg, a dark red splash of blood is growing larger by the second, 'Jesus I'm hit, Jesus get a medic quick. I'm fucking bleeding to death.'

Twelve Platoon's stretcher-bearer immediately begins to move forward to check on his soldiers but the platoon commander has other plans.

'One more step and I'll shoot you myself!'

The young officer has immediately realised the severity of his platoon's situation. Stopping in his tracks, he calls to his platoon, 'Stay calm and carry out the mine drill, clear around you first and then clear a path toward the man in front of you. The sooner we get the area safe the sooner we help our wounded mates.'

The platoon stretcher-bearer instantly realises his platoon commander is correct, he screams to Pillows, 'Put pressure on the wound, use your hand or thumb, as much pressure as you can bear'. He then draws his bayonet and prods his way forward to assist the injured men.

The Machine Gunner

Pillows chooses to ignore the medic's advice. He can see that Fletch is beyond help and Spanker looks a horrid mess. Blood is spurting from the remnants of his leg. Ignoring the risk of mines and his own loss of blood, Pillows drags himself and his M60 forward, past his section commander's jerking body. He knows he could trip another mine. Instant death was possibly between him and his scout but it would only be him this time as the rest of the boys are in mine drill. Each movement is a mixture of leg pain, fear of setting off a mine and a sudden difficulty in breathing. He reaches Spanker and quickly examines the seriousness of the injuries. He has to stop the massive loss of blood as quickly as possible. Pillows grapples unsuccessfully with a shell dressing. Giving up he pushes his bayonet through Spanker's torn pants just above the mangled part of Spanker's leg and twists it several times to form a tourniquet. Spanker's blood stops spurting and slows to a trickle. He can do no more than that. He is first and foremost the section's main firepower. If attacked, his M60 has to be ready to respond. Again ignoring his own injury Pillows attaches another 100 round belt of ammo to the 50 round belt on his gun and takes up a defensive fire position.

'Hurry fuck you, my vision is all blurred. I can't hold out much longer', He calls through a strangely shallow breath. He gasps for more air, 'Hurry fuck you, hurry.' His throat is desert dry yet his lips feel wet. He wipes the back of his hand across his mouth and looks at the result. Bright frothy red blood. He is beginning to feel tired as if he could just drift off to sleep. He struggles against the sensation, 'Hurry fuck you I can't keep it happening up here', he begins to shiver with cold. How can he be cold?

At the other end of the patrol line, the HQ group and I are responding. With bayonets drawn, each man is gently prodding the earth around them at a 30-degree angle marking out a circle of safety. I clear my area quickly. My mind is already at work, I know the company needs communications and I have already decided that an elevated aerial is our best hope. I also know which tree to try for, thanks to my earlier observations.

Slipping out of my shoulder straps, I undo the side flap of my backpack and pull out a metal plumb bob with its long coil of cord, quickly unfurling enough to ensure that the plumb bob can be launched skyward without being dragged back by the attached cord. Should I grab the water? I decide there's no time to unclip and scrummage around when we've got men bleeding up front.

'Get me communications and get it quick', screams the Captain. 'I have wounded up front and need a MEDIVAC.'

The three signals operators stare at each other and then, as one, stare at the artillery FO who shrugs his shoulders.

'No hope in this spot', he calls back to the acting commander.

I am more optimistic, 'Try and relay through Alpha Company. If you have no luck there search some frequencies for a chopper, you might get lucky', I call to Jacko, who is setting up a ten-foot aerial on his own sig set.

I now swing the suspended plumb bob back and forth in my right hand then slowly let it rotate around and around gathering momentum, my eyes fix on a single branch high in the tree to my right.

'Another mine up here', screams a digger from the front section.

I stop the swing of the plumb bob and squat down on my haunches. I am feeling rattled, the second mine means the patrol is probably inside an unmarked mine field. I need to hit the target first time. After a few slow breaths to calm my nerves, I prepare myself for the task. Again, the plumb bob begins spinning around my hand. My eyes fixed on the target above.

'Heads down. This thing might set off a mine when it comes back to earth.'

The metal object launches skyward and all in the immediate area watch it arc through the air toward the high branch, passing directly over it and falling back toward the ground on the other side. I drop back down onto my stomach and all heads press into the earth as the plumb bob crashes through leaves and small branches, finally hitting mother earth with a muffled thud.

Looking up I can see where the bobbin has landed. About eight meters to the right of the patrol line. I now need to retrieve it so I can suspend an aerial on the cord that now stretches over the branch high above.

Eight meters in a possible minefield may as well be a thousand meters any place else. I am dry, bone dry and need a drink desperately but I can hear a man screaming in pain up at the front of the patrol. I leave my M16 and reach for my trusty bayonet, then begin the slow laborious task of prodding and clearing a path to the plumb bob.

'Forget the bloody bayonet, walk over, and get the damn thing', I hear the acting company commander call out. 'I've got wounded men and need a damn Dustoff.'

I hesitate, do I obey the order or obey my training? I ignore the command and continue to clear slowly with my bayonet.

'I said walk for it man and that's a bloody order', barks the Captain. 'People are bleeding to death while you prod around.'

Suddenly Sandy's booming voice calls out, 'You tell my sig to walk for it one more time and so help me I will come over there, rip your head off and shit down your feckin throat. Sir!'

'Thank you Sandy, thank you', I call back and continue slowly and methodically clearing a path to the plumb bob.

'I've got another jumping jack back here', comes a cry from the rear of the patrol line.

My fear increases two-fold. This means only one thing, the whole patrol are inside an unmarked mine field. We could be surrounded by the little beasts of death.

I am now feeling quite faint and struggling to remain conscious. I am dehydrated and hyperventilating with fear at the same time. I rest and place my face on the dirt in front of me, slowly gathering the willpower to keep going. The earth smells of compost, my mind momentarily flashes back to my grandfather's vegetable garden. It is now a bittersweet smell. A scent of security, the safe little world of my grandfather's back yard. Now it is the smell of death and decay. Just a few more feet, a few more feet. I force my head back off the ground and continue the careful prodding.

'Come on soldier, hurry up, there are men bleeding to death up here', the Captain barks anxiously.

My bayonet slides into the dirt and stops against a solid object. 'Shit', I croak through my parched voice box. I carefully clear around the object buried in front of me. Gently with the bayonet tip, I move the soil back until I see the unmistakable first signs of the jumping jack. With my fingers, I move aside the earth and stare at the mines prongs. I have to move my hand clear as it is shaking violently. I grip the bayonet tightly to help stop the shaking. Get a grip, get a grip, a calm soldier is a live soldier, I say to myself.

'For God's sake man what is the hold up? I need to get a Dustoff in here', the Captain yells.

'You ignore the man and take yer feckin time son, Doc's up front with the wounded boys already, remember yer trainin', Sandy calls out reassuringly.

I call back, 'I have one here, a bloody mine right in my face', my voice croaks coarsely, 'and no soldier is goin' to tell me to hurry up. Shut that officer up Sandy or so help me I'll turn around and shoot the bastard.'

'Okay boy', Sandy calls back in a calm voice. 'Okay, you know what to do. Mark it with your giggle hat on a stick and gently move on, you're nearly there son. Just keep your cool and we will all be Jim Dandy won't we?'

He pauses then calls out again, 'Remember our talk young fella, dig down inside you and find that extra somethin'. Just like ya promised ya would.'

I pick up a broken stick and sharpen the end with two whittles of my razor sharp bayonet, push it into the ground beside the mine. Next, I pull my giggle hat from my head and rest it gently on the stick. Two long breaths through a parched throat and I commence the gentle prodding again, moving inches closer to the metal plumb bob. Finally, I am close enough to reach out with my trembling right hand and grasp it firmly. Carefully I turn to head back along the path I had cleared. I try to stand but cannot. My legs seem weak and the ground in front of me is rocking. Once again, I push my face to the ground and close my eyes. The smell of death and decay is snorting up my dry nostrils.

Get it together, get a grip. I promise you Sandy, I promise you I will get the job done, I whisper into the dirt in front of me before summoning up the courage to keep going. Hands and knees, one in front of the other, I mumble under my breath as I crawl back to the sig set.

Once there, I tie four hitches up the ten-foot aerial and connect one end of the claymore cable. Next, I connect the other end of the cable to the 25 set and then slowly hoist the aerial skyward, carefully ensuring it remains vertical so that it will reach up through some of the tree canopy.

Once in place I take up the handset. My top teeth have stuck to the inside of my top lip. I force a dry tongue between teeth and lip.

'Zero alpha, zero alpha, this is four, radio check', I croak. I wait for the response.

'Four, call sign four, this is zero alpha. You are weak but readable. Where the hell have you been? Over'. The reply I am so desperately hoping for.

I look up at the acting company commander who has crawled along the cleared track to my area. I make no comment just pass the handset over to the Captain. I crawl a couple of feet to his right along the path I have cleared to reach the plumb bob. Just far enough away to control my urge to strike the Captain with the butt of my M16.

The world is swirling around me, blurring the edge of my vision. I am trying to swallow but cannot. My throat is so dry it seems the passage has stuck together. A hand taps me on the shoulder. I look up and see Sandy's yellow teeth smiling from behind the black and green cam cream, a water bottle in his hand.

'Reckon yer throat would be drier than an old nun's pussy right now. Get this in you boy.'

I gulp down one small mouthful then another before again pushing my face into the dirt.

'Best damn sig I ever served with', I hear Sandy say. I drag the canteen to my lips for a third swig. The water, like nectar, a magic elixir, and the sweetest and most beautiful thing I have ever tasted.

'Dry as a nun's pussy. Where do you get these sayings from?' I croak back at Sandy.

'You stick with good old Sandy son', came the gruff reply. 'I'll teach you the English language the way it's meant to be spoke.'

'Yeah, I'll stick with you Sandy', I croak as I take a final gulp from the canteen. 'How many of the boys are down?'

'Three down, one dead.'

'Oh shit, who?'

'Fletch, damn it, poor bloody Fletch. It was your little mate Spanker tripped the mine I'm afraid. Looks bad, lost his legs I figure. One's already all but gone.' Sandy shakes his head as he tries to imagine what it would be like to tread on a mine but quickly shakes out the vision and stares back at me. 'Thanks to good old Poofy Pillows, Spanker should live, and thanks to you we can get that Dustoff in and get those boys out.'

'Thanks to you, I didn't obey that prick of a captain and end up with a leg or two missing myself.' I am trying to come to terms with the news but still in a state of exhaustion rather than shock.

'You let me deal with that son', Sandy replies. 'He's not a prick, he's a good man. Best he makes these mistakes with me around to see him right.

He won't ever forget that he could have killed you in his attempt to save the other boys. He's a better officer for the experience. One day he will be a colonel or a brigadier and he will always remember to put his soldiers' safety at the top of his planning.'

I look up at my mentor, 'You're the boss Sandy.'

Sandy smiles, 'Yeah, I'm the boss and you're the sig. Best damn sig I ever served with.' He smacks me gently across the top of my head with an open palm, 'Now give me back my water bottle ya greedy, selfish bastard. This war is thirsty work and I just might need a drink myself.'

Placing the bottle back in its pouch on his web belt Sandy stands up and turns away from me. He heads carefully along the cleared track to where Doc is treating the two wounded soldiers.

I lie silently for a while. My head is clearing but I need more water. I lift myself from the ground and crawl back to my sig set and backpack. Ignoring the acting company commander, I dig through the pack and grab my collapsible water bottle, take a long swig then stare at the Captain.

The officer looks up. A pale white face stares back at me. It suddenly flushes red. Embarrassed! I pass him my water bottle.

'Thirsty work eh?'

The captain nods and takes the bottle, puts it to his lips and tilts it enough for a small swig then passes it back. The radio crackles to life.

'Four zero alpha this is Dustoff, inbound Echo Tango Alpha, three mikes. Over.'

The captain raises the handset, 'four zero alpha, roger. It's a litter job for two and a return flight for our Kilo India Alpha. Out.'

The captain pulls a smoke grenade from his web shoulder strap and prepares it for firing. 'I'll get back to the wounded boys and pop the smoke when you give me a call, it's a yellow', he says to me. He passes the handset over and nods in the direction of the mine I had found. 'Thanks soldier', he clears his throat. 'Thanks.'

I nod. It was as close to an apology as I would ever get from this officer but it was good enough.

In the distance I can hear the Dustoff.

Whop   Whop   Whop   Whop   Whop

I listen to get a mental bearing on the chopper's location and flight path. 'Dustoff this is four, turn port nine o'clock and watch for smoke shortly.' I can hear the chopper change direction and head almost straight toward the patrol's location.

Whop   Whop   Whop   Whop   Whop

DEMONS AND GARGOYLES

Once the Dustoff manages to lift out the dead and wounded, greater care is taken to clear immediate areas around the patrol. In all we have located five anti-personnel mines and assume more are buried in our immediate area. Nightfall prevents a withdrawal from the area or a proper night harbour being established. The patrol is scattered in an extended line with instructions to bed down in pairs and take turns on night watch. Two hours on, two off.

We company sigs manage to get a second aerial into the trees and establish a communication link for artillery support if required. There is no time for a hot meal or drink. A quick snack straight from a C ration can and a few gulps of the precious remnants of water is all I have to sustain me through the long night. That, and an inability to stop thinking about what had happened today. I force myself to make a new entry in my notebook.

Most diggers are all too aware that the mine which killed their mate was an Australian mine. A hand-me-down from the infamous Dat Do disaster, when the Australian Task Force Commander decided to lay down a large blocking mine field. The Australian command then made the mistake of assuming that ARVN forces would conduct careful patrols to ensure the enemy would not sneak into the marked mine area and lift then re-plant the mines all over the provinces. 'Graham's folly' became the worst tactical mistake of the Australian involvement thus far. Poor bloody Spanker.

This is no longer a history lesson. This is the death of one of our own and the legs of another. My mind fills with dread about tomorrow. How will we extricate ourselves from this location? I worry about a possible assault by enemy at first light. Overriding all these thoughts is the fate of the men killed and injured.

I did not know Fletch well. He seemed okay as far as section commanders went. A national serviceman of 22, deferred from service to complete his electrical apprenticeship. Nevertheless, once called to arms he did not complain. Like most 'nashos', he would not have volunteered for army service but he was patriotic and of the old school in his belief that if your country calls you should respond. It was that mature attitude that stood him in good stead when it came to promotion. Now he is dead. It was all over in a minute or two. It would not have mattered if Doc was right there beside him just minutes after he was wounded, with the jugular torn and the bleeding unstoppable the man was dead before Doc could even administer morphine.

Pillows has a large wound in the upper thigh, a smaller piece of shrapnel punctured his lung and he did not even know about it. Doc calls them perfect wounds, not too much damage but good enough to put old Pillow-biter out of action for two or more months. This means an early flight home to Australia. 'Bloody earned a trip home, earned it with sheer guts', Sandy had snorted. The captain has bigger plans and has already spoken by radio to the CO about recognition for Pillow's disregarding his own wounds to help a mate.

Spanker is the tragedy. His right leg all but blown off below the knee with extensive damage to his thigh muscles. His left knee is shattered irreparably. An artificial joint might save the left leg but Doc says the muscle damage to the lower left leg might be too extensive, he could lose that as well. There is also damage to the lower intestine and Doc guessed the gall bladder was damaged. At least his genitals are relatively intact. Not fatal stuff but not a life to look forward to either.

I had grown to like Spanker, the dry humour and cheeky smile. I remember that night in the Jade bar steam room when Spanker stood with bottle in hand to back up Nunger against the Americans. He was no more than 20 years old, his life changed forever.

Wingnut earned his pay today. Five mines pinned and lifted, only one with an anti-lift device that Wingnut disarmed with consummate ease. There are more out there for sure but his advice to the Captain is to mark the area on the chart and back out as carefully as possible. Seems the Captain has decided to listen to people who know their job.

Maybe someday in the future, after the war is over, some engineers will come back and lift them but it is unlikely. Mines have been buried all over this country and not all will get recorded like this lot. Mines will still be here 20 years from now and probably still capable of exploding if tripped.

From my position I can see Doc and Wingnut in the fading light. They have had a terrible time today. One desperately trying to keep a badly injured digger alive, the other risking death as he disarmed mines. I can also hear them talk, trying in their own crazy way to unwind after the day's horror.

'I've got a friend back in Aus who is a plastic surgeon Wingnut, he could pin them ears back onto your scone and make you look less like a circus freak', Doc says in a lowered voice. 'Right now you look kind of like a VW with both doors open.'

Wingnut looks up indignantly, 'Girls like my ears, gives them something to hang onto when I'm down on the pussy.'

Doc continues his observations ignoring Wingnut's reply, 'Yeah I heard you have a unique way of eating bananas. Fixing the ears is easy but I can't see any way we can fix what's in-between them.'

'What do you mean by that arse hole?'

'Well you just can't fix something that ain't there can you?' Doc responds. 'Vacuum my dumb Vee Dub Beetle of a man, just vacuum.'

'Not vacuum fuck knuckle. Grey matter and lots of it. You're just jealous because you're so stupid', Wingnut retorts, anger creeping into his voice.

'Grey? Did you say Grey?' Doc sits up and looks into Wingnut's ear. 'You're right, there is something in there but its brown mate. I can see it with my own eyes, brown. Smells like shit. I reckon your head is full of shit Wingnut.'

Sandy's large frame is suddenly looming menacingly over the two men, 'If you boys don't shut up I'll put something into both yer feckin heads starting with a bit of common sense, even if I gotta hold you both down and put my dick in your ear to feck some sense into you.'

The two young men are instantly in a state of fear and lie back down into fire positions hoping Sandy will not deliver a swift kick of his GP boot into both of them.

Sandy now follows the nights com cord over to my sleeping spot and squats down close beside me. 'I'm with the Captain tonight so yer on ya own, don't worry about sig shift. I, the FO and Captain will look after that tonight. Just get what rest you can but remember there is no harbour perimeter, we are all on the edge so sleep with one eye open.'

I nod. Sandy's appearance lifts my morale. I want to tell the man he is my hero and thank him again for pulling the Captain into line, 'Take it easy on the two boys Sandy they both had hard jobs to do today and it ain't as if the Nogs don't know we are here, is it?'

Sandy winks at me, 'You let me worry about those two and what's best for 'em young fella. Truth is I keep 'em together because I like to hear them bitchin' at each other. It gives me some amusement in times like this.'

I am overcome with a cheeky desire to joke with my senior non-com, 'You like them don't ya Sandy, go on, admit it. I bet you even like me.'

'Hate the feckin lot of yas I do, but we are all members of the combat club, that's all that counts young fella. Special club this one, not like that

Melbourne Club or some toffy rich prick's club. Don't need no money to join our club. Nah, we pay our membership under fire. Any man eligible for membership to our club is special, even little pricks like you and the Doc and that pointy-eared abomination who calls his self a sapper. Ya feckin special and don't ever forget it.'

'Yeah, and ya like us don't ya? C'mon give me a big hug and then go kiss the boys an' tell 'em your sorry you spoke so rude to 'em.'

Sandy smiles, gives a wink before gently pushing my head face down into the dirt, 'Hugs and kisses! You been around poor old Pillows too long son. I'll think about liking you lot when we all get back to Aus. In the meantime my answer is that I hate the feckin lot of yas.'

As Sandy returns to his night spot I realise how dark it has become. It will be a long uncomfortable night. No hooches, no silks, just lying still with rifle and web belt ready, resting heads on forearms and cat-napping until first light.

As I lie here, I am thinking about what the enemy may be up to at this moment. In fading light, I make a short entry.

> *Those mines were put here for a reason. Was it to guard a base or was it just plain cunning and bastardry? If the enemy wants to have a go at the patrol, tomorrow morning is the best time. Get us when we are most vulnerable. The enemy will know that the patrol will carefully retrace its steps and back out of the mine area. Charlie could set up an ambush at the edge of the minefield. They know where the mines are laid, we don't. The enemy is in control of this situation.*

The one comforting factor for me is that I know that our patrol will have radio comms tomorrow. The task force will set up an aerial retransmission station.

> *Artillery and air support will give us back the edge we need. So what will the Captain do? How will he plan the withdrawal? Wish the OC was here right now, but Sandy can advise the Captain. The captain has*

realised the wealth of experience he has at his beck and call. Sandy is right as usual. The bloke will probably end up a bloody good officer.

What little sleep I manage is fitful and frightening. Visions of burning bodies, legless friends and enemy soldiers creeping toward me in the dark holding bayonets in their teeth, their lips and eye sockets eaten away by maggots. My innocent little girl's head and broken teeth. These demons and gargoyles will probably haunt me on many future nights.

First light stand-to is followed by friendly artillery fire guided in as close as possible to the rear of the patrol line.

This has two purposes, firstly, to clear or move any enemy plans for an ambush, and secondly to explode any mines in the area. After the barrage I make a new entry in my notebook.

Artillery landing 'danger close' is always frightening. The ripping sound as the shell heads toward you followed by that moment of silence, then the world around you crunched by a deafening roar and a shock wave that passes over the body no matter how flat you force yourself to the ground. Shrapnel and shock waves tear at the trees, small branches cascade to the ground and your ears ring regardless of how carefully you try to protect them with hands. The FO is using delay shells, designed to hit bunker systems. The idea is to delay the actual detonation for a split second allowing the shell to penetrate into the ground before exploding. In this particular case these shells are less likely to spray the patrol with shrapnel and more likely to detonate any mines. He is walking the shells right up as close to us as possible. Good thing I trust that FO. I would be shitting my pants otherwise. Come to think of it I am shit scared, good thing my arse is empty.

The shelling stops, it's now Wingnut's turn to earn his pay. With Nunger and the support section gunner right behind, he begins the steady task of clearing the path back out of the area. He will clear until he decides that our patrol is out of danger. Ten meters, a hundred meters, it is Wingnut's call.

After 30 meters, and only one more mine found, Wingnut makes the call and the patrol members rise carefully and follow his marked path to safety.

No enemy in sight, they had bugged out either when the artillery started or were probably never there at all.

The battalion commanding officer has decided to pull the company back to the Dat once we are clear of the minefield. A short hike to a clearing big enough for a chopper evacuation, then it is hot showers and all the water and alcohol I can drink.

With luck I can drown the knot deep in my guts. Try to drink away my grief for my good friend whose only claim to fame was that he shot a monkey.

Investigating Whom?

The M16 is bucking in my hands. It's muzzle climbing to the high right as I empty a 20 round mag on auto. I am standing legs apart, left well forward of the right. My weapon is locked against my right hip, the smell of smoking gun oil rises from the hot barrel.

With the magazine empty, my finger moves up and presses the release button, the empty mag drops to the ground alongside eight others. My left hand reaches into my web pouch and produces another full mag. I push the mag upward and home into the weapon and hit the bolt release to drive another round into the weapons chamber. I move the safety catch from auto to semi and brace again. I send another 20 rounds into the earth bun in rapid succession.

Even though I have been in combat situations, including a successful instant ambush, this is the first and only time I have fired my weapon in Vietnam. I'm at the Nui Dat firing range.

I have been allocated the job of 'burning off' old ammunition, lots of fun but it will mean a big clean up job on my M16 when I get back to my tent. Still, at least I can feel the power of an uncontrolled shoot, just letting rip with the M16 without concern about accuracy or saving ammo.

'Hey John Wayne, get your arse back here', Nunger calls from behind me.

I empty the mag, and let it drop to the ground then move back one pace and hold the weapon up to check the chamber is clear before offering Nunger a chance to examine its safety.

'Okay, that's clear.'

'What's up?'

'CSM wants you at his hooch, quick smart. Don't worry about the mags, we'll get them and I will inspect the Gat when you get back from wherever you're going. I'll make sure the thing is so clean I can suck the flash suppressor and not taste cordite.'

I release the bolt onto an empty chamber, flip shut the chamber dust cover and push home a fresh mag of ammo, check the safety is on and make my way quickly to Sandy's hooch.

'For feck's sake, you should be wearing better greens than those around the Dat, son', Sandy gruffly addresses me as we walk up to Company HQ. He walks around me, brushing the dust off the back of my shirt.

'C'mon, in the feckin Rover, too late to change now.'

'What's up? Where we going, Sir?' I ask inquisitively. I note that Sandy has slipped on his warrant officer armband which is seldom seen in Vietnam as soldiers rarely show rank to possible enemy.

Sandy does not reply, he crunches the car into gear and speeds off down the road 50 meters then slams his foot on the brake. As the vehicle skids to a stop, Sandy stares straight into my eyes, 'What the feck have you been up to? Tell me now so I can decide whether to back you up or cut off yer balls.'

'Nothing, Sir, nothing. What's goin' on?'

Sandy stares right through me for a moment searching for a sign that I am telling the truth and that I did not know what is up. 'Okay yer wanted at Task Force HQ for questioning. You are allowed to bring a friend as a support person and guess what, you chose to bring me because ya feckin like me a lot. And that's an order soldier.' He pauses then continues, 'Now I don't know what the feck this is about but think carefully before you answer any questions. Be a dumb grunt, 'I don't know about that Sir, I'm just a private type of answer'. Got that?'

'Yeah, got that Sir', I reply. I am confused as to what is happening or why. Sandy pushes the Rover back into gear and drives toward HQ.

'Come in soldier, eh, you too. Thank you Sergeant Major, take a seat, this is informal at this stage.'

I sit down in the metal chair, Sandy beside me. I notice with quiet amusement how Sandy sits upright to attention. Clenched knuckles on his knees, a soldier to the bone.

We are inside a barren Nissen hut furnished with two chairs in front of an aged table behind which three men in clean pressed greens sit sorting papers from several manila folders. I recognise one of them immediately. It is the clean skin tourist, who flew in with the CO to look at the bunker hospital.

'I recognise you, young man. You were out at that damn underground hospital. You called in the chopper to lift us out, didn't you?'

'Yes Sir. That's right Sir.'

The officer turns to the other clean skins, 'Unbelievable place. The enemy had actually built an underground hospital out in the jungle. I have some photos back in my room worth a look. Unfortunately the underground shots are a bit dark because I did not have the right equipment, but I'll tell you the story and describe what we saw. Unbelievable place!'

I can sense the contempt oozing out of Sandy's pores as the three men in freshly pressed greens chat away about their experiences. Finally, one of the clean skins starts to shed some light on the purpose of the meeting.

'This is an informal inquiry at this stage, we are gathering information. You can relax and talk freely in this room. You are not under trial and not under oath. Do you understand soldier?'

'Yes Sir.'

'Good. Sergeant Major you may speak if you feel it necessary to assist either us or the young soldier, but this is not a court, we don't need to advise this boy to shut up or play dumb. You know what I mean, we don't want you telling him to just shut up, now do we. Understood?'

'Yes Sir, I would never give that advice if an investigation is needed, Sir.'

The officer opens the manila folder in front of him and produces a stack of black and white photographs, spreading them loosely across the table in front of me.

'Recognise this incident?'

My heart takes a wild leap into into my throat and I struggle to push back the sickening bile and stop myself from vomiting as memories flood back.

'Yes Sir', I reply, trying to hide my quivering voice as I stare at the photo of the headless child.

'Take a good look son', the clean skin says.

'I don't need to Sir. It's planted in my brain for life.' Suddenly I feel the sticky sensation between my fingers and rub my hands on my greens.

The clean skin shuffles through the photos until he finds the one he is looking for.

'Is that you standing back there?'

I look at the photo. I can see a slightly blurred image of myself in the group of ARVN soldiers. The clean skins have obviously drawn a circle in black texta around me in the group.

'It's me Sir.'

'And here, this is you isn't it? Are you standing over the dying man on the ground?'

'It's me Sir, yes Sir, it's me standing there.'

'Who did that to the enemy soldier? Who disembowelled the poor wretch?'

'Not me Sir, no Sir, not me. I wouldn't even do that to a sheep killing dog, Sir.'

'What's this got to do with dogs soldier?'

'Nothing Sir, well sort of. I don't think you would understand, Sir.'

'Where was your commanding officer? The subby son, where was the liaison officer?'

'Don't exactly know, he was there somewhere. It was a bit chaotic at the time.'

The other clean skin in the group now speaks, 'A freelance journalist sold these photos and an interesting story to an Australian press reporter last week. Fortunately, the bastards back in Australia had standards and sent the information to us. They have allowed us to bury it but we want answers soldier.'

The Kraut, the fucking Nazi bastard. I had forgotten all about the man. Of course, he had grabbed a ride with the ARVN troop that went out looking for the VC assault party. He must have come back to the village with the two prisoners. He was there, taking photos, the dirty war monger.

I try to regain composure.

'What answers Sir? We were in the wrong place at the wrong time. We couldn't stop ARVN doing what they did. That was done by their commander. He has the authority from his own government to execute Viet Cong from what I understand.'

'You call that execution soldier, do you? We are obliged to prevent any breach of the Geneva Convention soldier.'

'Permission to speak Sir', Sandy cut in. He had been viewing the photos also.

'Yes Sergeant Major.'

'Well Sir, I don't know much about this incident, but I can see from the photos that this soldier was alone amongst a large group of ARVN. He couldn't stop that even if he threatened to shoot someone Sir. I mean, damn it Sir, he is just a damn private, not a general, Sir.' Sandy shuffles in his chair, 'My understanding is the same as this soldier's, Sir. If we are working with ARVN troops, we must respect their chain of command and their authority as representatives of the South Vietnamese government. Regional commanders have the authority to execute Viet Cong, Sir. We can't tell them how they should do it. They Sir are not signatories to the Geneva Convention as we are.'

Sandy's face is beginning to glow bright red with anger, 'Perhaps Sir, the politicians and generals back in Australia should give some clear guidelines to 20-year-old boys as to how they are supposed to react in a no-win situation SIR! Like when we capture prisoners alive and healthy and hand them over to the allies for interrogation knowing damn well what the poor bastards will have to endure SIR! Last tour I witnessed American CIA throwing prisoners from a chopper hovering 500 feet in the feckin air SIR! Perhaps Sir you could advise this boy what he should do next feckin time he is out there SIR!'

Sandy is putting himself out on a limb for me but he does not have any concern for his own career, he is angry and finally venting that anger. He pounds his right trigger finger onto the photos lying across the desk. 'Twenty or more years I have given my country, twenty years Sir, but never did I imagine some young boys like this soldier here would be placed in a situation like this. Don't condemn this boy for the senseless arrangements made by our political masters, SIR.'

The room is silent for a while. Stunned by the old veteran's outburst the three officers take a moment to regain their composure. Sandy sits back in his chair. Returns to the sitting-at-attention position. The three officers look at each other. I can see that they are shocked by Sandy's outburst but they also have got his message loud and clear.

The interview re-commences. 'Did the liaison officer attempt to talk to the ARVN commander about what he was about to do soldier?' A clean skin asks.

'I wouldn't know about that Sir, I'm sure he tried Sir, but like the CSM said, we were out of our depth and the LO is just a subby Sir. The ARVN bloke was much higher rank, a regional commander.' I am now beginning to feel a little more secure. Sandy is right as always. I could not have stopped the execution and could not be held responsible in any way, shape or form.

'Were you using illegal substances?'

This next question throws me completely.

'No Sir, of course not Sir. What illegal substances?'

'Drugs son, smoking drugs?'

'No Sir, I wouldn't do that Sir.'

'Was the liaison officer using drugs soldier?'

'I wouldn't know about that Sir. I'm just a digger Sir. A grunt, that's all.'

'According to our information the LO was so under the influence of drugs he could hardly keep his eyes open. We have been led to believe he has been using the damn stuff regularly. The journalist claims he shared dope in your hut. Were you involved?'

'No Sir! I wouldn't know about that Sir, I'm a private Sir. Just a soldier that's all. Officers don't share anything with diggers, particularly a fill-in like I was Sir. I mean I was just a short stand-in while the usual sig was on leave.'

'Was the LO using drugs or carrying drugs at any time you were with him soldier?'

'I'm a sig Sir not a batman. I don't look after his kit. He's an officer, he didn't share information with me Sir. You know that's the way it is with officers and diggers Sir. I wouldn't know what he does when he is not with me.'

'Permission to speak, Sir?' Sandy cuts in again.

'Yes Sergeant Major.' The clean skin replies almost painfully expecting another outburst. But Sandy has calmed down, he speaks slowly and carefully.

'Well Sir, if you want to know about the officer Sir, I think this soldier can't answer that question. I don't know of any young officer who would get that personal with a soldier in the ranks. What this soldier has told you is correct. He was simply there for a few days while the normal operator was on leave. Our battalion and company records will confirm that Sir. Now about this young soldier who is sitting in front of you. If you want to know if this soldier smokes dope Sir, I can answer that for you. He is the best damn sig I have ever served with and I've served with a few good ones in my time. A feckin professional soldier, pardon the French Sir. But one thing I guarantee you, he is too professional to let down his guard. He doesn't do any drugs

Sir. I'll bet my life on it, in fact I have bet my life on this man and he didn't let me or any other digger down Sir.' Sandy pauses a moment, 'That's all Sir. I just don't want this damn good soldier caught up in something he ain't got no control over, Sir.'

'Thank you CSM.'

The three clean skins look at each other for a moment. Finally, the one who flew into the bunker hospital speaks.

'Your CSM has a high opinion of you son, as does your commanding officer. I've known him since our days in the academy and I value his opinion. And yours of course CSM, though you might choose your words about our prime minister and his commander in chief more carefully next time.'

Sandy defiantly pushes out his chin but says no more.

Another clean skin talks, 'We won't be asking any more questions for now but we will want you back. There will be a formal inquiry. Get that word soldier, formal. We want you to think very carefully about the LO.' He looks at me straight into his eyes. 'It is not you we want to sort out Private, it's the liaison officer. We cannot have an officer who might dishonour the finest institution on God's earth. You can help us son, a few carefully chosen words from you and it is all over. Think about it, a simple acknowledgement that you saw this officer with drugs and we won't ask anymore questions of you or about you. Get advice from your CSM.'

'We are on ops again in the next day or two, Sir', Sandy interrupts.

'Sorry CSM, he may be a good soldier but he is also a key witness to get this trash officer out of our army. He won't be going on ops.'

'Excuse me Sir', I interrupt 'this young officer should not be a scapegoat for the actions of an ARVN commander. He had nothing to do with that execution.'

'I don't give a tinkers cuss about the damn execution soldier. Those two Nogs probably deserved what they got! I care about an officer of this army, my army, using drugs', snaps one of the clean skins. 'We have a proud heritage soldier and I damn well intend it stays proud.'

I sit motionless. The sudden realisation that these men are more concerned about someone smoking dope than they are about a brutal execution causes a deep dull pain in my chest. This is not what I consider part of a proud heritage. I will be in the clear if I dob in the young officer which will no doubt mean my old pal Johnno would take a dive also. What was it about mateship, about loyalty that really mattered? Loyal to an army that turns a blind eye to a brutal murder by its allies! Or loyal to confused young men fighting a war that could never be won?

In this instant, I decide to give my loyalty to Skip and Johnno. They may be stupid and unprofessional. They may have lured me into similar stupidity but I am no dobber. Not even to save my own neck.

The three men sit back in their chairs, each staring directly at me. One finally says, 'This matter is strictly confidential, and believe me, we mean strictly. Got that?'

'Yes Sir', both Sandy and I answer in unison.

The Rover is parked at the end of Luscombe airstrip, Sandy has removed the armband, 'You should have told me the whole feckin story about that village.'

'I did tell you.'

'Not like those photos showed it to be. Feck son that explains why you have been so feckin different since you re-joined the company.'

'What do you mean? Why are you and Nunger saying I'm different? All the lads telling me I'm changed, I ain't.'

Sandy ignores my question and looks me straight in the eyes, 'Forget the Sir bit for a moment. Imagine we're out bush, the buddy system, ya mate. Yer not feckin lying to me about the drugs are ya? 'Cos if you smoke that shit, I never want to see your ugly face again.'

'No Sandy. For fuck's sake, no. I don't smoke shit, except for them Lucky Strikes you put me onto.'

I love this man like a father. I am lying to the best soldier I have ever, will ever, serve with but I couldn't tell him the truth. It was not just the fear of Sandy's reprisal, this man had mentored me and it would break his heart.

'What about the young subby?'

'I wouldn't know about that Sir. I'm just a dumb grunt Sir.'

'Well I'll be fecked. Yer coverin' up for a feckin subby. A 90-day wonder and he ain't even a grunt. Feckin' army intelligence subby.'

'I wouldn't know about that Sir and I don't trust any clean skin! That young subby ain't taking a fall for that execution. Let the world see what a filthy war we got ourselves into. Publish the fucking pictures, let them see, don't hide it and dump it on a subby with some crap about drugs.' If the subby took the odd joint so fuckin' what! How about we let the fucking public see what sort of war we are really fighting. How about we show Australia how our allies treat prisoners. Fucking don't jump on some silly subby with a few fucking grams of ganja. I won't have him hung and quartered. I won't sell what little sense of self-respect I have left.

Sandy looks right through me, his dark eyes drilling a hole into my soul.

'Drug users are shit in my eyes and pogo subbies aren't any better. Put them together and they are not much more than firing range targets in my feckin mind, but if you feel you got to cover up for the bastard that's your business. From this day you're no friend of mine.' Sandy starts the Rover again and then looks at me, 'They want to get him soldier. They want their pound of flesh and I say to you now I hope they get the feckin little arse wipe. He doesn't belong in my army.'

'That's exactly the point Sandy, that's exactly the fucking point', I am responding angrily now. 'He doesn't belong and never did belong. He isn't one of us for fuck's sake. It's the army and the government that put him in that village. He's just a spoilt little rich brat stupid enough to speak a bit of Nog. Think about it a minute will ya before you go off at me. Blame the army.

Your army, Sir, not his, he is just a half trained, scared little boy miles from home with no mummy to cover up his mistakes.' I am panting, I can feel my face flushed with anger, 'Sorry for yelling Sandy, Sir, whatever you want me to call you right now, but Jesus Sandy, drugs or no drugs, you don't know what it's like to see a little baby girl with her head cut off. Killing that Cong ain't anything to compare it with. I'm fucked if I know how I can live with what we went through, so I don't know how that young subby can either. He has enough to live with as it is. I ain't going to drop him into more shit just to please those clean skins. Friendship or not, that's final.'

The Sergeant Major

Sandy switches off the vehicle's engine and stares across the airstrip, thinking about what his young signaller has just said. He has never been a fan of the modern national service, particularly officer training. The army forced to do in 90 days what should take two or four years of intensive training at Duntroon academy. Too many good young national service officers have died trying to lead from the front. Courage is no substitute for good training and good training is not enough. There needs to be a couple of years' experience attached to it before you send a mere boy off to war in charge of 30 soldiers. Most are good men but some young conscripted officers are as much a hindrance as a help.

Sandy decides that Brian is right. His beloved army failed this young man. The army should have insisted to their political masters that conscription for active service was not on.

'I'll have a word with the OC on the quiet and get him to talk to the CO. The career man can pull strings. His mate is one of the investigating officers.' He looks at me yet again, shaking his head from side to side. 'Alright, we are still a team you and I, but you won't stand a chance as a witness in any court martial. They will grill you to death because they know you're covering for him. You will be under oath son. They catch you lying under oath and you're in Holdsworthy MCE for a long stint. We got to get you out of it somehow.'

The Rover's engine kicks over and we start moving again. Sandy's mumbling angrily to himself, 'Feck me with a feckin pace stick, whatever happened to this man's army? What happened to the days when we just got drunk and into fistfights? Bust a few heads, spend a night in the guardroom under lock and key, then confined to barracks for a week, that's the old army I loved. What happened? Feckin national service that's what happened.'

REST AND RECREATION

ROUND EYES, WOW, big brown bottomless buckets of starlight staring through those round eyes. Red hair and freckles, I can't believe it, she's got freckles!

I sit on the edge of my allocated bed, arm stretched out as the nurse feels for the vein ready to plunge in the large needle to extract some of my blood.

'You know it is not wise to stare at a girl like that when she is about to shove a needle into you.'

'Sorry', I can feel my face blushing bright red.

The young nurse smiles, a beautiful bright smile radiating from her lips like a beam of sunshine dancing in a mirrored room.

'I'm used to it I suppose. At least you're not undressing me with those eyes, more than I can say about some of you diggers.'

I quickly look around the room so as not to do exactly what the nurse has suggested young soldiers do. A small room, barrack like, with just a few beds and the usual steel lockers and steel desks. Not like a hospital at all, the window has heavy weld mesh on the outside. I am amused, security to keep men out or keep them in? I am aware that the draw of Vungers is strong amongst soldiers, to be in Vung Tau Hospital and fit enough to slip into town is quite an appealing idea. I note the absence of any other kit on the other beds. I have the room all to myself.

The nurse extracts the needle with its contents, turns and walks to the mobile tray she has wheeled in with her. I take the opportunity to run my eyes up and down her body. Attractive but not the movie star type of beauty. Trim but one would guess not the perfect figure hiding under the green slacks and baggy shirt. Not perfect but who wants perfect? Men just want a woman who is lovely on the eye. But that red hair, it is pulled back tightly into a bun, I fantasise about it falling down naturally to her shoulders. Then there are the freckles. Now that is something special.

I had forgotten about freckles since arriving in Vietnam six thousand years ago.

Freckles said in big loud words, 'AUSTRALIA' and I am now swimming amongst those freckles. I want to ask those freckles to marry me and share my life forever or at least share a bed with me. The freckles are now staring back at me. I feel myself blushing red.

'Do you know when I get more tests?'

'Urine and blood is all I know about', she replies smiling through her wonderful freckles. 'I just take your blood pressure and pulse for fun', the smile turning to a cheeky grin. Four gigantic eyelashes flutter like butterfly wings stretching in a morning light.

'Oh, I assume this is about my fall from the chopper some time back, my wrist is still giving me hell.'

The nurse looks at my wrist and takes it in her own hands. I melt as I feel her soft warm hands. I pick up a very slight fragrance, not perfume but perfumed soap. I visualise her standing in a shower. She suddenly moves my hand and wrist. Gently but firmly moving the hand sideways then up and down. I wince on the downward movement.

'Did you ever get this X-rayed? There is a lump in there. Could have a ganglion.'

'We don't carry portable X-ray units on our back when we are on patrol.'

'Okay, I'll talk to the doctor tomorrow. Might pay to take you over to General and have it looked at. Meanwhile you're confined to this room for the rest of the day and night, a meal will be delivered.'

'Some of the boys from the battalion are in the hospital. I got a mate kicked a mine. I'd like to catch up, pass on a few messages from back at the Dat.'

'I know the soldier. He's going to be air lifted home tomorrow.' She looks sad, 'War is so cruel, he is so young. It's unfair what happened to him. Give me any messages and I will pass them to him before I come off duty tonight.'

'I'd rather see him myself, we got this kind of joke. A monkey thing happening between us, I think maybe I could cheer him up a bit.'

'Sorry, orders are orders, you stay here. But when you get back to your unit tell all his friends that despite what's happened to him he somehow finds every opportunity to cause havoc in the ward. Last night he pretended he was asleep and as the nurse pulled up his bed sheet he reached out and pinched her on the bum, very naughty indeed. We nurses are officers you know. Privates are not supposed to pinch officers on the bum.' She then points to the doorway, 'In your own best interest, let me warn you that there is someone on the door to monitor all movement in and out, but there are plenty of books and things on the rack over there. Find one you like and make the most of this moment. Just lie back, read and sleep. Most diggers would kill for a chance to do that.' She stops and blushes, 'I don't mean kill I mean...'

'That's okay. 'I know what you're trying to say. Hey! I might enjoy the stay if you come back and chat for a while. I mean only talk and stuff, honest. It's just been a long time since I spoke to an Aussie girl.'

The big brown buckets between the round eyes seem to soften for a moment as the freckles stretch to accommodate the beaming smile.

'I'm sorry, I really am, but I can't. It is hospital policy. I will tell your friend that you have tried to see him but orders prevent it. I'll tell him all the boys back at the battalion are wishing him a quick recovery.'

The Army Nurse

Lauren stared at Brian for a moment seeing no more than a boy, far from home in a tragic world. After completing her training at the Royal Adelaide Hospital, Lauren was about to take a placement at the Children's Hospital when it dawned on her that the army needed nursing staff. It seemed such an adventure at first being amongst all those young men filled with their childish egos. An opportunity to serve in a medical combat unit was an adventure she had to chase.

That was then of course, only eight months ago! Now Lauren sees the horrors of senseless killings. Now Lauren is run off her feet as a surgical nurse one moment and delivering bed pans the next. Shattered bodies, not virile young men with childish egos. Or boys like this one, in another world he might have been quite a catch, but now he is a lost soul and no amount of medicine will help him find himself in this place called Vietnam.

The moment passes and she wheels the mobile tray out the door.
I produce my notebook.

> *Her freckles and that wonderful smile were the most beautiful thing I have laid eyes on in months. I try to re-create that feminine smell of her soap in my mind. I had forgotten those simple delights, perhaps I had never noticed them before I left Australia, took them for granted.*

I allow my mind to leave that pleasant space and think about the Spanker.

> *Should I disobey orders and try to break out and go over to the hospital and see him, or should I just admit the truth to myself, that the orders give me an excuse to avoid staring at my own worst nightmare?*

Looking at Spanker's mutilated body will only remind me that I might be next. I need to change the focus of my thoughts so I get up from the bed and wander over to examine the books.

A reasonable sized paperback catches my eye, 'The Quiet American' by Graham Greene.

I scan through the pages in the novel, stopping at these words which leap from the page in front of me, *'Innocence always calls mutely for protection when we would be wiser to guard against it. Innocence is like a dumb leper who has lost his bell, wandering the world, meaning no harm'*.

I find these words disturbing. I lie back and stare at the ceiling fan.

Whop   Whop   Whop   Whop   Whop

I am hooked, no turning back on this disturbing concept. Quickly I return to the first chapter and read. Above the bed a fan turns. Turns and turns like the rotors of a Helo.

Whop   Whop   Whop   Whop   Whop

Regardless of my fascination with the paperback I have a sense of unease about the situation. Back at the Dat, Sandy told me to get my butt on the mail run to Vung Tau and report to the casualty unit at the hospital. I assumed it was for the old injury that I regularly complained to Doc about. I figured the D Company medic had finally organised someone to look at my back and wrist, but…!

'Oh what the heck, just like freckles said, enjoy the rest.'

The night passes with me absorbed in the book. I'm brought a barely warm but acceptable meal and I have a reasonable sleep. That is until a nightmare flings me out of bed and across the room headlong into a steel locker. The recurrent chopper crash nightmare, crash and burn, it often comes back when I am in base camps.

This morning I am sitting in an office in front of a grey haired Major wearing a white coat, a psychiatrist. I am distinctly uncomfortable about his presence in the hospital. The man in front of me is obviously an army reservist medical officer with honorary rank. Thinning grey hair almost bald in parts with a low forehead slanting at an awkward angle over bushy grey eyebrows then downward toward his oversized nose under which a small mouth provides a space between the rest of his head and an almost non-existent chin. His leathery thin neck is dominated by his Adam's apple, which moves up and down as he speaks. An army issue tie hangs untidily from within the collar of an oversized army issue polyester shirt. I conclude that the man is a turtle not a medical officer and amuse myself by imagining the man crawling up on a north Queensland beach to lay some eggs.

'Blood and urine tests found no trace of illegal substances', the Major says, while making notes on a file in front of him. 'Except for the alcohol that is. It shouldn't be that high unless you somehow managed to sneak out of here before the nurse took the sample.'

'No Sir', I now believe I've been sent here for tests to see if I was lying about the dope. Not that it would possibly show anything. I had not had a joint since the night of the attack on the village, too long ago for any trace to remain in my system. However, I have enjoyed more than a few drops of cheap whisky which I smuggle with me everywhere except on patrol.

'What's your poison son, rum or whisky?'

'Whisky, Sir.'

'Give it up son or at least cut back sharply, your liver will thank you for it one day.'

The Major is now looking directly at me. 'Rough night?' the man asks. 'Frightened the duty NCO when he heard you bounce across the floor and knock down the locker.'

I blush, 'That was just a bad nightmare. I ain't the only one with that drama, diggers often get the night yips when they're safe behind a wire.'

The Major nods knowingly, 'It comes because in safe areas you can get a deep enough sleep for sustained REM and when you do it's often an unpleasant experience.'

'REM Sir?'

'Never mind the jargon. What it means is that on operations, you boys are on constant machine gun watch every night and have your sleep pattern broken and you all sleep with one eye open. It causes a problem similar to sleep deprivation. You don't get into deep sleep often enough or long enough. That's my theory anyway.'

I shrug my shoulders, it will pass once I get back home and it don't seem such a big deal. 'So what am I doing here Sir? I mean seeing a shrink, seeing you Sir?'

The Psychiatrist

The Major turns away from his patient and stares out the window for a while thinking calmly. If I was a young man doing my thesis I'd love to examine the long term effects of this on these boys. In past wars soldiers were only tensed up when they were in the front line. No front line or rest area in this war. These boys are in it almost every day for almost 12 months. The brain is an amazing thing, it adapts and changes to meet its environment when under extreme pressure or life challenge. Will it adapt back to normalcy when the boys go home? No extreme pressure to re-adapt? Will their brains remain stuck in some sort of confused state between war alert and civilian boredom? I suspect there will be problems when they try to break the patterns back at home.

The Major smiles at the 'shrink' comment. 'Your Commanding Officer and I go back a long way son, a long way indeed. I was a young doctor in Korea. It seems it's in everyone's best interest that you are out of country for a spell, next week in fact.'

He is writing on a file in front of him. A few more notes then he continues his chat.

'You know how it is in this man's army son, orders are that you stay nearby, but I don't know that because I'm in a hospital unit not a battalion.

I decide you need immediate Rest and Recreation, war neurosis. Guess what? The paperwork gets jammed up in the system somewhere.'

I am stunned. Sandy's had a quiet word with OC. The OC's had a word with the CO. The CO has words with old friends and bingo! Until now I thought the military was too tight, too damn correct to tolerate this sort of old boy's network. But what the heck, right now all I am thinking about is my good mate Sandy and a chance for R and R.

'The trick will be in getting you on a flight to Australia without having some poor young digger miss out because you took his place', the Major comments.

'I want Taiwan.'

'Actually son, I would prefer you went home for a spell to be with family. You look pretty strung out.' The Major stares at my hands, noting that I keep rubbing them on my trouser legs. I stop rubbing but my fingers still feel sticky and wet.

'Not much of a family situation for me at home Sir.'

The Major stares for a while, obviously deep in thought about something that I could not guess at.

'No, you are going back to Australia young man. I'm sure we can get you on a flight with the Yanks to Sydney in no time flat. If not, I can arrange to squeeze you on a C130 taking the sick and wounded home. You will miss the one tomorrow but tragically there will be another soon enough. You can fly as an aide and help feed and comfort some of the stretcher cases.'

I sit upright, a new spring in my movements. This is all good news to me.

'So, what now Sir? I'll need to get back to the battalion to get things sorted.'

'Not a problem son. I'll speak to who I need to speak to and things will happen. You can head ba...', he pauses, looks closely at me for a moment. He opens his file notes and reads quietly. 'On second thoughts I'd like to keep you here one more night and arrange some observations.'

I shrug my shoulders. What do I care, probably this old bloke just wants to follow up that sleep deprivation and REM stuff.

'So it's back to the prison cell Sir.'

'I like to think of it as our psychiatric ward son. Off you go and enjoy the chance to have a decent rest.'

I return to my room, grab '*The Quiet American*' and start reading again. After a few pages, I lie back on my pillow and stare up at the ceiling fan turning above me.

Rest and Recreation! Five days in Sydney all paid for and no weapons, no fears, no night shifts. The war becomes an adventure again. I stare up at the ceiling fan mesmerised by its movement.

Whop   Whop   Whop   Whop   Whop

PART THREE

We share a table yet we are so far apart
I am conscious of your stare
Your awkward confusion
fearing that you pity me rather than accept me

My body gaunt, my own staring eyes
darkened by visions so far away
far far from this moment we share

So alone, my instinct knows only fight or flight
I envy your innocence. I resent your naivety
I sit at the table, an alien in this room
Uncomfortable that no soldier has my back

I long for those who talk softly with little to say
And my blood stained hands caressing the security
of an M16 resting across my lap

PLANET AUS

'Saint George I reckon, Balmain doesn't stand a chance. What do you think Brian?'

'Huh!' I snap back into the present conversation.

'Oh I wouldn't know mate, I've been out of country most of the season.'

'Don't get much time for rugby league over there I suppose?' The shoulder length haired Geoff inquires.

'No, no not really. Then again we don't think about stuff like that much either.'

'Hey, I heard that Trev Marshall got killed over there, sometime after Robby was killed?' Geoff asks, 'Remember him Bri? We all called him Surf. Him and Bobby Brown were our heroes weren't they.'

'Yeah, Surf, Bobby and Jacko. Good old Jacko, best board maker in Sydney I reckon.' I let out a long sigh, 'Poor old Surf is up in six set heaven with Bobby now mate. One gone in a pub incident the other in a war'. I try to move the conversation into another area. 'At least Jacko would still be around the beaches, that is providing his beer gut didn't get any bigger.'

'Plane crash or something?' Geoff asks, he would not be moved on to a cheery subject.

'His chopper got shot down', I respond, as a sense of inner guilt surges through my body. 'One of those things I'd rather not talk about.'

I am feeling out of place amongst old school friends. It has been a long time since I had sat with them in a pub drinking beer and making small talk. Too long! So far I have listened to Patrick explain how he is growing a dope plant inside his bathroom using ultra violet light which somehow seems of great interest to the rest at the table, and that William only had a pass in his European history assignment at university.

I ask, 'Why study European history, what good will that do you in Australia?' The group just look at me as though I am an alien from another planet.

'You have to study something', they respond in chorus. 'If you get kicked out of your arts degree your old man will make you go to work for a living.' For those at the table, this seemed to be the logical answer to my illogical question. Logic is not on my mind.

Just 70 hours ago I was in Vietnam wondering if I would still be alive in the next few days. Shortly before that I had seriously contemplated killing a Hoi Chan. I am still reeling from the horror of the mutilated little girl lying on the road, her head tossed to one side. Now I am tested with such issues as to who will win the rugby on Saturday. I do not see anything special about growing dope in a bathroom.

These old friends are like aliens from another planet. No! It is me. I am the alien from another planet!

The crowded saloon bar noises are also alien. This is partially due to my hearing loss from explosions and the constant tinnitus ringing in my ears. But there are also unfamiliar sounds that I cannot allocate to a place in my survival-programmed brain.

In the war torn jungle of Vietnam, every sound that my senses detect is instantaneously examined by my sub-conscious for a danger signal. Wind, heavy rain, a wild pig snorting or a monkey in the treetops. These are good sounds but any sound that did not fit was an early warning of potential danger.

This noisy room is sound overload. I am up tight, tense and my breathing is restricted.

I observe the strangers around me with care. Each face is scanned for a sign of indifference or fear, their eyes can tell me if they are friend or enemy, peasant or killer. My brain is now finely tuned to that world. Even in the more relaxed world of the boozer at the Dat there are distinct safety sounds and conversations between men in similar states of sub-conscious awareness. People talk much softer, laugh much louder in Vietnam.

This world of Australian voices with their unfamiliar discussions in unfamiliar surroundings added to unfamiliar sounds coming from all directions makes me feel tense and hemmed in. I need to get myself better positioned in the room so that I can at least know that all the sounds are in front of me, all the faces can be scanned. There is no tail-end Charlie covering my back in this place. I feel exposed and threatened. I look around for a table against a wall somewhere, preferably close to an exit door. There are no empty tables. I am fighting a strong urge to get up and leave the room. Near panic is nagging at my insides.

Fight or flight!

I cannot fight, there is no enemy. Flight is the only option my primitive senses are sending from the unconscious to the conscious.

Planet Australia is a million light years away from the brutality and reality of a war on the distant galaxy of Asia.

I look around the saloon bar, am I the only person with short back and sides? I feel alone and isolated. I almost feel like a monkey in a zoo as people stop and stare at me for a brief moment. 'Hey ain't you Brian? I remember you', they say, staring at my haircut and sunken eyes then uncomfortably moving off to another table.

I miss Wingnut, Doc, Sandy and the boys from Delta Company. Twice I have tried to get into a conversation tonight but on both occasions stop myself as I realise I am being stared at strangely. People shift uncomfortably in their seats and look around the room nervously. I realise I am swearing and cussing in ways never heard by these people but I can't seem to stop the foul language slipping through my lips. Even at home, my brother called me aside quietly and asked me to have some respect for our mother.

'What do you mean by that?' I challenged.

'Well you have said "fuck" at least three times at the dinner table and when you dropped the words 'little white mice cunts" while describing the Vietnamese police, I thought mum was going to faint.'

I feel an arm slip around me from behind, a kiss on the cheek and, 'Hello Brian. Gosh it's been a long time.' I look around to find my old school flame Rhonda smiling at me.

'Well what do you know then?' I reply as she sits on a chair beside me.

Rhonda has changed. A young woman develops considerably in three years. She is 20 like me, her hair hangs loosely past her shoulders. A flowing skirt with tie dye patterns hangs casually below her tiny halter neck top, her nipples protrude proudly through the cotton. Her eyes are slightly glazed and I can tell she has been smoking a joint. I remember Viper hospital and the bright nurse with big brown eyes and butterfly lashes. Rhonda's lashes are sadly no more than half-closed moth's wings hiding in the shadows of drowsy eyelids.

My mind slips back to those adolescent moments with Rhonda. Soft satin skin against my cheekbone, the sensual excitement as my hand ventured for the first time beneath her school dress, exploring the unknown world of her inner thigh until the delight of fingertips caressing cotton knickers.

Now I just look up at her saggy doped-up eyes lamenting what might have been for both of us.

'So what are you up to these days?'

Rhonda shrugs. 'I dropped out of uni. I'm just cruising. I'm thinking of going up to northern New South Wales, there are a couple of communes starting up there', she replies before suddenly getting excited. 'Hey I am learning guitar also. This guy I hang out with is teaching me. He said we could form a folk group, a new Peter, Paul and Mary deal.'

I nod politely, 'I thought Peter, Paul and Mary were still part of the scene. I mean Puff the Magic Dragon is obviously still around.'

Rhonda throws back her head and feigns a laugh, 'Ah yes good old Puff. So what about you. I heard you went to Vietnam?'

'Yeah, I'm only just back for a few days, it's called R and R. I go back early next week.'

'Bummer', Rhonda replies as her face changes its expression to one of stoned sympathy. 'It must be awful over there with all that killing and stuff. I just can't imagine you amongst those people, you're not a killer Brian.'

This statement has me a little confused. What killers is she talking about exactly?

'It's not so bad I suppose and I only have a short time left once I get back, before we come home to Australia.'

'Not so bad?' How can you call killing innocent women and children not so bad?'

'What women and children? We don't kill women and children.'

'Sure, sure. I know what I see and read in the papers Brian. Don't plead innocent with me about that war. It's terrible what you are doing to those people. You killed a whole village of women and children and don't try to pretend you didn't.'

This pressed a button in my psyche. The only dead children I saw were killed by their fellow countrymen, by communist terrorists.

I understand that children are casualties of war. We all know about that terrible massacre by that American platoon. But that was nothing to do with Australian soldiers. American bombing raids must cause child casualties and I do not like that anymore than the next person but Rhonda is insinuating that Australians are actually going around killing women and children as though it is a part of our job.

'What papers are you on about, some communist rag passed out at university or the main press? '

'Both, but the mainstream press don't tell the real story because they are anti-communist and on your side. I prefer to believe what I hear from friends in the movement.' She pauses, 'What's wrong with communism anyway? Why do you people just want to kill us?'

'Hang on, hang on, mainstream press on my side? For fuck's sake I ain't on any side. What do you mean "my people" wanting to kill you communists?' I shake my head then continue, 'Rhonda you got to understand that half the Australian boys in Vietnam are conscripts, draftees! The other half, people like me, we signed on to serve the democratically elected government of this country. That is supposed to mean we are serving the people of this country. We don't start wars and we don't finish them but I'll tell you one thing for sure, we don't go round killing women and children, so get your facts straight.'

'I feel sorry for you Brian. The government was only elected on a gerrymander. The real people of Australia don't want to see you people butchering innocent Asians.'

I can feel the cold rage bubbling up inside me, the little girl's head flashes vividly in my mind, my fingers suddenly sticky again. 'I don't butcher innocent Asians', I spit back at her as my voice drops an octave lower. I feel my face twist into the image of a callous cold blooded man filled with hatred and suppressed rage but I am unable to stop. 'I kill the terrorist scum that butcher little children because their parents chose to be anti-communist and I won't apologise for killing those bastards, not to you or any other person.' My voice increases in volume, 'Scum like that deserve to fucking die!' I look at everybody sitting around the table, some shuffling uncomfortably, others unable to make eye contact with my distorted angry face. I am aware that my cold words have left everyone feeling uncomfortable. Rhonda's facial expression is that of a child, frightened and frozen in shock.

I have lost my senses. I'm overcome with a mixture of rage, frustration and extreme embarrassment. I desperately want to lash out at any object, smash something. The embarrassment turns to fear as I realise I may lash out violently toward any person who tries to calm me. I'm afraid of my own potential to become dangerously aggressive. Fight or flight! I stand and quickly leave the room.

Outside I wave down a taxi, climb in the front and give him my parents' address. I sit in silence as the cab moves through the streets. Still the anger burns within me, I have never experienced such inner rage. What is happening to me?

'Army?' the taxi driver asks.

'How do you figure that?'

'People your age with short hair are either army or police. You're no copper I can see that.'

I ignore the cabbie and sit quietly, still trying desperately to gain some sense of inner calm.

'Vietnam?' Again, the cab driver is asking more questions than I wish to answer.

'Yeah.'

The cabby shakes his head. 'Should take all those long haired pooftas and put them in the army if you ask me. Send them to Vietnam that would sort the hippy bastards out', he says angrily. 'My mates died fighting the Japs so this country could be free and what thanks do we get, a bunch of long haired poofta commies trying to hide from doing their duty, that's what we get.'

I look at the cab driver. In his own way he is just as offensive as Rhonda had been. I want to lash out with my fist and punch the man. I grab my right fist in my left hand and squeeze it as tight as possible. Just sit tight, don't do anything stupid, make small talk until you are safely at home.

'You in a war?'

'The big one, WW2 son. You think these little pooftas would at least be man enough to fight in a little war like Vietnam.'

Little war! My vision now blurs out of focus, the inside of the taxi seems to swim around me. Sit tight, just sit tight, you will be home soon, don't blow up now, keep the small talk going.

'So what did you do in the big war mate. What unit did you serve in?'

'Not important, what is important is that I was there son. I did my bit for my country and I suppose you are too.'

'You suppose do you? Ever kill anyone, see people mangled and bloody, ever shit or piss your pants you were so scared?' I ask, the hot uncontrollable rage suddenly turning into a cold callous sensation but one that I feel in control of.

The cab driver shifts uncomfortably in his seat, 'Long time ago son.'

'So tell me, how do you strip and assemble a Bren gun? What's the safety procedure for a 303 mate? Cyclic rate of fire for an Owen gun? No vet can forget those things. Tell me what you did in the big war why don't you', I snap at the driver.

'Well I wasn't infantry son, not exactly', the cabby replies awkwardly.

'What were you then mate?' I push, 'Artillery? Armour?'

'Doesn't matter', the cabby replies as he realises he is dealing with a young man on the very edge of violent madness.

'Biscuit bomber or base waller I bet. I reckon you biscuit bombers know all about real war not like us stupid Vietnam vets who only fight in little wars.'

The cab driver remains silent for the rest of the journey.

I pay the man and walk toward my mother's front door but stop and sit on the front fence. Get a grip for fuck's sake, what's happening to me, I'm going bonkers. Come on, deep breaths, get a grip, can't let mum see me like this.

I dislike the naivety of the young people my own age but have nothing but contempt for fools like that cab driver. Rhonda may be idealistic and misguided and I was hurt by what she had accused me of, but at least she knew that war is wrong, even though she is innocent to the truths of international economics and politics. Nevertheless, she is wise in believing Vietnam is a war Australia should not be fighting.

I begin to calm and regain some self-discipline. I've got to get control of this shit or I'll end up killing some poor bastard.

As for the cab driver! I have no time for men who judge people by the length of their hair. It usually means they also judge people by the colour of their skin. I have come to know first-hand that the Sandys and Nungers of this world are men to be respected and befriended. There is an old saying that there are no atheists in foxholes. I disagree with that but I have learned first-hand that there are no racists in foxholes, no homophobes, only scared men trusting each other with their lives.

I have no time for old farts who claim they fought the real war while Vietnam vets are on holiday. Vietnam has more than its share of pogos, but WW2 had plenty of wankers and pogo wallers also. The ones who talk the most usually did the least.

I look down the road with its streetlights casting a dim glow over my childhood memories. Suburbia at its Australian best. My trusty notebook is with me. It has become a habit now. I just have to make notes each day.

> *Little boxes in neat little rows with low front fences that say to everyone, 'this is my territory'. I've pissed in these four corners of the fence line, marked my territory. Little boxes filled with ticky-tacky.*
>
> *This is where I grew up but it just isn't home anymore. I have not lived at home with my parents for more than three years but the sense of alienation is far greater than simply living away. It is as though I had only lived here in a past life. A life now dead, never to return. The memories are some other person's memories and that person does not exist anymore.*

I miss my mates back in 'Nam.

Tomorrow I will have to face Milly. Robby's girlfriend has asked me to meet her for coffee at the local milk bar. Jesus, what can I tell her, poor bloody Milly!

A vehicle pulls around the bend and drives up to the driveway entrance. My father is home at last from another night of working overtime. He needs to make more money to buy a bigger house or some other dream that has pushed him into the life of a workaholic, while my mother sits at home lonely and isolated from other women.

'Is that you Brian?' He asks of the shadow sitting on the fence.

'Yeah dad, just me.' I tuck the notebook away.

My Father climbs out of his car and stretches to loosen up his back and shoulder muscles after the long drive from his city office.

'Well seeing as how you are home, why don't I grab a bite to eat and then you and I can go down to the Returned Services club and have a game of snooker with my old cobbers.'

I look at the man in front of me. A workaholic and when he's not working he's getting drunk at the RSL or the golf club. What sort of life is that? Poor old mum in there with his tea kept warm in the oven. I think she prefers it when he goes down to the RSL, it gets him out of her hair.

'Thanks for the offer dad, but I think I'll give it a miss.'

'It's been a couple of days now Brian and you haven't wanted to mix with my cobbers down at the RSL. They want to meet you son and welcome you to the league.'

'I'm not in the league dad.'

'Well, yes you are son. I signed you up and paid the membership myself. I'm damn proud of you son. It's a great honour to see your name on the members' board right under mine.

'I'm sorry dad but not tonight, some other time maybe.'

'Robby's dad has been asking after you son, he wants to see you, talk about young Rob, about what really happened, you know what I mean. All the army told him was that he was killed in action and that he served his country proudly. Rob was your friend and you were nearby when he was killed, you could explain things to his dad, put his mind at rest.

'Nearby, I was a thousand or more meters away pissing in a helmet when Robby went down. Jesus dad, what do you want me to tell the poor man? His son was talking on the radio and a rocket-propelled grenade exploded in the tree right beside him, blew off half his shoulder and turned his head into pulp. Do I tell Rob's old man that, do I? Let him know what he missed out on seeing because they wouldn't let him view the body?'

I can feel my face flushing red with anger. Am I going totally mad with rage these days? 'Sorry I didn't get a photo, his mum would love that wouldn't she?'

'Calm down son, calm down, that's not what I meant. I'm sorry, it must have been hard and, well I don't know.' Dad pauses in thought then continues, 'Perhaps you could say a few nice things about Rob and tell him he had a brave son who gave it all for his country, that sort of thing.'

I shake my head, 'I have agreed to meet with Milly tomorrow, you know, Emily, Rob's fiancée.'

My father stands silently for a moment, 'I did not know he was engaged.'

'Jesus dad you met her at the airbase the night we flew out to 'Nam.'

'Oh that's right, there was a young girl there wasn't there, I just thought she was a pick-up, you know what I mean.'

'She is a wonderful young woman who loved Robby more than life itself. They fell in love at school dad, she was the best thing that ever happened to him, and now I have to look her in the eyes and I just don't know what to tell her.' I pause a moment, 'I feel so guilty dad, I was drinking beer and joking about the war when poor Rob was hit. I wasn't there for him. I mean I couldn't have saved him but I could have at least been there to look after him and treat him with respect just so Milly would know that he had me there to care for him. I feel so fucking guilty dad, Robby died while I made jokes and pissed in a hat, I am ashamed.'

'Well son, perhaps you could just tell this girl a bit of a lie. You could do the same for Rob's dad, and his mum I suppose.'

'No more bullshit about war dad, no more. It's time to tell the truth to the world about war. Rob died scared and afraid in a muddy bit of jungle, fighting a stupid war that Australia should never have got itself mixed up in, and you know what else dad? I'm getting on a C130 transport and flying back to that stupid war in two days and I'm shit scared that I might end up just like poor Rob. So the last thing I want to do is go to a RSL club with a bunch of people who had their war years ago, forgotten or exaggerated the truth and don't have to worry about what might be waiting for them in a couple of days.'

My father sits on the fence beside me, 'I am scared for you son, your mother is worried sick about you going back over there. You're not making things any easier for us you know. You say nothing, you won't mix with our friends and just seem to brood all day. Can't you just talk to me son?'

I sit quietly for a while allowing the inexplicable anger inside to gradually reduce then respond calmly, 'In the last war, your war, did you ever kill anyone?'

'No son, not exactly. I was on a naval ship, I guess the vessel sort of killed people and all of us on it were a part of that. But I never personally killed any Japanese. No I was down in the engine room. Not like being in a jungle full of tigers and things like you have been.'

I smile, tigers! 'So far I've never seen a wild cat when I patrolled the jungle. I heard one once, it was first light, just before stand-to. It moved in close to the perimeter and I heard it. I smelt it dad! The big cat stopped just beyond my sight, just stopped and no doubt examined us from the distance. Then it purred like a pussycat, a deep rumbling purr, after a while, it moved on. I stared at the soldier lying beside me and we both simply raised our eyebrows in unison, smiled the smile of two diggers living on a mixture of stress and adrenalin. I shrugged my shoulders; he shook his head and I saw him return the safety catch on his rifle to safe. I looked down at the safety catch on my M16 and realised I had moved it all the way to auto instinctively. Without thinking, I was preparing myself for the kill! I guess I am just a well-trained soldier, prepared for killing instinctively but don't squeeze off a burst until your enemy looms large in your sights.'

I draw back hard on my cigarette, 'Death at five meters dad, that is what jungle warfare is all about and you know what? I haven't squeezed that trigger in anger so far during my tour of duty. Others near me have. I haven't had to. I'm too busy on other tasks.' I stare at my father, 'I know that I will squeeze that trigger without hesitation should the moment present itself dad. I am prepared to kill another human being without hesitation, prepared to forgo all mum's teachings about humanity. It's a strange feeling to discover that I really am a trained killer, not just trained but actually able to do it. Dad I have stood over a man who had his intestines ripped out so he could die an agonising death. Fuck I just stood there and did not even care.'

I gaze into my father's eyes, 'Funny you mention tigers. It's strange how these memories keep me awake some nights, not the memories of grinding tank tracks, exploding claymore mines and screaming enemy. Sometimes I have nightmares about that shit. Only sometimes. Mostly I am kept awake by simple moments, not the dramatic ones. Always that jungle dad! I cannot stop thinking about it, I lay on my bed at night and it is vivid in my mind. Its mud, its leeches, its snakes and its enemy soldiers. Here I am back in Australia on leave for five lousy days, yet I lie awake at night, homesick for that putrid decaying mass of greens and browns. The smell of death, that anticipation for the unknown danger just beyond the next clump of bamboo.' Tears well in my eyes, 'It haunts me dad. I sometimes think a part of my soul is still wandering in that jungle, searching for me amongst the death and decay. It cannot find me and sadly, I cannot retrieve it. It remains in that jungle, it is the sorrowful and lonely soul of an Australian digger. What the Vietnamese call a Buon Co Doc Uc Dai Loi.'

My father twitches nervously, uncomfortable about the discussion, wanting to share some wisdom with his boy but not knowing what to say. He simply has no advice worth passing.

'You will be alright son, you are just, well, sensitive about things. That's not your fault you aren't like most men I suppose, it's probably a fault from your mother's side of the family. I probably failed you son, left you with your mother too much, you did not really toughen up much as a child. I am sorry for not doing that for you. Just, well just don't say these things in front of your mother, I mean about being ready to kill people. We don't want to upset her do we? We do not talk about these things son. Not like that, I mean not the way you talk about them. Joke about it or tell some sort of yarn but do not talk like that to other men son, it's a sign of weakness. You have to be a real man from now on.'

For a long moment, I just stare at my father not knowing if I love him or despise him for his response to my attempt to cross a psychological bridge. What's the point? What's the fucking point in trying to explain what I am going through?

'I'm sorry dad, I really am. I should not have talked to you about it. What say we all go out to dinner tomorrow night? Mum loves to go out to dinner, we could go somewhere special, that Chinese Restaurant you take her to on your wedding anniversary. Let's get my bro to come with us, be a family for a change.'

My father's eyes light up. 'Great I'll go tell your mother', he replies and walks to the door, stops, looks back at me and goes inside.

I sit on the fence long enough to finish another cigarette and prepare my mind for a night in my mother's favourite Chinese Restaurant. The last thing I want to do in the next two days is to sit in a room that serves noodles. I know mum loves to go out for Chinese food washed down with a glass of Barossa Pearl and I want to see her have a happy moment before I go back to the war.

I butt out my smoke, poke a finger into the ground and bury the butt in the hole. I instinctively check the ash has not left a tell-tale sign that I was here, an enemy soldier could not see it. Realizing what I am doing I smile wryly. You're right Sandy, 'ya can take the digger out of 'Nam, but ya can't take 'Nam outta the digger'. I shake my head slowly as I recall Sandy's words, then enter the house and walk into the kitchen. My mother is washing the pots used to cook my father's dinner. Father has grabbed his plate from the oven and sits in the lounge room to watch TV while eating alone.

Mum looks up and smiles, 'Dad tells me you want us all to go to the Peking Swan for dinner tomorrow night. He rang Rob's mum and dad and told them you would be there tomorrow night if they want to talk with you. Sort of suggested they might like to, well sort of, just turn up, you know.'

My heart sinks and a big knot forms down in my stomach. I force back the urge to storm into the lounge room and wring my father's neck.

'Something wrong darling?'

'No mum. I might just go to my room and read for a while.'

I lie on my bed staring at the ceiling. First, I have to face Milly, but how can I look Robby's mother in the eyes, knowing that she will feel guilty because she will be wishing it were her boy standing there instead of me.

I just lie there wishing I was back in Vietnam. Back where I now belong! Wingnut told me this would happen. Home ain't home anymore!

Humiliation

I am sitting staring at the grey haired psychiatrist who is reading the brief file in front of him. He shuts it and looks up at me, 'So, how was the trip?'

'Yeah, good, nice to see people you don't have to worry about. I would have preferred Taiwan to Sydney but, then again, you don't get too many free trips abroad do you?'

'Did you have any trouble with the family back home?'

I choose not to answer that question and instead pose a question of my own, 'So what am I doing back here? I thought you were doing the CO a favour and getting me out of sight for a while.'

The officer looks up again and stares straight at me. 'Careful son, careful what you say and just be thankful for friends in right places. I was assured by your commanding officer and your company commander that you, young man, could maintain confidentiality'

'Sorry. Of course I can', I look away, staring at the wall uncomfortably.

'What do you think of the army chaplains back at the battalion?'

'God botherers are not my cup of tea.'

'You had a talk with one of them?'

'Some time back, stuck his nose in where it wasn't wanted.'

'I've been checking up a bit while you were away. You worry me soldier, the nurses provided some concerning reports of your sleep patterns and the chaplain seems to confirm my worries. Nightmares and booze, a bad mix.'

'So what are you saying Sir? What makes me so different from my mates?'

'The difference is I don't get to see them. I did get a look at you and I did not like what I saw. You are strung out son, past it. I have the story and photos from your CO of what you went through in that village. It matched the nurse's report about you screaming in the middle of the night, the second night I had you stay in the hospital. I have seen the photos of that little girl son. What those bastards did to her…'

I am getting nervous, shifting in my chair.

'Okay, so I was strung out. We all are. I am no different. I've had a good break and I want to re-join the company.'

'You're not re-joining any company son, not while I have a say and I do have a big say.'

'You're saying I can't cut it. You're calling me a drop out and I ain't. I won't ever let my mates down, Sir.'

'I'm sure you won't let your mates down son. I don't know what it is with you grunts, it's the training I expect, damn brain washing if you ask me. Don't let your mates down, one for all, all for one. What is it you say? "No Jackman in this unit" or some such crap. No son, I am damn sure that you will go right back out there and somehow hold it all together on the outside. Nevertheless, inside you are a spent force. You're burnt out and past it. You're bloody dangerous.'

He looks at me, shakes his head and continues, 'I'm sorry I can't put it any softer to you soldier. As a psychiatrist, not as a soldier, I can't let you go back into the jungle with a rifle in your hands.' He holds up a photo of me standing over a disembowelled man, my face cold and emotionless.

'Christ almighty, I'm not sure what you will do if you get your hands on some poor young Vietnamese boy and decide he is an enemy before the proof is there.' He points to the photos.

'You watch others do this and eventually you become one of them. I don't want to see that happen to a young man like you.' The officer drops the photos back into the folder.

'You have done enough for your country son and your country won't give a squat down shit about what you have been through.'

He pauses, looks at me with sad caring eyes, 'More than enough, you deserve a break. God knows you earned it.'

Tears are rolling down my cheeks, tears of anger and tears of humiliation.

'You don't understand Sir. Please don't do this to me. I'm not a coward.'

'Coward!' The officer snaps back angrily. 'Coward my arse, no one is saying you're a coward. For God's sake, what do they teach you grunts? I get boys from other units screaming to get out of the war. Two days ago I had to assess an idiot from Services Corps who deliberately shot himself in the leg so he could be sent home. Not you grunts. No way grunts can call it quits, don't let your mates down.' The Major stands, takes two paces and stares out of the window. 'Bullshit!' He snaps angrily. 'If I had my way son none of you would go back out there. I cannot stop this war but I can stop you. You're self-destructing and you don't even know it.'

'Don't send me home Sir. Think about me and what I want. I don't need your head shrinking stuff.'

'You're not going home son. I have had a chat with your CO, he needs a new signals operator and he fancies you will do a good job. You have a broad skill base from what he tells me.'

'Oh great, the CO's sig.'

'You don't like your commanding officer son?'

'Can't say I do.'

'Well you should. I do not personally know a finer soldier. If we had more like him there would be less people in your situation.'

We sit in silence for a while.

'Look son, it won't be known by anyone. The CO's signaller is being sent home, he has finished his national service. You are slotted in behind him. It's normal procedure. No one will know about this discussion. My file will get buried so deep it will never surface.'

'I will know. I will have to live with it, won't I?' I respond and point to the small plastic container on the desk.

'So what now? What's with the pills there with my name on them?'

'I'm treating you for depression son. I think you're as close to severe clinical depression as I've ever seen in a man who can still function. Any other young fool would be curled up in a bed for months. You're running on motor, just self-discipline from your damn brainwash training.' The psychiatrist again examines the photos, flipping through them one by one. He grimaces at the picture of the headless child. 'You're in control soldier but only just. In layman terms, I'm concerned that if you snap, fall of that precipice you're balancing on… well it's either a total depressed shut down or maybe even worse.'

'Such as?'

'Since this incident, have you had trouble controlling the urge to lash out, particularly at Vietnamese, not just enemy, any Asian? For that matter could you suddenly find yourself attacking any person for no reason at all. A stranger, a friend, a lover! Have you experienced anything like that son?'

I am silent, my mind is racing back to my plans to kill the Hoy Chan. I had been obsessed with murdering the man. The inexplicable rage I felt toward the taxi driver back in Australia.

'No Sir, I'm fine. No thoughts like that, Sir'.

The Major studies my face no doubt noting the sudden pale complexion.

'You can lie to me son, I do not care about that. However, I do care about you lying to yourself. You could do something irrational if you fall off that precipice. It's my job, or if you like, the army's job to detect these things before they happen. It would be our fault if you did. There are some in this bloody army who do not seem to care but I do. I am responsible for your mental health and I damn well intend to do my duty.' He turns and looks out the window. 'My duty is to you son, not to the army.'

I stand in silence, scared that the old shrink might be right. Finally, I clear my throat.

'Yeah, okay, so I take the pills and I'll be just fine.'

'It's a mild anti-depressant. It won't stop you functioning, just ease that gut knot you talk about.' He pauses, 'One other thing son, depression is very real, you can go into some scary places, have thoughts that you wouldn't normally have.'

'What shoot myself or something like that?'

'Something like that, or worse! Shoot someone else.'

'Don't worry about that Sir, it's not my style.'

'Somehow I believe you son', the Major replies, 'but take care won't you, and remember that I am available if you need me. Your CO will see to that if you just ask him.'

I walk away from the hospital area. I have to meet up with a chopper heading back to the Dat. Sighting a rubbish bin next to a building, I walk over, lift the lid and drop the tablets into it. Not my style. Not my fucking style.

Whop   Whop   Whop   Whop   Whop

The Huey is slipping through the air on its mail run back toward Nui Dat. I sit quietly watching the landscape below. I add to my notebook…

> *Clinical depression! Is that what they call it? I just thought I was fucking miserable that's all. Fuck the lot of them. What's so bad about finishing the tour in a safe cushy job as the CO's sig. Hang around the firebase or the Dat, change his codes every day, maybe get to fly in one of those new choppers he uses now, the Kiowa.*

I look out and see the chopper's next point of call before reaching the Dat.

We are obviously stopping at the Horseshoe to pick up some diggers or mail. It is a base which stands out in the flat terrain like dog's balls. It's a natural defensive position, formed from an ancient volcano or maybe even a meteor hit back in pre-human times. It was used by the French as a base before we got into this Asian war and supposedly by the Japanese when they had invaded the country in WW2. Now it's the Australians.

Who next? This country has been shit upon for hundreds of years.

The chopper hovers at the landing strip inches above the ground as two soldiers climb on board. Artillery boys I figure, heading back for some R and R.

I nod. They nod. No words spoken.

Once again, we are in the air, banking over and making for home. The Dat.

Whop   Whop   Whop   Whop   Whop

GENEVA CONVENTION, GENEVA CONVULSION

'HEARD ABOUT WHAT happened to the CSM Delta Company while you were on R and R?' The battalion regimental signal's officer is staring at me with emotionless eyes. I feel a cold chill down my spine and a sudden tightening of the knot in my gut.

'Sandy! What happened? Is he alright?'

'He'll live. Should make a full recovery but they are sending him home in the back of a C130 any day now', the officer replies. 'Talk about bad luck. He was just standing up to direct an APC about where to park with the company supplies when suddenly the thing runs over an anti-tank mine. It killed the poor driver. The CSM Delta caught a bit of the tank track in the stomach. Big slither of it, like getting run through by a sword I suppose.'

'No one else hurt?'

'No, both Dutch and Jock were right there but didn't get hit by a thing. Poor old Jock thought he was in a safe pogo job after his arm infection. He gets sent back with Delta Company and ends up scraping a poor bloody driver out of a busted up APC.' The signals officer shakes his head. 'By scraping I do mean scraping. It went off right under his seat. Jock took it hard from what Dutch tells me. Keeps mumbling that he was supposed to direct the

APC into the area but the CSM told him to take a break and went to do it himself. Jock reckons the CSM is carrying his wounds.'

I stand silently letting the bad news sink in. He is carrying my wounds because I was off in Australia avoiding a court of inquiry. At least Sandy is alive and will make a recovery. I am wondering about Jock. If the man is shaken up and feeling guilty he should be sent back to a base job. I understand guilt and its impact on self-confidence. Lose that and you start making mistakes. Without Sandy's support after the chopper crash, I would be a basket case. Who would support Jock?

'Maybe I should get back to Delta. I know how their OC likes to operate, he might need me now that Sandy is out of the war. Jock can get back and sit in the CO sig position.'

The captain looked dispassionately at me, 'Sorry soldier, I have strict orders from the Colonel himself. He insists I put you into the vacant CO signals position. Makes sense I suppose, you have good command post training and experience. The work you did with Delta Company will be useful to the CO.' The officer laughs quietly. 'What amuses me is why the CO requested you. He must have complained to me a dozen times about you and how you wouldn't let him speak to the D Company commander during combat situations.'

'Following orders', I reply with a cheeky smile.

'The CO figures a Colonel's orders are more important than a Major's orders soldier. Maybe he wants you as his sig so he can clip your wings a little.'

I ignore the Captain's reply.

'Who is taking over as CSM Delta?'

'Platoon Sergeant, Eleven Platoon, has been promoted to CSM.'

It's Doug, perhaps its better I'm not back at Delta. I doubt we two could get through the tour without a clash of personalities.

'Well Sir if I'm going to be CO sig I better get familiar with that new chopper he taxis around in.'

'You got two days at task force to learn how to use the multi-channel radio equipment in the back of the thing then you will be sent out to the firebase. From then on you don't stray more than 10 feet from the Colonel's arse. Got that soldier?'

I nod, then stand and leave the signals officer's tent and go straight to the signals store and speak to the sergeant, who simply hands me a sheet of paper and an order, 'Report to task force sig centre. I don't want to see your ugly face for two days.'

That afternoon I walk to the vacated Delta Company area in Nui Dat and collect my meagre belongings. With my kit over my shoulder, I wander into the tent used by Sandy and sit quietly on the man's bed. I pull out the notebook.

Sandy's steel trunk is already packed and ready for transport back to Australia. The bed is stripped back to its plastic cover and the old green mozzie net neatly folded and placed at one end. The sand-bagged wall at the base of his bed has scratches in the tin sheet separating the outer sandbags from the inner tent, each scratch marking the nights Sandy spent in this bed. It was one of the CSM's little habits. He would look at the scratches and say, 'Not enough feckin scratches are there? Always out in the feckin scrub.'

'I'm going to miss you Sandy. Feck this, feck that and feckin Tabasco sauce. I'm going to miss it all.'

I sit silently for several minutes, remembering the moments, the wisdom and the friendship. Telling myself that when I get back to Australia I will look Sandy up, maybe even try to get a posting to whatever battalion Sandy is attached to. However, in the dark recess of my mind I know we might never serve together again. Sandy has disappeared from my immediate world just as so many diggers have. They've been wounded, killed or simply sent home as their national service time is completed.

Once again, I am denied an opportunity to say good-bye. This time it's the one man I trust and care about like he is my father and I can't even thank him. At least he is not dead like poor bloody Robby. Why am I writing in this bloody notebook? I only kept doing it for Sandy and now he is gone. It's not a notebook, just a waste of dunny paper.

Finally, I drag myself out of the empty tent and wander past the company boozer. Stopping once more to look at the gentle slope where I had sat with Sandy after the disaster with the chopper.

I promise you Sandy. I promise you I'll never let you or any other digger down.

I reach into my pocket and pull out the notebook. With my heel I dig a hole in the ground and drop the book into it then I spread some dirt over the top. Sandy can't order me to pick up the feckin notebook this time, it's a curse on me this fucking notebook.

Hitching my kit back over my shoulder, I make my way to task force signals centre to commence a crash course in Kiowa communication systems.

The Company Quartermaster

Behind Brian the D Company staff sergeant stops stacking the boozer fridge and walks over to where he has seen Brian digging a hole with his boot. He scrapes back the dirt. Staff knows only too well that the boys in Company HQ have taken a special interest in Brian's notebook. They haven't read any of it except maybe Doc. But they all tell him to keep writing. They want him to tell a story of war on their behalf. Even Staff's old mate Sandy allowed Brian extra moments to scribble a few words out in the field.

Jesus, poor bloody Sandy. They will fill his stomach with plastic intestines and he will probably shit into a bag for the rest of his days. But Staff understands how much Sandy cares about young Brian. Staff knows the story of Sandy's son, an illegitimate child to a runaway teenage girl when he was a young fella in a Salvation Army home. They took the girl away to have the baby, which he was told was a boy. He never saw them, not the girl, and not his little boy. Half caste kids don't get left to half caste abo parents. They got adopted or raised in institutions. But Staff had sat in the sergeants mess with a drunken Sandy who had told him that young Brian is that son he never had, and never will love as a father. Sandy had taken young Brian under his wing for all the wrong reasons but he just couldn't help himself. How would Sandy feel right now if he knew that young Brian had given up on his dream to write a book for his own son to read one day!

Three days later I re-join Support Company and commence my new task as CO signalman. I also hear rumours about an American Patrol entering a village. Capturing a young woman, dragging her into the bush, raping then killing her.

The matter has been brewing for some time as press editors struggle with the implications of releasing such a bombshell of a story. But now it is out in the open and the world's attention is focused once again on Vietnam and an American atrocity. Once the media decided to release this information, they turned into a frenzied mob seeking details of any possible misconduct. They also released information they had known for a long period of time but had chosen to cover up.

It seems to me the emphasis is more on sensationalism than unbiased reporting. More importantly, the emphasis is on American indiscretion while totally ignoring the countless atrocities performed by Viet Cong terrorists.

Unfortunately, this also means Australian soldiers in this war are now under the microscope. Would the photos of the village execution turn up in the Sydney Morning Herald or some other rag? I can only assume they won't because someone influential within media circles has allowed it to remain hidden. They can't come out with the pictures now in case the whole truth emerges about their own cover up.

Australian troops are largely innocent of any war crimes but this won't stop civilians making an association with the American atrocity.

'We don't butcher innocent Asians,' I had snapped angrily at my old school flame when back in Australia. Now it appears that we do. At least some of us!

I can imagine young Rhonda shaking her head in disgust. She would be thinking that I had lied to her and that all soldiers were committing atrocities in this war.

But what is an atrocity?

I am struggling with my emotions. I had witnessed the brutal execution of two men without trial and one disembowelment. What of the slaying of the family with the fat boys and the little girl? An act of terrorism that brutally ignored all sense of human decency. Vietnamese, not Americans or Australians committed those acts.

I cannot imagine Australians butchering each other, civil war or not. Yet I am aware of the desensitising effects of war. After witnessing enough brutality one becomes accustomed to its presence. Not unlike an ambulance driver in a big city, the sight of blood and death becomes part of the job. So it is with soldiers. The killing becomes part of the job. Where next does the human mind go?

Where had I gone in that village? To the edge of the precipice like the psychiatrist claimed.

Would Australians butcher each other in a civil war? The more I think about this question the more I realise that Australians are human just as Vietnamese are, or Americans. After all, Nunger is always pointing out to us that we whities had butchered and slaughtered many Indigenous Australians when we colonised Terra Australis.

What about the young Viet Cong soldier with the multiple gunshot wounds?

Did I not witness a medic killing the boy? Oh yes it could be justified but isn't that what happens in war? We justify one act and are numbed by the experience. Soon we justify other acts and so forth.

My mind slips back to a conversation I had with my grandfather's brother, a grand uncle who had served in Gallipoli. A younger me had asked him about what they had done with the Turkish prisoners.

'We did not take prisoners.'

'Didn't some try to surrender when you overpowered their trench lines?' I had asked.

'Wouldn't know boy. We just put the bloody lot of them to the bayonet. Only good enemy is a dead 'un', the tough old man had replied dryly.

I have felt the rage, the cold anger and desire to kill. I have experienced the mob mentality that sweeps people along in hatred and revenge. The old Major, the psychiatrist, understood what had happened to me and now I begin to grasp what the man was talking about when he refused to let me back in the field. The primitive beast is deep within us all. We control it with religion and laws and we hide it even from ourselves. But war brings out the worst in human behaviour.

What if I was with that American platoon? What if I saw a friend killed and was filled with adrenalin and anger? What would I do if my platoon commander gave the order to shoot villagers?

The answer scares me! I honestly do not know the answer to the question. The proper and correct answer is so obvious. However, I am aware of my almost uncontrollable rage in the hotel while on R and R, something inside me has snapped since I came to this war. I am now afraid of my own anger, the capacity to become a cold calculating violent human being. Somehow, I have to find the ability to feel pain and compassion again.

My beast given its opportunity to emerge has tasted its frightening freedom. I must return it to its cage. If I can!

Still, I have adjusted to my new role as CO signals operator. I've discovered that the rumours are true about the 'Singing Colonel' who insists that all flights are accompanied by the chopper crew singing out of key.

I am averaging eight to ten hours flying time each week in the back seat of the new Kiowa command helo. With much prompting by my commanding officer, I have learned the words to songs by Elvis, Johnny Ray, and half the regular Australian singers on Brian Henderson's Bandstand television program. When not singing or flying, most of my spare time is spent in a fire support base or back in Nui Dat. Any contact and the CO invariably wants to be in the air trying to supervise operations. He leaves his operations officer to manage the command post at the firebase. This routine has its advantages but it also drives most field soldiers a little batty. Too many cooks spoil the broth. Having both the ops officer and the CO constantly wanting answers to questions, while the field commander tries to manoeuvre his soldiers in a battle causes considerable frustration.

My experience with Delta Company's commander was that the CO was generally not wanted in the area while a firefight was occurring. I have already had one argument with the CO about flying directly over company positions on the ground when no contact is occurring.

'The men spend days silently moving through the jungle so that the enemy doesn't know where they are. Then we fly right over them and let Charlie know that Australians are in the area', I had snapped at the CO.

'You worry about doing your job as a signals operator soldier, let me worry about the enemy', was the curt arrogant reply from the Colonel.

'I just tell it as I see it Sir', has become my standard reply. I am unconcerned if I offend him. In fact, I don't give a tinker's fuck.

When not in the air with the CO, I am rostered to do command post duty as a signals operator. It's a problem to roster me on regular shifts because the CO can grab me on short notice. This means I tend to be an extra person rather than the main operator. A bonus as I can assist with message decoding and perform those extremely important tasks such as making coffee or acting as a go-for to grab cold drinks etc. when the Nui Dat mail chopper arrives.

It is just past midday and I have finished my watch in the firebase command post. No action today, just SITREPS and a constant flow of LOCSTATS to plot the movements of the two rifle companies out on search-and-destroy patrols.

I emerge from the bunker and wander over to the inner pit where I sleep when not on command post duty or flying with the CO. The soldiers pit at a firebase consists of two eight-foot long trenches dug into the ground about six feet apart and pointing toward the perimeter wire. These sleeping pits are covered by sandbags to protect against mortar attack. Both pits are joined at the back end by a fighting trench from which the two soldiers can direct their weapons on any enemy attacking the base. Over the fighting trench is a low-slung hooch to keep the sun and rain off the men inside. Crude but comfortable enough providing the tropical rains are kept out of the hole by the hooch.

I share this pit with another signal's operator. Dave is a corporal signaller who works the command post. It is his second tour of Vietnam and like Ray back in Nui Dat, he is glad to have this job after doing time with a rifle company on his first tour.

Dave stands out amongst others for two reasons. Firstly, he has a badly hooked nose, the result of a fistfight many years ago, the break never properly attended to. Secondly, he has a slow Queensland drawl when he speaks. A Yellow tinned XXXX Beer man who claims all things Queensland are wonderful and all things New South Wales and Victorian are bad. He never mentions the other states of Australia because he assumes they exist in a state of half world, half myth. For Dave, Australia is simply the east coast and the rest doesn't matter. He is determined to leave the army when his contract expires.

'I'll take my savings and buy a commercial fishing boat. Imagine that aye, paid to go fishing', he tells me repeatedly.

'So what do you know today Dave?' I ask as I sit down in the pit under the hooch which is stretched over the top to keep the hot sun off us.

'I know it's hot and dusty and I know I got bit by the biggest centipede in living history and it stung like shit, that's what I know.'

'Those big red bastards with the black legs?'

'Yeah, that's the one, ten feet long and meaner than a Gook with a Gat in his hands.'

I ignore the slight exaggeration, it is true these beasts can grow 12 inches and along with the giant scorpions and the horrible red or orange RTA bugs, the centipedes are not a popular bed mate inside the pits. Unlike the RTA bug however, Dave will not die or be paralysed by the centipede's bite.

I pull the tab on the cold can of Coke I grabbed when the midday mail run arrived by chopper, I take a long swig and pass the can to Dave.

'Take a swig on this goffer mate. What do you make of this story about the Yanks dragging that girl out of the village?

'Nothing surprises me about this war. Why not anyway, Viet Cong have been raping and butchering civilians for years and getting away with it, about time they got some of their own back I suppose she was probably a Viet Cong sympathiser any way.' Dave swigs from the can and passes it back to me. 'You know they killed over 3000 non-combatants in Hue when they overpowered the city. When the Yanks and ARVN won the Emperor's Forbidden City back they found the lakes floating with dead bodies, their hands tied behind their backs. They were just thrown in to drown. Took local teachers and even buried some of them alive. So it's okay for them to kill and butcher thousands but if some Yanks rape some girl or kill a couple of hundred it's a war crime. I don't get it mate.'

'Can't accept that one mate it's just too personal, actually grabbing a defenceless person like that, besides, how do you know she was a Viet Cong sympathiser?'

I have some knowledge of the Tet capture of Hue. 'I think they called the place 'The Citadel', that's what this Chinese Vietnamese bloke told me. The NVA got inside and the Yanks had to fight building to building to get it back. Apparently, they even called in air strikes on the buildings. Destroyed a whole bunch of historic buildings.'

Unbeknown to Dave, I have seen firsthand what the Viet Cong can do in the name of independence. Yet since my trip home and with time to reflect, I cannot accept the tit for tat response Dave is offering. I am trying to use logic to re-cage the beast that escaped my soul.

'Two wrongs don't add up to one right, got to have some standards, don't you? That's why the Geneva Convention was created', I say to Dave. In my mind are OC Delta's constant attempts to ensure that strict standards of being an honourable soldier are understood and upheld.

Dave looks over at me, a sneer below his crooked nose, 'What a lot of shit that thing is. It is like the Marquis of Queensbury Rules for Boxing. It's okay to punch the shit out of some bastard as long as you do it by the rules.' He reaches out, grabs the nearly empty can from me and finishes its contents. 'Do all the brain damage you like but don't hit below the belt. What a lot of bullshit. Let me ask you how come the Geneva Convention says it's okay to drop not one, but two atom bombs on a defeated nation and kill hundreds of thousands of women and children, but it ain't okay for some platoon of Yanks to kill a couple of hundred Cong supporters? That bloke Calley or whatever who led that platoon into the village a couple of years ago, why is he worse than the bloke who dropped an atom bomb on Japan?

I have no simple answer to that question.

'Well it's got to be wrong to walk into a village and start shooting for Christ's sake. You've got to draw a line somewhere. You've got to be the good soldier, the honourable soldier. Somehow, you just have to. Somehow.'

'Honour aye, thats where you draw the line?' Dave responds. 'They gave that bloke who flew the bomber that killed 200,000 people a medal mate, the Congressional Medal of Honour. Get the two last words clear here, "of Honour". He shakes his head, 'Draw the line my arse. If they are serious about drawing any lines, it should be at the front door of the army recruiting office. It should read, "Only young men willing to kill and maim innocent people are accepted beyond this point". They should piss off that Geneva Convention shit and tell the fucking truth. War is about killing and death and fucking destruction. The only rule is to stay alive while you stop others from staying alive.'

Dave's brutal summing up of war does not shock me. Regardless of my attempts to re-cage my inner beast, I remain callous.

'You missed your calling mate; you should be a catholic nun with attitudes like that.'

'Don't get me started on that lot and their inquisition mate', Dave responds dryly. 'Holier than thou bastards. They are responsible for more death and destruction than anyone else in history if you ask me.'

I look out from under the hooch sunshade, across to the outer perimeter wire and beyond to the edge of the cleared area around the base. The heat haze is mixing with the dust and causing an orange and brown mirage of wavering light.

I feel strangely lost and confused by all that has happened to me these last months. Back in Australia, life was so simple and innocent, naive really. Just believe what your parents, your teacher or your local politician tells you. Don't ask the ethical questions and don't demand facts, figures and documents of proof. Just stick your head up your arse and be an average unenlightened Australian citizen. She'll be right mate, put some more snags on the barbie and open another tin of beer.

Now my life is a confusion of ethical dilemmas. No black or white, good or evil, right or wrong. Just different responses to different situations. No response acceptable to everyone. The best response is to shut out emotions. Do whatever you need to and get home safe.

I look at Dave, 'These Nogs hate us mate. I spent some time in a village not long back. At the time I thought they did not make eye contact because of some culture thing but now I realise they just hate us.' I stretch my leg out to avoid it cramping, 'When I came over here I thought it would be different, that we would be appreciated because we were defending these people from terrorists. We ain't defending them Dave, we are just making the whole thing worse for them and they hate us. They don't like the Viet Cong either but they know that in the end we will go and the Viet Cong will win, the sooner that happens the sooner they can get on with their miserable existence without bombs and bullets. That is what a South Vietnamese officer in that village tried to tell me, I did not believe him then. I believe him now.'

'You think too much Brian that's your bloody problem,' Dave advises. 'Good soldiers don't think about reasons, they just do their job. If they think too much or ask too many questions, they just get themselves all screwed up in the head. Stop thinking about right and wrong, just do what ya gotta do and stay alive until wakey. Why don't you think about joining me and going halves in a commercial fishing boat, we could be a team back in Australia.'

I ignore Dave's offer.

'I just got back from Australia not long ago on R and R. I reckon this latest village shit is going to make life hard for all of us Dave; those bastards doing that to some girl. The people back home will tar us with the same brush as the Yanks. It's the beginning of the end mate. They won't want us in this war after this and they will march in the Australian streets like they are over in Europe and America.' I shake my head and make a final comment, 'Suppose that's a good thing really, it will get us out of the war. But I feel as if we are in nowhere land. The Gooks we are supposed to be helping hate us and back home more and more Australians are hating us.'

Dave looks across at me, 'And I hate them. They already march in Australia so this will just be more of the same. Every war we've ever been in has had some do-gooders claiming we should not get involved. They are always wrong. We always win. In the end nobody listens to them.'

'No mate, we won't win this war and as for those peace freaks, until now it's been a bunch of worried mums and some fun loving uni students. After this, it will be serious stuff. No one will want us in a war where our allies butcher innocent women and children en masse. I don't think I want us here anymore. I sure don't want me here, trouble is I don't really know where I want to be.'

'Tell that to the jet jockeys dropping napalm on villages', Dave remarks. 'Tell that to the B52 bomber pilots. They will say, "So what's new?" I think the difference between you and me is attitude. You think this Yank officer is a war criminal. Me, I am like most people who have had a gut full of the Viet Cong terrorists. I think the Yank is a fucking hero. Just like the bloke who dropped the atom bomb on Japan.'

'This war is killing us mate, those bastards that raped that girl, they aint no fucking heroes', I reply as the sticky sensation re-appears between my fingers and the vision of a headless child flashes into my mind. 'Inside our souls it's killing us. What scares me is that I hear what you're saying and don't agree with you. But I don't know how to have an argument about it, I know from personal experience that I ain't much better than those Yanks myself.'

The Corporal Signaller

Dave looks over his crooked nose at the deeply troubled man beside him. Wondering what secrets lay hidden behind those sad troubled eyes. Brian used to be such a cool soldier, always ready with a joke. He was always willing to buy a beer after training back in Aus. Everybody liked Brian back then but now he is a distant angry or downright miserable soldier who stares endlessly at nothing as though he is seeing things that nobody else can see. And what the hell is it with his hands, he rubs and rubs them on his pants endlessly. Something strange happened to the poor bastard but it seems that it is strictly out of bounds to talk about it. Dave knows there are rumours, but Dave knows better than to ask.

'Them rumours. I don't know and I don't friggin' want to know what happened to you out in some village Brian but I'll tell you what I do know. You're okay mate. You really are an okay digger. I like you, we all do, put whatever happened in that village behind you mate. Stop thinking about the politics and the right and wrong of war. As I said, you are a damn good digger. That's all you are supposed to be.'

TAOR

A STRANGE SCRATCHING sound emanates from the earthen wall centimetres from my right ear waking me from a half sleep. I stare up at the corrugated steel sheet covering my personal bunker pit. My pre-prepared grave.

Above that iron sheet, three layers of sandbags help keep the heat from burning me. Nothing however can stop the humidity. My body shines with a thick layer of perspiration. This pit is little more than two meters long and one meter wide. As I lie here on my back I can quickly access the small luxuries of war. Dug out of the compacted earth to my left is a small shelf where I keep a water bottle, a packet of Lucky's and a spent mortar shell filled with butted out coffin nails. To my right, shortened star droppers have been hammered into the side of the pit walls and my 9 mm Browning handgun hangs from one in its holster, my web belt and ammo pouches hang from the other. Outside my sleeping bay, the fighting pit is similarly arranged with dug out shelving for grenades and spare ammo. My sidekick, Dave and I have positioned our weapons at the ready on rough-hewn shelving made from empty artillery ammo boxes. Simply fashioned stools are positioned at each end of the fighting pit. When not used to sit on they become the access and exit stairs.

I am down in my sleeping pit taking a break from the monotony of staring over barbed wire at barren, heat-shimmering dirt between the firebase and the tree line. Dave is sitting out in the fire pit scrawling a letter to his wife. He occasionally glances outward but constantly checks movement within the perimeter, more concerned about a sergeant or warrant officer wanting someone for a work detail than he is about any enemy that may be lurking in the outer tree line.

'Want to say hi to me missus Bri?'

'Hi missus', I call back. 'Tell her I said that you have been a faithful hubby, only sex you've had since you got here is with your right hand.'

'Not even that', Dave replies. 'Too bloody hot for wankin'. Anything else you want me to write? How about I get her sister to write you a bit. You would like her Bri.'

He pauses and scratches his head, 'I was serious when I suggested you and me could go halves in a commercial fishing boat. I reckon you and me work together better than most blokes. We would be a great fishing team.'

'Nah, you don't need a loser like me Dave. We might get on sharing a bloody fire pit but a business partnership is another story altogether. I don't think I could stick at fishing year in year out. I ain't even sure I can stick out another month in this bloody pit.'

I am too interested in the scratching noises coming from within the wall next to me to participate in benign jocularity with my pit buddy. Was it another centipede? Or a more sinister RTA bug digging its way into the pit. I lie here silently, deciding that when I die I want to be cremated, not lying in a hole in the ground silently waiting for the bugs to attack.

My mind flashes back to yesterday's flight with the CO. Bravo Company had detected an enemy camp but instead of attacking as a company of riflemen, the CO had arranged for an American air strike. I had a bird's eye view from the command chopper as the spotter plane zoomed in on the knoll and let loose two white phosphorus missiles. I heard B Company commander screaming into his radio, 'No, No wrong knoll!' But it was too late. The F4 Phantoms screeched in at close to the speed of sound, the first dropping two 250 pound bombs, and the second aircraft spilled two canisters of napalm. As the canisters spun toward the knoll, I could still hear the OC Bravo Company calling, 'Wrong fucking knoll you fucking dip shit pilot'.

The Napalm canisters wobbled and tumbled toward the wrong target while the F4 climbed almost vertically skyward. Its pilot was not on the same radio frequency and unaware of the mistake was now determined to show off its superior power, he threw the jet into a victory roll as it climbed. The knoll erupted into a yellow, then red and orange bloom of death. The flames bubbled and boiled up from the knoll, horrific yet beautiful until the dirty grey black smoke rose after it. A stench of jellified kerosene found its way through the open door of the Kiowa chopper as it sped over the wrongly bombed knoll. I recalled trucks pouring hot melted tar on new roads back home and knew that when I returned home, road works would never smell the same again.

The CO called zero alpha, 'The foxtrot 4s struck the wrong knoll. Are there any friendlies or local village people on that second knoll? God I hope not.'

'This is zero alpha, no friendlies on that knoll. Over.' The CO waited and again asked 'Roger, this is niner, what about locals? Over.'

Silence.

'This is niner I want a damn answer, is it possible we bombed civilians? Over.'

'Zero alpha, ahhh, we don't know. Our India November Tango has no info on that location, we were not tasked to check that knoll. Over'

'This is niner, ahhh, re-check grid references given to the air strike team, ahhh….. contact Hotel Quebec and warn of possible media storm if word of this gets out. Ahhh oh shit just make sure the mistake was not at our end ahhh. Out!'

I was quickly on the chopper's internal line, 'No mistake at our end skipper I have re-checked the grid references we passed to the spotter plane. They obviously just got slack and hit the obvious knoll instead of the smaller one.

If memory serves me correctly, I patrolled that area with Delta and there is only an abandoned temple ruin on that knoll.'

'I hope you are right son. God I hope you are right!'

'I am right. It was a beautiful old ruin skipper. Hopefully some of it will survive the bombing.'

Suddenly my mind is brought back from the monumental mistake of yesterday's war, to the current moment and Dave's cursing from the attached fighting pit.

'Oh oh, here comes trouble, A4 is on the prowl.'

A4 is the nickname given to the Support Company CSM. An A4 being the sheet size and number for a military charge and the Support Company sergeant major is fond of charging soldiers with the most minor and trivial breaches of military law and conduct.

I quickly climb out of the underground section and do a quick check that all is in order as I watch A4 heading directly toward our pit. The Support Company CSM is not making a direct line to Dave and me without a reason. I know that with all things A4 moves with a purpose, no energy is wasted in general conversation or in mixing with his soldiers.

A4 is intensely disliked by Support Company soldiers but it doesn't seem to bother the man. He acts as though being disliked is almost a badge of honour and he makes extra effort to press people's buttons. For some reason he has a distinct dislike of me.

The Support Company CSM stops at our pit and looks straight at me through his steel grey eyes which are tucked below an overabundance of eyebrow hair. 'Your lucky night soldier, you got a TAOR to lead and an ambush to set for tonight.' He's almost spitting out the words in his curt unfriendly tone.

I roll my eyes, to date I have avoided all TAORS and have not had to cop an ambush.

'What do you mean by lead, Sir?'

'We are short of real soldiers mister and I figure that you are not protected from earning your pay just because you are the CO's sig.'

'Baggy arse CO sig, Sir. I don't lead shit. I just follow the crowd and volunteer for sweet fuck all 'cos as you know only too well, good grunts don't volunteer and bad grunts definitely don't volunteer. Sir.'

'You must have sucked that Delta Company OC's cock then soldier because he was on to your real OC about giving you some stripes when you were attached to Delta. Consider that I just volunteered you and that you just agreed, otherwise I might just have to hit you with insubordination', he pauses arrogantly before pressing home his position of authority. 'Let's see now, that should be good for a month of cleaning shit pits in full web kit.'

I ignore the threat of an A4 charge and look at my own upper arms. 'Don't see any stripes Sir. No stripes and no lead of any TAOR. I reckon the last thing the CO would want is a dumb baggy arse digger like me leading a group of Australia's finest youth.'

'You'll do as you're ordered soldier. Don't ask me why you didn't get a promotion. You're a mystery boy to all of us. One minute you're the darling of Delta Company, next thing you're CO sig with strict instructions that only the CO is allowed to clear you for active combat duty.' He sniggers, 'I smell a coward myself, either that or you sucked the CO's cock just like you sucked OC Delta's. I don't know what you got up to that created all this fuss. Care to tell me the real story son.'

I ignore the comment and play my ace card. 'So, the CO cleared me to take out a TAOR did he? Orders are orders Sir. Only the CO can clear me for patrol work.'

'The CO ain't here is he? He flew to Saigon chasing pussy and in his absence I figure you can do your bit like every other soldier. You know how to read a map, you know how to call in artillery and you probably know more about patrolling than most of the little wimps in this firebase. So you are going to take the patrol.'

I detest this man, he is a mean snivelling troublemaker and not popular even with senior NCOs. He is the only infantry CSM I have come across who made the rank of WO2 without serving overseas somewhere. He has quite a bit of cheek saying diggers in the firebase are wimps when he has only done three weeks of support company patrolling. This netted only one brief contact by assault pioneer platoon kilometres away from the bastard. But I am not about to challenge him further. I know with the man's mean streak he would hold a grudge forever.

'Who do I have and what area?'

'You get who I decide to give you and you patrol and ambush the area the operations officer orders you to patrol and ambush. Now get your arse to the CP for briefing.'

A4 turns and walks away to annoy or bully some other soldiers.

'He's a cunt ain't he?' Dave responds once the man was out of hearing range.

'Cunts are useful Dave and very nice to be with. He ain't no cunt that's for sure but I once trod in some dog shit and that reminds me of him.' I pick up my M16 and climb out of the pit.

In the command post the operations officer is relaxed and matter of fact in his attitude and briefing.

'We have an intelligence report which says some local Viet Cong are moving between these two relocation villages along one of these many creek lines to get together and plan some terrorist activity.' The ops officer points to the pencilled track lines marked on the map spread in front of us. 'Our guess is they will use one of these two tracks here or this dry creek bed.' He pauses long enough for me to pencil in the walking tracks on my own chart. 'We have arranged for Charlie Company to set ambushes along them. Our problem is they might just choose to use this one here', he points to a smaller creek line. 'It's a bit indirect in that it meanders between the villages but there is an outside chance they might use it. That's where your ambush patrol comes in.'

I study the chart in front of me. I had learned a lot from OC Delta Company and from Sandy. 'It's the least obvious route so in my opinion it's the most likely route they will use Sir. How much faith have you got in this intelligence report? '

'As much as can be expected. It's an agent report not a SAS recce observation so it's less than fifty percent chance. But they did say the meetings occur on a full moon to help the little bastards navigate at night. It happens to be a full moon tonight but it's cloudy and overcast so tonight's not the best night possible for them, but we want to cover all tracks anyway.'

Again, I examine the dry creek line. 'All they need to do is follow the creek line along here and not head up the wrong fork. They don't need a clear sky or the full moon. Down in the dry bed they will use torches because no one will see them shining down there.'

The ops officer looks at me, 'I have another TAOR out already so this is a make shift TAOR and ambush. You get a motley crew because I think there is little chance of a contact.' The ops officer moves his finger to a new point on the map. 'Be a little deceptive and patrol out to the edge of these rice fields to let any locals have a look at where you are probably heading. Once you move back into the bush set a new bearing to the creek line and set up an ambush in a good spot.'

I spread my own map across the table and begin marking and calculating. Looking for clearings to avoid and for best locations for a rapid helo evacuation in case the small patrol runs into a large enemy force.

'What's my backup?'

'You got our Mortar Platoon sitting here in the firebase with four tubes at the call of whoever springs an ambush tonight. Apart from that you're on your own.' The ops officer points to another area on my chart, 'Some armoured personnel carriers are over in this area. Get their most current location from the duty officer before you take off.'

I lightly mark the general area where the cavalry vehicles are operating, it's about an hour's bash through reasonably rugged scrub from my approximate ambush site. I am not happy. If I get into serious trouble, the only fighting force that can come to my rescue will be the three Charlie Company ambush patrols. They will have to abandon their own ambush sites and close up together before coming to my aid. I cannot rely on them, particularly at night or first light next morning.

'You said I had a motley crew, how motley?'

The ops officer shrugs his shoulders, 'Best the CSM could scrape up, not a lot of experience amongst them, though he did manage to get one of the trackers from anti-tank platoon. That is about all I can tell you I'm afraid.'

'I'm going to ask for extra claymore mines, Sir.' My mind is now planning the safest possible ambush technique for deployment with inexperienced soldiers.

'Take whatever you need soldier. If there are any questions from the Q, tell them to talk to me.' The officer looks at his wristwatch. 'CSM will have the patrol lined up by the number five-gun position in 30 minutes so you better get your shit together and be ready to meet them.'

I nod and leave the command post making my way directly to the Q storeman.

'Det cord Froggo, lots of det cord and some det caps, I got a bank of claymores to rig up tonight. It's cleared by the ops officer'.

Froggo, the storeman, raises his eyebrows. He knows I am the CO sig so he isn't going to question me. 'Fifteen length between mines?' he asks. 'I'll crimp the buggers if you like.'

'No thanks mate, you measure and I'll crimp the caps on. No offence meant, but if they do not go off it's my responsibility not yours. I'm in a hurry mate, let's get these buggers rigged.'

We set about our task with cold calm professionalism. We are creating the connectors to a set of mines which, once set in place, will be capable of killing up to 20 human beings instantly. Our minds are more concerned with time than the carnage this weapon will cause once detonated.

Thirty minutes later I have a backpack full of claymores for someone to carry and a radio set on my own back. I'm looking at the men I will lead out from the wire, two signals linesmen, a digger from hygiene section, a cook, the operations officer's batman, a transport mechanic, a mortarman and Chucka, the tracker I had met in Vungers 10 lifetimes ago. I feel like I've been set up and in a hopeless position. I have never led any patrols in Vietnam and know the men who now stand in front of me expect me to be a seasoned digger. The only thing I can do is act confidently and look like a veteran of many patrols and contacts. I do my best to sound and act like Sandy or Nunger.

My eyes go straight to the tracker from anti-tank platoon. Chucka is the only combat experienced digger amongst the group, 'Sorry Chucka, you're it for scout.'

Chucka looks around at the group, 'Suits me, think it best I am. What's in the bag?'

'Claymores, lots of the bastards'

'Better give em to me, not sure these blokes have set many up before'

I hand Chucka the claymores and next look at the mortarman who is carrying the GPMG. He is short but stocky in build, what he lacks in height is offset by broad shoulders and thick forearms.

'You love that thing or hate it?' I ask. 'Because I only want a machine gunner who would rather sleep with his M60 than sleep with his wife.'

The mortarman lifts the gun muzzle to his mouth and kisses the flash suppressor, 'I'm not married and I'm willing to sleep with anything female. This little darling looks downright sexy mate. Just a bit worried about who is carrying the spare barrel.' The mortarman is looking at the cook who is standing in excited anticipation. The spare barrel is strapped to his back.

I now run my eyes over the young soldier from catering corps. He has a short shock of greasy, bright red hair cropped above a pimply face. He's barely 19 years old and has no sign of the wrinkles and scars regularly seen on diggers who have spent time in the field.

'You know what to do with that thing Cookie?'

'Sure, I did some training with these things. All things mechanical are fine with us cooks, they don't call us fitters and turners for nothing.'

'They call cooks fitters and turners because you fit perfectly good food into an oven and turn it into shit. Just do whatever the gunner tells you to fucking do and don't ask him any fucking questions. Okay?'

The cook nods. I now look at the mechanic. Another fresh face with big thick glasses that would have prevented the man being accepted as a grunt. He is certainly too fresh faced and emotionally young to be placed in any combat situation.

'Can you see the end of your dick if you aren't wearing those binoculars on your ugly face?' I stare at the mechanic who shuffles nervously. 'Fucking Coke bottles with cam cream, that's what you are.' I shake my head from side to side in an obvious expression of contempt.

'Let me get this straight, a tucka fucka and a grease monkey with Coke bottles for looking glasses are volunteering to do an ambush with some grunts. What is your fucking problem?' I stand between both men eyes darting from one to the other. 'Why would you want to do this? The rule of all good grunts is never ever volunteer for any fucking thing in this mans' army.' Both men shift uneasily.

'I thought it would be a good idea to get out with you blokes and have a real go at this war', came the mechanic's reply.

I look at the young man with his thick-rimmed glasses and a trace of unfinished acne showing through the cam cream, obviously placed carefully on his face in front of a mirror and designed to make him look like a Hollywood war hero.

'Welcome to the real war mister, and it ain't about enemy it's about long walks with too much shit to carry and a fucking sleepless night, you got that?'

'Yes Sir.'

'Not Sir you Coke bottled bastard', I respond quickly. 'Don't fucking insult me with "Sir!". I'm a fucking baggy arse and proud of it, the name is Brian.'

The two men stand silent.

'If just one of you step out of line or fuck up my patrol I'm going to rip off both your arms, plug them in each ear, get on your back and ride you around this country like a fucking push bike. I hate fuckin' volunteers.'

I look away then suddenly look back at the two inexperienced soldiers. 'Fuckin' hate them', I sneer, trying desperately to hold a straight face and noticing Chucka having a quiet giggle off to one side.

I'm now satisfied that I have bullied the two young men so they are as miserable as possible. 'You will listen to me and you will live if any shit spills tonight. I may be a pig of a man but I want this patrol back here tomorrow alive and happy, even if you hate my guts for eternity.' I then calmly address the rest of the small patrol.

'Okay, I've got the sig set and we are carrying a shit load of claymores because I like my ambushes to go off with a big bang. Once we are out about 500 meters from here we will poke our nose out along the dry rice field so the locals can see us and think we are setting up an ambush near there. We then move back into the tree line and change course out of sight.' I pause to make sure each man is getting the message that this is going to be a long walk at a fair pace.

'Another thousand and we will set up an ambush along a dry creek bed that the ops officer thinks the Gooks might be sneaking along tonight.'

I run my eyes over every member of the TAOR patrol and change my voice to an octave lower, 'We do it my way, not the way some other bastard might have done it the last time you did a TAOR, and we don't say jack shit to anyone about how I do it.' I look at the group, 'Any questions?'

The group remains silent. I point to the opening in the wire, 'Once we get through the maze it's a 165 bearing, until I say otherwise Chucka. Just check back at me every 20 or so meters and I will keep you on bearing with hand signals. I'll do the paces and you concentrate on what's up front. We will have to move at a fair clip so you concentrate on that risk and only that.'

I call in a radio check and advise that we are moving beyond the perimeter. Once confirmed and clearance given, I give Chucka the nod and the little band of misfits makes its way through the perimeter wire maze.

After crossing the cleared area around the firebase, the patrol moves into scrub country, thick enough to provide cover but not awkward jungle. Chucka is experienced at his work, he's normally a backup for the dog handler. It is his job to cover the handler as a second scout or pick up a track once the dog has pointed. Scary stuff! Dogs only point if the enemy is almost in your face. For this patrol however, the risk of contact is minimal. Minimal or not, I ensure all precautions are taken and followed by the patrol members. My main concern is locating the dry creek bed in time to do a decent recce and find an ideal ambush site. I do not wish to push them so fast they get sloppy but I want time up my sleeve to set up the claymore ambush.

The patrol reaches the dry paddy area and we walk in the open long enough for any locals to see us. We then move back into the cover of the bush and set a new bearing for the creek line which is a klick away.

After 1,135 paces along the new compass bearing, I call a halt and indicate a mini harbour be formed. I then squat down with my chart. Chucka joins me.

'By my paces we should be on the creek line now', I whisper. 'I normally pace pretty well over this type of scrub.'

Chucka looks around, 'Landform indicates we are close to something, it's only a slight dip but it's noticeable.'

'Okay, you and me will have a squiz.' I look at the patrol members and with my left hand form a circle between finger and thumb and place it over my left eye. I wait until I am satisfied that all members have seen the recce signal and motion Chucka to move off.

We move only 30 meters through the undergrowth before we come across the dry creek line. I set myself at the top, on the ground, my M16 ready to provide covering fire. After a thorough visual search of the area to my front, I give the young soldier the nod to proceed.

Chucka slips down into the dry creek line and squats for a look. He moves a couple of meters along the line then turns and climbs back up beside me. He takes great care to leave no trace or footprints that could warn any enemy moving along the dry creek bed.

'Some recent movement but nothing I can pick as Nog. Could be enemy, could be animal.'

Right now I wish I had Nunger along, but Chucka is doing his best. I indicate that I want to follow the creek line to sight an ambush. This time I lead out with Chucka covering.

Another 50 meters and I find just what I am looking for. The creek line turns into a sweeping bend with short shrubby scrub right up to its edges. From where I squat, I can get a clear vision straight up the creek after the bend.

I check my map to confirm the bend in the creek is clearly marked. This gives me confidence that my navigation is accurate and I can call for mortar support with some certainty as to where the shells would land.

There is good cover to hide a couple of soldiers. We move back away from the creek line about 25 meters and check out the area for a mini defensive night harbour. Perfect. I nod to Chucka to head back to the patrol.

Back with the patrol, I call in half of the group and draw a mud map in the dirt. I give the first of two identical briefings. 'We will move to a position behind the bend in the creek line just here', I point with a stick. 'I will set up a bank of six claymore mines facing down into, and up along the creek line at the bend. I will run the wire back to a spot just here', again I point. 'It will be a split roster tonight, two men manning the clacka with a com cord running from that position 15 to 20 meters back to the patrol harbour. In the harbour, everyone will be in shell-scrapes just in case I need to call in mortar support.'

I stop to make sure the group is understanding what I am describing.

'Another claymore will be placed 15 meters from the perimeter and sighted along the com cord line. The gun will also be set up facing along the com cord line. If Charlie walks down the creek line, he will most likely be using a torch. If you are on the clacka you wait until the enemy is in this killing field.'

I again point to the area on the bend of the creek bed. 'All you do is squeeze off the claymores with your eyes shut, ears covered and head down. And I mean head down, the concussion blast from these things is 16 meters and they will only be about 10 meters in front of you. As soon as the big fucking bang happens, you get your hand on the com line and slide back to the harbour where we will be set up in case Charlie survives and comes looking for us. If he does he will walk into another claymore and an M60 machine gun.'

'That's it?' the cook asks.

'Yeah, that's it. I ain't sitting awake all night with you lot lined up in a standard ambush, you will fidget and fart all fucking night and tip any enemy bastards off. This way, only two at a time can make a fucking noise close to the ambush kill zone.'

I look at the small group then at the redhead, 'You can set up a roster while Chucka and I set up the ambush. Leave me out of the roster because I am awake all fucking night and doing the radio checks.'

The cook nods, 'I don't know how to set up a split roster.'

I stare straight at him, I'm still the bully, 'You had better work it out real fucking fast mister because if you get it wrong the whole patrol is going to hate your guts come morning.'

I pause and look at the young man staring back at me from under his short thick blaze of red hair, 'And put yourself on the death watch, middle of the night. That way you are getting a taste of the real war which is what you wanted wasn't it?'

I run my eyes across to the others, 'Now you lot bugger off back to perimeter defence and let me brief the rest of the patrol.'

Once the second group is briefed, the patrol follows Chucka into the harbour site behind the ambush area where I sight each soldier's position and collect the claymore mines and det cord. There is 30 minutes to last light.

I direct the mortarman to move three meters out into the scrub as a listening post while the rest of the group quietly dig shell-scrapes in the soft soil. As the patrol commence their task Chucka and I move to the ambush site and set up the bank of mines.

Once back in the ambush area I connect the claymores to each other for a simultaneous explosion, using 3 meter lengths of det cord to which I had pre-crimped detonator caps back at the firebase. At each site, I lie down behind the mine sighting to ensure the killing field is covered with overlapping mine blasts. The fragmentation pattern is about 60 degrees and the kill zone some 50 meters. The mines facing directly into the creek bed need to be set close together to ensure maximum fragmentation into the restricted area. Two additional mines are sighted in both directions along the bend in the creek line where the full 50 meters of kill capability will be deployed. I then ensure each mine and the det cord covering them are concealed from view by foliage and move back to the detonating area.

With Chucka covering, I quietly prepare two shallow pits for the shift soldiers to lie in. Once completed I leave Chucka at the site and run the green communication cord back to the night harbour, tying it tightly between the trees so that it can easily be followed in the dark.

The mortarman returns from his listening post and sets up the final claymore mine. I take a quick radio check and send the code word to tell base that we are in position and ready. Finally, I drop down behind the last claymore to ensure it is sighted for maximum effect. A minor adjustment and double check of the detonator and I'm satisfied that all is ready.

Back at the night harbour, the group have settled into their shell-scrapes and the mortarman is now quietly digging pits for Chucka and me.

I move to the cook, 'Let's see the roster Cookie.' The cook hands over his best effort, I study it in detail. 'You got some help, didn't you?' The Cook nods. 'You might just pass as an honorary grunt if you keep up the good work. Just change Chucka from last watch to first watch, he is already out there. Start the second watch with the mechanic with Coke bottles for eyeglasses now so that

Chucka is off in one hour, the mechanic in two etc. Got that?' The cook nods and re-scribbles on the sheet. I hesitate a moment. 'Change yourself from the midnight shift to an early morning one, sometime after 4.00am.'

'Why?'

'If the Gooks do come down this creek it will probably be between 12 and 3 am. I would rather have a grunt on the clacka Cookie, nothing personal, just that the linesmen have had extra training in ambush drills and what to do if the claymores don't fire.'

The cook looks back at me, 'What do you do if the claymores don't fire?'

'Shit your pants Cookie, shit your pants. But grunts are trained to shit their pants quietly. If there's a lot of Gooks they will let them go through. If it's just one or two they will zap the little fuckers with their rifles.'

'I could do that', the cook responds naively.

'You still might have to Cookie. Who knows what will come down that creek and when. I'm just putting the most trained diggers in the most likely time slot but Charlie might not be thinking like me.'

Once finished, I go to each soldier and tell them when they are on watch and who they have to wake. I lead the mechanic to the site where Chucka lies ready. I draw a quick picture of the night harbour and explain to Chucka where his pit is and whom he has to send out when he comes off watch.

I move back to the harbour and radio in the SITREP to the firebase requesting a silent defensive-fire mortar target 500 hundred meters to the front of our harbour where I can guide fire onto the creek line if the ambush is activated. This is generally not a standard procedure. A distance of 1000 meters should be set for the first rounds as an extra precaution against poor navigation but I am confident of my position. The bend in the creek line is clearly marked on my map, as is the nearby fork. I want the first mortar rounds hitting the area as quickly as possible if the ambush is sprung.

The sun's red ball slides gently behind the trees and over the horizon followed by ever darkening shadows that gradually envelope the patrol's ambush harbour. I, like the others, allow my eyes to relax and adjust to the blanketing darkness, a last check to identify distances to significant trees and shrubs. I expect patrol members to take a final glance at the disappearing shell-scrapes and notice the diggers to their left and right. They need to take a final scratch of closely cropped hair, a sip from a water bottle and clear a dry throat.

It is now dark. The group settles in for the long wait. I will receive radio checks on the hour all night to help me stay awake while allowing the others to get some rest if they possibly can. The ambush radio check is a simple arrangement, there is no talking from the ambush patrol. Zero alpha will call me and I will respond with two clicks on the talk button if all is well. I will send three clicks if at any time I want the fire base to arouse the mortar platoon ready to provide support.

The sounds of night in the bush starts on cue, the noises comfort me. I understand fear and what it does to a man. Particularly in a blackened jungle.

I have discovered that fear is more intense in moments such as this, during an actual contact, the fear creates adrenalin surges. All concentration is directed toward the task of killing or surviving. The shakes come later but usually when I'm in a safer situation. Night fear is about the imagination and the tricks that it plays. A digger is most vulnerable to fear when he is trying to stay awake with nothing else to do or think about but the bloody enemy. I recalled the night spent alone on gun sentry. Never again, I know the signs now. I just hope none of the inexperienced diggers with me tonight get the night panics and spring this ambush unnecessarily. I know from experience that while the night is noisy there is no enemy walking along that creek. I tell myself repeatedly that the chances of a contact are minimal. After a while I relax. An hour passes and I can make out Chucka quietly returning and sending out the mortarman.

The radio comes alive as the zero alpha sig operator whispers quietly for a comms check, I pick up the handset and depress the talk switch twice.

Hours pass, it is now 0420 hours and all is proceeding smoothly.

I guessed that if any enemy were moving about tonight they would do it between 0300 hours and 0400 hours. That time has passed and I am beginning to relax and curse myself for volunteering to stay awake all night on the radio set.

Suddenly a cold chill runs up my spine and that strange metallic taste is in my mouth as a sense of danger causes adrenalin to flow. I trust my gut feeling, I know such feelings usually have a logical explanation. I am now alert. I try to identify the cause of the premonition. It is the silence. Too silent!

Either there is a night cat on the prowl or the enemy is walking along that creek line. I am betting it is enemy. I curse myself for changing the cook's roster but reassure myself that I had wired up the claymore mines properly. If the enemy is coming, the mines will not let the young redhead down.

I check that my M16 mag is locked home and I remove the plastic cap from the upturned magazine ready to flip it over if needed. Next, I feel in the dark for my bandolier of magazines to ensure they are by my side. I turn up the volume on the sig set to maximum, depress the talk switch three times, pause a moment then repeat the warning to zero alpha. Finally, I push my head down into the shallow shell-scrape with eyes shut so as not to be night blinded by a sudden flash. One ear is pressed hard against my right shoulder, the other is covered by my left hand. If my gut feeling is correct the whole world is about to explode.

Drop Short

THE THUNDEROUS ROARING boom created by six claymore mines detonating simultaneously causes a shock wave even back in the small harbour. I can only hope that the two diggers on ambush shift have followed my orders and buried their heads and covered their eyes.

Around me in the harbour the patrol is startled into awareness. I can hear the mechanic asking people close to him what is happening.

'Shuddup, shut the fuck up Coke bottles', Chucka calls back to the mechanic.

'Finger outside that trigger guard gunner', I call to the pit beside me. 'We should have two very scared diggers sliding along the com cord any second now.'

'I can hear them coming', calls back the mortar man holding the gun ready. 'Or at least it had better be them'.

'Hold your fire fuck-knuckle, hold your fire until I fire', I respond.

The two diggers from the ambush crawl into the perimeter area. 'Don't shoot for fuck's sake it's us'.

'Shut the fuck up and get over here', I reply.

The two diggers crawl past the gunner and over to my shell-scrape.

'What have we got?'

'I think there was about six of them. I don't know really, I only saw two, but the torch light was way ahead of what I thought were the actual people I saw so I just pressed the clacka like you said', the red-haired cook replies.

'In your fucking pits boys I'm calling in the tubes', I take the handset and call the fire support base.

'Zero alpha, zero alpha, this is six bravo in contact. Fire mission Foxtrot Golf two. Over.'

'Roger that six bravo, ready fire mission, Foxtrot Golf two. Over.'

'Foxtrot Golf two, one tube fire. Over.'

'I read back, Foxtrot Golf two, one tube ready to fire. Over.'

'One tube ready fire, now out.' I respond then call out, 'Heads down mortar in coming.'

The distant 'poink' can just be heard, then the long wait as the mortar launches through the air toward its target. Next, the explosion, almost 500 meters to the right of our position.

'This is six bravo, left one hundred, drop one hundred, one gun fire. Over.'

The radio crackles into life repeating my call. I confirm and another mortar shell is sent into the night sky, exploding much closer to the position this time.

'Drop one hundred, danger close, one gun fire', the message immediately read back to confirm.

Again the mortar tube sends its shell skyward, the explosion sending live shrapnel through the tree line about 9 metres above my head.

'Drop five zero, I say again five zero, danger close, one gunfire.' I call out to the patrol, 'Heads down this one's hot.'

The explosion is close enough to send a shock wave over us and live shrapnel is hitting the trees, three to six metres above the ground. I will not take the risk and call it any closer.

'Repeat, I say again repeat. Out'. The intention is to confirm the accuracy of the mortar setting.

Again, the shell lands exactly where I want it to explode. I feel a real sense of satisfaction that all is going as planned. Now it's time to send a message to any enemy that may still be in the area. I talk into the handset.

'Target, lock on two guns, I say again target. Lock on two guns. Three rounds, fire. Over.'

I hear two distinct 'poinks' in the distance. I call for the patrol to keep their heads down.

Suddenly the earth around me vibrates with an almighty thump as a mortar round lands almost on top of us. Already another two rounds being fired from the base.

I grab the radio handset. 'Check fire, check fire. Over.'

Another two rounds explode. One where it should, the other right amongst the patrol.

A blinding flash, I feel almost lifted off the ground by the concussion blast which seems to push my eyes back into their sockets. My ears not just ringing but screaming. I call on the radio, 'Check fire, you dumb cunts, you're dropping short.'

Silence!

All I can now hear is the high-pitched ringing in my ears.

'Sound off, are we all okay?' I yell out to the patrol.

Each digger calls out. One short! My heart is racing now, 'Who the fuck is missing?'

'Where is fuckin' Coke Bottle?' I hear Chucka call.

'Oh Jesus that's all I need', I mumble to myself as I crawl out of my shell-scrape and make my way to the mechanic's position.

As I crawl closer I can hear a groaning noise, I grab the pen light torch from my shirt pocket and shine it onto the mechanic. The man's face is covered in blood and his hands cover both his eyes. I reach out, pull his hands away from his face and find the problem. The soldier's spectacles are shattered and broken glass has ripped into his eye sockets. The spectacles are missing, there is a deep gash along the top of his skull and one ear is hanging by a thread to the side of his face.

'You had your fucking head up, had to have a look didn't you?' I call out loudly, but the mechanic does not register that he has heard me.

'Chucka, get over here with two gunshot bandages and wrap up this poor prick's face.'

Chucka crawls over and glances at the mess in the dim light of the small torch.

'Fuck, what a mess', he says as he rips the shell dressing from the butt of his M16 where it was taped ready if needed. 'You better call in a Dustoff'.

I slip back to the radio, 'Zero alpha, this is six bravo we have a Whisky India Alpha from friendly fire, alert Dustoff. Over.'

A quiet and calm voice comes back to me over the radio. 'Six bravo this is sunray minor. I understand you have taken a mortar round in your own position, is that right. Over.'

'Damn right, two rounds dropped short. Get a setting on that second tube and find out who is fucking responsible because I want some bastard's balls on my breakfast plate. Over.'

'Calm down son, calm down, it could be a problem at your end with the LOCSTAT.'

'Bullshit, fucking bullshit', I snap back. 'Get me a fucking Dustoff and get it quick. I got a man down here in trouble.'

'Dustoff alerted and in bound 10 mikes. What is the enemy situation? Over.'

I speak calmly into the set now that I know the chopper is on the way. 'This is six bravo, we sprung an ambush on three to six enemy soldiers. Either they are dead or they have bugged out. We will have to wait 'til sunrise to confirm enemy casualties. I will be off air while I ready the CASEVAC. Out.'

I slip over to Chucka and have a look at his handy work. The wounded soldier is still in a state of shock, only groaning from time to time. Chucka has covered both his eyes with the first bandage and used a second to secure the ear to the side of the young man's head. There is little that can be done to the gash across the top of his skull. Like most head wounds of this nature, the bleeding has slowed rapidly and now needs only a dab with a sweat rag to keep it reasonably dry.

I grab my larger army torch from my web strap and a hand-fired parachute flare from my left ammo pouch. I have no strobe light, which is the preferred method for the pilots so I will have to use torch flashes. A flare can be fired to warn the chopper that something is going terribly pear shaped at the last moment.

'It will be a stokes litter so get one of the boys ready to lift him on and strap him in. The pilot won't like hanging around any longer than he has to', I call to Chucka, who simply nods and carries on with his task.

Whop   Whop   Whop   Whop   Whop

I can hear the chopper in the distance, so I move back to the radio, 'Dustoff this is six bravo, I hear you. Over.'

'Ahhh…. Roger, six bravo. Is this a litter drop? Over.'

'Six bravo. Yes, shine a light. Over', I reply, as I start to search the night sky through the treetops. The aircraft lights become visible in the distance. I stop breathing for a moment, the picture of a burning chopper flashing in my mind. Sandy's words come back to me. 'Look me in the eyes and promise me.' I start breathing again and press the talk switch.

'Dustoff I have you visual. Kill your light and turn starboard three zero. Over.' I watch as the small chopper light changes direction then blacks out.

'More right and five hundred, watch for my marker. Tree height at 18 metres. I say again six zero, stay at two five meters and you won't need illume over us to advertise yourself for a RPG. Over.' I flash my torch skyward in groups of three then two flashes.

Whop   Whop   Whop   Whop   Whop

'Six bravo this is Dustoff, I have flashing, confirm two five as safe hover. Over.'

'Roger to two five meters. Give me a count. Over', I respond. I want to make sure the pilot is picking up my light and not a cunning enemy light.

'Ahhh …. This is Dustoff, I make three two, three two. Over.'

'This is six bravo. Roger. We have him ready for a litter. Drop it on the flashlight. Over.'

Whop   Whop   Whop   Whop   Whop

The chopper looms over our small patrol. Its black outline blotting out the moon, creating an ecliptic vision, silhouetting the dark black rotors as they cut and claw at the thick tropical air.

The litter quickly drops and I make out the silhouetted medic staring down at us. As the litter hits the ground Chucka and one of the linesmen lift the injured mechanic onto the litter and strap him in. He then gives me a wave.

'Dustoff this is six bravo, he is all yours. Thanks for the service. Over.'.

The chopper immediately climbs skyward while still winching the litter up and disappears over the treetops.

Whop   Whop   Whop   Whop

I talk into the handset, 'Zero alpha, this is six bravo. Dustoff complete, we are setting down until first light. Detailed SITREP in the morning. Over.'

'This is zero alpha, roger that. Do you want illume? Over.'

'Negative. Out', I respond.

I crawl to each soldier's shell-scrape and reassure them that the wounded digger will live and we are all going to be safe until first light.

The patrol settles down to wait for morning. I am still feeling the high pulse rate and fear. It is not just the close encounter but guiding a Dustoff into an area where enemy might be has also strained my nerves to a raw edge. I could not live with myself if another chopper is shot down while following my directions.

I desperately want to have a smoke and a bit of a cry. I am the leader here and the inexperienced soldiers with me are looking for me to stay cool so they can believe they have nothing to worry about. I promise you Sandy, I fuckin' promise you. Morning light cannot come too soon.

Morning After

'Six bravo this is tango alpha two one. We have cleared along this side. Do you want us to look over the other side? Over.'

I smile and press the talk switch on the handset and reply to the armoured personnel carrier commander, 'Thank you tango alpha two one, we have this side covered. Please hold your position while we move in and have a closer look. We would love a ride home when we finish the search. Over.'

'Two one wilco to both requests. Just call the cavalry if any Indians are on the prowl, we will be there with bugle blowing. Out.'

I waited until first light to crawl down to look at the ambush killing ground. Two dead bodies lay in the dry creek bed. I'm not prepared to clear the area on my own so I had called for backup and the cavalry is coming to the rescue.

I hold a grudging respect for all APC crew members. 'Turret heads' most grunts call them. They often come to the aid of grunts in trouble when we are a long way from base and exhausted by battle. The cavalry also provides a lift home. Uncomfortable but better than walking. All grunts know the story of the Battle of Long Tan. The turret heads were there, without them the diggers would have been in very serious shit, a possible mass funeral rather than a presidential citation.

I decide that the two dead Viet Cong are probably local VC part-timers on their own, but I do not want to take any chances. If they are part of D445 or attending a meeting with the regular VC unit then there is a possibility that the VC has now set their own ambush. There is no reason why the enemy might not ambush the ambushers and catch us out as we search the bodies.

The APCs find nothing in the most likely places Charlie would set up a counter ambush, so it is time for the patrol to have a closer look. I position the machine gunner to cover up and along the creek in the opposite direction to the area the APC's are protecting. I distribute my few soldiers to cover flanks and nod for Chucka to slip down into the creek bed. Chucka carries out a basic inspection then gives me the all clear sign. I slip down into the creek bed and motion to the redhead cook to follow.

'You sprung the ambush so you can have a look at what war is all about Cookie', I whisper to the wide-eyed and excited redhead.

Once in the dry creek bed I look at the now pale young soldier and point to the damaged torch taped to the end of a long stick. 'Two, not six Cookie. Never was six. Just two cunning little bastards carrying a torch on the end of a long stick.'

'What do they do that for?'

'VC figure that if they walk into an ambush the main fire power will be directed at the torch light, so they poke it way out in front on a stick. Gives them a better chance of survival.'

I point to the place where the bodies lie in the creek bed, 'That's why I sighted the claymores on the bend, two of them were sending frag down each way, not just directly to the front.'

The cook moves over to examine the bodies.

'Not so fast tucka fucka', I snap. 'Let me and the Chucka decide whether we touch them or pull them over with a rope. Could be booby trapped.'

The young cook immediately freezes. Chucka is having a closer look, checking all around both bodies for any sign of tampering.

'This one copped a payload and died instantly', he says. He moves over to the other body. 'This one tried to crawl away but died from blood loss. I can't see any indication that they have been tampered with.' He carefully examines the M1 carbine on the ground beside one of the bodies. Satisfied it was not booby-trapped he lifts the rifle and clears the chamber.

'Captured from the ARVN I suppose. Do you want me to have a fiddle?'

'Gently does it', I reply, noticing the young cook moving further away from the bodies.

Chucka slides his hand under the first corpse and feels for any grenades or booby traps. Slowly he draws his hand back and wipes the blood on his hands over the shirt of the body. 'Clear.' He moves to the second corpse and carries out the same procedure. 'Nah, on their own mate, just two locals out for a party meeting after curfew.' He then points to the body of the VC who had tried to crawl away, 'By the way, this one's got tits.'

Chucka rolls the body over, opens the shirt on the body and exposes a pair of female breasts as he goes about a more detailed search for any documents the VC may be carrying. He pulls the shirt back over her shoulders, checking under armpits, and then drags her long black pants down to her ankles to check for any items taped to her legs. There are few large wounds on her body. They are small pin-holes where the claymore mine's deadly payload penetrated from her right side and smashed vital organs inside.

'I don't think we need a cavity search do we boss?' He calls to me, 'Stinks pretty bad.'

'I wouldn't. You shouldn't', I reply, staring emotionlessly at the woman's vulva.

'Hey check out the Gat she was carrying', Chucka comments inquisitively.

'What the hell is that old thing?'

I move over and examine the weapon. I run my finger gently across the dry sand around the weapon feeling gently for a wire or any sign of disturbed dirt. Once satisfied there was no booby trap I pick it up and release the old hand action bolt, remove the round and look in the chamber. Next, I look for the magazine release catch, finally removing the small magazine and examining its contents. Three more rounds.

'You know what, I think it's an old Japanese World War 2 rifle, only four rounds. Probably all the ammo she had for the old gat. Hell the damn thing's almost as long as the little Cong bitch.'

The cook comes in closer and stares at the body, 'Jesus, I killed a woman, that isn't right mate. I didn't mean to kill no woman.'

My mind flashes back to my first taste of death in war, 'That ain't a woman Cookie, that's an enemy soldier.'

'No gender shit here mate', Chucka remarks as he rolls her onto her stomach to examine her back, and then turns her over again like a sack of potatoes leaving the corpse twisted in a heap.

'It's the sort of thing that would make that ball breaking bitch back home proud ain't it.'

'What are you talkin' about Chucka?'

'You know that sheila what wrote that Female Unicorn book.'

'Greer', I respond. 'And it ain't Unicorn you dumb tracker, it's Eunuch. I'll cut off your balls so you will get it right next time.'

'Yeah well, I don't read books like that. I'm strictly Superman comics and stick books mate. So how am I supposed to know? All I know is that bullets and bombs don't give diddly-squat if you are a man or a woman. She could kill just as well as men do.'

He leaves the dead woman lying bent and contorted, stripped half-naked, long black pants around her ankles and shirt wide open. The woman has no documents or additional weapons. As far as Chucka is concerned her carcass is irrelevant to the task at hand. Moving over to the other body, he commences the same grizzly task of stripping and searching for documents. 'Talk about the evil eye, get a load of this Gook's face will ya.'

I glance impassively at the second corpse. Shrapnel hit the man on the side of his face and somehow caused one eye to pop out of its socket.

Still hanging by nerve ends it stares back at me blankly. 'Must have been told to keep an eye out for Uk Dai Loi', I comment dryly.

'Don't look at me like that mate', Chucka says to the dead enemy. 'I'm just doin' my job and earning my pay, you're the sucker that got between me and a safe trip home.'

Our eyes meet for a moment, we both smirk, the callous smirk of men who have seen too much. The redhead is not looking at the dead soldier's injuries. He has walked over to the young woman and is trying to re-dress the body.

'It just ain't right to see a woman like this', he says. His hands are trembling as he lays her neatly on her back, straightens and closes her legs and drags her tattered black pyjama pants up over her hips. Next, he gently buttons up her shirt covering her exposed breasts. 'It just ain't right.'

I stare impassively at first but gradually something pricks my callous soul. It's a distant memory of an innocent young soldier who almost fainted when he discovered that a dead enemy soldier had in his possession a poem written to his girlfriend.

I look at the dead woman on the ground but am unable to feel any remorse. I only have a numb emotionless sense of a job well done, another kill for the battalion's statistics. Yet I know I should feel some sense of sorrow or guilt maybe. What has happened to me, how have I become so cold?

Cookie had pressed the clacka on the claymore. It won't matter how many people try to explain to him that he is not the one who started this war, not the one who sighted the mine that killed her. It was my sighting that destroyed this woman. He is just another young kid with ethics and values, placed in a no win situation.

'Don't worry about dressing the bitch', Chucka remarks. 'You're a cook, treat it like it's just dead meat mate, a leg of lamb or pork. Besides, we're just going to drag her up to our ambush shell-scrape and shovel some dirt on her.'

I snap my head around and look at Chucka. The man is as cold hearted as I am. I hold a finger up to my lips 'shush'. I point toward the bush line as a sign for Chucka to move out of the area. Chucka shrugs his shoulders responding immediately to my direction. Somehow, I have retained enough humanity in my tortured soul to know that the young cook needs this moment to help him come to terms with what has happened. After a few minutes, I move over close and examine the job Cookie has done dressing the body.

'You've done all you can for her Cookie. I'll get another man to bury her if you like.'

'No, no it's okay, I killed her. I want to bury her even if it's not a proper grave', the redhead replies trying desperately to stop his voice from quavering.

Through the gaps in the trees, a morning sun casts its rays of light. The warm rays caress the dead woman's face casting a golden sheen over her pale blue-yellow skin then dance over the blood soaked black clothing that had been torn open in a callous methodical act of war. She now lies neatly on her back in front of us with her arms across her chest.

I stare at the peasant woman. Is she young? Well maybe. It's sometimes hard to tell if a dead body is 20 or 30. The way they die causes the face to change. This is not the peaceful made up body in a swanky Sydney funeral parlour, it's a girl who died in agony. Red hot steel ball bearings from the claymore mine burned her vital organs.

Somewhere deep inside my stomach a small pang of pain reminds me that this was once a human being with feelings. She is someone's daughter, sister or girlfriend. For a moment I want to push such thoughts from my mind, force myself to think that it's just another Cong, another scum bag butcher. But no! I remember the balding grey haired shrink back at Vunger Hospital. No! Let it hurt, don't fall off the precipice. Put that beast back in its cage.

I reach into my shirt pocket and produce a plastic cigarette case, pull off the top and tap out two fags, push one of my Lucky Strike between the pale soldier's thin tight lips and pass him my Zippo cigarette lighter. Cookie opens the Zippo and runs his thumb across the wheel. As flames touch the end of the cigarette, the young man draws back hard before raising trembling fingers and pulling it free of his quivering lips. Slowly he lets the smoke expel from his lungs. 'Thanks.'

Noticing the engraving on my Zippo, the young man holds it to the morning light and reads the inscription: '*When I die I will go to heaven; I have done my time in hell.*' 'Sums it up pretty well don't it', he says, as he hands back my lighter.

'Welcome to the real war Cookie', I reply as I light my own smoke and then tuck the lighter back into its plastic cigarette case. 'Welcome to the real war.'

I do not turn and walk away as all my instincts tell me to, instead, I kneel beside the dead woman. 'Let me help you soldier. Let's lift her gently up to one of our pits and cover her with my spare hooch before we put some soil on her.'

Post Mortem

The Support Company's sergeant major is standing straight to attention alongside me. I stand quietly and look around the confined underground bunker space.

The commanding officer's personal underground bunker. About nine feet long and six or seven feet wide. The walls are lined with corrugated iron, it has a duck board floor and beams are supporting a sand-bagged roof. In one corner is an army issue stretcher pushed up on its end to get it out of the way. Against one wall a fold-up table, set up with a variety of charts stretched untidily across it. An army issue-folding armchair is propped in another corner. The confined space hums with the constant chatter emanating from an ANPRC 25 radio set wired to an additional speaker so that all general conversations on the zero alpha push is monitored.

Regardless of the situation the CO has at hand, I know he is primarily concerned with the war situation involving his soldiers. Bravo Company has been chasing enemy out in the field with the help of a tracker dog and the CO likes to stay tuned to any possible contact that may occur. The radio is therefore turned to full volume which drowns out the endless noise created at a fire support base.

He is pacing up and down within the confines of the bunker, a few short steps, and a quick turn and back the other way. Agitated, trying to decide what to say, how to handle the situation confronting him.

Finally, he stops pacing and looks up at the Support Company CSM.

'I left distinct instructions, no damn it, orders that this man was not to be in the field on patrol. You send him out in command of a fighting force. What do you think I should do about such a breach of military discipline CSM? What should I do to you for being so damn disrespectful?'

The CSM shuffles slightly. 'We were short of experienced men to lead the group Sir. I understood this man was recommended for promotion to full corporal when he was attached to Delta, and as CO sig he would normally carry one stripe Sir.'

'What the hell has that got to do with disobeying my instructions?'

'Experience Sir, I needed his experience. The man knows more about patrolling than most at the base. I understood he is very highly regarded by the OC and CSM in Delta Company, Sir.' I can see the concern in the CSM's eyes, he is in trouble, and he decides to pull the ace from his hat. 'You were not here so I checked with the operations officer and he said okay.'

This last comment leaves the CO a little stumped. The operations officer agreed to send me out with the TAOR. The commanding officer could not discipline the CSM without also taking action against his next most senior officer. He stares at the corrugated wall. 'And tell me sergeant major, why in hells name were you not able to lead that patrol?'

I am enjoying the tension of this moment. This is a rare opportunity to see the CSM red and blushing, his career threatened by an angry lieutenant colonel. A4 made a rapid rise through the ranks by snivelling up to commanding officers, not by getting offside.

The CSM speaks again, ignoring his commanding officers' subtle accusation of laziness or cowardly behaviour 'With due respect, Sir. It's probably just as well this soldier was on that patrol. It could have been a major cock up with a less experienced man on the job.'

The CO turns and looks at the CSM. 'Not the point CSM, I recognise that this man is an experienced soldier but there are other issues you do not need to know about.' He walks over to the table and looks at the chart spread in front of him, noting the marks indicating the ambush site and the harbour position.

'I should bust you back to sergeant for such a breach of my orders', he says to the CSM without bothering to look him in the eyes. 'Consider yourself very lucky and get out of my sight', he pauses a moment then speaks again. 'And from now on CSM you will lead future ambush patrols from this fire base. That is an order. I will inform your Company Commander and the Operations Officer of my order. Now CSM, right now get out of my sight.'

The Support Company CSM quickly turns and climbs up the stairs leading out from the small bunker. I stand waiting for my turn, whatever that is to be.

'Who gave you instructions to set up an ambush that way soldier?'

'I decided it was the safest way to go considering the quality of soldier I had with me Sir. I mean they're good diggers I suppose, but drivers, cooks and bottle washers are best kept behind the wire Sir. It's noisy in the field, can't lay still long enough for a standard ambush and untested if the enemy react and sweep around our flank.'

The CO nods. 'Just as well you had them in shell-scrapes I suppose. God almighty, I don't need to have my own boys killed by friendly fire at this point in time, do I?'

I shift uncomfortably. 'Sir my LOCSTAT was pretty damn close. It was not me who fucked up, it was the mortar boys. First tube was fine, they stuffed up the setting on the second tube.'

'I flew over your position grid and description soldier, there is no doubt according to my calculations that you were within a 50-meter radius of that grid reference you gave. What we don't know for sure is why the mortar dropped short. According to the platoon commander both tubes were set exactly where they should have been.'

'Or the bastards are covering up their mistake Sir.'

'Damn you soldier, don't push your luck', the CO snaps. 'My young officer would not cover up a mistake damn it. I can only assume we had two faulty charges which caused the drop short. These things can happen in warfare son.'

I stand silent trying to gauge the situation. Of course people cover up mistakes. I was myself an example of a cover up in which the CO had a significant role. Maybe it is just swings and roundabouts. My turn last time, a mortar sergeant this time, what difference does it make in the end. The main thing is that nobody intentionally stuffed up. My mind runs back to the incident at the bunker assault, poor old Henry shot by a friendly from another section. There should never be blame or scapegoats in these situations, people are doing the best they can in extremely difficult circumstances.

I assume the CO is not happy that I was back in the field, but also possibly concerned about any friendly incident inquiry that would bring attention back to me. I have no idea what happened at the investigation into Skip and the drugs but I am just as keen as the CO for my name not to come up anywhere.

The CO sits down in his chair, hands together in a praying formation with the fingers twiddling, deep in thought. 'Fortunately the boy's wounds are not fatal, one eye lost but they think the other will be okay and we did manage to kill two enemy with your clever little claymore ambush technique. You damn well need to get a swift kick in the bum for setting up an ambush like that without permission. You're not SAS soldier, you're regiment and that means you do it as your regiment has trained you to do it.' He shakes his head. 'Not to mention the breach of the one-thousand-meter rule. I need soldiers who follow orders son.'

'There were no orders on the set up. I was told to set up an ambush Sir. It's called initiative.'

'You're sailing close to the wind son. You know that we have clear methods of doing everything in this mans' army, in my Royal Australian Regiment. And you chose to do your own thing, didn't you? Well I don't think this man's regiment needs individuals, it needs men who do the job the way they are trained to do it.'

I feel anger welling up inside me. You pompous prick of a man, I am thinking. I get sent out with a bunch of pogos and I get two damn enemy kills, not to mention that my own supporting fire nearly wipes out my patrol. If I hadn't broken the rules he would have dead Australians on his mind. Fuck him.

'Don't look at me like that soldier', the CO barks, as he notices the contempt on my face. 'The very reason you are not a corporal is that you are a rebel soldier not a professional soldier. The only reason you are here instead of MCE is that I want no drug scandal in my battalion. I was protecting my boys from a scandal son. I was not protecting you.'

'I might be a rebel soldier but I am also a live soldier Sir, and so are those men who went out there with me.'

'Don't give yourself too much credit son. You would probably be just as alive if you had a proper ambush setting.'

'Care to get out of your precious little chopper Sir and have a good look for yourself. See the fucking war from where diggers see it. I'll show you just how fucking lucky we were, damn it.' I am furious with the commanding officer and have thrown all concern for military protocol out the window. I have spoken before thinking and now realise that I truly am sailing close to the wind.

The CO sits quietly in his chair fuming with self-important rage.

All I can do now is wait for him to call in the regimental police.

'You might have been lucky soldier I'll grant you that much, but army training isn't about luck. It's about discipline and procedure. I was considering a stripe for your arm. Now I'm considering having you thrown in a cell for 14 days for insubordination.'

I stand staring at the corrugated wall behind the CO. Right now, a couple of days in a cell would be welcome.

The CO looks me square in the eyes, 'You think I don't know what you and D Company OC were doing when you were his sig son?' He asks before responding to his own question, 'Of course I did. You kept me busy so the Major could play boy soldier, didn't you?'

'The OC Delta is the finest officer I have ever served with Sir. I would follow that man down the barrel of a loaded howitzer if he asked me.'

'A fine platoon commander son but a bloody irresponsible company commander. It is no accident that young officers are leading the casualty count along with scouts and gunners. It is because they try to lead from the front. Damn it I can accept that sort of zeal from a subby, or a full junior officer but a Major is a different story. He is more important than me damn it. If I am shot out of the sky, there is an operations officer in the command post and a company commander on the ground. What happens when the company commander takes a bloody round son? Who makes the calls then? Do we pull a platoon commander from his platoon? Do we rely on the CSM to make decisions for a whole company? Or do we try and fly in a company captain who is not in touch with what's actually happening? Come on son, you tell me.'

I stand silently. The CO continues.

'I cannot question his courage or his commitment to his lads, but he is not a good role model for the likes of you, he damn well encourages rebel behaviour. OC means officer commanding not gung-ho leader. A good OC is a live one and one who demands that military practice is by the book.' The Colonel stands and walks up to within inches of my face, 'You young man could have a solid career in the army if you got that rebel chip off your shoulder and started being a true professional.'

The radio speaker crackles into life, 'Zero alpha this is one, we are in contact. Over.'

The CO immediately springs into action. 'Don't you go too far away soldier I might need you in the air shortly. Now get my codebook up to date and make sure I have fresh water in one bottle and some snack food to chew on just in case we are up in the air for a while.'

With that, the CO scurries up the short stairwell and heads off toward the command post bunker. I stand for a moment, quite incredulous at the pompous CO. I am a signaller not a batman and yet I am now filling water bottles and putting lollies in the bastard's flying kit. I calm a little, maybe I am just as arrogant as him in my own stubborn way!

I reach over and grab the CO's code folder from the table and run a check on what needs to be brought up to date. It dawns on me that the CO was actually going to promote me but because I chucked a shitty he's decided against it. Story of my fucking life.

The radio set on the battalion frequency is now providing details. Alpha Company is in contact and calling for gunship air support. I listen in as the operations officer advises that gunslinger has been alerted.

Gunslinger! My attention is snapped toward the radio speaker. That means we have Yank Cobras instead of our old Hueys. It should be quite an experience to see them in action from the air, I don't want to miss this one.

I snap the code folder shut and grab the CO's web belt, climb out of the bunker and head straight for my own pit to get things ready. As I move over toward my pit I notice the Kiowa starting its engine, the rotors turn slowly at first then gradually get up to full revs ready for take-off.

I run to my pit as fast as my legs will take me. I will be in the air soon and the pompous prick of a CO wants a fresh bottle of water. I notice Chucka walking toward the command post

'What's up?' I can't help but see Chucka is looking angry and agitated.

'They sent a dog out without back up again, that's what's up', he snaps angrily. 'I'm supposed to be the cover man for the dog handler and they keep sending him out without me.'

'Count your blessings. Shit you're just back from a fucked up ambush, enjoy the break.'

'You just don't get it mate', Chucka responds. 'They get some poor scout to back up the dog handler. Scouts are good mate but this is a specialty. I know that dog almost as well as the handler does. I know the dog's 'point' mate, I'm trained for this. One day, mark my word, one fucking day some poor bastard will die because that bastard CSM wants people like me to do gun shift and TAORs around the firebase instead of what I am trained to do.'

For a brief moment I look at my new friend, unable to comprehend how he can be angry that he is being spared the dangers of tracking a wounded enemy. I notice the CO coming out of the command post bunker and running back to his own bunker to grab his webbing.

'Gotta go mate. Catch you when this lot gets sorted out', I yell to the angry young man. 'I got a gut feeling we are in for a long couple of days.' I grab my kit and quickly fill both my own and the CO's bottle. I check that my M16 has no round in the breach and the 20 round magazine is placed in my left web pouch with six others. I check I have smoke grenades in case I am required to mark out an area on the ground. As I scurry toward the Kiowa I flip through my personal sig operator's folder to make sure all codes are up to date and begin the mental exercise of memorizing the frequencies I will need.

Once in the back of the aircraft, I pre-set the VHF frequencies starting with the battalion's network, next the company network and then the administration network. I would not need the artillery frequency as the battle is out of range for artillery support. Finally, I check the FM band to ensure I am on the right air support push.

After pulling my head set over my ears and adjusting the mouthpiece to a comfortable position, I flick the radio onto the battalion's network and push the talk switch, 'Zero alpha this is pronto niner. We are ready to fly, radio check. Over.'

Command Post replies, 'Loud and clear'. Next I try the administration frequency, 'Zero bravo, pronto niner ready to go airborne, radio check. Over.' Again, I get the 'Loud and clear'. I do not call a radio check with Bravo Company as I know they are too busy with the battle to play toy soldier to the CO signaller. We will be right over their heads shortly and comms are all but guaranteed. I push the switch to intercom and speak to the pilot, 'I'm set back here so you can lift off as soon as the boss puts his arse through the door.'

'Errr, okay', a nervous and unfamiliar voice responds. I look forward as the pilot turns in his seat. A new pilot is at the controls, a young baby-faced kid looking nervously over his flight plans and checking instruments.

Shit, I hope this is an easy flight. Last thing I need is a beginner at the controls if we have to do some fancy flying. The commanding officer climbs into the aircraft beside the pilot and pulls his head set on.

'I assume your set back there pronto.'

'All set boss.'

'Okay pilot, let's go. Chop chop son', he calls to the baby face holding the cyclic. The pilot revs the motor and begins the ascent. The nose tilts forward and the Kiowa climbs rapidly to the east then circles over the firebase before heading directly toward the firefight. I look down to the base below, adjust my seating position and smile as I hear the CO on the intercom.

'Full steam ahead son, we got a war to fight and I'm in a hurry. I got some American Cobra gunships arriving over the fire fight and I want to get there before they do.'

'Yes Sir, I'm getting up to speed now', the young pilot replies nervously.

I sit back and rest my head on the rear bulwark. There is nothing to do now until we are near our destination. Over the radio, I hear the company signaller call, 'Zero alpha this is two, request Dustoff. Over.'

'Damn it, someone's hit', the CO calls over the intercom. I guess that the dog handler or back up scout has been cut down in the initial contact.

'Okay son', the CO calls to the new young pilot. 'We have a routine in these situations. We like to have a bit of a sing-a-long while we fly, ain't that right back there pronto?'

'Yes Sir. You sing it, I put up with it.'

'Ignore the cheeky soldier in the back seat son', the CO says to the pilot. 'What's your favourite song son?'

'Err, I don't know Sir.'

'Mmm! Ever watch Bandstand on TV growing up?'

'Well, yes Sir I did.'

'Good, I'll sing a song and you join in. That's an order son.'
'Yes Sir, you're the boss Sir.'
'Damn right I am.'
The chopper speeds toward the battle.
Chudda   Chudda   Chudda   Chudda   Chudda

DUSTOFF NEEDED

CHUDDA   CHUDDA   CHUDDA   Chudda   Chudda

The humming chudda chudda of the Kiowa Command helicopter creates a different sensation than the deeper, slower whop whop of the ubiquitous Iroquois UH-1 Huey helicopter as it speeds across the Vietnamese countryside toward a battle on the Long Khan and Phuc Tui provincial border.

The young Australian army pilot officer is working the cyclic and foot pedals almost too vigorously, veering the aircraft left then right to prevent any enemy soldier on the ground from sighting a surface to air missile at the little chopper. Occasionally he pulls back on the cyclic control and increases the collective for speed, sending the Kiowa skyward, and then pushes the cyclic forward to send it toward the treetops. The low level flying accentuates the speed of these dangerous evasive manoeuvres.

A tropical landscape careens beneath the helicopter skids in a blur of greens and browns. There is the occasional splash of a different colour as the Kiowa scuds across Vietnamese workers in their fields. Their black pyjama-like clothing and conical hats contrast against bright scarves and the odd decoration on the yokes of their beasts of burden.

The Commanding Officer

Lt Colonel McCellen looks across at the junior pilot officer almost wincing at what confronts him. A boy in a man's uniform, his pilot's helmet too large for the almost pubescent head beneath it, a facial expression showing a mix of determination, anticipation and fear. Are these boys getting younger, or am I getting older, he asks himself? A highly competent scallywag in the back seat and a pimply kid on the controls. I am just getting too bloody old for this shit. Time to look for a desk job when my work is done on this tour of duty. Bloody pilot is chucking the bird around so much I am getting bloody motion sickness.

'Cut the bloody jet jockey crap and fly this thing straight damn you', The Colonel barks at the pilot.

'Evasive manoeuvres, Sir.'

'Crap, bloody crap! Climb up off the treetops before you start collecting branches on your bloody skids and take us straight to our destination.' With that, he begins singing over the intercom: *'Bye, bye, bye, bye baby good-bye. See you in the morning at the break of day, just a little kiss and I'll be on my…* Hey do you know this song Lieutenant?'

'No Sir.'

'What about you back there soldier?'

I push my foot down on his internal talk mode button. *'I get so lonesome when we're apart, don't leave me lonesome and please don't break my heart.* Col Joye, more your generation Sir. I think my great, great grandmother had a crush on him. I'm a Stone's man personally.'

McCellen turns and smiles and I realise we have developed a grudging respect and a love/hate relationship with each other in just a few weeks. Okay I am a cheeky, self-opinionated rebel. All armies have people like me, and the Australian army seems to produce a few too many larrikins as far as this CO is concerned. But…

'Damn scallywag aren't you pronto. But you know your songs so I will let the old age joke pass THIS TIME', he mutters into the intercom.

'So don't get too cheeky young fella. I'm not much older than you. Stones… Rolling Stones, huh! What songs have they got son?'

As is his practice, the Colonel finds it easier to sing or talk to keep his own and his companions' minds off the impending danger we are careening toward.

'How about *Satisfaction* Sir? Or….hang on… I got a call coming in.'

I have no time to finish my answer. My headset comes alive with the sound of the company commander involved with the battle ahead.

'This one's for you Sir. I'm putting you on the Bravo Company frequency.'

Sitting behind the Colonel, I am monitoring the bank of three VHF and two FM radios. I can flick from channel to channel or direct specific frequencies into the CO's headset. With the CO, the pilot and me operating the communications we can talk to three locations at once. If required I can monitor two additional stations.

The use of code names and call signs enables signallers and commanders to make sense of the garbled jargon passing through the ether on the thousands of frequencies used by Australian and American forces. The commanding officer's common code name is 'sunray' and his radio call sign is 'niner'. On air, I use the call sign 'pronto niner'. This allows those below to know that I am up in the air with the CO and can relay messages to and from my superior officer.

I know from air chatter that we are heading at high speed toward Bravo Company's battle with the Viet Cong. The rifle company engaged a medium sized enemy force in relatively thick jungle late the previous afternoon, killing one Viet Cong and inflicting several casualties or so it appeared given the blood trails leading from the contact site.

The company commander had called in the tracker dog and handler to hunt down the wounded soldiers. A Huey had delivered them at night, ready to get started the next morning.

During today's chase, the tracker dog had led Four Platoon, radio call sign 'two one' into a fortified enemy position.

Bravo Company is now pinned down by a well-armed enemy force and have taken one casualty. Their forward scout was hit by small arms fire while acting as back-up for the tracker dog and its handler. The platoon commander has requested a casualty evacuation, known simply as CASEVAC, call sign, 'Dustoff'.

The rifle company is operating at the extreme edge of artillery support. For this reason, the Colonel has arranged for the American forces to provide two deadly AH-1G Cobra Gunslinger helicopter gunships to support the ground troops.

Chudda   Chudda   Chudda   Chudda   Chudda

With the CO on the battalion's frequency talking to the company commander about the current state of the battle ahead and below, I flick to B Company's internal frequency and pick up the agitated platoon commander calling into the ether.

'This is sunray two, one, where is that Dustoff? Over.'

'Two one this is pronto niner. Dustoff won't come in until gunslinger has arrived to cover. Do you have a Lima Zulu ready? Over', I ask, hoping that the platoon had somehow found or cleared a landing zone to the rear of the actual contact area.

'This is two one, you think we got time to do any gardening down here, drop a litter and winch him up. Over.'

This curt reply tells me the wounded boy is in trouble on two accounts. He is badly wounded and he needs a stokes litter. The contact is heavy and they have not been able to move him back to a safer area. Of more immediate concern for me, no chopper pilot likes to hover over a fire fight lowering a winch, it makes them a sitting duck for enemy ground fire.

I call back to the platoon commander below to buy time and reassure him, 'Two one this is pronto niner, bushranger, errr, gunslinger Echo Tango Alpha is five mikes. I will chat with Dustoff now. Over.'

'Thanks pronto niner, thanks. Out.'

I flick onto the FM air combat band and drop the pronto tag. 'Dustoff, this is niner, I am in call sign two one's area, where are you? Over.'

'Ah-h-h! hello niner, this is Dustoff two four zero, we are inbound, Echo Tango Alpha two mikes. Confirm your combat push and I will talk to you there. Over.'

Great. The American drawl tells me we have a chance to get that boy out of there by winch. Yank pilots seem unconcerned about getting their choppers shot full of holes. I give them the coded frequency, pause, and then advise them that it is a winch job, assuring them that gunslingers will arrive shortly to provide protection. I wait to receive their answer knowing that the pilot is considering the lives of his crew in addition to his own. Will he go in or will he say no?

The radio crackles back into life, 'Roger that niner, we copy and are ready when the gunslingers get hot, switching to your combat push now. Out.'

I throw my head back. I love these Yanks! My heart is racing as the adrenalin surges through my body. The hunt, chase, kill and rescue. It does not matter which it is. As soon as it is on, the fear rises inside me, my suddenly dry mouth is filled with a foul metallic taste, my vision becomes crystal clear, mind sharpens and nerve ends tingle with anticipation. I hate being scared and yet … it feels like a rush of morphine to my soul.

I depress the intercom switch and speak to the Colonel, 'Dustoff in-bound Skipper. They will need direct gunship cover. It's going to be a winch and litter job.'

'Damn that platoon commander. Why can't he move the boy back? We have to move the boy back,' the CO responds.

I roll my eyes. Don't ask me, I think. How do I know if he can move him back, you pompous prick? I'm not on the ground am I? I do however know the platoon commander down in the firefight. A young officer respected by all ranks and I am quite certain that he would move the wounded soldier back if it was possible.

'Get me his frequency', the CO calls. I immediately flick the CO to the company combat push and put myself on the battalion's frequency, to pick up any requests on that line. I know the CO has little chance of changing the decision made on the ground. Being a lieutenant colonel in the air means little to the boys down there getting their arses shot at.

No sooner am I on the new frequency when my earphones crackle into life, 'Niner, niner this is two zero, sunray. Over.'

'Two zero this is pronto niner, my sunray is on your internal push. Over.'

'Thank you pronto, please advise niner that Victor Charlie has a fifty cal down here, probably tripod mounted. Over.'

The officer commanding B Company or the OC as is the common term, has just given me the one bit of information I do not want to hear.

Shit, an anti-aircraft gun is all I need this close to wakey. I push down on the intercom, 'Skipper there is a fifty cal anti-air down there, get this chopper back down on the tree line or get the hell out of here.'

The pilot immediately banks over to clear the area but the CO comes onto the intercom, 'Get back on course damn you Lieutenant and don't you sit in the back seat telling me how to fight this war son.'

Oh that's just great, the pompous career man wants to be a fucking hero, does he? I know that my commanding officer has no direct battle experience despite his extensive military career. It was all attaché and administration work in Canberra.

The man can fly up here above the battle but he cannot hear the high pitch snap of the rounds as they pass his ears. He's only heard that strange 'pop pop' sound as enemy rounds search the sky. He can't hear the scream of men injured or burning. He has not seen the carnage committed to a body when metal projectiles tear flesh and shatter bone. The career man only gets to see the boys, 'his boys' as he fondly calls them, in a hospital after the doctors have done their best. The stench of fear, the clinging odour of death in the tropical heat is washed away with a generous splash of antiseptic.

As the Kiowa returns to its original dangerous course my mind flashes back to my first taste of combat. A young man with a gaping hole in his chest. Bright red blood frothed out of both his chest wound and his mouth as he struggled to stop himself from drowning in his own blood. I am snapped back instantly to the present as my headphone assaults my eardrums with the high-pitched screaming of the CO through the intercom.

'Get out, get out …. out to the right.' I look up to see the CO hitting the pilot's left shoulder with his right fist which is only hampering the pilot's ability to manoeuvre the aircraft.

Through the jungle canopy below, the green tracer from the 50 cal machine gun is snaking up at us. In an instant, the whole scene before me seems bizarre and surreal, slow motion happening in double quick time.

Am I watching my own death about to happen?

Chudda   Chudda   Chudda   Chudda   Chudda

The Kiowa kicks hard over to the right and falls sharply as it banks. With the gravitational force jamming my stomach upward into my chest, I sit mesmerised as the tracer rounds pass along the side of the aircraft and through the rotor blade area. I hear the pop, pop, pop, pop as the 50 calibre rounds pass by the chopper at twice the speed of sound causing mini sonic booms.

Green tracer, not NATO orange, must be Russian! I am amazed at my clarity of thought as I sit waiting for the rotor blades to disintegrate and send the tiny aircraft plummeting to the earth below. Gravitational force is now pulling my body in different directions as the Kiowa is flung hard onto the left side and commences a rapid climb before diving again. I experience a moment of panic tearing at my chest as the trees rush up at me but suddenly the Kiowa levels and scuds across the treetops. It is under control; the pilot is performing evasive manoeuvres.

'Are we hit back there, are we hit?' The pilot calls in a quivering voice.

I feverishly scan the rear cockpit area for the tell-tale signs of weapon damage. Nothing.

'I don't think so, everything back here looks okay.'

The chopper again skims meters above the treetops, away from the contact area. Being low to the jungle canopy an enemy cannot see the helicopter coming until it literally passes over head. It is the safest place to fly when anti-air is looking for you.

The young pilot is overdoing the evasive manoeuvres. He's throwing the little bird hard over, left then right then back to the left again. Without a seat belt to restrain me, I am tossed around the back area, no longer held steady by natural G force. I grab the signals console in front of me and put my head down between my elbows trying to fight off the motion sickness that is beginning to overpower me, caused as much from the fear, as from the violent motion. Bile is rising in my parched throat, burning my oesophagus, somehow, I hold it down.

Oh fuck, oh fuck I thought I was out of it, out of the pointy end in a safe job. I swallow back the bile. Now this happens, why now, when we are almost home.

The CO has regained his composure and is again talking to the platoon commander below. He hits the intercom switch, 'How many smokes have you got back there?'

I belch and my mouth fills with bile. I try to ignore the burning and spit the yellow and black substance on the floor and hit the talk button, 'Two, one yellow one blue.' I always carry a couple of smoke grenades in case the chopper must put down. I grab my water bottle and swallow enough to ease the burning sensation. Not now, not a fucking bout of indigestion on top of a shit scared dry throat. Maybe it's a heart attack. I should be so fucking lucky.

'There is a bag of them under the rear seat', the nervous call from the young pilot rings in my ears. 'In the satchel under your feet.'

I look down and see the well-padded bag. I open it and find the smoke grenades. Of course! It's a command helo isn't it?

A new worry confronts. Why would the CO want smoke?

My fears are answered soon enough as the CO calls back to me, 'Get that door open. We are going to drop the smoke down to the boys. They are short and will need it to guide in the gunships.'

Worry now turns to gut wrenching fear, my intestines twist into a tight ball and my sphincter muscle snaps tight as I steel myself for another slow pass over the area being sprayed by an anti-air machine gun. I am not angry with the CO for insisting we return into the firing line. I know the smoke grenades are essential. Why the boys had run out I do not know but that is academic now. If the diggers below are short, then the Kiowa must deliver. Without smoke the Dustoff and ongoing gunship support cannot happen. I take a deep breath and clench both fists several times before letting the air rush from my lungs then I suck in more air to steady nerves. Here we go, keep it together. I shove the door open and feel the blast of air rushing by.

'Give me a call when we're over them', I call back through the intercom.

The little chopper has flown in a broad 360-degree arc and is now heading back toward the contact area, still pitching in evasive manoeuvres to avoid any ground to air rockets. Up ahead the green tracer from the enemy gun still speeds skyward in a set of short bursts. It is testing the air for a lucky kill. It's a fishing expedition of green death, sweeping in arcs, hoping to hit us as we fly over.

'Stop that stupid evasive action and go straight at it son!' The CO barks at the pilot.

'We are going to be sitting ducks up here once we get over the top', the pilot winces, fear clearly discernible in his quivering voice.

'Hold your nerve son, hold your damn nerve and do what I order you to damn well do', the CO barks back at him.

'*I can't get no, sat-is-faction, I can't get no!*' Hey back there. I'm not so old I don't know about the damn Rolling Stones. Sing with me boys, '*I can't get no sat-is-faction.*'

As we spit out the words to the song, we can see whiffs of blue smoke rising from the trees ahead. Further ahead red smoke has found its way through the jungle canopy. The CO stops his Mick Jagger impersonation and calls on the radio, 'Two one, I have blue and red. Over.'

'On blue, on blue', the platoon commander replies. 'Enemy approximately 50 meters in front of, or north of, the red smoke.'

My heart is pounding through my chest as we near our target. No time to sing now. I hope this pilot can hold his shit together, no second chances if he panics.

The chopper starts to slow, above the smoke and over the treetops, ready to perform a flare manoeuvre, which will bring the Kiowa's nose up suddenly and stop the helo in a mid-air hover. Green 50 calibre tracer pop, pop, pops past the flimsy aircraft.

I imagine that all enemy soldiers below us are now trying to sight the Kiowa. I know I will not be able to tell if they are firing at the chopper with their rifles as the enemy rarely use tracer in their general assault weapons. The 'snapping' from AK 47s is barely audible above the high pitch rotors and internal whining. I lean out the doorway, feeling exposed and vulnerable, waiting for an enemy round to smash into my body. Silly really, I think calmly, as if a thin alloy and fibreglass door can protect me from an AK round.

My arm is now stretched out, holding the bag which is being blown around by the rotor blades. My muscles feel like rubber, I am unsure if I can maintain a grip on both the bag with one hand and the aircraft door surround with the other.

'Don't panic, keep it together', I call to the pilot, afraid that any unpredictable manoeuvre by the pilot will fling me outward to my death.

'Don't drop 'til we are right over them', the CO calls back to me.

G forces push me forward then upward as the chopper flares over the blue smoke drifting through the trees from below. The pilot lifts the chopper's nose too high and its tail rotor is almost clipping tree tops. He over-corrects, pushing the nose too low and flings me forward into the radio console. 'Fuck!' I scream as I snatch at the radio console to stop myself being flung out the door. Somehow I manage to retain my grip on the smoke satchel.

'Steady damn you son, steady. Come on son keep us level and clear of those trees', the Colonel yells to his pilot who gradually brings the aircraft under control.

I stare downward, make out a digger lying on his back and waving his arms. I let the bag drop down through the trees. Suddenly a popping sound turned into a 'clang' as a small hole appears in the chopper's floor to the left of my squatting body.

'Drop is complete', I call to the pilot. 'Get out of here. They have us, they have us damn it, we are now targeted.'

Whoosh!

A dark black object rockets past the tiny aircraft, missing it by no more than a few meters. 'That was close! Get out of here quick', the Colonel screams to the pilot.

Chida   Chida   Chida   Chida   Chida

The chopper is suddenly at full revs as the Kiowa pitches over for a fast getaway to the right of the red smoke indicating the enemy area.

The pilot is suddenly screaming aloud on the intercom, 'Jesus please, Jesus help me!'

Whoosh!

Another black object scuds past just in front of the aircraft leaving a tell-tale smoke trail from its tail. Half-praying, half-panicking, the inexperienced pilot is getting the aircraft out of shape. The little Kiowa begins to slide sideways through the air toward the jungle's canopy, its rotor pitch now screaming as the blades cut desperately through the tropical air trying to find some lift.

As the branches of the treetops come rushing toward me I decide my greatest fear, my worst nightmare is about to become a reality. 'Don't let me burn', I cry aloud in panic, thinking I should jump clear and grab at the branches.

Was it common sense or legs frozen with fear? I do not know but I remain glued to my canvas seat instead of jumping. I sit waiting for the crash.

Chida   Chida   Chida   Chudda   Chudda

The little bird begins to win its battle with gravity. Slowly its rotor blades grip the tropical air. Somehow, it holds itself up and gradually pulls away.

'Oh God, oh dear Lord thank you my Lord', the pilot is screaming over the intercom, his talk switch obviously jammed open. He is a total jelly at the controls and both the CO and I are at his mercy. I can see the CO reaching over to the pilot and fiddling with the young man's equipment.

'Get a grip on yourself son, get a grip', the commanding officer is yelling to the pilot.

The Kiowa moves clear and again starts speeding across the treetops but the young pilot's legs are trembling so much he seems unable to control his foot pedals. The bird is kicking its back end 60 to 80 degrees from side to side erratically.

'Climb up you silly bastard, you're too shaken to be this close to the trees. Your legs are shaking like jelly, you'll kill us all', the CO calls to the pilot. The pilot eases the cyclic back between his legs and the bird climbs into the sky.

'If I climb up we will be a sitting duck for anymore surface to air missiles', the pilot screams hysterically back at the CO.

'They were not missiles fired at us son, they were bloody rocket propelled grenades. Get right up high and out of the way, as high as we can safely get this fucking thing', the CO orders. 'RPGs can't hit us up there in the clouds.'

'Yes Sir, I'm sorry Sir, I'm trying.'

'Sing with me Lieutenant, sing with me. *Don't leave me lonesome and please don't break my heart.* Sing fuck you!'

'Yes Sir. *Bye, bye, bye, bye, babe*…Oh God I can't Sir!'

I throw my head hard back against the padded rear bulwark sucking in a deep breath to stabilise the panic gripping my chest. I can tell by the young officer's voice that the pilot is crying.

'Don't lose it mister, do as the damn CO says and fuckin' do it now!' I call over the intercom. 'All together now *bye, bye, bye, bye baby good bye.*'

The Colonel joins me on the intercom and we sing together.

461

'See you in the morning at the break of day, just a little kiss and I'll be on my way…'

'Come on fly boy, sing!' The Colonel yells.

As the aircraft crawls skyward, the young pilot adds his quivering voice to ours, *'bye, bye, bye, bye, baby goodbye…'*

'Call sign two, this is gunslinger hot shot one. I have a bird flying clear of blue smoke is that you good ol' boys?' The radio is alive again.

The gunships are here at last. Damn the CO, if we had only waited a couple of minutes we could have dropped that smoke with air support.

'Gunslinger this is two, one. We are on blue and releasing more to pinpoint our position. Victor Charlie is five zero past the red to the north, in line with the blue, copy. Over.'

The platoon commander responds from the ground below.

'Ahhh… gunslinger, that's a copy. Heads down Aussie, I'm hunting Gooks. Over', comes the arrogant reply from the gunship pilot sitting in his amour-plated killing machine.

'Give 'em hell', the platoon commander replies.

From the left, below the Kiowa, I can see the two black Cobra gunships. One back and one banking over to dive and strike. It drops down over the approximate enemy position and lets its mini Gatling guns loose on the jungle canopy. It fires so many rounds that the tracer is a constant orange-red blur. The grenade launcher spits out a spread of 40 mm grenades onto the enemy below.

As it climbs, the second gunship comes on the air, 'Hot Shot 2 here, I got me a bead on that anti-air tracer, time to put a spike up his mudda fuckin' arse'.

Christ almighty, I am thinking, Australian gunships or bushrangers always do a dry run and fire some white phosphorous to verify they are hitting the area the troops on the ground want, but these Yanks are going straight at it.

I watch in awe as the second gunship dives and unleashes all his missiles at once. The mighty war machine almost shudders to a stop in mid-air as a dozen high explosive and four white phosphorous missiles dart into the approximate area that the 50 cal has been firing from. The ground below seems to shudder, treetops fling wildly about from the concussion waves then erupt in flames and thick white smoke.

'Goddamn, had me a trigger failure hot shot one, all my damn rockets gone at once.'

'Shhhoooeee, some rush there boy, I sure did see a blast', hotshot one responds. 'How is that Aussie, we get them little Gook mudda-fuckers or did we hit some of you good ol' boys?' The first pilot is calling to the platoon commander below.

'You're on target, I say again on target, but be a bit more bloody careful for God's sake. Over.'

'Hotshot one, roger to you. Hey hotshot two check our spare push and see if we got gunslingers nearby who want some trade, we gonna need more goddamn rockets.'

The air crackles again, 'Hotshots one and two this is gunslinger white hawk heavy fire team we want trade, give us your location man.'

An eight-figure grid reference is sent across the airwaves.

'White hawk heavy that's a go for us, we're jest five mikes out and headin' in for some fun. You hotshot boys jest keep them Gooks shittin' their jammies 'til we git there.'

Hotshot one then speaks to his companion, 'Well I got damn rockets, we will use my mother's 'til white hawk arrives in five. For now we can take turns with the Gatling guns and let the Dustoff do his run damn it.'

'Hot shot two wilco, let the fun begin'. The invincible war bird banks over to do its job on the helpless enemy below.

I call to the CASEVAC Huey, 'Dustoff this is nine, Dustoff niner, can you start your approach? Over.'

'Eeerrh-h-h-h… in bound now, have that boy ready to fly.'

I wait for an answer, nothing, I call to the platoon below.

'Two one this is niner. Did you copy Dustoff coming in for pick up. Over.'

'This is two, one roger. Out. To you, Dustoff two one, right over the blue. Over.'

'Ahh-h-h … … Dustoff, I copy.'

The little Kiowa is now at maximum height. Up until this point I have been listening to the talk and staring like a stunned mullet at the reckless and brazen gunship pilots. Now I am aware of my own state. I'm exhausted, physically I'm tired to the bone, my mouth is desert dry, my right hand is shaking almost uncontrollably, and my left hand, which I used to drop the smoke has no feeling in it at all. I realise that both my legs are stretched out and pushing against the forward bulkhead so hard that my thighs are trembling from over exertion. I wonder if my bladder held? I glance down and am relieved to see that my crutch is as dry as my mouth.

Feeling just as gut-rotten bad as I do after a contact on the ground, I remind myself that flyboys earn their pay in this war as much as grunts do.

The airwaves sing in the headset again.

'Two one this is Dustoff, we have your boy and are goin' home. Over.'

'This is two one, thanks Yank, we owe you a beer. Over', the platoon commander replies.

Overhead in the Kiowa the CO becomes animated again.

'Dustoff this is niner, how is the boy? Over.'

A long pause follows, too long.

'Ahh-h-h, Dustoff here, come back on the Fox Mike push.'

I flick the CO onto the FM frequency and listen in. A long pause and the pilot comes on the air.

'Head wound, not good. We will by-pass Viper and take him straight to main. Over.'

'Thank you, Dustoff. Out', a sorrowful reply from the CO.

The airwave is silent for now, we are deep with thought. The young man has obviously caught a bad head wound, probably better off dead.

The intercom crackles with the young pilot's voice, still shaky and quivering.

'We need fuel Sir.'

'Home son', replies the suddenly tired battalion commander. 'To the Dat not the firebase. Let's go home and juice up. I need a damn word with you once we touch down'.

I cut in, I can see one small and three large black dots on the horizon. The gunslinger heavy fire team is racing in for some trade. 'Skipper we better stay as long as we can those gunslingers are gung ho cowboys, you might need to pull them into line.'

'OC can do that if needed son, we need fuel or we will be on the ground ourselves in no time. I don't want you, me and this blithering idiot to be parked in a clearing out here waiting for friendly support. There are bloody bad guys all over this bit of jungle.'

The Kiowa pilot wipes tears from the bright red cheeks of his humiliated face. He banks the chopper over and heads at full revs toward the Dat. At last, the chudda chudda is taking us toward safety not battle!

The CO is back on the combat frequency, talking to the company commander at the firefight. I flick myself over to the battalion's zero bravo frequency to check that supply for the company is being arranged. Immediately I can hear the command post signaller reading back the encrypted message to the B Company signaller.

'Zulu Zulu, Mike, Foxtrot – November, Charlie, Zulu, Golf', the read back goes on and on until a final, 'Over'. Then comes a reply from the company sig, 'Two bravo. Out.'

The battalion operations officer comes on the air calling for the serial number and first initials of the young soldier in the Dustoff.

I pull the head set from my ears. I do not want to know who is in that Dustoff chopper with a hole in his head. Right now I just need a smoke to calm the nerves. I want this jelly-legged pilot to land without crashing and some whisky to hit that knot. That lump deep in my guts! I stare at the hole in the floor and across at the exit hole in the closed door. Oh Jesus, how many other hits did we take? I grab my water bottle and force some water down my parched throat. Get me home you God fearing little prick of a pilot, just get me home.

The commanding officer has turned in his seat and is trying to say something to me. I stare back at him indifferently. The CO motions for me to put my head set back on.

'Fuck off!' I yell back over the noise of the little Kiowa. The CO looks shocked for a moment, then makes a waving gesture with his hand and turns back to the front.

I rest my head against the rear bulwark. Adrenalin has kicked back in and spit is filling my mouth, causing a strange sensation of a bone-dry throat and sloppy wet lips. I swallow hard to force the spit past the golf ball sized lump in my throat. I take another long swig from my almost empty water bottle. God I need a smoke.

Chudda   Chudda   Chudda   Chudda   Chudda

OLD EYES MEET

THE COMMAND FLIGHT had stopped briefly back at the Dat while the Kiowa was checked for serious damage, three hits to the fuselage but deemed superficial. As it was considered airworthy the CO ordered a quick refuel before returning to the combat area.

From my privileged position in the Kiowa, I could see a visibly scarred jungle below. The gunships had done a nasty job on the enemy position, probably more effective than an artillery barrage because of the acute accuracy of strikes by the air to ground rockets.

Charlie had dug in, but it was not a fully fortified bunker system that Bravo Company had found. It was being constructed and not completed. The Australians had upset Charlie's plan and the enemy had obviously decided to retreat and live to fight another day.

While platoon two-one had laid on covering fire, platoons two-two and two-three had swept over the position to find almost nothing. The CO had directed the pilot to land at the battle site and we met with the company commander to brief him on what little we knew of their wounded digger's fate; he was in surgery and may not live.

We wandered over the captured bunker system and viewed the carnage of battle. Fortunately, the CO was not carrying a camera. I could see the look of contempt on some soldiers' faces as we walked past and heard one mumble to his mate 'fuckin' tourist now it's safe', not realising we had been the ones that gave them the smoke to help direct the gunships.

We then flew back to Nui Dat and the CO went to his hut, me to my tent and a chance to collapse on a real bed. The Dat is a place of constant noise, particularly in the Support Company area. Luscombe airfield runs down the side of the rubber trees where the company tents are located, and the battalion's helicopter pad is no more than 60 meters down the gradual slope from this position.

Regardless of the noise, I am drifting in and out of sleep, half-drunk from the whisky stored in my trunk. Cigarettes are not helping undo my gut knot anymore but whisky always helps. As I lay in my own sweat, I think about the days battle and how close to death I had come.

But that was then. For now, I am safe. I have grown to love and appreciate real beds, as opposed to muddy ground or a thin string hammock endured when in a rifle company. In this new job as CO signaller I have the luxury of many extra moments in the Dat. Moments to laze in my new-found love which is a plastic covered green mattress with a sheet and an army issue green towel draped across to stop it sticking to my back.

For a moment I let down my emotional and psychological guard, leave my two weapons out of immediate reach with their chambers empty and magazines secured in a web pouch.

I just lay there emotionally exhausted wishing I had stayed in my zero bravo job.

In my half-aware state I hear, 'Hey Bri! The CO wants you.'

I feel something sharp or cold on my chest. Startled, I leap out from under the mozzie net. Graham, a linesman from signals platoon, is standing beside my bed with an ice-cold can of Coke, looking stunned by my cat-like leap from bed.

Without thinking, I line Graham in my sights and punch him in the left side of his head. I swing again but miss as Graham falls back over the sand bagged blast wall.

'Don't ever do that!' I scream hysterically. 'Never, ever again!'

White with fear, Graham got to his feet and ran clear of the area. From the next bed, Ray the admin command post sig operator, peers at me while shaking his head from side to side.

'Bit jumpy mate?' Ray says with a wry, knowing smile.

I look across to Ray, embarrassed. I am calming down and feel stupid. In my half-drunken sleepy state, the cold can felt like a sharp knife. It had triggered a flash-back fear of the bushman scout trying to beat me to the kill. It never happened of course. It never will, the little Nog has done a runner somewhere. But for that split second I reacted as though my life was at stake only to discover that I had punched a digger in the face because the man was offering me a can of Coke.

'Graham was trying to tell you the old man wants you up in his hut, asap. Go see the boss and I'll find Graham and remind him that he shouldn't startle diggers just back from combat', he pauses, then continues briefly. 'Don't worry, he'll be okay about it.'

I pull my shirt over my sweaty sticky back then slip my 9 mm Browning pistol and gun belt around my waist. Once done I head for the exit, stop momentarily to grab my M16 rifle, kitted web belt and the code book just in case we are in the air again.

As I stroll up the hill to the CO's hut, I am expecting to be officially charged with something or other for telling the CO to fuck off earlier that morning. I am not concerned about a couple of days in a cell and a week of extra duties. The battalion is close to completing its tour of duty and the punishment may result in my not having to fly with the Colonel again.

At the top of a slight hill, some small huts with tiny verandahs sit side-by-side, a little larger than the four-person tents used by the diggers. The huts are privileged turf and provide the CO, the Administration Company Commander, the battalion Operations Officer and the Regimental Sergeant Major a little piece of heaven in this place called Nui Dat.

To the left of the huts and just along a sealed piece of road is the above ground battalion Nui Dat command post where signallers monitor a 24-hour service to troops in the field, called the Zero Bravo Administration HQ.

'Come in soldier', I hear the CO say from the darkness of his hut. I enter and allow my eyes to adjust to the dim light. I can see him sitting alone in an army issue-folding armchair, a bottle of Johnny Walker Black Label whisky on a coffee table beside him. Overhead the tired old ceiling fan is slowly turning to move the still stale air.

Whop   Whop   Whop   Whop   Whop

Damn rotor blades, I muse, choppers and ceiling fans. I swear they will haunt me forever.

I study the CO's features for the first time, how strange that I never bothered to note any detail before this moment. Up until now all I ever saw was a colonel, a sort of big boss with no real detail except the rank on his uniform. The battalion commander is in his late thirties or early forties, a touch of short-cut, grey hair showing along the sides of his head and a thick bushy moustache hiding his top lip, his open neck shirt shows signs of chest hair just below the shave line. There is little sign of a weathered neck or face, so common amongst professional grunts with a lifetime of outdoor activities. The deep wrinkles on his brow are recent and caused by strain, not the harsh Australian sun.

'I am flying over to visit young Mark, you know, the boy we got out this morning. I just don't understand why he was up front as forward scout', the Colonel shakes his head slowly. 'He has only been in the country a couple of weeks. A replacement conscript for God's sake. Surely the bloody section commander would have put an experienced man up front to cover the tracker?'

I stand silently. Was the CO questioning himself or was this question aimed at me? I decide to answer the question. 'Dog handlers are supposed to have their own trained support team from the anti-tank tracking platoon. It's a common, and if you want my opinion, bloody dangerous practice of

Support Company's sergeant major to send the dog handler out alone and rely on the platoon in the field to provide backup, Sir.'

I pause then speak again spitting out the words, 'Don't blame the section commander, blame your Support Company CSM out at the firebase. He's the one taking short cuts so he can keep more troops at the base for other duties.'

I am now experienced enough with war on the ground to know that the men in the field get tired and nervous. The new fresh digger probably asked to do the job to show everyone he was a good soldier and the section commander probably thought, stuff it, my scout is on a knife-edge, why not let the new boy have a go!

I am wondering to myself whether I know any Mark in this battalion, did I ever meet this wounded bloke? I cannot put a face to the name. After a pregnant pause I nod sympathetically to the career man.

'How is he, Mark? Will he pull through?'

In the dim light, I can see the CO's face turn grey. The man suddenly looks old, very old.

'He's alive son, that's about all. He took a round through his temple, it came out the left eye socket and took away a good part of his frontal brain area. It's a god-awful sight looking at that boy. Half his head is missing, it's just not there.'

A proud man, the CO cannot look me in the face for the moment, as he looks away to fight back tears and regain his composure. 'God-awful sight, I would rather he was dead maybe we should just let these ones pass away.' He clears his throat, 'Just a boy. Just a boy.'

I usually hate this bastard, the way he refers to all of us as 'his boys'. Now I feel for him. We really are his boys, aren't we'? The CO has a mother to contact when he gets home. He is feeling the weight of command right now and I am glad it is the CO and not me.

'What is it with you soldier? I can throw you in the cell block for the contempt you showed the Support Company Sergeant Major.'

I stiffen. 'I tell it as I see it, Sir!'

The Colonel smiles a sad but affectionate smile.

'I cannot argue with that. I should kick your arse but at least I can always know where you stand on any situation'. He shakes his head slowly, 'Only this very morning I was trying to tell you that you could be a fine soldier, your trouble is not how you perform under pressure in the field son. Your bloody problem is that you think most people around you are arseholes. You are an arrogant son of a bitch. The truth is the army is full of arseholes but only arrogant bastards like you are so obvious in your contempt, the rest of us show a bit of military protocol.'

He throws his code holding folder to me, 'I'll get you to change my code book now, the situation's settled enough for me to hop over to Da Nang and visit the boy for what it's worth.' He again pauses to regain his composure and stop his quivering voice before continuing, 'He won't even know I am there you know but I feel I should sit with him a bit. His mother would want that don't you think? I'm sure she would want me to do that'.

'I'll be flying back early tomorrow, so be at the chopper pad ready to go at 0600. We will operate out of the firebase, not here. I feel so damn guilty sitting here in comfort while my boys are out there.'

I had the next day's codes in my leg pocket, so I quietly remove the old and replace them with the new. As for the CO's last comment I say nothing. I stopped feeling guilty about anything long ago. It was a sense of duty mixed with survivor guilt that had led me from a safe pogo job into the sharp end six long months ago. Now all I want is to stay safe, to stay alive.

I examine the updated codebook to double check I had correctly placed the cryptos in order and that each page is slipped into its protective plastic cover. I then recheck the back-ups at the rear. Satisfied, I drop the codebook on the coffee table and stand back. 'That be all Sir?'

The CO looks up at me.

'That's the first time I have had a Kiowa command chopper really tested in combat you know, great little bird. Took three or was it four hits and didn't miss a beat.' He raises both eyebrows. 'The system of having a signaller on board to manage all the frequencies was a real bonus, it took some of the weight off me and the, ah-um, Pilot. The boys on the ground no doubt found it easier?'

I stood motionless in the dim light waiting for the hero lecture or the dressing down because I had told him to fuck off.

'In the chopper when you told me to fuck off, or get fucked or whatever you screamed at the time, I was trying to thank you for doing a great job. Having a digger that has done it on the ground before is a real bonus in the air. Next time I might even swallow my pride and take some advice.' He pauses, 'You know, the anti-air advice you gave the pilot?' Again, the Colonel pauses for a moment to pick up a towel and wipe perspiration from his neck, 'Thank God you were also right about that bloody air strike the other day. The Yanks are denying the mistake of course and we will all just shut up about it and thank our lucky stars no media got wind of the stuff up, but God we are lucky that old temple was abandoned long ago. Even if we did destroy a piece of history by mistake, we can't be blamed for killing civilians.'

'This time', I quip sarcastically.

The Colonel nods in agreement and takes a short swig on his whisky. 'We make a pretty good team you and me. Different taste in music and we can't sing to save ourselves, but we work well in a tight spot.'

I stand motionless, stunned by the compliment. Maybe the career man is not such a prick after all!

'You have got to avoid the Col Joye stuff Sir, stick with the Stones. It's easier to spit out the words when your bum-ring is snapped tight and your scared shitless.'

The CO allows the corners of his lips to curl upward, 'You would have missed Col and the troop when they did their show two months ago. You were still with Delta Company weren't you, on operations?'

'Yeah! On ops with Delta, I also missed Big Pretzel dancing in her bikini damn it. We were stuck in the bloody jungle while the lazy bastards back here could get entertained. But that's my luck Sir.'

The CO chuckles quietly and points to the bottle of scotch. 'Help yourself son, you earned it. I won't go into details about why Big Pretzel is called Big. It was a great show, Bev was great, big voice for a small sparrow and Patty sang all her hits. I must admit I even liked those silly stomp songs. As for Col, well Col is Col. They don't come any better son.'

I reach down and grab the bottle, pour a good splash into the green plastic mug on the coffee table and swallow it down in two gulps. The hot burn deep inside has become a real comforter, better than smokes. It somehow takes that sick-knotted gut feeling away for a while. 'Well thanks for that update on what a good time you had Sir, it warms the cockles of my tender heart knowing what I missed out on. Shit happens, I guess'.

'You guess! No guesswork son, shit happens period. Not just to you, to every soldier at some time, give yourself another swig, it's a small consolation for missing the show and it's also a quiet thank you for your efforts today.'

I pour another good splash of whisky into the mug then look back at the career man, our eyes meet for a moment of mutual respect. Staring at each other through two sets of eyes that have seen too much sorrow. Thousand-year-old eyes.

Only the tired old ceiling fan breaks the silence.

Whop   Whop   Whop   Whop   Whop

'We will be home soon son, home soon. It is only weeks away when you look at the calendar', the CO says wistfully. He looks away to indicate an end to the conversation. 'Get your arrogant arse out of my sight and be at the chopper pad when I return.'

I swallow my drink and leave the commanding officer with his whisky and his worries. I quietly slip out the fly-screened door and wander back down to my humble tent.

Graham is at the tent. A sheepish freckle face peers from under short hair accentuated by a fringe cut straight across with scissors by some inept or drunken digger.

'Sorry Bri, I didn't want to startle you, just wanted to catch up, that sort of thing', Graham mumbles apologetically.

'My fault Buckets. Sorry for that black eye you've got showing up already. Look. I just need space right now. I'm strung up real tight like an over wound spring just ready to snap and I'm exhausted. But thanks for the cold can'

The Linesman

Graham looks at his gaunt colourless companion. This man is no longer simply a friend. He is a ticking time bomb. He needs help, but not right now. Graham looks over at Ray who indicates with his eyes that Graham should quietly leave. He lowers his eyes and leaves the tent quietly.

Ray leaves with Graham. He knows from experience that all I want at this moment is to be alone in my bitter misery.

I reach down to my steel trunk and pull out the bottle of whisky. It is only Johnny Walker Red Label, or a locally pirated version of it, not the fancy Black Label the Colonel has access to, but at least it is a 40 oz bottle with plenty still left in it.

'Here's to you Colonel, you're not so bad, just a career man that's all', I say aloud as I raise the bottle to my lips, stopping for a moment then toasting again, 'and here's to you Mark whoever you are, or whoever you used to be, you poor sorry bastard.'

I strip off my greens and sink back into bed, troubled by the CO's comment about feeling guilty. Something happened to me six or seven months ago or was it six thousand years ago. A journey into darkness which culminated in a week of professional incompetence and a moment of brutal madness. Now I will have to live with not only the memory but with the ever-curious soldiers who have been denied the facts. My fingers suddenly feel sticky and wet. I rub them feverishly in nervous jerks. Images of thick semi-congealed blood flashes into my mind. Quickly I sit up and swallow back down the vomit that has begun its caustic journey from my stomach.

There will be no career for me in the army. Soon as my times up I'm gone. Off the face of the planet where I will never have to face these bastards again.

I reach for the water bottle under my bunk and take a long swig to remove the burning in my oesophagus. Oh, Jesus I hate that burning. I lie back in my bunk.

I can hear a chopper heading off from the nearby battalion chopper pad, probably a late run to the fire support base with a load of mail and extra rations. As it flies over head the whop, whop, whop shifts my mind back in time, nine months ago to my early experience in this war. Nine long months. As I think back, I realise Graham was there the night Robby was killed.

The combination of vomit and whisky settles in my stomach. I wipe my hands on my towel. Another swig of whisky and a warm glow replaces the tight knot deep within me. Eyes shut. I slowly drift off into a state of half sleep remembering that time back in the company boozer, laughing with Graham, Singo and Ray. The night with Uncle Ho's hat. It seems so long ago.

Whop   Whop   Whop   Whop   Whop

Morning Sky

'Psst, Brian me mate, Brian, Brian.'

'What ....' I sit up with a start. Heart pumping, I look around me. I am in the tent at Support Company lines and Ray is standing at my feet, which he gently touched while trying to wake me carefully.

'Wakey, wakey me old son. Your time to get ready to fly out to the fire-base', Ray says in a quiet calm voice.

I now realise where I am. I had fallen into an exhausted sleep after my visit to the CO's hut, re-living my past six or more months in my dreams.

These nights of long dreams are becoming more common now that I am not required to do night shift. This creates a new problem for me, distin-guishing dreamtime from real time. I sit quietly for a while allowing dry eyes to adjust to early morning light, steadying my breathing and collecting my thoughts. I recall that the CO wants me ready to fly out to the firebase at first light. I untangle myself from the mozzie net and reach for a smoke.

It is early light, that magical moment when dark starts to turn. No stand-to here, this is inside the Dat with its endless routine of sig shifts. The stand-to routines are out on the perimeter.

I struggle to my feet and walk out the back of the tent. I reach for the plastic jerry can full of water and pour a good splash into the hand basin sitting on the crudely fabricated table and bury my face into the basin. I grab an old bit of torn towel, dip it into the basin and rub green army issue soap over the wet end. I use it as a flannel to wash under my arms and down around my crotch. That task complete, I reach for the razor and soap kept nearby. Peering into the mirror, I see a grey faced man, not the young boy who once stared back at me. The man in the mirror has drawn cheeks and his lips are squeezed tight like two thin lines in the middle of his face. Eye sockets deep and dark reflect brown eyes buried within dull grey-white balls that dart constantly from one place to another no matter how hard I try to stop their movement. Like a dead man's eyes attached to a living body. That man in the mirror is me.

A quick scrape with the razor. 'Fuck the teeth', I say aloud then grab my little dobey kit and walk back into the tent. I lift the flap on my pack and push the dobey kit in and sit back down. I pull on fresh greens and lace up my GP boots.

'So what's the word Ray?'

'All good mate, all good. You won't be flying out with the old man this morning, he is in-bound to Task Force HQ, but you still need to jump on the morning mail run 0600.'

'HQ! Not another fucking op I hope?'

'No mate, it's just the opposite. We are closing ranks, pulling back to basics only and getting the battalion ready for the home run. Still patrols and all, but not so aggressive. Its pack up time mate. They will close down the fire base within 72 hours and operate out of here 'til wakey.'

'Bullshit. How do you know?'

'I decoded the message on my shift that's how. Message for the admin OC, and the old man came on the blower about ten mikes ago and said to get you on the mail run just the same.'

'Well fuck me with passion, you reckon this is good news, or what?' I respond as I grab my kit and throw it over my shoulder. 'See ya soon mate, see ya soon.'

'On the ferry', Ray answers and smiles back. 'Now get your arse down to the pad or you'll miss the mail run.'

The mail run Huey flies in low over the rubber trees, turns sharply and puts down on the battalion's pad. Some boffins load on a few items in boxes and the bag of mail.

I casually wander over, still beaming with the thought of reduced operations. This means less chance of another episode in the air with the CO still trying to earn a Victoria Cross while I sit shitting my pants in the back seat.

The door gunner gives me a friendly wave. As I climb on board, I point to my M16 with the magazine removed to reassure the door gunner that there will be no possibility of an accidental weapon discharge. I notice the spare head set and pick it up, slipping it over my ears I flick the talk switch, 'Good morning my good fellows, what a lovely day this will be, don't you think?'

One of the pilots up front looks around at me and smiles back, his voice comes back over the headset, 'We're heading to the firebase not Vungers. What are you so chirpy about digger?'

'It's a beautiful morning that's all. It's just a beautiful morning.'

'Man's gone troppo if you ask me', the door gunner cuts in laughing. 'I think bamboo is growing in his brain.'

I look around and smile at him again, 'You fly boys are such a miserable lot, aren't you? Not like us grunts, we are always happy to be in a war.'

The pilot now cuts in, 'Hey Mick, try and get that head set off him before he makes me want to puke and make sure he's got his mag off his gat. Happy grunts worry me. I only like 'em when they're miserable and fucking mean.'

'Mags off', The door gunner responds.

'Well if that's the way you feel, I'll just mind my own business', I say jovially.

The rotor pitch changes and the Huey gives its traditional little shudder then lifts effortlessly off the pad climbing quickly to about 2000 feet.

I sit with one of my legs dangling over the side of the open doorway, looking down over the land below me. The buffeting air is comforting and I know from experience that if the chopper banks over, its G forces will help to hold me in place and prevent me from tumbling to my death as long as I also have a grip on a load ring in the floor. Soldiers are not supposed to sit like this but after a while the door gunners gave up trying to make us sit fully within the aircraft. I begin singing through the intercom, '*Bye, bye, bye, bye, bye, bye, baby goodbye.* You guys know the song?'

'Shut the man up will you', the pilot calls back to his door gunner. 'A happy grunt who can't sing is worse than an angry Cong.'

I stop singing. 'Yeah but I am better looking than a shitty pilot', I reply jokingly 'and according to your girlfriend I am better in bed too.'

'That's better', the pilot replies. 'Now you sound like the typical grunt I am used to putting up with.'

I stare out the chopper's door to the landscape below. In the morning haze, a shimmering white mist detaches itself from mother earth and rises gently from paddy fields and tree lines blanketing the landscape with a see-through creamy white tulle, a scene from a magical, mystical fairy-tale stretches before me. As far as the eye can see the place is beautiful. The rice fields and paddy buns form a giant patchwork quilt. Roads and streams run like red and brown ribbons among the straight long rows of rubber planta-tions. In the distance, the prominent Long Hai mountains seem to rise from the ocean and disappear behind cotton fluffy wisps of cloud. The Nui May Tau mountains and their jungles no longer ominous and foreboding, now a magnificent, rich dark green. Little villages and hamlets dot the landscape.

Curfew is lifted after first light. I can see the villagers moving out with their beasts of burden to work their fields as they have worked them for endless generations, as they will continue to do for many generations to come. Not even war with the most powerful country on earth can change the rhythm of Asia.

No wonder the French wanted to keep this place.

I have forgotten how to retain a happy state without the use of alcohol. I am now a miserably addicted depressed digger. My brain hungers for that feeling of depression when the alcohol is not there to fuzz the edges. My mood becomes sombre as I study the vista below.

So much death and destruction, so many lies and untruths and the poor bastards in those villages and hamlets are just stuck in the middle of the whole mess. They will still be there long after we have gone, they will endure our war. Despite their suffering, they will endure.

There is no military technology that can defeat passion and endurance. Bombs and missiles can only kill people not their ideals. What did Nguyen say to me, they will outlast your army because they will out-die your army, something like that, and he was right. We destroy so much for nothing.

My hands feel sticky with blood again. I rub them against my trouser legs, turn them over to look at white knuckles, and wipe them on my shirt. Trembling, I ask myself a very scary question. Do I somehow like being in this war, while pretending to hate it so much? Am I becoming an animal, an adrenalin junky? All the way with LBJ! I do not know the answer.

I do know some things though, I will never trust a politician again, never believe what I read in a newspaper and never march alongside those sad old bastards in the RSL. Reminiscing past glories many of them never had. They have betrayed me with their stupid values. Serve your country and your country will be proud of you. Proud of what?

'Hey smiley, what happened to the good humour then? Did you really think we were flying you off for a blow job in Vungers?'

I snap out of my self-inflicted misery, look over to the door gunner and flick the talk switch. 'Just reminiscing. How long you got to go before you're out of here?'

'Too fucking long mate.'

The Huey is at several thousand feet now, the sun is rising, changing from bold red to orange, the mist begins to evaporate over the trees and paddies. It's a picture painted on pure silk stretched below us, quivering in the sudden heat. The chopper blades whop, whop, whopping blend with the humming of my headset. I do not flick the talk switch, instead I quietly sing to myself, *See you in the morning at the break of day… just a little kiss… I'll be on my way… home!'*

The gunner shakes out his monkey strap and climbs around the pole set from floor to ceiling on each side of the Huey to support the fold away canvas seating. He sits beside me and swings his legs back and forth over the side looking down on the country below.

'Sometimes I got to ask myself, how could you have a war in such a beautiful place?' The gunner says as he shields his eyes from the morning glow.

I smile and stare out at the magnificent panorama. For the first time since I arrived in Vietnam I can appreciate, truly appreciate, rather than hate, the environment.

'I know what you mean. I've been asking myself the same question.'

We sit there looking out, lost in separate thoughts as the chopper blades cut through the air sending us toward the fire support base.

Whop   Whop   Whop   Whop   Whop

BUON – CO DOC - UC DAI LOI

THE THICK TROPICAL air has a fresh new smell of salt in it.

It is 0100 hours and I have been standing on deck with several other diggers for the last two hours waiting for the HMAS Sydney to pull out of harbour on the tide.

Most have gone to their mess decks to string up their hammocks and get some sleep but a group have stayed awake, talking, reminiscing and wondering.

Talk of home, sweethearts and family mingled with memories of friends now dead and thoughts of the diggers who would still be here after we have steamed out of the harbour.

Another battalion and another tour of duty. When they arrived I desperately wanted to go to them and warn them of what really lies ahead, but I know they will not listen, just as I had not listened. They will have to walk that line between life and death before they can possibly listen to a veteran and understand, truly understand the futility of war. This is why every generation in Australian history is littered with war veterans. Now, a thousand more naive young boys are taking my battalion's place.

More fodder for the canons. More names on cemetery slabs.

The lights of Vung Tau are in the distance. Curfew has come and gone but still the lights are there, and in the air, always the sound of aircraft.

483

I move away from the others and stand alone, thinking and leaning on the safety rail staring down to the black dark water far below. Watching as the navy divers maintain their rubber duck patrol around the ship's hull.

I am amused, I simply cannot imagine a Viet Cong terrorist swimming out in the filthy, polluted harbour water and sticking a limpet mine to the hull of the aging aircraft carrier. If the bastards weren't killed by the pollution in the water, the damn mine wouldn't stick to the rusty old hull anyway.

I know as all soldiers do that the old HMAS Sydney has been saved from the scrap heap to ferry troops to Vietnam. There is severe rust throughout the ship, some places are clearly marked as out-of-bounds due to structural hazards and I can see gaping rust holes on the flooring of the anti-aircraft gun mounts. When this war ends so does the old aircraft carrier. It's an indignant end to a war machine, downgraded to ferry then sold for scrap metal.

Upon returning from R and R I have been dislocated from my mates in Delta Company and have had trouble reconnecting with them since becoming the CO signals waller. Equally, I seem unable to re-connect with old friends in signals platoon. I feel the last months in Vietnam have left me a stranger amongst friends, as if I am detached from my body, watching myself talking and interacting with those around me.

I have become what Skip had called Buon Co Doc, sorrowful and lonely. I struggled unsuccessfully to learn the language from Skip and Nguyen. I have come to admire these Vietnamese people. The real people, not the dogs of war whom I still think of as murdering scum.

My fellow diggers still laugh and tell racist jokes about the Vietnamese, jokes about death, but the talk is shallow, the laughter thin. Awash with ignorance!

I am no longer innocent or ignorant.

I know something my fellow diggers do not! Yes I know I am insane. They are not yet aware of their own condition. Still in denial. But years from now they will struggle with their own war baggage, just as I am struggling now.

Or at least some of them will. I am not the only one amongst us who has been fucked up by this war.

Only Chucka seems close to me as a friend these days. The young digger I met playing the guitar in the Jade bar that first trip to Vungers. Since hanging around the firebases and sharing that fateful TAOR patrol, I have formed a bond with the tracker from anti-tank platoon. Somehow a fellow traveller. A loner, for whatever reason.

As was now the norm, my mood is sombre. Buon', as Skip would say. So, finally I am going home, alive and safe.

Yet this is not a time for celebration. I worry about the future of the innocent people of this country. My mind constantly flashing back to the tiny girl. Each time I think of her I reach down and automatically rub my hands on my thighs then rub them together, self-aware, yet again, of the habit that has formed. I stare at my hands; I turn them over to look at my knuckles in the dim night light and then wipe them on my shirt. It is a bad habit I have formed, I hope it passes once I find a new life back in Australia.

I reach into my pocket for my pack of Lucky Strike. My fingers still feel sticky, so I rub them against each other and on my shirt again before flipping back the lid on my Zippo and striking the wheel. Pushing the flame up to my smoke, I suck in the strong dry tobacco fumes, all the way back, deep down to the lump. Staring at the flame for an eternity, finally flicking the lid shut. The metallic clap of the Zippo lid snaps me back to the present time.

I hear the sounds of laughter and the odd hooray and realise that the old rusting aircraft carrier is slowly moving. The Vung Tau ferry is taking us home at last.

Glancing at the blackened landscape I notice the Long Hai Mountains silhouetted against the moonlit sky.

Wingnut is back there somewhere, with the new battalion on ops probably. He signed up for an extension as he always said he would, his voice sending me a chilling message, 'I belong here, not back in Aus. You'll be back too mate, you're not welcome back home but you're always a part of a team here.

You belong to something. You don't belong to nothin' back home. You will be back, I know mate, I've been home and it ain't home anymore.'

I had experienced a hint of what Wingnut was trying to tell me when I had returned home on R and R.

Sandy's words in the firebase are also haunting my soul. 'Ya can take the feckin soldier out of Vietnam, but you can't take feckin Vietnam out of the soldier.'

Was that what Wingnut was trying to say?

What happened to the cheeky young larrikin who climbed off a plane almost 12 months ago, full of fun, seeking an adventure? Will he ever be found again deep inside or is he forever a Mat Linh Hon, a lost soul wandering the jungles forever? Or buried out there alongside the church, with the little china doll?

What of me when I get home? No longer the Uc Dai Loi. What will I do with myself without a war to fight? Can I leave this place behind me? Will it haunt me forever?

A Buon Co Doc Uc Da Loi!

A flick of my finger and the cigarette flies over the side dropping to the water far below. I turn to walk to the stairs that lead down to my mess deck, I stop, go back for one last look at the lights disappearing in the distance.

The breeze is up now with the boat speed assisting, the blast of fresh air smells good. Clean, unbelievably clean. No smell of death and decay. I linger, as though something is pulling me back to the country and to the war. The knot in my stomach is now a dull ache with a strange tingling sensation up through my chest. One last fag, I pull out my pack of Lucky Strike. God these are the most horrible fags I've ever tasted.

Memory of the night fight floods back, the fear, the pain as the dead shrapnel hit my chest, and the sense of stupidity when I realised I was not really wounded. Then, in the morning light, the sight of my hooch peppered with tiny holes.

A shiver runs down my spine, 'Change yer brand', Sandy had said as he threw me the packet of Lucky Strike. I have smoked the damn things ever since. Superstition and premonitions are silly really but they've helped me get through the tough moments.

Well I don't need the good luck fags do I? It's time to piss them off and smoke something decent. I pull the half-empty packet from the plastic protective case and throw them into the water. I remove the Zippo and look at the two halves of the plastic container I have carried for months through hell and back. I kiss the side of each piece and let them drop into the purple-black water with its boiling and yellow phosphorescence dancing in the grey-white foam, furrowed by the old aircraft carrier's bow.

'A funeral for the fags at sea. My parting gift to a God forsaken shit hole. Leave the shit where the shit belongs', I say aloud, 'and now for the Zippo.'

My thumb moves up to flip back the lid one last time. Suddenly I am aware of the rough edges caused by the deep engraving on its side. I hold it to the moonlight. The red paint that smeared the original engraving is all but worn away, yet I can still make out the words…

'When I die I will go to heaven; I have done my time in hell'

A cold chill descends through my spine, another premonition maybe. Have I done my time in hell? Or… Is this just the beginning? With a flick of my wrist, I launch the Zippo into the darkness.

I take one last look back. I turn and walk away.

PART FOUR

Once we were soldiers
Boys in young men's bodies
Boasting the boldness of naivety
and suppressed insecurity
Victims of political folly, placed in harm's way

While you of our age learned how to live
We learned how to kill
While you learned of love
We learned how to hate

Our service no longer required
Cast aside as collateral damage
Like fallen leaves
prey to the winds of circumstance

What has become of us
We with nothing more than shiny medals
Hanging from coloured ribbons

Left to grow old
Our years condemn
We wander among you
Aliens in our own country
Where are we now?

FINAL ENTRY

It's neat, that's how I would describe the place. I always had a different idea of what an Aboriginal mission settlement would look like. I guess I am like most white Australians. My knowledge of the original inhabitants of this land is limited to a few documentaries. A movie about a girl called Jedda and a tennis player who the sports commentators always accused of 'going walkabout' if she ever showed any lapse in concentration. Yet, my closest friend, my hero, was of black blood. Right here, just to the right of where I stand is his mother's gravestone.

The small church is the focal point. That makes sense because it was once an Aboriginal Mission. But there is no dust or kangaroos like most Australians tend to imagine. There are lots of small bush flies as is always the case anywhere in outback Australia. But this is no run-down dump full of no-hopers. What grass there is gets cut and watered regularly and there are a few flower beds here and there. Many of the roads are sealed and the small houses scattered around are in pretty good shape. Lived in, but loved.

The kids look healthy and most of the adults we have met are in reasonable shape though a few have the tell-tale yellow eyes that suggests they are heading for an early grave. They are friendly folk. Once they know who we were or are and why we have come they welcome us and talk proudly of our friend's mother. She has been dead many years and her little home smoked long ago by the elders, so we can hear her name.

There is a strange mix of Christianity and traditional ways. The church is well attended on Sundays and alcohol is banned on the property. Some of the old fellas, and sadly some of the young uninitiated lads have moved into Ceduna to drink themselves into an early grave. But folks here are proud of their little place and maintain the little church and its Christian graveyard with love and devotion. They also sing their songs and have their sacred ceremonies at special places. We are not permitted to witness those. But that is not what Doc, Nunger and I are here for.

For the three of us of course the real reason we are here is to bid farewell to our old mate Sandy. I shouldn't use his name. But I have still not quite come to terms with his spirit business. I know the old bugger would want me to respect his people's wishes and I am trying as best I can.

Doc came and got me from ward 17 in the veterans' hospital. Good old Doc, he has never stopped caring about the boys from Delta Company. Doc is active in the Vietnam Veterans' Association, fighting for our rights to decent medical care for that damn Agent Orange poison the Yanks sprayed all over the jungle. Now he talks about this new thing called PTSD. Something about a new kind of shell shock or war neurosis. I don't really understand what he is on about.

He says that I have it.

I don't know about this new PTSD diagnosis. I just figure I have made a big mess of things since we came home from 'Nam. I got married and had two kids. My daughter was born with no nose, just a great big hole in her face. Cleft palate they said it was. I figured it was the damn poison they sprayed on us in 'Nam.

I took to the grog a bit after that, just blamed myself for the poor kid's face. There was lots of surgery to fix things but every time I looked at my little girl I had visions of another little girl with her head cut off. I never told anyone, not even Doc.

My little girl died on the operating table. Fifth attempt to rebuild her tiny helpless throat and tongue.

As for my son? He hates my guts. I left his mother with the lot didn't I? Yeah that's me isn't it. I just walked out and went bush for three years. Drowned my sorrows in whisky. But at least I didn't hang myself like poor old Jock, he just didn't cope with life after we got home. Maybe I should've though, I thought about it a lot. Doc tells me a few of the boys from our Batallion have just gone off and killed themselves.

OC saved me for a while. He got Tiny and me to go to Saudi Arabia and work for him on his new business as a security service provider for the oil pipelines. Money was good and I couldn't let OC down so I stayed off the grog. But then OC started behaving funny. Motor Neurone Disease is what the specialist called it. Once he got the diagnosis he just went for a walk one night and never came back. We found his body about a kilometer from number six pump station. He had his Magnum in his mouth and the top of his head was missing. A simple note…

'Better to die a warrior by my own hand than waste away. PS Tell Doc he was probably right about the water in that damn river.'

The Pipeline Security Company's contract was void with OC's death. Tiny looked around for a new adventure, I went back to my whisky.

Tiny left me to sleep of my bender at an airport in the middle of the bloody Arab desert and flew off to join the Rhodesian Army. They were hiring experienced jungle soldiers to put down the Blacks who wanted to take over the country. But Tiny was a good cobber to his old army mate, he left a wad of money in my pocket and a ticket back to Sydney. I haven't heard from him since. Doc said he heard he got involved in some gun smuggling for the CIA. Another military coup in the name of democracy I suppose. Just a rumour mind you, but anything to do with the CIA is all about rumour. Like the rumour that Jacko was killed fighting against the Indonesians when they took over Timor. Bloody hell, he just wanted to play cello for the Sydney

Orchestra. What happened to the poor bastards dreams? Bloody National Service, that's what.

My son is now on his way to becoming a teenager. He looks me in the eye when I come over to visit and just says to me, 'Why dad, why did you just leave us. Poor bloody mum hasn't even got a stinking dollar from you to help raise me.' He is right of course.

'Yeah son I sure am a bastard', Is all I can say. 'You and mum have every right to hate my whisky sodden guts.'

'But why dad?' He keeps asking me.

I can't answer, I just can't talk about it. How do I tell him that everything I touch just turns to shit? How do I tell him about the nightmares, the dead boys with their heads crushed, my little china doll with her teeth smashed and dead eyes staring at me. Her ghost screaming inside my brain calling me a fool. Do I tell my son that every time a chopper flies overhead I think I can smell poor old Surf Marshall's burning flesh? How do I tell my son that I am just a failure at everything I do? It is much easier to just be a bastard.

Nunger went back up north to his tribal home land. Got all political about land rights. He is hard to talk to these days. Just seems angry about everything to do with us white Australians. Doc is the only one he stays in touch with. But most of us stay in touch with Doc. At least he seems to know where to find us.

Doc is a lawyer. He went back to university and got his law degree just as he said he would. But Doc isn't a good lawyer. He doesn't chase the big bucks. The stupid bastard does public defending and spends all his spare time helping Veterans with their pension claims. Nunger says Doc has put in weeks of work helping with the land claim for his mob up north.

Of course, like Nunger, Doc is political himself now. He wants to run for a seat in the Labor Party.

I tried a few things when I got back to Australia from the Middle East. Skip offered me some work as a security guard at one of his father's nightclubs. I stuffed that up when I came to work so drunk the police arrested me thinking I was a troublesome guest not an employee. Skip said to me that he couldn't help me anymore. Old Johnno his sig mate is now Mr Pure and Noble. A school principal for some toff private school in Melbourne. Bet they would get a shock if they knew he was a dope head in 'Nam.

Speaking of schools, Doc tells me that Dutch is a student counsellor at some Catholic School. He has six kids of his own. There was a seventh but he died of a brain tumor.

Like I said, Doc knows where all the boys are. Sky Pilot, the preacher, well he stopped bothering God and now runs a Buddhist meditation retreat up near Dorrigo, northern New South Wales. FO is a sailing bum who travels up and down the east coast of Australia in a big old ketch with his wife. They run a sly tourist business, a sort of shared cost holiday deal.

Mick the stupid storeman is a second hand car salesman in Wagga Wagga. He is president of the local Liberal Party branch. Doc and he are friends these days. I can't figure that out. How can a Labor bloke like a Lib? Or vice versa? I just can't work anything out these days. What's the point?

Wingnut is some sort of international business man. He has two kids and both were born with big problems. One was born deaf and the other is sort of slow. But good old Wingnut and his missus started making toys and learning aids for their kids and next thing Doc hears about them is that they have a small factory and export these things all over the world.

The Spanker lives in Perth and has a job with the Olympic Committee for Wheel Chair athletes or some such thing. Poor bloody Spanker. But he always was the sort of bloke who could make the most of any situation. I wish I was like him in the personal guts department.

Good old Pillows is the best story of all. According to Doc he has a fancy clothing hire shop in Kings Cross somewhere with his boyfriend. He is on the organising committee for the Sydney Gay Mardi Gras and he is editor of a gay newsletter called 'Pillow Talk'. The army brass gave this guy a Military Medal for what he did to save old Spanker when that mine went off. I can't stop seeing the funny side of it all. The bloody homophobic army gives a bravery medal to a leading figure in the Sydney Gay movement. Good on him I say.

Speaking of bravery medals. Well Doc got a South Vietnamese Cross of Gallantry with Bronze Clasp for his effort at the bunker attack. He should have got a Bloody Victoria Cross if you want my opinion. I should know, I was there and saw it with my own eyes.

I don't see too many of the old signals platoon diggers. I know that Ray became a regimental sergeant major and has a son who just finished his officer training at the Duntroon Military Academy in Canberra. Bucket Arse is an Occupation Health and Safety Representative for the NSW Public Transport union.

I'm glad I didn't take up Dave's offer to go halves in a commercial fishing boat. He got caught out in a big storm off Townsville and him and his crew all drowned. Dave's widow had a kid just like mine with a bloody cleft palate. Doc says there are lots of us vets with kids that got cleft palates and other problems. He still insists it was the chemicals in 'Nam that caused so many diggers to father kids with medical hassles. He wants the Government to own up. What's the point? It won't help our poor bloody kids knowing that will it? Who pays for their extra special needs? Not the bastards who made the stuff or the bastards that ordered it to be sprayed all over the bloody donga.

Apart from the Delta boys and the sigs I also heard that the crazy Chucka stayed in the army for a few more years but then just up and went bush. Nobody knows for sure where he is, some say down in Tasmania. Others reckon he is up in the Kimberley Ranges somewhere. Just living off the land. And the poor bloody cook who pressed the clakka on that night ambush. Well I ran into him at a fish and chip shop in Bankstown. He owns it. He got married but couldn't have kids of his own so him and his missus adopted a Vietnamese girl whose parents did not survive the trip out to Australia. How about that for an act of fate. Kill one, save one. It's the least he can do to ease his conscience I suppose. I hope it all goes well.

And then there was our beloved Sandy. Poor bloody Sandy. Oh shit I used your name again old fella. Sorry. He made it to the rank of regimental sergeant major in some desk job shifting paper around an office in Canberra before they pensioned him off. Cancer of the bowel. I never did see him again, too ashamed to look him up I guess.

At least he found his home after they discharged him. He found his birth mother's place called Koonibba. Sadly she had died before he could meet her but the people here knew who he was, they welcomed Sandy home.

He stayed here. He died here.

Doc, Nunger and I are all the old army lads who came to farewell our mentor. Doc drove me down in his car. He made me promise to go dry for the whole trip and reckons I should go back to an adult education school that Whitlam started before he was shoved out of office. Doc wants me to be a writer.

Nunger made the trip down to Ceduna by plane. We came to say our farewells to our best mate.

I say to Nunger, 'At least he is back with his real mum. Back at her home land.'

But he goes off his tree at me, 'This ain't his mother's home Brian. They didn't just take away her boy. They took away her land. She is of the coast people, where the whales sing.'

Nunger looks sad, angry but sad, 'They took away her dreaming, most of her stories, they even took away her whale songs.' He shook his head and looked down the hole at the plain wooden coffin.

'And they deprived him of his stories, all he ever knew was foster homes, Salvation Army boys' homes and the real bloody army. He fought for this country, for the government that took away his mother's boy, took away his own life as a free boy, and what thanks does he get? A bloody hole near a bloody white man's church far from the sand dunes and the call of the great whales.'

'He loved the army Nunger', Doc interrupts in his quiet calm voice. 'He loved being a soldier. He cared about the men who he trained and took charge of, including you, don't forget that when you get all angry and high and mighty. How many times did he give you a second chance, teach you to be a proud Murri. He taught you how to organise and lead people. He even got you away from the booze and the brawling. He did it because he was a true soldier in every way. Don't ever forget that Nunger, he loved the army and never regretted the day he put on his uniform. If it wasn't for this man and his love of the army and his care for you, you would just be a drunk ex-vet instead of a leader in your community.'

Doc picks up some coarse sand and throws it onto the top of our old mate's coffin. 'He taught you how to be a leader and he would want you to lead by example, not by a great big chip on your shoulder.'

Doc looks at me next and gives me a talking down, 'And what about you Brian? Are you going to spend the rest of your life staring at the bottom of a whisky glass, boo hooing yourself about those poor bloody kids in that village. Do you think he would be proud of you? You were like a son to him. It's about time you tried to become at least half the man he believed you could be.'

I am shocked, 'You know about that. The village thing? I made San.. I mean the Sergeant Major promised he would never tell any soul about that trouble.'

Doc reaches into his bag and produces my water stained and weathered notebook.

'He never broke a promise when he made one Brian. It's all here, I can read between the lines. You threw it in the mud remember. Then you buried it out near the Delta boozer while the company was on ops. But Staff wasn't. He was stocking the fridge and saw you dig a hole with your foot and bury it. He asked me if we should leave it buried or dig it up and give it to our CSM when we got home. I told him to give it to me for safe keeping.'

He points to the coffin, 'It would have broken the man's heart if he knew you chucked it away again. Besides, I figured one day you might want it back.'

I stare at the notebook in his hand. I am both deeply touched that he has kept it and very angry that he has read it. I don't know how to respond.

'Maybe you are not so different to that father of yours Brian, your son needs to know what happened to you. Take this home and write your story then give it to your boy. It doesn't matter if it is never published. It will mean something to your boy one day.'

He is staring right through me, his eyes penetrate my soul like a stiletto knife.

'Turn this into a book Brian. With a bit of luck other young boys will read your story so they will know the truth about war. Most of us vets can't write the truth like you, we only write John Wayne crap. It's time one of us had the guts to tell it how it really was, how it felt deep down behind the pretence of being macho males.'

Doc passes me the notebook. It's stained by mud and some dead tropical mould or fungus that Doc has obviously tried to clean away. I tilt it up and look at its side. The pages are a bit wrinkled and faded in places. I open to the first page and stare at the blotched ink that has smeared slightly from the wet and tropical dampness but it is still legible.

There is an old man standing quietly by the exit door, he is all alone…

I stare down into that deep, deep hole and try to imagine the tough old bugger looking back up at me. I can hear him calling out to me from his grave. 'Promise me, deep down inside you will find that extra something. Promise me.'

I look back at Doc with tears in my eyes. 'I promised I would never let him down you know, I fuckin' promised him and just look at me. Fuck.'

'So', Doc says to me, 'keep your fucking promise damn you Bri. Keep your fucking promise to the man who loved you like a son.'

'I'll try if that's what you think he would want. For him I'll try. I owe him that. Have you got a pen Doc?'

Doc doesn't have one but Nunger digs into his pocket and finds a Biro.

Nunger says, 'Make a final entry into your notebook Brian. You decide what the last page must be. After that it's all up to you whether or not you keep that promise.'

Doc and Nunger leave me alone with my old mentor's box at the bottom of the open grave. They say they are going for a long walk while I decide what my future is going to be. Good mates even after all these years. They want to give me time to contemplate what has become of me. I sit down next to my old soldier's grave looking down at his box for a moment and then make this last entry you are reading…

For you my son, and maybe, just maybe, for a whole lot of mother's sons. What will I tell you as you venture into life as a young man? What were my thoughts all those years ago, the year I turned 20? How did it all begin? How will I start? Where will I start?

Well, I suppose it started back in the airbase, looking at the old man who came to bid us farewell. I can understand now his sad and sorrowful face. He knew what we had yet to learn. It's my turn now. My turn to be the old man watching others go to war.

I thought I was so grown up. I thought I knew everything I needed to know. Like all young boys in men's bodies, I thought I could conquer the world. But in truth, I just did not understand what I was really getting into.

I was only 19.

Acknowledgements

I love reading novels. My favourite is without a doubt *To Kill a Mocking Bird.* That beautiful story of Scout's youth and innocence blended with her fathers' goodness and wisdom has inspired endless other writers to create similar novels of childhood learning.

What writer of sea going adventures has not been inspired by Patrick O' Brian's novels, which accurately mix the historical facts and events of Nelson's Navy with his fictional Captain Jack Aubrey and ship's Surgeon Steven Maturin.

Erich Maria Remarque's novel *All Quiet on the Western Front* set the scene for many war novels. Youthful innocence and desire for adventure. Cruel and brutal instructors training young men for war and of course the horror of war itself. We have seen this theme repeated in novels and movies ever since, more recent examples being *Full Metal Jacket* (Vietnam) and *Jar Head* (Desert Storm).

Although my love of books has never been confined to one particular genre, I have, because of my own military service, enjoyed a well-written war novel on many occasions. These readings influenced my own writing style.

When I chose to write my novel, I decided that fiction and fact should not be greatly removed from each other. This is, in a sense, historical fiction capturing an insight into a real war fought by real people. The heroic Surf

Marshall and his crewman Beaver are fictitious characters but during my personal tour of duty two Australian choppers were lost, one supporting South Vietnamese near Long Hai and another supporting the Third Battalion at Long Khan. Surf and Beaver represent those courageous men who gave all to support us grunts on the ground.

Throughout the novel, there are incidents that have 'some' origin in an actual event changed sufficiently to maintain the novel as fiction while at the same time giving the reader a taste of reality. Many veterans including myself have struggled with Post Traumatic Stress Disorder, but we generally manage to get on with our lives and build our own families and futures. Sadly, there are those, like our character Brian, who really have struggled. I hope that, as a result of this novel, the reader will have a greater appreciation for these men and how hard it is to come to terms with such brutal events that occurred at a time when they were just young boys in young men's bodies.

We have since Vietnam, and will in the future, send more young Australians to wars in different lands. Let us respect those who suffer not just physical injury but the psychological wounds of war. Their history needs a place also, be it in fact or historical fiction.

Unlike pure but dry history there is no detail of dates, references to military maps or records in my novel. But history in its dry form fails to record such things as exhaustion, fear, racism, passion or malice from an intimate perspective. These things were and are real, therefore they are as much a part of history as those dry details we wade through when studying our past. Many autobiographies also fail to touch these issues from an intimate perspective, yet true history is richer for their inclusion.

So! Armed with my own personal living history I simply sat before a computer and allowed my mind to tell a story about fictitious characters struggling through a historical event that we in Australia and the USA call the Vietnam War. What the Vietnamese call the American War. I allowed fingers to caress the keyboard without any real concern for dry historical accuracy or respect for the pure English language.

I would follow up with a second, third (or fifteenth) re-write and additions. Much to the frustration of my wonderful partner Grace who tried helplessly to edit my rambles into some form of reasonable spelling and grammar only to discover I had re-written many pages. I remain for life, indebted to her patience and her positive support. Dear friend Gillian Anderson gave so much of her time providing this document in edited format and encouraging me to re-write it in an autobiographical form even though it is a novel. I am so grateful to my sister Eileen for reading and correcting.

As the novel reached its final stages, I read my work from a different perspective. I ask myself, *who has influenced my writing style?*

The answer of course is that many writers of many genres have influenced my work, but one or two writers stand out above all others. I cannot help but notice the influence of Australian author John Hepworth on many of my descriptions of tropical jungle and the chaos of combat. I considered rewriting these scenes, to change the style and be my own unique self-styled writer. I chose to leave the work as I had created it. I was in fact honouring the creative style of a wonderful author. Most writers do this without realising that what they have transferred from their mind to their novel has been inspired by others. It is the greatest form of flattery. There is another influence here. Peter Haran, whom I respected as a soldier when I served, and who's book *Trackers* is a masterpiece.

Joseph Heller, of *Catch 22* fame. Graham Greene's *Quiet American* and of course Facey's *A Fortunate Life*. And the powerful novel *'The Thin Red Line'* inspired the theme for this story There are many others too numerous to name but their influence can be gleaned from these pages. Finally, and importantly, there is always present in my work, the influence of Erich Remarque whom I shall quote one last time…

> *'This book is intended neither as an accusation nor as a confession but simply as an attempt to give an account of a generation that was destroyed by the war.' All Quiet on the Western Front*